"I SEE YOU QUICKLY FORGOT YOUR DETERMINATION NOT TO MARRY."

In the halo of light cast by the candle she held, she looked stupefied. "Why would you think I was going to marry?"

"Roger told me so. I saw no reason to doubt him, considering the passionate kiss you shared that afternoon. What was that about?"

Gina hiked her shoulders up in a dismissive shrug. "Merely a scientific experiment."

"Never have I seen two people derive so much pleasure from *science* before. I, too, volunteer for the experiment." He took the candlestick from her and set it down on a chest of drawers. "I am always delighted to do whatever I can to advance *science*."

Justin took her face in his hands and settled his mouth on hers in a deep kiss that sent her senses reeling.

"How does that compare to Roger's kiss?" he growled fiercely.

Like a diamond to a cheap paste imitation.

SCARLET LADY

MARLENE SUSON

AVON BOOKS ◆ NEW YORK

This is a work of fiction. Names, characters, places, and incidents either are the product of the author's imagination or are used fictitiously. Any resemblance to actual events, locales, organizations, or persons, living or dead, is entirely coincidental and beyond the intent of either the author or the publisher.

AVON BOOKS
A division of
The Hearst Corporation
1350 Avenue of the Americas
New York, New York 10019

Copyright © 1997 by Joan Sweeney
Inside cover author photo by Debbi DeMont
Published by arrangement with the author
Visit our website at http://AvonBooks.com
Library of Congress Catalog Card Number: 96-95179
ISBN: 0-380-78912-4

First Avon Books Printing: May 1997

AVON TRADEMARK REG. U.S. PAT. OFF. AND IN OTHER COUNTRIES, MARCA REGISTRADA, HECHO EN U.S.A.

Printed in the U.S.A.

RAI   10   9   8   7   6   5   4   3   2   1

To Ruth Ryon and Myrna Oliver,
special and treasured friends

Chapter 1

London, 1833

As the Earl of Ravenstone read the letter from a woman he had never met, a Miss Georgina Penford, his incredulity and anger increased with each line.

For a moment after Justin finished the infuriating document, the only sound heard in his library was that of the carriage traffic outside in Grovesnor Square. He could not remember anyone, even a man, daring to question and criticize him as this Penford woman did.

Justin looked across his walnut desk at his secretary, Terrance O'Neill, who had called the infuriating document to his attention and said dryly, "I see why this female—whoever she is—is still *Miss* Penford. No man in his right mind would shackle himself to such a damned insolent harridan."

The brazen, meddling harpy dared to take Justin severely to task for his "cruel and negligent" guardianship of his fifteen-year-old half sister, Melanie.

Cruel and negligent, hell! He bought Melanie whatever she wanted—not that she wanted that much, unlike her greedy mother.

1

Justin was also expending a huge sum to educate her at Lady Neldane's Academy in Kent, the premier boarding school in England for the daughters of the nobility. He was quite certain it was money wasted, for as nearly as he could tell the silent, sullen Melanie had not a brain in her vacant head.

"From the nature of her letter, I thought surely you must know her," Terrance said.

"The only Penford I know is a jovial, charming viscount. Clearly this old harridan could not be any relation to him. Apparently she lives near where Melanie's maternal grandparents did in Sussex."

After his father died when Melanie was still a baby, her mother had returned to live with her parents, taking the infant with her. Melanie had remained with the elderly couple until they, too, had died in quick succession last year.

Justin pictured the Penford woman in his mind: a hatchet-faced spinster who hated everyone, a dried up old prune in her fifties or sixties with grim, disapproving eyes and a thin mouth turned down in a perpetual frown.

"Do you have any other unpleasant business, Terrance, to call to my attention before I leave for Charles Lyell's geology lecture?" Geology fascinated Justin. Had he not been heir to an earldom and its duties, he would have become a natural philosopher, specializing in the subject.

"Lord Plimpton and Lord Ingleham called on you four times today and three yesterday," Terrance replied. "They are determined to see you. I fear if you do not give them an audience soon, they will set up a vigil outside the house to catch you as you leave."

Justin folded the maddening letter from Miss Penford. "Let them try."

"Did your lordship note that letter is dated three

months ago? She sent it to Cornwall, and it's taken that long to reach you here in London. In view of the delay, I thought you would want to answer it immediately."

Glancing at the letter's date, Justin noticed for the first time Miss Penford's address above it: Umberside, Sussex.

Umberside—what a coincidence. G. O. Douglas, the reclusive natural philosopher whose geological theories so excited Justin, lived there. Only this morning Justin had been reading Douglas's latest paper published in the *Transactions of the London Geological Society*, in which he theorized that the Alps had been carved by glaciers.

Justin yearned to discuss Douglas's provocative theories with him, but the man was a hermit who refused to see visitors.

"Miss Penford can wait one more day for her answer." Justin dropped the letter on his desk. "I will not be late to Lyell's lecture."

Justin's reply would singe the impertinent female's eyes and teach her not to stick her nose—which undoubtedly was as long and pointed as her fellow witches'—into his business.

Carriages clogged the streets around the building where Lyell was to speak, and it took Justin's equipage several minutes to travel a half block. He wondered irritably whether everyone in London had decided to attend the lecture. At least the rain that had been falling intermittently all day had stopped for the moment.

As Justin put his head out the window to check how far from the corner he was, a groom opened the door of a handsome chaise ahead of his. A woman in a vivid scarlet pelisse and matching hat descended from it.

He heard her tell the groom, "The lecture hall is just around the corner." The lovely, melodic timbre of her voice sent a strange shiver of pleasure through Justin. "I will get there more quickly on foot."

Certain she was right, Justin opened the door of his own carriage, jumped down, and followed her toward the corner.

As he passed her chaise, he looked inside, curious to see who her companion was, and saw she had none. That surprised Justin, for ladies did not attend public lectures without an escort.

She did not move with the fashionable languor common to women of the ton, but with an assured, no nonsense stride that he found refreshing. When they reached the corner, he was only two or three feet behind her.

As he rounded the corner, Justin's step slowed at the sight of a man clad all in purple. *Damn, Lord Plimpton!* He stood apart from the crowd, eagerly scanning the faces of the lecture-goers in search of someone.

Beyond a doubt, that someone was Justin. His peers knew of his deep interest in geology, and he would naturally be expected to attend a lecture by so eminent an authority as Lyell, the author of *The Principles of Geology*.

His gaze still fixed on Plimpton, Justin started to back around the corner just as the woman in the scarlet pelisse abruptly changed direction and crashed into him.

Caught by surprise and afraid their collision would draw Plimpton's attention, Justin grabbed her and pulled her behind the three-story stone building on the corner, out of Plimpton's sight.

She was more petite than he realized, coming barely to his shoulder, but then he was an unusually tall man. When Justin felt the soft curves of her exquisitely proportioned body against his, the embarrassing strength of his physical response to her so disconcerted him that he hissed, "You might look where you're going, madam. You are lucky I did not knock you down."

She looked up at him. A nearby gaslight illuminated a pixielike face dusted with freckles. Her pert little nose turned up at the tip, and her eyes sparkled with good humor.

Her dark hair had been swept up into a chignon beneath her hat, but willful tendrils drifted down about her face and teased her slender neck in an artless, natural way that Justin found charming. "Why the devil did you turn so abruptly?"

"I was trying to avoid the poodle."

He looked down in surprise at the ground, then frowned. "What? I see no poodle—nor any dog at all, regardless of its breed."

Her eyes glowed mischievously. "Pray, look more closely at the man in purple."

Justin did so and burst into spontaneous, appreciative laughter. Plimpton was so thin and fine-boned that he looked as though a middling wind would easily blow him away. His narrow face boasted dark button eyes. Although he was only twenty-nine, seven years younger than Justin, Plimpton's very fine, very curly hair had turned prematurely gray. On rainy days such as this one, it always frizzed up uncontrollably, looking exactly like a poodle's topnotch.

Why had Justin never noticed the striking resemblance before this intriguing woman pointed it out to him?

She responded to his laughter with a smile so brilliant that it warmed him like a fire on a frosty night. To his surprise, he found himself wondering whether she was married. Not since before his own ill-fated marriage had he wondered about a woman's marital status.

She looked to be in her early twenties, past the usual age when a well-bred woman wed. "Does your husband allow you to attend these lectures without him?"

"I have no husband, thank God."

She said this with such fervor Justin stared at her in surprise. He had yet to meet a woman of her obvious breeding and education who was not desperate for matrimony. "You sound remarkably pleased about that."

"Oh, I am," she assured him, her smile growing even more luminous. "I am quite on the shelf. It is the greatest relief to me."

Although she sounded sincere, he was skeptical she could truly mean that. "What makes you so adamant against matrimony?"

"Husbands."

Her succinct answer startled Justin into asking, "You dislike men?"

"Not as long as I don't have to marry one."

The humor and mischief in her eyes charmed him. She was not a beauty, yet he, who was rarely attracted to far lovelier members of her sex, found himself drawn to her. He could not remember when he had met a more provocative woman.

Justin looked toward Plimpton, still scanning the crowd. A tall man who resembled Justin in height and coloring rounded the opposite corner, and "the poodle" hurried toward him.

"Quick," Justin whispered to the woman, taking her arm, "if we hurry, we can make our way inside before the poodle notices us."

They succeeded. From the number of people crowding into the building with them, Lyell's lecture would be packed. A surprisingly large number of the audience were women, including several ladies of the ton whom Justin knew.

Once inside the door, he stopped to look for Lyell while the woman continued on into the lecture hall. She stood out in her vivid scarlet pelisse among the other women's pastel shades, like the brilliant sun against a bland blue sky.

Justin was so absorbed in watching her that he nearly missed his quarry. "Mr. Lyell," he called as the theorist passed him on his way into the hall. "Would you spare me a moment?"

"Of course, Lord Ravenstone." Lyell stopped beside Justin. "I am honored to see you here tonight."

"I have a quick question for you. You must know a natural philosopher in Sussex named G. O. Douglas?" Justin wanted Lyell to intercede with the recluse to arrange a meeting for him.

Lyell frowned. "Only by letter, I'm sorry to say. I even offered to go to Sussex to meet him. He wrote back he was very sorry to have to refuse, but he entertains no visitors."

If Douglas refused to meet with Lyell, one of the recognized giants of contemporary geology, he would certainly reject a request for an audience from an amateur like Justin.

"Such a pity," Lyell said with a sigh. "Douglas's theories are so provocative that I would enjoy discussing them with him, as I know you would, too.

Now pray excuse me, my lord, for I must begin my lecture."

Justin followed Lyell into the stuffy hall, packed with about three hundred people. He scanned them for the woman with whom he had collided and discovered her seated in the center of the third row. She had already shed her scarlet pelisse, revealing a matching gown of chaley, a twilled silk and wool fabric. In the light of the hall, her hair was the shade of fine chocolate.

To his disappointment, all the chairs around her had already been taken. He had to settle for one near the end of the first row beside a corpulent gentleman with gravy stains down his coat. When Justin turned his head, however, his chair afforded him an excellent view of her face.

Whenever he looked her way as Lyell lectured, she appeared deeply engrossed. Once or twice, Justin saw her nod her head in silent agreement with the speaker.

He watched her admiringly. The world was too full of meddling harpies like Miss Georgina Penford. It needed more intriguing women like this Scarlet Lady.

Georgina Penford felt *his* eyes on her. She was still unnerved by her collision with the dark stranger. The peculiar thrill that ran through her when she'd crashed into his hard, muscled body had shocked her. Now, as he turned in his seat in the front row to study her, she felt the same sensation again.

She paid little heed to men, so why did this stranger have such an effect on her? Perhaps it was the unyielding strength she sensed about him. She wondered who he could be? He had neither the look of an aristocratic dilettante nor of a natural philosopher, but of a man of the world, used to commanding others and being obeyed.

His raven black hair was thick and curly. Piercing brown eyes, so dark they looked almost black, were set in a face that was too sharply planed and angled to be handsome. Yet in combination with those penetrating eyes, his face was both arresting and harshly intriguing—the face of a dark and dangerous pirate. A little shiver ran through Georgina.

He was not a man to be crossed.

His subdued clothes were distinguished only by the excellence of their cut and fabric. No fashionably embroidered waistcoat nor heavily frilled white shirt was visible in the wide expanse between the lapels of his blue coat.

When Lyell entertained questions, Georgina asked about aspects of his uniformitarian theory that speculated today's world was not the result of catastrophic upheaval but of forces still at work—ice, water, wind, and volcanic fire.

Then the harsh-faced stranger inquired of Lyell, "Have you read G. O. Douglas's article in the new *Transactions of the London Geological Society*?"

His question so surprised Georgina that her head swiveled toward him.

"I have," Lyell answered.

"Do you agree, as I do, with his theory that the Alps were carved by glaciers?" the stranger asked.

"Yes, as Mr. Douglas points out, it explains why we find so much order in the distribution of rock blocks in the Alps."

Georgina felt inordinately pleased that the dark stranger had already read the paper. She looked at him, and their eyes met, kindling a disconcerting heat within her. He smiled at her, drawing attention to his sensual mouth. She wondered dreamily what it would be like to be kissed by him.

His smile softened the harsh lines of his pirate face. She remembered Melanie Alexander once describing her hateful half brother as looking like a pirate. Lanie should see this man, and she would know what a pirate really looked like.

Poor Lanie. Georgina had received another heart-rending letter that morning from her. She was so miserable at that dreadful school where her brother and guardian, Lord Ravenstone, had sent her. He was so uncaring of her welfare that he had not even deigned to answer Georgina's letter to him about his ward. And she'd written it *three months* ago.

Rude, heartless man. Should Georgina ever have the misfortune to meet Ravenstone, she would blister his ears with what she thought of him and his treatment of Lanie.

Chapter 2

⧫⧫⧫

When Lyell left the lecture podium, he was immediately surrounded by members of his audience, seeking a private word with him. On another night, Justin might have been one of this group, but tonight he hurried in the other direction, intent on catching the Scarlet Lady before she could leave the room.

She confounded him. The strong physical attraction he felt for her was startling enough, but Justin, who heartily endorsed the prevalent view that man was the superior sex, was truly amazed that any woman could grasp geological theory as she clearly did.

To Justin, women were frail, childlike, emotional creatures whose minds could not grapple with matters of substance. They had to be protected from their own foolish natures and passions. Certainly his late wife, Clarissa, had been a spoiled child in an adult's body.

He pushed his way through the crowd toward the woman. She carried her scarlet pelisse over her arm. Her chaley gown of matching scarlet lacked the ridiculous overabundance of furbelows that were currently the style among those in the first

11

stare of fashion. The refreshing simplicity of her attire pleased him. So did its color. "Scarlet is most becoming on you," he told her. "Few women would dare wear such a vivid color."

She bestowed her marvelous smile on him. "The climate is dreary enough. I see no reason why I should dress to match it."

Her clear, musical voice reminded Justin of a fine set of church chimes. A faint, pleasing scent of gardenia wafted over him.

"The new issue of the *Transactions* only came out today," she said. "I was surprised you had already read the Douglas article in it."

"I am a great admirer of Mr. Douglas," Justin said. "Whenever I discover one of his papers, I read it immediately."

Her smile grew even more brilliant, and it provoked an intense physical reaction in Justin.

Meaning to compliment her, he said, "You have a most remarkable grasp of geological theory for a woman."

To his astonishment, her bewitching smile vanished instantly, and her eyes narrowed into an angry glare. "How kind of you to say so, sir." Her voice would have frozen boiling water.

Why the devil would she react like that to his praise, Justin wondered in bewilderment.

She turned to leave him, but he caught her arm, determined not to let her escape him until he learned her identity. "Wait, I have not seen you before. Are you from London?"

"No, I came to town to hear Mr. Lyell's lectures."

He could not believe any woman would travel to the city merely to attend lectures on geology. "Do you mean to stay in London until the series has ended?"

"Yes, that is my intention."

Thomas Skagit, a rotund, white-haired acquaintance of Justin's, came up to them. "Ah, Lord Ravenstone, you—"

"*What!*" The woman's startled exclamation stopped Skagit in midsentence. She stared at Justin as though she had just been told he was a murdering fiend. "*You* are the Earl of Ravenstone?"

He nodded, much taken aback by her obvious revulsion to him, a novel experience indeed. Usually when women discovered he was an earl, they tried every coquettish trick in the book to engage his interest. He said wryly, "Apparently you have heard of me and not favorably."

"Most unfavorably." Her voice was edged with icy disapproval. She looked as though she intended to say more, much more, but she looked around. People were already staring at them curiously. She gulped visibly, as though trying to swallow her spleen. Then, without another word, she turned on her heel and marched away.

"Wait, Miss whatever the devil your name is," Justin called.

She ignored him, striding rapidly through the crowd in her eagerness to escape him.

Skagit asked, "Who is she? I was hoping you would introduce us. I'm a widower now, you know."

Justin could scarcely conceal his irritation. Could the fat, silly fool not see that he was far too old for the woman, whoever she was?

"She's a most comely creature, most comely indeed," Skagit continued. "Her smile is truly extraordinary."

Justin agreed completely on both points. By now, she had disappeared into the crowd. A combination of his height and her bright scarlet gown helped him locate her again as she left the lecture room.

He struggled through the crowd toward the door she'd used. When he finally reached it, however, he saw no sign of her.

He hurried outside just in time to see her groom hand her into her chaise. By the time he maneuvered his way through the people on the steps, the equipage was rolling away.

Justin had no time to wait for his own carriage. Instead he hailed a passing hackney and ordered the driver to follow the woman's chaise. "There's an extra guinea for you if you manage to stay behind it until it reaches its destination."

The man, clearly determined to win this reward, followed the coach with reckless alacrity.

Justin leaned back against the leather seat, wondering whether he had lost his mind. He did not chase after women, married or unmarried. In fact, he did not even like them very much, except when they warmed his bed.

So why the hell was he doing this?

His late wife had cured him of both affection and respect for the weaker sex. His marriage, when he was not yet twenty-one, had been arranged by his father. Within a quarter-year of the wedding, Justin had come to cordially dislike his extravagant, self-absorbed wife whose wild temper tantrums became legendary among the servants at Ravencrest, his county seat in Cornwall.

When Clarissa died of typhus four weeks after their third wedding anniversary, Justin determined never to subject himself to the misery of marriage again. That had been twelve years ago, and he still regarded wedlock as nothing but a damned snare for a man. He was quite content to let his title and all that went with it pass to his younger brother, Henry.

The hackney rounded a corner to the left at a fearsome pace, forcing Justin to grab the hand strap to keep from sliding across the seat.

What the devil could the scarlet lady have heard about him that prompted the disgust he'd seen in her eyes? Justin knew he was respected by men, and he could think of no lady who could honestly complain of his treatment of her.

But then, he reflected bitterly, what woman was truly honest?

The hackney turned again, this time sharply to the right. Justin heard another coachman attacking his driver's parentage in loud, pungent terms.

Since Justin had been widowed twelve years ago, a great many women had set their cap for him, but he had never been guilty of leading on any of them. Unlike many aristocrats who felt their titles gave them leave to do whatever they wanted, Justin's private code of honor did not permit him to seduce young ladies or another man's wife, nor to require his housemaids to satisfy his needs.

Instead he turned to various high fliers of the demimonde, who were never guilty of foolishly mistaking lust for that romantic nonsense called love. With them, it was simply a business arrangement—value given for value received—and he made clear from the beginning their liaison would be temporary.

His mistress of the moment was well paid to please him. Justin considered this a far more honest relationship than matrimony, which among his strata of society was about uniting an ill-suited man and woman to gain strategic alliances, fill family coffers, and produce suitably blue-blooded heirs.

The hackney, which had been making a bewildering number of turns, finally slowed to a stop. When Justin inquired about their location, the coachman replied, ''In Chesterfield Street. Yer chaise be stopped up ahead.''

Justin stuck his head out the window in time to see the woman in scarlet rush up the steps of a handsome townhouse. She did not knock but opened the door and disappeared inside.

Noting the address, Justin pulled his head back inside the coach. He smothered the urge to get out and knock on her door. Learning where she lived was enough for tonight. He'd call on her tomorrow.

He told the driver, ''You've earned your guinea. Now take me back to where you picked me up.''

As the hackney started up again, Justin chuckled out loud as he thought of how surprised the scarlet lady would be when he called on her tomorrow.

Georgina dashed into Nancy Wilde's townhouse, uttering silent thanks the door had not been locked. The noise of her entry brought Nancy's butler running, his face reflecting his consternation at this surprise invasion.

'' 'Tis only me, Burton. Forgive me for not knocking first.'' As Georgina shut the door behind her, Ravenstone's hackney continued past Nancy's house. She should have been delighted to be rid of him. Instead disappointment pricked at her.

She'd never before met a man who had stirred her interest as he had. Georgina had been delighted when he'd sought her out after Lyell's lecture. When he'd smiled at her, odd sensations had coursed through her, and she'd wondered again what it would be like to be kissed by that sensual mouth.

When she'd discovered he was Lanie's rude, negligent guardian, she was dumbfounded and appalled. She should have delivered the scathing indictment the heartless beast deserved, but she could hardly do that in so public a forum as a lecture hall, with three hundred interested witnesses looking on. It would have been the talk of London by morning.

Instead Georgina turned on her heel and departed before her unruly tongue could get the better of her.

Then he had dared to follow her. What a surprise he would have had if he had followed her into this house.

Its owner, Nancy Wilde, the reigning queen of the demimonde, appeared, her beautiful face as alarmed as her butler's had been. When she saw Georgina, her expression turned to dismay. "Gina, you cannot come here like this. Your reputation will be in shards if anyone saw you."

"I do not care if the whole world sees me here," Georgina said stubbornly. "I am proud to count you as my friend."

"And I am most fortunate to have you as mine, Gina, which is why I am so anxious to protect you from scandal. Your papa would be horrified to learn you are here."

"Papa would never censor whom I see," Georgina replied with absolute certainty. "He has not argued with me about such matters since I refused to have a debut season when I was eighteen. He has too much respect for my intelligence to play the tyrant with me."

"What a rare man," Nancy remarked dryly. "Too many think all women of inferior intelligence and regard it as their male duty to tyrannize all females under their control. You are far more fortunate in your father than I was in mine."

"I was very fortunate in both my parents."

Nancy led Georgina into the small drawing room done in pastel shades that complimented the courtesan's blond beauty.

As Georgina sat down on a delicate peach brocade wing chair, one of a pair, she said, "How handsome your new home looks, Nancy. Are you happy with it?"

"Very." Nancy settled in the other wing chair. "It is what I have wanted for so long. Ironic, is it not, that I bought it and own it in my own name, but the world automatically assumes it belongs to Lord Conington?"

The legendary courtesan enjoyed her pick of men eager to be her protector. Currently the Marquess of Conington occupied this sought-after position.

"What does it matter what the world thinks?" Georgina scoffed. "You have achieved the independence that is so important to you."

Men might see only Nancy's beauty and charm, but Georgina admired her for her sharp intelligence, wit, and the determination and financial acumen that had made her wealthy in her own right—and consequently independent.

While many would condemn Nancy for the means she'd used to attain this end, Georgina was not among them. She appreciated too much how hard it was for a woman to make her way in the world.

"To what do I owe this surprise visit, Gina?"

"A man was following me."

"Dear God," Nancy exclaimed in alarm. "Do you have any idea who he was?"

"That dreadful Lord Ravenstone." Georgina felt

a twinge of conscience for applying that adjective
to him. In truth, she'd thought him fascinating—
until she'd learned his identity.

"Ravenstone followed you!" Nancy exclaimed. "I
cannot believe it. He is not the kind of man to do
such a thing. Where did you meet him?"

"At Lyell's lecture."

Nancy smiled. "Was it hate at first sight?"

"Actually, no," Georgina confessed. "At first I
liked him, especially after he told me how much he
admires G. O. Douglas's articles. He even asked Lyell if he had read the latest one. I was astonished."

Nancy's eyes gleamed teasingly. "Perhaps Ravenstone is the man of your dreams."

"Dreams, hah! The man of my *nightmares*!" Georgina shot back. "Why, the arrogant, patronizing cad
had the nerve to tell me I had 'a remarkable grasp
of geological theory *for a woman*.' "

That remark had infuriated Georgina, but her
heated reaction to it had stemmed in part from the
unsettling effect he'd had on her.

"But why would he follow you?"

"He was piqued because I walked away from him
without taking proper leave."

Nancy's eyes sparkled with amusement. "Undoubtedly a unique experience for him. Women
generally run toward him, not away."

"I cannot understand why." Georgina realized as
these words left her mouth that they were a lie. She
understood better than she liked.

"You and Ravenstone could have a lively discussion on the subject of marriage, Gina. He thinks
men have by far the worst of the bargain."

"How could he possibly think that?" Georgina,
the heiress to a large fortune, was convinced that

marriage would far more likely rob her of her security than provide her with it.

"Why don't you ask Ravenstone? I should like to be privileged to hear that . . . uh, conversation."

"Perhaps I will." Georgina felt passionately about this subject. "A wife has no rights to her own property and fortune—even her own children. Look at my poor aunt, turned out without a penny by her mad husband and then denied access to her small children."

"Not all men are like that," Nancy reminded her. "Your own father is not."

"No, but Papa is most unusual. He both loved and respected Mama. They had the most wonderful marriage."

Georgina thought wistfully of her parents' union. She would settle for nothing less than the loving, sharing, egalitarian relationship her parents enjoyed.

Although she'd never been in love herself, she knew love had been the indispensable ingredient in her parents' very happy marriage. "I am lucky that I am wealthy and have no need to marry merely for a home and a husband to support me. The only man I would consider marrying is one like my father, who respects my opinions and encourages my geological studies."

And who loves me.

"But I have given up hope of finding such a man." Georgina tossed her head stubbornly. "I shall never marry."

"You cannot dictate to your heart whom you will love, Gina. Love happens—often with the most unexpected people."

"Well, it has not happened to me at all."

"I wish you would not scorn marriage as you do.

The right man could bring you enormous joy and pleasure and happiness."

"If it can be so wonderful, why do *you* eschew marriage?"

"I am able to reap pleasure outside of marriage, but a woman of your social standing has not that option," Nancy replied. "You must marry or you will become a social outcast."

"I care nothing about what society thinks! You know that. Better to be a pariah than married to a husband like Lord Ingleham, who is squandering his wife's inheritance on gambling and other women. She knows she will be left destitute, and she is helpless to stop him."

Nancy studied her thoughtfully. "Lord Ravenstone would never throw his wife's fortune away. It would violate his code of honor. Besides, he is not a careless man with money."

"I wish Ravenstone's code of honor contained something about his duty to his sister."

"Perhaps he sees his duty to her differently than you do, Gina. He is not irresponsible or malicious. Hot tempered, yes, but spiteful, never."

"If the fool does not remove Lanie from that dreadful school to which he sent her, she is going to run away."

A half-smile tugged at Nancy's lips. "Ravenstone can be called many things, but a fool is not one of them."

" 'Tis a disgrace the way he ignores poor Lanie."

"From what you told me, I collect she much prefers him to ignore her."

"She does," Georgina admitted, then her temper fired again. "But he is to blame for that, too. He's terrorized the poor girl."

Nancy looked skeptical. "Frankly, I cannot imagine him mistreating her. For all his careless manner, he takes his duties seriously. And why did you lead him here? He must think you live here. I wonder if he will call on me tomorrow."

"I could not resist hoaxing him," Georgina confessed. "I know how skilled Burton is at getting rid of unwanted male callers. I wish I could see Ravenstone's face if he calls and Burton tells him, 'Nancy Wilde is not at home to him.' He will think he followed you home."

"Ravenstone knows I am not you. He was my protector once."

A weird little pain stabbed at Georgina. "For how long?" Her voice suddenly sounded a little shrill.

"A year." Nancy's eyes grew dreamy. "Justin was the best lover I ever had."

"Why do you say that?" Georgina's experience in such matters was nonexistent, and she did not like being ignorant on any subject. "What makes him, or any man, a good lover?"

Nancy's eyes turned soft and dreamy. "Justin is most accomplished at giving a woman enormous pleasure. He is a tender and generous lover."

Georgina frowned. "But you said he was miserly with his money."

"I do not mean that kind of generosity."

Then what kind had she meant?

Before Georgina could ask, Nancy said, "Nor did I say he was miserly with his money, merely that he has a reputation for not being careless with it."

But Georgina remembered Lanie's mother, Ravenstone's stepmother, insisting, "a more clutch-fisted man never existed."

"If you loved him, Nancy, why did you send him away?"

"It was the other way around." Nancy's expression grew pensive. "I made the mistake of falling in love with him and telling him so."

"Why do you call that a mistake?"

"Justin does not believe romantic love exists. He mistook my avowal that I loved him as a brazen attempt to make him more generous to me. I was very young then, and I was so hurt he could believe that of me I made matters worse. I was thinking with my heart, not my head. I never repeated that mistake. A woman in my profession cannot afford to do so."

"And that dreadful man has *no* heart!" Georgina cried. "None!"

"In all fairness to Ravenstone, he was always absolutely honest with me, which is more than I can say of many men. He made it clear from the beginning he regarded our relationship as a business arrangement beneficial to both of us."

"A business arrangement!" Georgina was horrified. "How romantic he is!"

"In my world, that is precisely what such connections are. I violated our arrangement by falling in love with him."

"How could you fall in love with him?"

Nancy shrugged. "Can anyone truly answer that question?"

"Do you still love him?"

"No, that was years ago, not long after his wife died. From what I heard of her, she would have soured any man on marriage."

"What kind of man disparages his dead wife?" Georgina demanded indignantly.

"He did not do that. I heard it from his friends, not from him. Justin never mentioned her name to me."

"After the way he treated you, I am astonished you defend him."

"He is a good man, but a formidable one. You would do well to remember that, Gina. I would not want him as my enemy."

Remembering Ravenstone's dark pirate face and the power that she'd sensed was leashed in his strong body, Georgina did not doubt Nancy spoke the truth. A little shiver went through her at the memory of those hard eyes.

And a strange desire to stare into them again.

Chapter 3

Justin dragged his wayward thoughts from the Scarlet Lady he'd encountered the previous night and back to the letters and invitations piled on his desk awaiting his response. It was not like him to let his mind wander while he gave instructions to his secretary on how to answer his mail.

He scanned the top letter on the pile, a request from the steward at Ravencrest that he travel there to inspect work that he had ordered done.

A visit to his Cornwall estate was overdue, but Justin kept delaying it. Although he loved the land and the countryside, he hated the drafty and uncomfortable house, built in Tudor times. It was rambling, inconvenient, and poorly situated. Worse, it was filled with unpleasant memories, especially of his late wife.

His secretary watched Justin with a bemused expression on his ruddy young face. "Why are you looking at me like that, Terrance?"

"You seem remarkably distracted this morning, my lord. So unlike you, it is. Mr. Lyell's lecture last night must have given you much food for thought."

"Yes, it did," Justin prevaricated. Once he disposed of this tedious stack of correspondence before him, he intended to visit the real source of his distraction.

He did not understand why he should be so anxious to see her again, but as he contemplated visiting her, the boredom that seemed constantly to plague him like a lingering case of the ague vanished.

His curiosity about her and the prospect of her company spurred him to deal more quickly with the matters at hand.

The final letter in the pile was from Lady Neldane, the headmistress of the exclusive boarding school his half sister attended:

> It pains me to tell you, my lord, that Lady Melanie is alarmingly silent and taciturn for a girl her age. She keeps very much to herself and makes no effort to form friendships.
>
> She has made no progress whatsoever in needlework, music, and dancing, the subjects crucial to a young lady's success in the world. Her teachers have begun to despair.
>
> I urge you, my lord, to visit your ward and exhort her to do better.

Justin smothered a groan. He could think of nothing he wanted to do less than travel to Kent to urge his sullen, silent sister to perform better in school, especially when he was convinced she was incapable of doing so. How unfortunate that Melanie had not inherited their father's intelligence instead of her mother's bird wit.

He handed the sheet across his desk to Terrance. "Write Lady Neldane that I am attempting to work a visit into my schedule." It would be a very long time before Justin managed to do so. "Tell her, in the meantime, to keep me informed about my sister's progress."

"You have a day free Tuesday next, my lord," his secretary said eagerly. "Shall I set it aside on your calendar and write Lady Neldane you will be there then?"

Although Terrance was an excellent secretary and Justin valued him highly, he fervently wished the young man would not *always* try to be so damned helpful. "No," Justin said more sharply than he'd intended.

His secretary looked so puzzled that Justin felt obliged to fib again. "I have private plans that day."

Terrance colored slightly. "I see."

He didn't see at all. His blush betrayed that he assumed his employer would be spending the day with his current convenient. Well, Terrance was dead wrong. Justin would be happy never to see her again. Like too many of her predecessors, she had become greedy and wheedling, two qualities Justin would not tolerate in a woman. She had earned her congé from him.

Justin would have given it to her before now had he found a woman whom he desired enough to replace her. But he had not.

Nancy Wilde still stirred his interest, but Lord Conington was her protector now. Justin would never trespass upon another man's turf, no matter how elastic the connection might be.

He and Nancy had been lovers once long ago, but it had ended badly. The fault had been his. The wounds Clarissa had inflicted on him during their marriage had still been raw, and the distrust for all women she had instilled in him, at its zenith. Had he and Nancy met a few years later, perhaps . . . but

Justin was not a man to dwell on what might have been.

"Are we finished, my lord?" Terrance asked.

"Not quite." Lady Neldane's note had reminded Justin of the letter from Miss Penford, and he plucked it from his desk.

Justin would give Miss Georgina Penford the setdown of her life for her unwarranted interference in his business and her baseless allegations about his negligent guardianship of his half sister.

But were they baseless? An unexpected twinge of conscience plucked at him. He could not deny he'd seen very little of Melanie in the years he'd been her guardian, but he'd been assured in letters from both her and her grandparents that she was very happy with them in Sussex.

Miss Penford seemed most incensed that Justin had failed to take his orphaned sister into his own home, either at his Cornwall estate or in London.

"Melanie is your father's daughter and has as much right to live in the homes of her father as you do," she'd written.

But he could not send his sister to Ravencrest because the house was closed. Even were he to open it for her, he could not let her stay when he himself would not be there to supervise her.

He shuddered at the thought of living again in that damp, drafty pile of stones where he had been so miserable.

As for London, the last thing Justin wanted was a sullen schoolroom chit residing under his bachelor roof. Nor did he think his sister, who clearly disliked his company, would welcome the arrangement any more than he would.

He'd made extensive inquiries into boarding schools for her and been assured Lady Neldane's

Academy was the very best to be had and the choice of England's most elite families for their daughters.

Justin's eye fell on another sentence of Miss Penford's letter that particularly irked him. "If you must be so cruel as to deny her a home with you, Lord Ravenstone, then let her live with me."

As if he would ever allow his sister to come under that meddling harpy's influence. Glaring at the letter, Justin cleared his throat to begin dictating his response, then decided to answer it himself rather than shock his secretary with his astringent reply.

"Never mind, Terrance, I will write out my own answer. You can go now."

As his secretary left the library, Justin seized his quill pen and, in a bold hand and caustic language, vented his anger on Miss Penford for her impertinent, unwarranted letter.

He folded the scathing reply, sealed it with a wafer, and franked it. He slipped the letter into his coat pocket, intending to give it to his secretary for posting, and promptly forgot it in his impatience to see the scarlet lady again.

Justin did not bother to order his carriage. He lived only a short distance from her address. Given the heavy London traffic, he could walk there more quickly. As he headed toward Chesterfield Street, two men suddenly flanked him, one on each side.

"We know you will not object to our accompanying you on your walk, Lord Ravenstone," the Earl of Ingleham, on his left, said.

Too late Justin remembered his secretary's warning. He objected very much to Ingleham's company, but he was trapped. He smothered a groan. "But you do not know where I am going."

"It does not matter," Ingleham assured him.

Justin glanced at the man on his right. *The poodle.*

The Scarlet Lady's appellation for Lord Plimpton with his button eyes and nose and frizzy gray hair was so apt that Justin had to bite his lip to keep from laughing aloud again.

In fact, he thought satirically, both his callers resembled dogs. Ingleham's bushy brows, pointed ears, flowing, unkempt gray beard, and long mustache reminded Justin of a schnauzer.

"Lord Ravenstone, you must help us save this great nation from those damned radicals intent on destroying it," Plimpton squeaked. Even his yapping voice sounded like a poodle.

"Yes, it is your patriotic duty, Ravenstone," the schnauzer added.

Why the devil was it whenever some fool wanted something from Justin, he always presented it to him as his patriotic duty?

"You know I have no appetite for politics." Justin had lost it years ago. Even if he hadn't, he had no sympathy for the policies Ingleham and Plimpton advocated. Members of the most reactionary clique in the House of Lords, they opposed anything that so much as hinted at narrowing their power and prerogatives.

"That traitor Viscount Penford, who betrayed his fellow peers by campaigning to enlarge the voting franchise, now plans to betray his entire sex by giving women power, which everyone knows they are incapable of wielding rationally," Ingleham said.

Justin demanded impatiently, "What are you talking about?"

"Penford is drawing up a bill that would remove a wife's property from her husband's control and place it in her hands," Plimpton explained. "Her husband would no longer have any say over it."

"Can you imagine what a catastrophe that would

be?" Ingleham demanded. "Why, the country would go bankrupt."

At least Ingleham would, Justin thought wryly. The schnauzer had squandered his own considerable fortune, then taken as his second wife two years ago the only child of a textile manufacturer and sole heiress to her father's enormous fortune. Everyone knew Ingleham was going through her inheritance at a prodigious rate despite her outraged and futile protests.

The wheel of a passing carriage hit a puddle, sending up a spray of dirty water that forced Justin and his unwelcome companions to jump back.

"Everyone knows a woman's intellect and temperament is too inferior and weak to deal with financial affairs," the poodle yapped indignantly.

On this point, Justin concurred. A law giving wives such authority would be disastrous. He shuddered at what would have happened had his extravagant late wife controlled her fortune. It would have been gone within six months.

"Sebastian Dodd has also signed on to our cause," Ingleham said.

That ensured Justin would not back them. He was convinced Dodd was insane, which no doubt explained why he supported the schnauzer and the poodle.

Plimpton said mournfully, "What can Penford be thinking of?"

"I'll wager pounds to pence it wasn't his idea," the schnauzer said with a sneer. "His shrew of a daughter must have nagged him into it. That woman has a wasp for a tongue."

"A hive of wasps," the poodle agreed. " 'Tis no wonder she's still a spinster. No man in his right mind would offer for such an ugly, ill-tempered, old maid as Georgina Penford.''

Georgina Penford! Bloody hell, could it be Justin's correspondent was Lord Penford's daughter? ''Does she live in Sussex?''

''Aye. Her father has an estate near Umberside,'' Ingleham replied.

She had to be the female who had written Justin. He belatedly remembered he'd failed to give his reply to her letter to Terrance for posting. The woman must be much younger than Justin had thought, for Lord Penford was only in his late forties. ''How old is Miss Penford?''

''Twenty-six,'' Plimpton answered.

''I don't recall ever seeing her in London,'' Justin said.

''She is such a dreadful antidote that her father wisely decided against wasting his money on a London season for her,'' Ingleham said scornfully. ''She was never introduced to society.''

Justin stopped in front of an imposing building of Portland stone, determined to rid himself of his companions. ''I must leave you here, gentlemen. I have an important meeting.'' Indeed, he did, although not in this building.

''With whom?'' Ingleham demanded. ''I hope not Lord Penford. His office is in this building.''

''So is my solicitor's,'' Justin said truthfully. ''I was unaware Penford had one here, too.''

''Will you help us save the nation from women's folly and imprudence, Ravenstone?'' Plimpton asked eagerly.

''Let me think it over. I will contact you.'' *About the time hell freezes over.*

Inside the building, Justin hurried down a hall to an intersecting corridor that led to a side street and turned left. He passed a short, rotund man hurrying down a stairway.

"Why, Lord Ravenstone."

Justin stopped, turned, and looked back at the rotund man who had reached the bottom of the stairs. He blinked in surprise as he recognized the jolly face accentuated by bushy salt-and-pepper eyebrows. "Lord Penford, always a pleasure to see you."

And it was. Justin enjoyed Penford's quick intelligence and keen humor. The viscount's radical politics had made him a pariah with many of his fellow peers, but not with Justin, who admired and respected the man's courage and compassion for others.

Justin remembered the caustic letter in his pocket and pitied Penford that he was saddled with such a virago. "And a coincidence, too, for I wrote to your daughter in Umberside only this morning."

"Are you carrying on a secret correspondence with Georgie behind my back?" Although Penford's tone was amused, he studied Justin with the eye of a father assessing a prospective son-in-law.

Justin recalled what the schnauzer and the poodle had said about Miss Penford. No doubt her father hoped to pawn his dried up shrew of a daughter off on anyone he could find. Well, Justin was not the man.

"I was replying to a letter from your daughter in which she took me severely to task for my guardianship of my sister."

"Ah, yes, the Dortons' grandchick is your sister." Penford gave Justin a shrew look from beneath his bushy brows. "I hope Georgie was not too hard on you."

"She was very blunt." Infuriatingly so.

"Georgie is always extremely candid," her father said indulgently. "It is one of her charms."

Justin did not find her candor in the least charming. "I must warn you, I was equally blunt in my answer to her."

"I hope you haven't posted the letter yet, for Georgie is not in Umberside but here in London."

"Actually, I have it in my pocket."

"Give it to me. I'll deliver it myself."

As Justin handed the letter to Penford, the viscount said sympathetically, "Must have been hard to have a schoolgirl thrust on you as your ward."

At least one Penford understood. "Damn difficult. She was a virtual stranger to me." When Justin had collected Melanie after her grandparents died, he'd been dismayed to discover what a sullen, unpleasant girl she'd become.

"Your daughter seems to think I should have Melanie live with me, but a bachelor's London residence is no place for a schoolroom chit." Justin would be forced to hire one of those elderly, horse-faced chaperons for her. The thought of such a woman and his petulant, morose sister living under his roof froze his blood.

Penford tucked Justin's letter into his pocket. "My daughter is extremely fond of Melanie. After her mother died a few years ago, your sister spent so much time at Penfield, I began to think I had two daughters."

Knowing what poor company his sulky, silent sister was, Justin said with concern, "I hope she did not make a nuisance of herself."

"Not at all. She is always welcome at Penfield."

Justin suspected that for once Penford, usually the most honest of men, was not being entirely candid with him. "I appreciate your kindness to her."

"Nonsense, she is a bright, delightful girl."

This statement convinced Justin that Penford was sacrificing truth for tact.

"You must join Georgie and me for dinner one night."

Not if Justin could help it. Just the thought of dining with Penford's harridan daughter gave him indigestion.

"Good day," Penford said pleasantly. "I will see my daughter gets your letter."

"I doubt she will be pleased," Justin warned.

"I'm certain she won't," Penford said with an odd smile.

A few minutes later, Justin banged the knocker at the house in Chesterfield Street. The butler who answered gave him a surprised, appraising look.

"Tell your mistress that the Earl of Ravenstone wishes to see her immediately." Justin's imperial tone coupled with his title was guaranteed to win admittance from even the most reluctant and snobbish of butlers.

"Yes, my lord. Let me show you into the drawing room, and I will tell her."

Justin was ushered into a room decorated in soothing pastels. He would have expected a more vivid color scheme for the Scarlet Lady. He strode over to a pier table and examined a Sevres porcelain of a man and woman in ball dress.

Hearing the swish of skirts behind him, he turned slowly, wondering what the Scarlet Lady's reaction had been when she'd learned he was here. No doubt she'd been much flustered.

He saw his hostess's face, and his jaw dropped.

Good God, Nancy Wilde! He was so stunned at seeing his former mistress he blurted, "Bloody hell, what are you doing here?"

"This is my home."

The implications of that staggered Justin. It had not occurred to him that the woman he'd met the previous night could be a member of the demimonde. She neither looked nor acted at all like a high flier, but like a well bred young lady of quality. Clearly he'd been wrong. Only another member of the demimonde would have dared come here as she had. The lady's reputation must be as scarlet as her garb.

Her unorthodox behavior—attending a public lecture alone and professing strong distaste for marriage—should have warned him just how unconventional she was. Still . . .

Momentarily at a loss for words, Justin looked around the room, assessing its value with a shrewd eye. And a surprised one, too, for Nancy's current protector was noted for being stingy with his blunt. "You do not seem startled to see me here."

"I'm not. When I heard you'd followed Gina here last night, I expected you would call today."

So the Scarlet Lady was named Gina. He liked the name, which must be short for Regina. His mind ran rapidly through the women of Nancy's world, but he could not recall a single one with that name.

"Gina must be a new addition to the demimonde." Why the devil did his innocuous observation cause Nancy to stiffen and look so furious?

"Very new," she replied icily.

Her sudden coldness startled him. Could it be Nancy was jealous of the newcomer? "What is Gina's surname?"

"I cannot tell you without her permission. She might not desire to know you better."

Justin could think of only one reason why a woman of Gina's calling would not welcome an earl's attentions, and it did not please him at all. "Why? Because she currently has a protector?"

Nancy looked as though she were weighing how to answer him.

He frowned. "I want the truth. Does Gina have a lover presently?"

"No."

The enormous relief he felt startled him. He no longer needed to ponder whom he wanted to succeed his present mistress.

Eager to see Gina again, he asked, "Where does she live?"

"I cannot help you, Justin. I have never called upon her. She comes to see me."

Justin suspected Nancy was lying. He had never known her to do so before, and his estimation of her sank. But he would gain nothing by accusing her. Instead he said brusquely, "Then I must commission you to deliver a message to her for me. Inform her that I wish to enter into a business arrangement with her."

Nancy stiffened. "The kind you and I once had?"

The hard edge to her voice convinced him she must indeed be jealous of Gina. "Yes. Tell her I am prepared to be very generous."

"Should you not be thinking of marrying again and producing an heir, rather than acquiring another mistress? How old are you now, thirty-seven?"

"Thirty-six, and nothing would ever persuade me to marry again." Just the thought of doing so made his jaw clench painfully. "Once was too much. I am quite happy to have my title and fortune pass to my younger brother, Henry."

"I remember you used to regard Henry almost as a son. Where is your brother now?"

"In Berkshire, restoring a neglected estate that I recently purchased there. Promise me that you will tell Gina of my offer?"

"I shall when she calls upon me again, but I have no idea how long that might be."

Justin bridled impatiently at this answer. Nancy's amused expression prompted his suspicion. Not entirely trusting her, he said sharply, "Promise me you will tell her the very next time you see her. Do I have your word on that?"

"You do." Nancy looked as though she were enjoying some private joke. "I am as eager to hear her response as you are."

Georgina could not concentrate on the huge blade-like tooth of a prehistoric creature that she was analyzing in her workroom at her father's London house. A dark, harsh face set with deep brown eyes kept intruding on her thoughts, and the harder she tried to push this image from her mind the more stubbornly entrenched it became.

The butler appeared in the workroom doorway. "The afternoon post has arrived, ma'am, with a letter for you."

She set the strange tooth down on her worktable and took the letter. The nearly unreadable handwriting told her it was from Ravenstone's sister, Lady Melanie Alexander, her second letter in as many days.

Hurriedly Georgina broke the seal and opened it. The ink was badly splotched by tears. As she deciphered Lanie's atrocious handwriting, her heart ached for the unhappy girl.

"Clearly you do not like the contents of your letter."

Georgina looked up. Her father stepped into her

workroom. She smiled, always delighted to see him. "I did not realize you were home, Papa."

"I just arrived." He nodded at the paper in her hand. "Who wrote you?"

"Lanie Alexander. The poor dear is utterly miserable at that dreadful school her brother insists she attend. She threatens to run away unless he removes her from it."

"That tactic will not work with Ravenstone," her father observed. "Such a ploy might have been successful with her grandparents, but she would be ill advised to try it on her guardian."

"Surely, you don't sympathize with that dreadful man!"

"I have known Ravenstone for more than fifteen years, and I have the highest respect for him. Nor do I envy him being saddled with responsibility for a schoolgirl he scarcely knows."

Georgina immediately jumped to Lanie's defense. "'Tis not her fault they are strangers, Papa. Ravenstone has made no attempt to get to know her."

"Be that as it may, she should be writing him, not you, of her complaints." Georgina's father crossed the room to her worktable.

"No doubt he ignores her letters to him just as he has ignored the one I wrote him. I don't know what to do. 'Tis a waste of time to write him again since he has not even the common courtesy to answer my first letter."

"Oh, but he has." Her father pulled a paper from his pocket. "Here is his reply. He gave it to me himself."

"Did he tell you why it took him three months to answer me?"

"Ravenstone is not a man who bothers to explain himself."

Georgina broke the seal on the earl's letter. His bold handwriting was considerably easier to read than his half sister's. But as Georgina scanned the brief contents, her eyebrows rose and so did her anger. Branding her a meddling ape leader, he hotly rejected her accusation that he'd neglected his duty to his ward.

Ravenstone concluded his fiery missive by admonishing Georgina to keep her long, pointed witch's nose out of other people's business in general and his in particular.

Sputtering with fury, Georgina looked up from the offensive note, shamed to think that, before she'd learned his identity, she'd found the insufferable, negligent scoundrel fascinating.

"His answer does not appear to please you," her father observed.

"The dolt does not care in the slightest that Lanie is miserable at Lady Neldane's Academy. It is an outrage to put a girl of her intelligence in that insipid school that cares only about molding her into a docile, obedient, mindless wife."

"But that is precisely why parents of the ton pay a fortune to send their daughters there."

"Thank God, you and Mama did not think that way," Georgina said with fervent gratitude. "I would have been as bored and unhappy as Lanie is. She writes that Lady Neldane thinks a student's most important achievement is learning to embroider a pretty sampler. How could Ravenstone think Lanie would be happy there?"

"Most likely he believes, as too many men unfortunately do, that a woman's intellectual capacity is limited."

"Which only shows you what a fool he is."

"Had you known his late wife, perhaps you would not judge him so harshly."

"Perhaps I would judge him even more harshly were I privy to her side of the story," Georgina retorted. "Only consider, if you were to hear the complaints of Aunt Margaret's crazed husband against her, you would think he was a most aggrieved spouse instead of a madman."

"I base my argument about the late Lady Ravenstone on my own observation of her, not on hearsay from her husband. Indeed, I never heard Ravenstone speak ill of her."

"Most likely he ignored her as he does Lanie. What Ravenstone should do is what you and Mama did for me—hire a tutor for her."

"I doubt he would share our radical ideas about educating young women. Remember how shocked everyone was when we hired Gareth."

Georgina gurgled with laughter. "Yes, they were certain he would seduce me. Such fools! I learned a great deal more from Gareth than from any of my governesses. Although that was not their fault," she added quickly. "Those poor women could not teach what they had never been taught themselves."

Her father picked up the tooth lying on her worktable. "Where did you get this, Georgie? I've never seen a tooth so large."

"Mr. Morton found it in Oxfordshire and sent it to me to see if I could identify it."

"Can you?"

"I am almost positive it belonged to a prehistoric beast that Dr. Parkinson named megalosaurus."

As her father laid the tooth down, Georgina glanced again at the angry letter in her hand. "Ravenstone makes it clear he will not let Lanie live with either him or us."

Her father gave her an odd smile. "Perhaps if you try to persuade him in person, he might relent."

The sudden gleam in Papa's eyes perplexed Georgina.

"I have always found Ravenstone a most reasonable man, once the facts of a situation were properly explained to him."

And it would give me a reason to see him again. Where had that thought come from? As if she should care! Yet her innards twisted in excitement at this prospect.

No doubt Ravenstone believed a mere woman, meddling witch though he might think her, would never dare to challenge him further. Georgina would teach him that she was not so easily cowed.

This time she would confront Ravenstone face-to-face in private.

He would not soon forget it.

Chapter 4

Justin tossed aside his copy of the *Transactions of the London Geological Society*. Unable to concentrate on what he was reading, he rose from his walnut desk. He could not remember ever having been so curious about a woman as he was about the mysterious Gina—or so eager to see her again.

He strode restlessly to the long windows in his library and looked down on the wide expanse of Grosvenor Square. How long would it be before Nancy Wilde would see Gina and transmit his message to her. He wanted her in his bed as quickly as he could manage it.

Despite Nancy's warning that Gina might not want him as a lover, Justin was not worried. No high flier would turn down a liaison with an earl. At the thought of her in his bed, his body responded as though he were a randy halfling again.

The rain that had been falling for the past hour had stopped for the moment, but the gray, gloomy sky promised this interlude would be brief. Only two equipages plodded through the square.

When one of them, a smart carriage, stopped in front of the steps to his house, Justin groaned, fearing he was about to be subjected to another visit by the reactionaries from the House of Lords. He watched as a footman jumped down, hurried to open the vehicle's door, and let down the steps.

To Justin's surprise and relief, no gentlemen emerged but rather a lady in a carriage gown and green pelerine. Although this cape hid the top of her gown, its colorful full skirt alternated wide vertical rose stripes with narrower ones that matched her pelerine. The wide brim of her green bonnet trimmed with roses hid her face from him.

He could not help smiling at the refreshing splash of color she made against the grayness of the day. No one else climbed out of the carriage after her. That startled Justin, for stylishly dressed ladies of quality did not call unaccompanied at the house of an unmarried man.

As she strode toward his steps, she raised her head to examine the exterior of his house.

Justin's breath caught. *The Scarlet Lady!* Could he be hallucinating? No, his eyes were not deceiving him. She was climbing the steps to his door.

He could not help grinning. Clearly Nancy had wasted no time in informing Gina of his proposition. And she was wasting even less time in accepting it.

Justin chuckled cynically. So much for Nancy's warning that Gina might not be interested in his offer.

Most men in his position would be angry at Gina for daring to come to his house like this rather than requesting him to call on her. Being so new to the demimonde, she must not have learned yet that a light-skirt never embarrassed a protector, past, present, or future, by coming to his home. But Justin was far too happy to see her to care in the least about appearances.

The front knocker sounded loudly and firmly. No timid, indecisive tap for his Gina. He smiled in satisfaction, certain of her reason for coming. Oddly though, much as he wanted her as his mistress, he felt a pang of disappointment that she had capitulated so easily.

Turning from the window, Justin hurried out of the drawing room. As he reached the staircase that led down to the entry hall, Gina's voice, clear and melodic, yet firm, drifted up to him.

"Please inform Lord Ravenstone that I must see him at once. I have important business to *discuss* with him."

The peculiar emphasis she put on discuss warned Justin he'd been premature in thinking she'd accepted his offer. Apparently they had some hard bargaining ahead of them. Would she turn out to be as greedy as his current convenient? That sobering thought was enough to lessen his interest in Gina.

His mouth tightened. He would, as he did with all his liaisons, set out for her in explicit terms exactly what he would give her and what he would expect in return.

Putney, Justin's butler, inquired of her in a haughty, skeptical voice, "What business would that be?"

"'Tis a private matter between his lordship and me."

Her voice was even frostier and haughtier than Putney's. Justin's estimation of her crept upward at her refusal to allow his butler to intimidate her. He liked a woman with starch in her spine.

"Whom shall I say is calling?" the butler asked.

"My name is of no importance," she answered coldly.

"It is if you expect his lordship to see you. He does not receive callers of *no importance*."

Justin, who by now was halfway down the stairs, intervened, "Never mind, Putney. The lady and I do indeed have business to discuss."

At the sound of Justin's voice, she tilted her face toward him. He wondered why her charmingly arched eyebrows raised in apparent surprise at his answer, but she said nothing.

As he reached her, he noticed that a chocolate brown tendril of hair had escaped the confines of her bonnet and drifted across her soft cheek. He had to curb an impulse to reach out and tuck the wayward lock beneath her bonnet, then stroke her cheek. He was surprised at how strongly he yearned to touch her.

Justin gave her as inviting a smile as he could muster. To his disappointment, she did not return it. "Please come up to the drawing room where we can . . . er . . . talk in *absolute privacy*."

He intended this as both a warning to Putney that they were not to be disturbed and a veiled hint to Gina that before she left, he would like to indulge in more pleasurable activities than talking.

He half-expected her to take umbrage at his subtle innuendo. Instead she looked him directly in the eye and said in a surprisingly flat, matter-of-fact tone, "Yes, considering the nature of our business, I think that would be best."

Her cool, self-possessed manner disconcerted Justin. He was used to women of her ilk, no matter how experienced and calculating, to act coy and uncertain at such moments as these. Would she be as brisk and no nonsense when she negotiated her price? Or when she was in his bed?

From the look in her eye, she was determined to drive a very hard bargain.

Not that she would succeed.

He looked her over critically. She fell short of the standard of beauty he generally required in his convenients. Yet something about her, her confident carriage, her laughing eyes, her vitality, or perhaps her brilliant smile—although he had yet to see it today—captivated him.

Justin glanced toward his butler. For the first time in memory, Putney's wooden, bored countenance had vanished, and he was watching them with lively interest.

Below stairs would be abuzz tonight, Justin thought wryly.

"Putney, bring us up a bottle of . . ." He broke off, uncertain of what was appropriate to serve. Justin had never before entertained a prospective mistress in his own drawing room. Such a thing was not done.

He decided to start with sherry. He disliked the wine, but after she had a glass or two, their negotiations would very likely go easier. When they agreed on the terms of their arrangement, he would have a bottle of French champagne brought up to celebrate. He had not an instant's doubt that they would soon be drinking to their new alliance and then consummating it.

"Bring us sherry," Justin told Putney.

"Please, do not have him do so for me," Gina said to Justin. Her pelerine brought out the green in her eyes, making them look more that color than hazel. "I do not care for sherry."

"Something else then?" Justin inquired.

"Nothing, thank you."

Her manner, like her voice, indicated a woman of

superior breeding. He wondered whether she had been forced into the demimonde after a wastrel father or brother had squandered the family fortune.

Justin recalled her antipathy for husbands. Could it be she was a widow left penniless by a husband who had gambled both his and her money away? Inexplicable fury gripped him at the thought some blackguard could have reduced her to the straits in which she now found herself.

He told Putney, "See that we are not disturbed."

Taking Gina's arm, Justin felt a little shiver run through her at his touch. That pleased him—his attraction to her was definitely not one-sided.

He longed to see her face light up with her marvelous smile that crinkled her face and brought such sparkle to her eyes. Hoping to promote this, he smiled broadly at her as he guided her up the steps to his drawing room, but her expression remained serious.

Justin had to content himself with breathing deeply of her charming gardenia scent.

He led her into the drawing room, which he rarely used. His mother had determined the decor: the delicate plasterwork on the walls and ceiling, the Louis XV tables, the fragile sofas and chairs covered in gilt and royal blue brocade. Justin much preferred the library with its warm oak paneling and sturdier, masculine furnishings.

As he shut the door, he asked, "Why would you not give my butler your name?"

"I feared if you were told it, you would refuse to see me."

That startled him until he realized that naturally Gina would assume he would not recognize her name and, therefore, would turn her away. "Oh, but you are very wrong about that," he said softly.

"You see, Nancy Wilde told me who you are."

"She did?"

Gina sounded so dismayed that he asked in surprise, "Why does that distress you?"

"I am shocked she told you. I made her promise she would not. I never thought Nancy would go back on her word to me like that."

"To do her justice, all she told me was your first name. I guessed the rest."

"How astonishingly astute of you."

She sounded so surprised that Justin did not know whether to be complimented or insulted. "I am generally reputed to be acute." *And she would do well to remember that.* "Nancy refused to tell me where you live. That's why I was forced to transmit my message to you through such an unusual intermediary."

"I wondered—" She stopped abruptly as Justin began to undo the fastening of her cape.

"I am quite capable of removing my own pelerine, my lord," she said sharply, vainly trying to push his hands away.

He gave her his most seductive smile. "But a gentleman loves to do little things such as this for a lady he admires."

"You admire *me*?" She was clearly incredulous.

He wondered why that should astonish her so much. If he did not admire her, he would never have made her the offer he had. "Very much," he replied truthfully.

"Despite my long, pointed nose?" she inquired tartly.

He looked at her blankly. Gina had quite the most adorable little nose, tilted up at the tip, that Justin had ever seen. It fit her pixie face perfectly.

"Whoever told you that must have been blind,"

he assured her kindly. "Your nose is charming."

She opened her mouth, then closed it again as though her voice had suddenly failed her.

Justin laid her cape over the back of a chair and gestured at the sofa nearby. "Please, do sit down."

The sofa would hold two easily, and he'd intended for them both to occupy it. But Gina sat in the middle, clearly expecting him to take the chair across from her as though she were a lady instead of a courtesan.

She must learn he was not a man who would be kept at bay. He squeezed down beside her. For a delicious moment, his body pressed against her soft curves.

Gina hastily slid to the far side of the sofa, as though his closeness burned her. His body, too, had responded so ardently to their brief moment of contact that he was startled.

He reached beneath her chin and untied the green satin bow of her bonnet, saying, "Your chapeau is charming, but I prefer to see your lovely hair."

Gina grabbed his hands, clearly intent on stopping him. Their gazes locked.

They both went very still for an electric moment.

Her eyes widened and softened. Clearly unaware of what she was doing, she ran the tip of her tongue over her upper lip, calling Justin's attention to how kissable her mouth was. He ached to taste it.

Looking dazed, she absently released his hands. He lifted her bonnet from her head and laid it on a satinwood table beside the sofa.

He could not keep himself from gently smoothing a few strands of her hair with his fingers. Her eyes widened again at his touch, and he felt her quiver.

If only she would smile at him. She still had not done so. He wondered if she was more nervous than she appeared. Trying to put her at ease, he said, "I think we will deal very well together."

"You do?"

Again Justin wondered why she should sound so amazed. "Yes, I do. I am delighted you were sufficiently intrigued by my message to call on me—and so promptly, too."

Gina stiffened. "Intrigued is hardly the word I would use to describe my reaction to it, my lord."

Justin was taken aback by the surprisingly icy edge to her voice. Attributing it to anger at his having commissioned Nancy Wilde to deliver such a private message, he said soothingly, "Well, whatever your feelings, I am very pleased you wasted no time in seeking to discuss my message with me, for that was what I hoped it would prompt you to do."

She stared at him as though he were deranged. "Are you saying that outrageous message was intended to bring me here?"

"Well, not here actually, but I did want it to whet your curiosity enough that you would ask me to call on you."

Her eyes narrowed angrily. "You have a peculiar way of whetting—"

He interrupted her with a smile, pointing out, "But it worked, did it not? You are here."

Her brows knit in a frown. Justin could not resist running his fingertips lightly down her cheek. His gesture clearly startled and surprised her, but he did not think it displeased her.

Still, it was too early to start that aspect of their relationship. First they must settle its financial details. "Tell me, Gina, what do you want from me?"

"Since I am here, I would think the answer is obvious." At last, she smiled at him, only a small smile, but it was progress. "I am persuaded you know the one thing I want from you."

Justin did not. He was certain only that whatever this sole desire of hers was, it would be very expensive.

In his experience, mistresses most wanted two things, a fine house to live in and jewels. Since he did not know her taste in the latter, he decided she must want the former. "Yes, I believe I can guess," he said dryly.

"I thought you could, given how astute you are."

Best he tell her what he was prepared to give her and test her greed. He said cautiously, "I have given much thought to this matter."

Again she seemed surprised. "You have?"

"I have, and I propose to let a house, a very comfortable house with a full complement of servants. Where should it be?" He waited for her to name one of London's most expensive streets.

Gina appeared astounded. "But, my lord, I neither want nor expect you to go to such ridiculous expense as that."

It was his turn to be astonished. Never before had a prospective inamorata expressed any inclination whatsoever to save *him* money. "What do you suggest instead?"

"Why not here with you?"

Justin choked. He was going to have to speak to Nancy Wilde about educating Gina in the ways of the world. She was far too naive for her chosen profession.

Furthermore, he could think of nothing worse than having his mistress living in his own residence. Why it would be as bad as being married. She would be constantly underfoot, demanding his attention.

He was careful, however, to phrase his rejection in more tactful terms. "Convenient as that would be for me, I am afraid it is out of the question."

"Why?" she looked genuinely puzzled. "It is a very nice house and clearly large enough to—"

"Society would be outraged by such an arrangement."

She frowned at him. "You struck me as a man who cares little about what society thinks. I see I was wrong."

He winced at the disappointment and disdain in her voice. "No, you were quite right, I don't care. But I am a gentleman, and I refuse to be responsible for exposing any lady under my protection to the censure that would be hers."

His answer clearly perplexed her. "What possible exception could society take to such an arrangement?"

Justin had no desire to instruct her in the niceties of society's expectations. Once they were in the bedroom, however . . . The thought of her lying naked beside him was so enticing that he had difficulty pulling his mind back to the present.

"I suggest you ask Nancy Wilde to explain it to you." He was growing increasingly impatient to undress Gina with more than his eyes.

A flush of embarrassment colored Gina's cheeks so prettily that Justin could scarcely resist kissing her.

"It is true I have been little exposed to society," she said, "and I am not entirely familiar with its expectations."

This meeting was not going at all as Justin had intended. He suddenly felt a need for something to quench his frustration.

Rising, he went to the table where a brandy decanter and glasses rested.

As he poured himself a glass, he asked her, "Shall I let the house after all?"

"Oh, no, please don't! Truly, it is such an unnecessary expense. I am happy to offer you my home instead. It is quite large and comfortable."

Justin felt a sharp, unexpected stab of jealousy, and ice crept into his voice. "May I ask from whom a woman of your young years acquired such a large, comfortable home?"

"Actually it is not mine. It is my father's."

"Your father's!"

"Yes. I am certain you would find it quite acceptable. My father prides himself on his hospitality."

Justin's jaw dropped. "Bloody hell, you mean he lives there, too?"

"Of course, but he will not mind an addition to his household."

"I cannot believe that!" Her papa was more likely to welcome Justin with a loaded flintlock.

"But it's true," she assured him. "I have already asked Papa about this arrangement."

"You've already asked him?" Justin echoed faintly. He took a large gulp of brandy before making his way back to the settee.

"Certainly. I would not take such a step without consulting him," Gina said as Justin sat down again beside her. "Papa is agreeable to the arrangement. Indeed he suggested I come here to discuss it with you."

"Suggested *you* come here!" The brandy sloshed dangerously in Justin's glass. "You have a most unusual father."

And undoubtedly an extremely greedy one.

"Oh, yes, I am very lucky. He gives me so much freedom to do what I want."

Gina's brilliant smile was so bewitching that Justin had to tighten his hands around his brandy glass to keep them off of her.

"Papa is the best father in the whole world," Gina continued.

It was all Justin could do to keep from snorting in derision. The "best father in the whole world" did not profit from his daughter's body. Justin was assailed by the unnerving suspicion that he had been mistaken about Gina's intelligence, that she actually must be quite simple in the head.

As for her father, Justin would have a hard time not killing an evil, greedy bastard who pushed his daughter into the demimonde. "I think it would be wiser for me to let a house."

"Oh, no, 'tis such a waste. I would much prefer you use the money to hire a tutor."

Justin's jaw dropped. "A tutor! Surely you are jesting."

"Not at all. I know it is a most unusual request for a girl, but I would be eternally grateful if you would do it."

Taking a sip of brandy, Justin studied her face suspiciously above the rim of his glass. "Do you perchance know a tutor I might hire?"

"Yes, I do."

His mouth tightened. "I thought so. Was he previously your tutor?"

"How did you know?" she asked in surprise. "My father hired him for me."

Her damned father deserved to be hung by his thumbs.

"I assure you Papa made certain that he was the very best."

"Was he?" Images of Gina and her "tutor" making love in various exotic positions fueled Justin's growing rage. He would show her just how wrong she was about her "tutor" being the "very best."

"Oh, yes. You would be amazed at all Gareth taught me."

No, not amazed. Incensed! What a fool Gina must believe him to try to cajole him into hiring her lover to entertain her when he was not about. "I will hire no tutor. I am not the inexperienced nodcock you obviously think me."

"Oh, but I don't think that at all, my lord, although I do think you do not understand women very well."

"To the contrary, I understand them far too well. You would be very wise to remember that in your dealings with me."

Justin's anger was warring with his lust for her. After her ploy about "her tutor," his desire for a liaison with her was fading. Still, he ached to taste her full, tantalizing lips, to caress her slender body, to bury himself within her. Her mere presence proved to be a potent aphrodisiac for him.

By now, he was certain of only one thing. He was tired of all this damned talking.

It was time he showed her what they might have enjoyed together had she not taken him to be such a stupid idiot that she could foist her lover off on him as her tutor.

Better yet, he would drive any thought of her damned teacher from her mind.

Chapter 5

Georgina watched in fascination as Ravenstone's hard eyes softened to a warm, turbulent shade of brown. His response to her visit confounded her. His behavior was so totally different from what she had expected. And far more congenial.

Nor was he nearly as uncaring about his sister's welfare as Georgina had thought him. His generosity in offering to rent a house for Lanie and to staff it with a retinue of servants deeply impressed Georgina.

She also applauded his desire to protect his sister from censure. He was absolutely right about a woman being the one who always paid the highest price when society frowned.

With a little more time, Georgina would surely be able to convince him to give up the idea of renting a house for his sister and let her live at Penfield instead.

Persuading him to hire her old tutor for Lanie would clearly be more difficult, but Georgina hoped that eventually she could bring him around.

She looked up at the sharp planes of Ravenstone's face framed by his thick curly hair, black as jet. His dark eyes glowed with a strange fire that kindled an answering warmth in her.

His mouth descended upon hers, and he kissed her. She was paralyzed, too shocked to protest, and his lips caressed hers lightly like a rose petal drifting on the evening breeze.

She had never experienced anything like it. Deep within her, excitement twisted and a strange ache gnawed at her.

Georgina would never have thought this big, harsh-faced man could be so gentle.

Instead of soothing her ache, though, his kiss intensified it. She was astonished to discover she yearned to be even closer to him, to have him hold her in his arms.

As though he read her thoughts, he folded her against him, and she felt the leashed strength of his muscled arms around her. An unusual spicy scent, which Georgina found very pleasant, clung to him. What a blessed relief from the dreadful heavy musk in which so many men drenched themselves.

The tip of his tongue teased her closed lips in a tantalizing way that made her feel warm and strange. A pleased little sigh escaped her. He took advantage of this opening, his tongue darting between her lips to explore her mouth more thoroughly.

Georgina started in surprise. She had never been kissed like that before. She would have pulled away from him, but his arms tightened around her. He cradled the back of her head with one of his hands.

The sensations he generated within her were so exciting that she could not bring herself to try to escape him nor even to protest. Perhaps, in a moment or two . . .

His mouth grew more demanding. She was swept

by a strange elation. *Justin is very accomplished at giving a woman enormous pleasure.* Before Georgina was quite aware of it, she was returning his kiss fervently.

Ravenstone raised his lips a fraction and murmured, his voice strangely thick, "So sweet, so delicious."

He kissed the tip of her nose and laid a trail of kisses across her cheek. His teeth lightly caught her earlobe and nipped on it. Then he traced the inner contours of her ear with his tongue, and she marveled at the twisting hunger she felt low in her abdomen, so remote from her ear.

His thumb casually—surely by accident—brushed the tip of her breast. His hand slid down the curve of her body and stopped at her waist. "What, no stays?"

"No, I despise them. They are so uncomfortable to wear I refuse to do so." Thinking she detected a hint of disapproval in his eyes, she asked. "Why are you looking at me like that?"

"I am surprised. Most women would not be seen without them on."

Georgina frowned. "Are you offended that I do not wear them?"

He shrugged. "No, as long as you stay as slender as you are, I will have no objection to your not wearing them."

His answer puzzled her, but before she could inquire about it, his hand moved to her belly. He stroked it lightly, and heat streaked through her. Georgina forgot all else. The pleasure she felt was so intense she gasped. She thought dreamily that this must be what Nancy Wilde had been talking about.

He lifted his head. As he looked at her, his eyes,

a hot liquid brown now, glowed with something she could not define. "So you like that, do you?" His voice was low and as soft as velvet, intensifying the ache within her.

"Yes," she admitted.

"I thought so." He sounded pleased with himself.

Without warning, he grabbed her around her waist and under her knees and lifted her onto his lap. She shivered as she felt his warm, hard body against her own.

"That's better." His mouth again fastened hungrily on hers in a deep, devouring kiss that robbed her of breath.

He stroked her ankle with his hand. She could feel its warmth through her silk stocking. Slowly, as their kiss continued, his caressing hand crept up her leg, like the slow, almost imperceptible rise of the tide in a calm sea.

By the time he reached her knees, she was so awash in strange sensations that she hardly noticed as he nudged them apart.

Her stockings ended just about the knee, and when he caressed the bare skin of her thigh above them, she clamped her legs together in shock, catching his hand between them. She jerked her mouth away from his and uttered a protest.

He lifted his head, and Georgina was stunned by the anger and derision in his eyes.

"Oh, come now, my sweet, I know what you are," he said mockingly. "Don't pretend to be the coy virgin with me. It does not become you."

His scornful words instantly banished the sensual languor that gripped Georgina. "Not become me?" she echoed, perplexed.

"No, it does not"—his voice took on a cutting

edge—"especially after you boasted to me about your *tutor*."

"What does Gareth have to do with this?" Georgina asked, mystified.

She tried to wrench herself from Ravenstone's hold, but his arm tightened around her. His eyes were no longer soft but hard as granite. "Let me go!" she cried.

"Not yet, my dear," he said coldly. "At the very least I insist you show me some of what your talented tutor taught you." His hand closed roughly around her breast.

The man must be stark, raving mad. Much alarmed, Georgina marshaled all her strength and gave him a mighty shove as she twisted off his lap.

Her unexpected move took him by surprise, and she gained her feet before he could recover.

"How dare you?" she hissed at him as she backed away. She longed to run from the room, but her pelerine lay over the back of the sofa and her bonnet on the table next to him. She reached out to snatch the bonnet, but his hand caught her wrist in a punishing grip.

"Let go of me!" Georgina tried to pull away from him, but he was too strong for her.

Justin yanked her down hard on his knee, fury blazing through him. "I will when I am finished with you." Damn this woman, she'd led him on until he was painfully aroused, then pretended such affronted innocence. As if they both weren't fully aware no woman of her profession was anything of the sort.

For a moment, she seemed bereft of speech, then she said in a scathing tone, "You are no gentleman."

He curled his lip in contempt. "I am a gentleman

only when I am with a lady. And you, my dear, are no lady."

"I am *not* your dear! And I *am* a lady! Kindly address me with respect."

"With respect!" He laughed harshly at the humor of a doxy claiming she was a lady to be addressed with respect. "And why should I do that?"

"Why?" She sounded incredulous. "If you had the smallest modicum of breeding to go with your title, you would not have to ask."

"My, what sharp claws you have, Gina." He felt her body stiffen.

"Don't call me Gina!"

"What am I to call you? Jade? Harridan? Doxy?"

"Doxy!" She was sputtering with rage. "First, I am a meddling ape leader with a long, pointed witch's nose! Now I am a doxy! You will address me by my name, Miss Penford."

Justin thought he must have misheard her. "What did you say?"

She regarded him as though he were a Bedlam lunatic. "My name, as you well know, is Miss Penford."

"Good God, *you* cannot be that dried up shrew, Georgina Penford."

"Am I to consider that a compliment, my lord?" she inquired acidly.

For a moment, Justin was frozen by shock. Then he let go of her with the haste of a man who had belatedly discovered he was holding a viper. She jumped to her feet and out of his reach.

"Bloody hell, I don't believe this!" Justin ran his hand distractedly through his hair, incredulity and embarrassment warring with frustration.

Discovering who she was did not cure his ache for her. If anything, it increased it, for now he knew he could never make her his mistress. What a damned comedy of errors!

Gina stared at him, looking as confused as he felt. "But you said Nancy told you who I was."

He stood up and took a step toward Gin—Miss Penford. She backed away from him.

"She told me . . ." He broke off, remembering the anger that had flashed in Nancy's eyes when he'd referred to Gina as a new member of the demi-monde. "Oh hell!"

Justin had made an unwarranted and insulting assumption, and Nancy had not corrected him. He was livid at himself for having done so, rather than heeding all the contrary evidence.

He had just made a damned fool of himself. And for a man of his pride and temperament, that was intolerable. He was so angry at himself that he vented it on the only other person in the room. "Why the devil did you go to Nancy Wilde's house last night?"

"To hoax you for following me."

"You sure as hell succeeded," Justin said in exasperation.

He studied her indignant eyes and flushed cheeks. How pretty she looked, even as angry as she was now. He wondered how Plimpton and Ingleham could have called her a dried up prune and an antidote? Not only were they fools, they also suffered from seriously defective eyesight.

As Justin watched her, he suddenly, to his astonishment, felt the most perverse yearning to take her in his arms and soothe and kiss her into better humor.

He was not such a fool as to try that, though. Instead he said, "I don't understand why you came to see me today."

"How can you say that—after telling me that insulting letter you had my father deliver was designed to bring me here, and that it succeeded."

Justin had forgotten about that damned letter, and he groaned in dismay. "Have you not seen Nancy Wilde today?"

"No, although why you should ask is beyond my comprehension."

Justin felt as though he had unwittingly stumbled into a quagmire and was sinking rapidly. "You had better explain to me for what purpose you offered your father's house," he said grimly.

She stared at him as though he were a simpleton. "That's obvious."

"Not quite as obvious as you think."

As I told you in my letter, if you will not give poor Lanie a home with you, then you should let her live with me so she can escape that dreadful school she despises."

Justin ran his hands over his eyes.

Miss Penford looked puzzled. "What other reason could you possibly think I had?"

Justin decided against enlightening her, which did not stop her from continuing with her campaign.

"If you accept my offer, you will benefit, too," she pointed out. "You will not have to go to the expense of hiring a separate house with a staff of servants for Lanie. I own I was very angry at you when you failed to answer my letter for three months, but—"

"I failed to answer it because you sent it to Cornwall, and it did not reach me here in London until two days ago. I was not pleased to receive it."

"So I gathered from your reply. I came here today only because I received yet another letter from poor Lanie. I cannot bear to see her as miserable as she

is at that dreadful school. I assure you, my lord, it
is highly distasteful for a meddling ape leader like
me to stick my long, pointed witch's nose into the
affairs of your family, but—"

"Miss Penford," Justin interrupted her. For the
first time that he could recall in his adult life, he felt
his face flushing with shame. "I apologize for my
intemperate remarks to you. I should never have
given that letter to your father."

"No, you should not have."

Her indignant tone spurred him into defending
himself. "But, by way of explanation, I was grievously insulted by your fallacious charge that I have
neglected my duties as my sister's guardian. Nothing could be further from the truth."

Miss Penford looked so incredulous that he was
moved to explain. "To the contrary, I made a dili-
gent search for the very best school for young ladies
of quality. I was assured by one and all that it is
Lady Neldane's."

"The academic standards of her school are a disgrace! Lanie is bored to death there."

"Miss Penford, Lady Neldane offers the very best
education that money can buy for a young English-
woman."

"How very sad then, is it not, that the very best
education money can buy for a female in this great
country is so inferior?"

"Inferior? How so?"

"For one thing, it offers no courses in science nor
in advanced mathematics, only simple arithmetic."

"Good God," Justin exclaimed, "of what earthly
use would science and advanced mathematics be to
a girl?"

"The same earthly use they would be to you or
any other man!" Miss Penford retorted hotly.

The thought of his sister trying to do advanced mathematics boggled his mind. Whenever he tried to talk to the chit, she could scarcely manage to string two words together. "Melanie would have no interest in such subjects," he said with strong conviction.

"How would you know?" Miss Penford's eyes radiated anger. "If you would spend any time at all with your sister, you would discover what an intelligent, lively young woman she is."

"*Melanie!*" he exclaimed in disbelief. "Are you certain we are talking about the same girl?"

"You would know we were had you deigned to spend even a small amount of time with your ward *as a responsible guardian would have.*"

Her accusation contained just enough truth in it to make Justin growl defensively, "I do not need you to tell me my duties as a guardian."

"You need someone to do so!" She glared at him. "I warn you, unless you pay Lanie more attention and provide her with an education commensurate with her intelligence, she will run away. And you, my lord, will have no one to blame but yourself."

"Nonsense," he scoffed. "Running away would require courage. Melanie is far too timid to do such a thing."

"You sadly underestimate your sister—and women in general."

Justin silently disputed that. The only woman he'd ever underestimated was standing before him now, angry as a hornet whose hive had just been destroyed. "If my sister is so terribly unhappy at Lady Neldane's, why has she not written me of her sentiments?"

"She has not done so?" Miss Penford was clearly

surprised. "But I thought . . ." Her voice faded away.

"No, she has not written me, not a word."

"Or perhaps her letters are lost somewhere between London and Cornwall as the one I wrote you apparently was for three months," she replied tartly.

He bit back a smile. Damn, but Miss Georgina Penford was hard to best verbally, yet he intended to do so. "Or perhaps the post was unable to decipher my sister's execrable handwriting. Ah, I see by that sudden gleam in your eye that you recognize how bad her penmanship is."

"I'm afraid I do," she admitted, flashing that wonderful smile of hers. "Please, my lord, will you allow Lanie to live with me?"

"I cannot—"

She interrupted him. "Don't you see, it is to your advantage to do so. Only think, you need not go to the expense of letting a separate house for her. I think society is ridiculous to condemn an orphaned little sister for living with her bachelor brother, but I defer to your more knowledgeable judgment on that."

Justin decided against further fueling Georgina's anger by trying to explain what he'd really meant. Instead, he asked, "And what about your old tutor?"

"If you will not employ him or another tutor to educate her, I will accept the responsibility."

Justin, wounded that Miss Penford thought him such a pinch-purse, said angrily, "I do not object to the cost, only the impropriety of having a tutor instruct a girl of her age. Nor can I allow my sister to live with a woman who is a friend of Nancy Wilde."

"Why not?"

"Because I must look out for my sister's best interests."

"So far you have failed miserably to do so."

Justin had been trying hard to keep his temper and his cutting tongue in check, but this unjust accusation unleashed both. "It would be disastrous for Melanie to have the slightest association with you, considering the company you keep," he snapped. "Her opportunity for a suitable marriage would be as dead as your chances of catching a husband are."

Miss Penford glared at him. "Is that why you are not married, my lord?"

Justin looked at her blankly. "I beg your pardon?"

"Have you not caught a wife because you were once Nancy Wilde's *intimate* friend?"

"I have not caught a wife because I do not want one," Justin said through his teeth. "The last thing on earth I want is to be married again."

"Then you apprehend perfectly how I feel about marriage."

"A woman of your station cannot feel like that. What else are you to do with yourself?"

Her eyes blazed with anger. "What else indeed, since you clearly think women are born solely for the purpose of serving men?"

"Who serves whom?" After his own experience, Justin felt intensely that men had by far the worst of the marital bargain. "It is the man who must protect and support his wife, and you should be damned grateful that we do."

Georgina elevated her upturned little nose in disdain. "Well, I am *not* grateful. No doubt, my lord, you think protecting your wives and daughters requires you to lock them away so that—"

"I have no wives, singular or plural, nor daughters either. And—"

"How fortunate! I cannot imagine a worse fate for a female than to be related to you."

His jaw clenched at this insult. "For your information, a considerable number of females have vied for the role of my wife over the years."

"Boasting, my lord?"

"No, stating a fact!" Plimpton and Ingleham had been right on one point. Miss Penford had a wasp's tongue, and he was tired of being stung by it. "Can you deny that women of our class are obsessed with marrying well?"

"No, but the blame for that lies with men."

"Balderdash! Is there nothing you do not blame upon my gender?"

"Women are desperate to marry, my lord, because it is the only respectable role they are permitted in life. If they do not wed, they become a pitied, unwanted appendage in the household of a brother or some other grudging relative. If no one takes them in, they must earn their livelihood in the only way they can, as a paid companion or a governess, both genteel forms of slavery."

Justin could not deny the truth of her argument. Frowning, he said, "I agree that is an unfortunate problem and probably without solution."

"A very simple solution is available, if only you men would permit it."

"Pray, what is that?"

"Equal education for girls and the right to control their money and property after they marry."

"A ludicrous idea," Justin jeered. "Everyone knows women have not the intellect to do either."

"No, not everyone *thinks* that, my lord—only antiquated fossils like yourself."

Wounded by this nasty barb, Justin retorted, "It is an indisputable fact women have no notion of finance and economy."

"That is a highly disputable male *myth!*"

Ignoring this comment, Justin said doggedly, "If a husband did not control his wife's finances, she—and perhaps he as well—would be left penniless. She needs his firm hand on the economic reins."

"Tell that to poor Lady Ingleham! Her profligate husband's firm hand is running through her fortune faster than the swiftest horse covers the course at the Newcastle races."

Justin winched at the accuracy of what Miss Penford said.

"You think it a great honor for a woman to have a man seek her hand in marriage, even though like Ingleham his sole interest in her is her fortune—or her bloodlines!" Georgina cried passionately.

"Not every man squanders his wife's fortune nor turns her into a brood mare."

"No, not *every* man, but far too many. Marriage is a terrible trap for a woman."

"What nonsense. It—"

"That is why I want no part of matrimony."

"Nor will you have to worry on that score," he lashed back scathingly.

"Yes, and as I told you last night, you cannot conceive of what a great relief that is to me." Miss Penford turned toward the door. "Much as I enjoy listening to your insults of me, I must go. Please, do not bother to see me out, my lord. Such politeness would fly in the face of your odious behavior to me this afternoon."

With that parting shot, she opened the door. With

head held high and back rigidly straight, she sailed into the hall.

Justin, who was about to fire a parting verbal salvo, closed his mouth as he saw several servants scattering hastily away from the vicinity of the door. Clearly his sparring with his visitor had not been as private as it should have been.

For the second time that afternoon, he felt the heat of embarrassment flushing his cheeks. It had not been his finest hour. Only very rarely had he been bested in duels of the tongue and never had a woman succeeded in doing so.

Until today and Miss Georgina Penford.

His pride sorely bruised, Justin promised himself this would not be the case if he ever had the bloody misfortune to meet her again.

Chapter 6

When Georgina returned home after calling on Ravenstone, she went to her father's library. He looked up from a document he was reading and gestured for her to take the chair beside his.

As she complied, he inquired, "Were you able to persuade Lord Ravenstone to allow his sister to live with us?"

Still fuming from her confrontation with that insufferable, arrogant wretch, Georgina answered hotly, "No, I did not. He is the rudest man I have ever had the misfortune to meet. You would not believe the insults he hurled at me." Her cheeks burned at the recollection. "I am convinced the man is deranged!"

Her father looked at her incredulously over the top of his spectacles. "What makes you think that, Georgina? Ravenstone has always seemed to me the most rational of men."

"You will not think so when I tell you what he said. After that disgusting letter he wrote me, he had the temerity to tell me that he admires me very much!"

Her father leaned forward as though she had said

something of great interest to him. He watched her intently.

"Why, he even said my nose is charming!"

"Yes, I can see that he insulted you grievously," her father said dryly. Something very like satisfaction gleamed in his eyes. "Was Ravenstone surprised when he learned who you were?"

"No, Nancy Wilde had already told him. I was so disappointed in her! Although in fairness to her, she would only tell him my name was Gina, which is what she always calls me. But he guessed the rest."

Her father frowned. "He did?"

He sounded so skeptical that Georgina smiled in sympathy. "I know, I was amazed, too, that he could be that astute."

"What reason did he give you for refusing to let his sister live with us?"

"He said he could not allow her to live with any woman who was a friend of Nancy Wilde's."

Her father's frown deepened. Georgina knew he did not approve of her friendship with Nancy, and she said hastily, "But what seemed to upset Ravenstone most was my proposal that he hire a tutor for Lanie. He called it improper. He is clearly a stuffy old fossil when it comes to women, and I told him so."

"That observation must surely have endeared you to him," her father said ironically.

"Well, he is an old fossil! He says society would censure his sister if she were to live with him because he's unmarried."

Her father frowned. "He told you that?"

"Yes. Don't you think that's ridiculous?"

"Georgina, perhaps you had better relate to me

precisely what he said to you, beginning with your arrival."

She dutifully complied. When she told him about the earl's generous offer to let a separate house for his sister and her own response to it, her father groaned, removed his reading spectacles, and rubbed his eyes.

"What is it?" she asked.

"Nothing of import," he said, his voice as dry as she had ever heard it. "Go on."

When she chronicled the earl's reaction to hiring a tutor for his sister, her father made a small choking sound and buried his face in his hands.

"Papa, is something wrong?" she asked in concern.

He shook his head from side to side with his hands still covering his face. When he lowered them, he said with a resigned sigh, "Tell me the rest."

Georgina decided to skip over the part about the earl kissing her and its aftermath. After all, Papa had asked only that she recount what Ravenstone had said to her, and virtually nothing had been said between them during that interval.

Instead she related the earl's nonsensical reaction when she told him he was to address her as Miss Penford. "And that after he'd told me he already knew who I was from Nancy."

Her father rubbed his temples.

"Do you have the headache?" she asked in concern.

"Yes, it is suddenly quite severe."

"I am so sorry, Papa. I shall have Cook make you a tisane as soon as you tell me if you can make any sense of Ravenstone's behavior."

"Unfortunately, yes. Her father rubbed his temples again. "I have warned you that your friendship with Nancy Wilde might give people the wrong impression of your character. I strongly suspect Ravenstone mistook you for another member of the demimonde and thought to make you his mistress."

"Surely not, Papa," she protested, uncertain whether she was horrified or amused. But when she thought of what had transpired between them in that context, it all made sense.

"My lord?"

This quiet query from his secretary jerked Justin out of his revery of Georgina Penford. He looked across his big walnut desk at Terrance, wondering how long he had been patiently waiting for an explanation of how he wanted the letter in his hand answered.

Since Georgina Penford's visit to him eight days ago, Justin had not been able to put the maddening hornet from his mind. Nor had he been able to stifle his desire for her, even though he knew full well he could not make an unmarried woman of her breeding his mistress.

"My apologies, Terrance." Justin looked down at the letter in his hand, an invitation to a country house party in Hampshire. He gave the missive to his secretary. "Send my regrets."

Putney appeared at the library door. "My lord, Lady Neldane is here to see you. She says it is most urgent she speak to you at once. She awaits you in the drawing room."

Justin jumped up from his chair, a sense of foreboding gripping him. Had something happened to his sister? He could think of no other reason for the headmistress of her school to call on him.

"That will be all for now," he told Terrance as he hurried from the library.

In the drawing room, Lady Neldane stood near the sofa where eight days ago he and Georgina Penford had . . . damn, how could he be thinking about that baggage now?

Lady Neldane's ashen face told Justin his supposition about Melanie must be correct. "What has happened to my sister?" he demanded.

"My lord, so distressing . . . I cannot conceive . . . I do not know . . . Nothing like this . . ."

Having no patience for her blubbering, Justin commanded harshly, "Tell me where my sister is."

"If only I could, my lord," she said mournfully.

"What! You do not know?"

"I fear Lady Melanie has disappeared."

Unless you provide your sister with an education commensurate with her intelligence, she will run away. And you, my lord, will have no one to blame but yourself.

Justin scowled at the irritating realization that Miss Penford's prediction about his sister, which he had ridiculed as nonsense, had been right. "Run away, has she?"

"We—we do not know for certain, my lord," Lady Neldane faltered, "but we believe so."

"How could you have let that happen?"

Her ladyship suddenly seemed to take a great interest in her glove-clad hands clasped together in front of her waist.

"It has never happened before, my lord," she hastened to assure him, still studying her hands. "As I have written you, your sister has been a most difficult student. Indeed, my lord, I fear she eloped."

"Eloped?" he echoed incredulously. "What makes you think that?"

"She was caught twice within a week sneaking

back into the school just before the rising bell.''
Lady Neldane sniffed disdainfully. ''From her disheveled appearance, it was clear she must have
been consorting with a man. Now, she may well
have run off with him.''

''I cannot believe that. She is but fifteen!''

''I suspect she fell prey to a fortune hunter seeking a rich heiress.''

If she had, the scoundrel was in for a great surprise. Their father had made no provision for Melanie, other than to dump responsibility for her on
Justin by making him her guardian. ''Have you no
notion at all of where she is?''

''We hoped she and her lover might be hiding
somewhere near the school, but we have searched
extensively in the area and—

''Extensively?'' Justin interrupted. ''How long has
my sister been missing?''

''Three days.''

''*Three days!*'' He was horrified that Melanie had
been gone that long. Contrary to what Georgina
Penford thought, he did take his duties as his half
sister's guardian very seriously, but he had firmly
believed he was doing what was best for her by
sending her to Lady Neldane's Academy. ''Bloody
hell, why was I not informed immediately?''

''Your language, my lord!'' Lady Neldane
gasped, looking as though she was about to swoon.

He had no patience with such missish women.
''My language be damned. My sister has been gone
for three days. Why was I not told at once?''

''We did not wish to worry you unnecessarily.''

''The girl is my ward, my responsibility,'' he said
acidly. ''As her guardian, it is my duty to worry,
unnecessarily or not.''

Lady Neldane's face tightened angrily, ''I did not

think you had that much interest in her, my lord."

"I assure you that I take a great interest in anyone in my care," he said in a frigid tone. "I should have been informed immediately of my sister's disappearance."

Lady Neldane's complexion took on a greenish hue. "Yes, my lord."

"Where the devil could she have gone?"

"She frequently wrote letters to a Miss Georgina Penford. Perhaps she might have some idea where your sister is."

Hope flared in Justin. Even more likely, Melanie was with Miss Penford. Justin seized on that possibility like a drowning man clutching a bit of flotsam.

"I have obtained Miss Penford's address in Sussex," the schoolmistress said.

"Miss Penford is in London, not Sussex." Justin would go to Lord Penford's townhouse immediately. If he found Melanie there, he would give Georgina Penford the trimming she so richly deserved for not informing him that his ward had run away from school and was with her.

"No, my lord," Lady Neldane said.

"No, what?" Justin asked blankly.

"Miss Penford is not in London. I went to her residence before I came here. I was told she had departed unexpectedly for Sussex."

Justin frowned. She had told him she planned to remain in London until Lyell concluded his series of lectures. Why had she changed her mind and left so soon. An ugly suspicion crossed his mind.

"When did Miss Penford depart?" Justin asked tersely.

"Yesterday morning."

Melanie would have had time to reach London by then. Was that why Georgina had departed so unexpectedly? Once his sister had come to her in London, had Miss Penford, in her pique at him, decided to teach him a lesson by hiding Melanie in Sussex?

Experience had taught him to expect the worst of women, and he was instantly ready to do so of Miss Penford.

An even uglier thought occurred to him. Perhaps running away had not been his sister's idea at all. Had Miss Penford gone to Kent and persuaded Melanie to leave Lady Neldane's Academy for Sussex in order to make her prediction to him come true?

Justin's volatile temper exploded. For an instant, the world around him turned red.

As his vision cleared and focused, he heard Lady Neldane asking in alarm, "My lord, what is it? Are you unwell?"

"No, why would you think so?" he asked curtly.

"You did not answer my question. Indeed, you looked as though you did not even hear it. And your face turned a most peculiar color, rather the shade of eggplant."

Justin did not appreciate being compared to an eggplant. "I am in excellent health," he said sharply. "But I must ask you to repeat your question."

"I asked if you wish to send a messenger to Miss Penford in Sussex to discover whether she might know where your sister is."

Justin would waste no time with a messenger. He would go to Sussex himself, certain he would find his missing sister there with the clever, conniving Miss Penford. He would set out early tomorrow on horseback. He should reach Penfield by afternoon.

And while he was in Sussex, he'd teach that damned meddling hornet to rue the day she decided to inject herself into his life.

Chapter 7

Justin's nagging anxiety that some harm might have befallen his sister grew stronger during the night, and he slept poorly. Should he have heeded Miss Penford's warning? Usually fastidious in his appearance, he did not even take time to shave before he set out for Umberside early the following morning.

He rode hard and changed horses frequently, rain plaguing him off and on much of the time. During these wearying hours of riding, he managed to quiet his fears for his sister's safety and to convince himself that he would surely find her at Penfield.

The longer he thought about her disappearance, the more certain he was that Miss Penford had been responsible. Melanie, timid little mouse that she was, would have been far too frightened to do anything so daring on her own.

The unconventional Miss Penford, however, was a different story. With his strong distrust of women, he was quite willing to convict her of having urged his sister to run away.

He scoffed at Lady Neldane's contention Melanie must have eloped with a lover. When he'd last seen his sister, she'd displayed no interest in the opposite sex.

Justin hoped he was right and not merely unconsciously trying to ease his own nagging guilt that he had failed in his duty to her.

He shifted wearily in his saddle, heartily wishing both Melanie and Miss Penford to perdition for all the bother and discomfort they were causing him.

He consoled himself with the thought that Umberside was the home of G. O. Douglas. If Justin could persuade the reclusive Douglas to meet with him before he left the village, this miserable journey would be worth it.

Splattered with mud and sick of the saddle, Justin reached Umberside shortly after noon. The village was larger than he had anticipated and appeared to be very prosperous with its neat hedges and freshly whitewashed cottages.

He halted his mount to request the direction to Penfield from a pedestrian on the village's main street, an elderly man with a thin fringe of wispy white hair around his mostly bald head.

The old man, who walked with the aid of a stick, examined Justin with critical eyes that, although watery with age, appeared to miss nothing.

"Follow this road out o' the village," he answered in a raspy voice. "You'll see its big house soon enough. And in another mile, you'll come to the gates o' Penfield on the left."

"Thank you," Justin said politely.

"Didn't waste no time, did you, coming to call on his lordship," the old man observed. "Him and his daughter only arrived from London this morning."

"I understand his daughter brought a friend with her, a young girl," Justin said with feigned casualness as he sought confirmation that Miss Penford had Melanie with her.

The old man looked surprised. "Only saw his lordship and his daughter."

Perhaps his eyes were not as good as Justin had thought. "How long have you lived in Umberside?"

"All me seventy-three years."

"Then you must know everyone in the village."

"Aye, me does."

Justin rubbed his hand over his unshaven jaw. By now the stubble there felt like a briar patch. "Tell me where I can find Mr. G. O. Douglas."

The old man's scraggly eyebrows snapped together in a frown. "Douglas? Ne'er heard o' nobody here called that."

"Then clearly you do not know everyone in the village."

The old man bridled at that. "I know every man what lives in this village," he insisted huffily. "No one here by that name."

Clearly it would be a waste of time to pursue the subject further with the old man, so Justin took his leave and rode toward Penfield.

Soon, to his left, he saw an impressive stone mansion built in classic Georgian style, crowning the tallest hill in the area.

At the estate's ornate wrought-iron gates, the gatekeeper came out to greet Justin. When he identified himself, the man regarded him skeptically.

What with the thick black stubble on Justin's face, his muddy clothes, and the unimpressive mount—the best of what had been available at the last posting house where he had changed horses—he could not blame the gatekeeper for doubting his claim of being an earl.

Finally, though, the man admitted him, and Justin

rode up the long drive. His wearying ride from London had given him ample time to convince himself of Miss Penford's culpability in his sister's disappearance. He welcomed his forthcoming confrontation with the little hornet.

He could even predict just how she would react when she saw him. First, she would deny any knowledge of his sister's whereabouts. Then she would lecture him that she warned him Melanie would run away, acting as though it had been his sister's idea to do so and not her own.

He dismounted in front of Penfield's long portico with its eight Corinthian columns, hurried to the door, and banged the knocker.

Miss Penford's voice, as clear and musical as fine chimes, drifted through an open window near the door. "Who on earth can be calling on us now when we have but barely arrived?"

For a man as furious as Justin was at her, her lovely voice had a disconcerting effect upon him. How the devil could he feel such pleasure at hearing it again?

A manservant wearing a large apron over nondescript clothes answered the knock. Seeing the unkempt, mud-splattered caller, his expression betrayed he thought the visitor unworthy of notice.

Justin disabused him of that notion with frosty hauteur: "I am the Earl of Ravenstone, here to see Miss Penford."

In the drawing room, Georgina started at the sound of Ravenstone's imperative speech. Her heart struck an erratic beat, and she forgot the bowl of newly picked roses and carnations that she was arranging. What could have brought the earl here hard on the heels of her and her father's own arrival?

Georgina felt herself blushing with embarrassment as she recalled her last meeting with the earl. Before she left London, she had called on Nancy Wilde, who'd confirmed Papa's suspicions.

"Justin called on me the morning after he followed you here and asked that I convey his offer to make you his convenient," Nancy said. "Your friendship with me gave Justin the wrong impression of your character."

Since her visit to Nancy, Georgina told herself she was furious at him, but sometimes she found herself wistfully remembering the wonderful sensations she had felt in his arms.

She abandoned the flowers and hurried into the entrance hall dominated by great pillared arches and a staircase of white marble veined with black. Fanciful pastel frescos of frolicking maidens and cherubs decorated the ceiling and the walls between the pillars.

On the two previous occasions Georgina had seen Ravenstone, his clothes and grooming had been impeccable. Now, between the ragged stubble, thick and black, on his jaw and his mud-splattered clothes, she scarcely recognized him. He looked more than ever like a pirate.

So why did a little shiver of excitement run through her as she looked at him? Disconcerted, she demanded, "What in heaven's name are *you* doing here?"

"You know very well why I am here," he replied brusquely.

"It pains me to contradict you, my lord, but I have not the foggiest notion." Despite her accelerated heartbeat, she managed to sound cool and haughty. "Unless, of course, it is to offer me another *business arrangement*."

To her surprise, he had the grace to flush, but when he spoke, his tone was sarcastic. "That's the price you pay for being such good friends with a woman like Nancy Wilde."

Georgina eyed his unkempt appearance critically. "Is that why you have chosen to call upon me looking so disreputable? A *gentleman* would have stopped at an inn for a bath, shave, and change of clothes before presenting himself to a lady."

Justin stiffened. "I apologize for my appearance, but I have ridden hard from London to arrive here as quickly as possible, and I have no time to waste."

"Since you have none to waste, then why, pray tell, have you come *here* at all?"

He glared at her. "I marvel at how baffled you manage to sound. As you know very well, I have come to collect my sister from you."

Georgina stared at him in blank surprise for a dozen seconds, then stammered, "I—I beg your pardon?"

"Stop playing games with me," he snapped. "I have had a long, arduous, and unpleasant ride from London, and I am in the devil's own temper."

"So I see," she retorted, uncowed.

"I came directly here rather than stopping to repair my appearance for two reasons. I wanted to make certain with my own eyes that Melanie is safely here and to remove her from your unfortunate influence as quickly as possible. Kindly summon her at once."

Georgina gazed at him in astonishment. "You truly are a lunatic! Lanie is at Lady Neldane's—"

Justin cut her off. "No, as you so accurately predicted, she ran away."

"Ran away?" Georgina cried in dismay. Her worst fears for the girl's safety had been justified.

"Yes. Now surely you want to remind me at length how you warned me she would do just that," he said sarcastically.

"Never have I wished so much to be wrong about anything as that. When did she run away?"

"Four days ago, but I was not notified until yesterday."

"She's been gone four days!" Georgina cried in horrified alarm. She forgot her anger at Ravenstone in her deep concern and fear for his sister. "Where can she be?"

Justin's expression changed from anger to confusion and apprehension. "You mean you truly do not know where my sister is?"

"No, I have no idea."

"Bloody hell!" he exclaimed in obvious dismay.

Ravenstone looked so worried that Georgina was surprised. She would not have expected him to be that anxious about his runaway sister. From the disheveled look of him, Ravenstone, in his concern for her, had driven himself very hard to reach Penfield.

"Lady Neldane thinks Melanie eloped with a lover."

"That sounds like something the idiot woman would think," Georgina scoffed. "I would be very much astonished if Lanie has done anything of the sort."

For an instant, Ravenstone looked relieved, then his face clouded again. "On what do you base your certainty?"

"Several things, among them her disgust with her silly classmates who could think and talk of nothing but young men who had caught their eye."

"But where can my sister be then?" He sounded

desperate. "Have you no idea at all where she might have gone?"

Georgina eyed Ravenstone in surprise. He was not such an uncaring guardian as she had believed him.

"I would have thought your sister would come to me. Where else could she go?" Georgina looked at him in belated comprehension. "But, of course, that is why you have come. You quite naturally thought the same thing."

Georgina's voice reflected her sympathy and understanding for what his feelings must be. That, in turn, seemed to vanquish the last vestige of his anger.

"Have you had any word at all from her lately?"

"Nothing since the letter that brought me to your house in London. Do you think I would not have notified you immediately if I had any knowledge of her whereabouts?"

His sensual mouth tightened, and Georgina's pulse raced as she remembered their kiss. "To the contrary, I suspected you might have encouraged her in this folly to prove your prediction was right."

"You do me a great injustice!" she cried indignantly. "I would never support her embarking on such a dangerous scheme. Indeed, I wrote her, urging her not to run away. But we have no time for such quibbling now. We must find her."

In her agitation, Georgina began to pace the floor. "Four days! Where can she be? I dread to think what might have happened to her."

"So do I," Justin said somberly, a bleak look in his eyes.

"Have you launched a search for her?"

"No, I am ashamed to admit." His voice resonated with his anger at himself. "But I was so damned certain I would find her here."

"That is quite understandable, my lord," Georgina said kindly. "I would have thought the same, had I been you. You must not blame yourself."

Her response was entirely different and far more compassionate than Justin had anticipated—or deserved. He was confounded, discomforted, and very grateful to her all at once. She clearly was as deeply concerned about his sister and her welfare as he was. Damn, but he should have listened to her warning in London.

He looked at her with a new perspective. Her red cotton gown was old and far from fashionable, but Justin hardly noticed. He had eyes only for its bright color and the tantalizing way it revealed her lovely figure.

A tiny smudge marred one cheek, and Justin had to stifle the urge to reach out and wipe it away with his thumb. He could think of no other woman who would have allowed him to see her as she was now instead of retiring to her room for a half hour of primping.

When she'd first stepped into the hall, Justin had been dumbfounded by the delight that he'd felt at seeing her again, despite his simmering anger at her. And now, to his surprise, sharing with her his apprehension for his sister seemed to lighten the burden a little.

Miss Penford said, "We must organize a search for her at once."

Clearly she wasted no time in fluttering and hand-wringing in a crisis as most women did, and Justin was deeply grateful. Fear for his sister gripped him. So did the realization that he had failed in his guardianship of her. He abhorred failure.

"Our servants are at your disposal, my lord."

"To whom are you disposing our servants, Georgie?"

Justin looked in the direction of this new voice just as Lord Penford strode into the elegant entrance hall in his riding clothes.

"Why, Lord Ravenstone," Penford said as he recognized the caller, "I own I am astonished to see you. You have come a long way to collect that dinner I offered you."

Before Justin could speak, Georgina cried, "The most dreadful thing has happened, Papa. Lanie has run away from school, and we do not know where she is. I would have thought she would come here, but she has not. And she has been missing for four days."

"So that is why you came, Ravenstone," the viscount said. "An excellent deduction on your part."

"Except that Melanie is not here," Justin reminded him.

"No, but your sister most likely will come yet," Penford replied, clearly unperturbed. "Where else could she go, if not here or to you?"

"But it does not take four days to travel from Kent to Sussex," Georgina cried. "If she were coming, she would have been here by now. I am dreadfully afraid something happened to her."

So was Justin. "You know my sister better than I, Miss Penford. Is it possible she might have gone to Dorton Hall, where she grew up?"

Georgina frowned. "I do not think so. She scarcely knows the distant cousin who inherited both the property and her grandfather's title when he died last year. Lanie felt strongly that it was no longer her home. The poor child feels she has no home at all, that she is an abandoned orphan. That's why I was anxious that either you or I provide her with one."

"I don't know where to begin looking for her," Justin confessed. "Perhaps I should leave for Kent immediately to see if I can pick up her trail."

Penford said, "It is late, and you look as though you have already spent too many hours in the saddle today. Stay the night here and leave early in the morning."

"Much as I would like to accept your appealing offer, I cannot linger while my sister is missing. I must find her."

"I suspect you have not eaten for hours," Penford said. "You must at least do that before you depart."

Penford was quite right in that regard. Justin had eaten nothing since a very early breakfast, and he was famished. He looked down dubiously at his mud-splattered clothes. "In all my dirt? Surely not."

"'Tis of no matter," Penford assured him with a jovial smile.

"Then I accept your kind offer."

Georgina said to the man in the apron, "Set a place in the dining parlor, Curwood. I will have his lordship served there."

As Curwood hurried off to do her bidding, she told Justin, "I fear it will be simple fare, for we only arrived this morning ourselves. But I did have cook make up a pot of Papa's favorite soup, which he always enjoys after he has been traveling."

"It sounds delicious," Justin said truthfully, "but I should at least like to wash my hands and face first."

Her father pointed toward an inconspicuous door. "You will find soap and water in there."

When Justin emerged after washing his face and hands and combing his disheveled hair into some semblance of order, Penford was waiting for him in the hall. Justin looked around for Georgina. To his disappointment, she had disappeared.

He followed his host into a bright informal room with a sideboard, a round dining table, and a half dozen chairs, all in mahogany. The woodwork had been painted white, and the walls hung with Chinese wallpaper. Its cheerful pink, white, and green floral pattern was repeated in the coverings of the thick cushions on the chairs.

French windows opened onto a slate terrace overlooking a small vale with a pond at the bottom of it. Justin silently admired the view over verdant grounds with artfully placed trees, shrubs, and flowers.

A light breeze, fragrant with floral scents, drifted through the open windows into the room. Even on the darkest and rainiest of days, this room would be delightful, Justin thought approvingly.

Georgina came into the room. "Your food will be here in a minute, my lord."

Her father went to the mahogany sideboard, where he poured his guest a glass of claret from a silver-and-glass decanter.

As he handed the wine to Justin, Penford said, "I fear I am late for an appointment with my steward."

"Please, do not let me keep you from him." Justin was delighted at the prospect of being left alone with Miss Penford.

Penford had scarcely left the room when a footman appeared to serve Justin a large bowl of steaming soup, thick with vegetables and beef, and a loaf of crusty, freshly baked bread accompanied by a pot of newly churned butter.

The food tasted as good as it smelled, and Justin

ate heartily. When he had taken the edge off his hunger, he said, "You told me, Miss Penford, you intended to stay in London until Charles Lyell finished his series of lectures. Why did you not do so?"

The angry glint in her hazel eyes was not the response he'd expected. "Now what the devil did I say to make you poker up like that?"

"Surely you have heard."

"Apparently not."

"The remainder of Mr. Lyell's lectures have been closed to women. Since the only reason I came to London was to hear his lectures, I had no reason to remain there."

Justin looked up from his soup. "I cannot believe that geology lectures could be the sole reason for any woman coming to London." His tone was lightly mocking. "What of the shopping and parties you wanted to attend?"

"I loathe shopping. Nor were there any parties that I *wanted* to attend."

"I have never yet met a woman who hated shopping," Justin said. Clarissa would have happily spent all her waking hours in that pastime.

"You have now," Georgina retorted.

A woman who preferred geology to shopping? Not bloody likely. To hide his incredulity, Justin took a piece of the crusty bread, still warm from the oven, and buttered it.

"Once Lyell's lectures were closed, I returned to Sussex. I much prefer it to the city."

Justin swallowed a bite of the bread. "When did you develop your great interest in geology?" He was still skeptical that any woman would pursue such a subject with diligence. Surely it was nothing more than a momentary whim on her part.

"I became fascinated the moment I discovered my first fossils in a quarry near here twelve years ago." Her expressive face lit up at the memory.

Justin understood why. He had first discovered geology in much the same way, but he had been eleven at the time.

"I realized I was seeing the history of the world preserved in stone and sand," she explained.

A felicitous way of expressing it, Justin thought. What an intriguing woman Miss Penford was. "Since you have such a long-standing involvement with geology, you must know Mr. G. O. Douglas."

For an instant, some emotion Justin could not read flashed in her face. Then she inquired, "Why would you presume that, my lord?"

"Because the man lives in Umberside."

"Are you certain of that, my lord?"

Georgina had an odd glint in her eyes that puzzled Justin. It was much like the one he'd seen when she'd told him Lyell's lectures had been closed to women. "Very certain," he replied.

"I know no man named G. O. Douglas who lives in Umberside nor, for that matter, anywhere else in Sussex."

Justin frowned. "He's a recluse. Perhaps you have not met him."

"I assure you, my lord, I have met every man in Umberside. It is part of my father's estate, and I am very much involved in the affairs of the village."

Her reply reaffirmed what the old man in Umberside had claimed. Disturbed, Justin stared out the French windows. Both Georgina and the old man had to be wrong. Douglas must live in the village, or at least in the neighborhood, but he was clearly going to be difficult to run to ground.

In the distance, Justin saw someone coming

across the grounds toward the house. As the figure moved closer, he made out a woman trudging along a meandering path that led to a side door in Penfield's rustic. Must be a servant returning from some errand, he thought, turning his attention back to Georgina.

"I am surprised your father left London with you," Justin remarked. "I had heard he intended to introduce a bill in the Lords on property rights for married women."

"After discussing his proposal with other members of Parliament, he concluded he has not the support to pass it."

"He's right on that score."

"To Parliament's shame."

Justin could not let her provocative comment pass. "I share the majority's view, and I assure you I feel no shame."

"So you admit you are shameless!"

Before he could answer, something outside caught her attention, and she went to the open French windows. "Who can that be?"

Justin saw she was looking at the woman he'd noticed earlier. She was close enough to the house now for him to see she carried a portmanteau. Yet her lavender dress with its great puffed sleeves and wide skirts was far too fashionable for her to be a servant.

Miss Penford exclaimed, "Why, it is Lanie! Your sister has come here after all. Papa was right about that, thank God!" She stepped through the open French windows and ran across the terrace toward Melanie.

A sudden, nasty suspicion nagged at Justin. Surely his sister's arrival at this moment could not be accidental. He had not thought Lord Penford devious, but now he wondered whether the viscount had left, not to meet with his steward, but to arrange Melanie's appearance. His newfound charity toward Miss Penford melted in the heat of his anger.

What kind of a fool did she and her father take him for?

Chapter 8

Justin started to follow Miss Penford outside, then decided against it. Instead he stood by the French windows and watched Miss Penford run to his sister, reaching her when Melanie was still a dozen feet from the slate terrace.

"Lanie, Lanie, where have you been?" Georgina's voice carried through the open French windows. "I was so worried about you."

Melanie dropped her portmanteau on the ground and threw her arms around Miss Penford, hugging her exuberantly. "Oh, Georgina, I am vastly happy to see you. I have missed you so."

His sister appeared to be as fond of Miss Penford as she claimed to be of Melanie. Her attention was so focused on Georgina that she did not even notice her brother standing by the open French windows.

Miss Penford stepped back. "Where have you been the past four days, Lanie? How did you get here from Kent?"

As if she did not already know, Justin thought scornfully, convinced that Miss Penford had transported his runaway sister here.

"I came on the stage."

"By yourself?" Miss Penford sounded genuinely surprised.

"Yes," Melanie responded proudly. "Oh, Georgina, it was such a grand adventure, even though it did take longer than I anticipated."

Justin had never heard his sullen sister sound so animated and excited. Nor could he believe the timid little creature would have had the courage to ride a common stage at all, and certainly not alone.

"I wish you could have been with me," Melanie said. "I confess I was not brave enough to take an outside seat, which I know you would not have hesitated to do. But, had you been with me, I would have joined you there."

Justin caught a glimpse of his sister's shining face as she looked at Miss Penford. Melanie clearly idolized her.

"But you ran away from Lady Neldane's four days ago, Lanie. Surely it did not take you that long to reach Sussex by stage."

"I did not know you had left London, and I went to your house there first." Melanie's happy face darkened. "I was terribly distressed and frightened when I discovered you were gone."

"Why did you not then go to your brother in London?"

"I would never go to him! He would only have packed me off to Lady Neldane's again without paying any heed to my complaints."

Most likely that was exactly what he would have done, Justin realized guiltily.

"Instead I thought of what you would do in my place, Georgina, and that carried me through."

"Did you not receive my letter in which I begged you not to do anything so foolish as to run away?"

Melanie stared silently down at the dusty toes of

her shoes, which peeked from beneath the skirt of her fashionable lavender traveling gown. The seconds ticked by.

His sister's discomfort startled Justin. Could it be this scene was not being put on for his benefit?

Finally she admitted, "Yes, but I could not bear that horrible school another moment. I beg you to let me live here at Penfield. I would rather be dead than go back to Lady Neldane's."

"I would be delighted to have you live with me, but—"

Melanie interrupted. "Oh, I shall be so happy here!" she cried with an enthusiasm Justin had never seen her display before.

"You did not allow me to finish, Lanie. I am happy to have you live with us here, but only *if* your guardian approves."

"But that cruel old man will never give his approval!" Melanie wailed.

Justin was not certain which of his sister's slanders stung him more, being described as cruel or as old.

"Why would Lord Ravenstone not permit you to live here?" Georgina inquired.

"Merely to be spiteful. He knows it is what I want."

"I think you are overly harsh on your brother."

Well, bless her! Justin was uncommonly pleased that she defended him to his sister. His earlier animosity toward Miss Penford was melting away like ice on a hot summer day.

"It is impossible for me to be too hard on him!" Melanie cried. "Mama always said he was the most odious, contrary man she had ever met, delighting in denying everyone within his power whatever they might want. She said a more clutch-fisted man never existed."

Justin was outraged to hear his stepmother's slanderous description of him, especially after he had given the greedy creature so much of what she'd requested from him.

Miss Penford took Melanie's arm and turned her toward the open French doors where Justin stood. "You can ask your brother now."

A shocked screech escaped his sister when she saw him. Real fear contorted her face. From her terrified expression, one would think she saw a wild boar instead of her brother. Bloody hell, what had he ever done to deserve that expression? All suspicion that the scene might have been staged for his benefit vanished.

Miss Penford tried to guide Melanie toward him, but she jerked away, panic clear in her blue eyes.

"No, no," she objected. "I—I look a sight. I must change my clothes and repair myself first."

"I had not thought you such a pudding heart." Georgina sounded disappointed.

"I am not!"

"I am greatly relieved to hear that, for you must ask—and receive—your brother's permission if you are to live with us."

Melanie promptly burst into tears, a favorite tactic of both her mother and Clarissa to get what they wanted. From Justin's past experience with them, he was certain he could count on it being at least five minutes by the clock before his sister's tears stopped.

"How can you be so unkind to me, Georgina?" Melanie sobbed. "If I ask him, he will only refuse me as he has done so often."

"Lanie, you know I cannot abide a watering pot,"

Miss Penford said sharply. "I am ashamed of you."

To Justin's astonishment, his sister's tears ended as abruptly as they had begun.

"I won't cry anymore," she promised.

Justin regarded Miss Penford with new respect. He began revising yet again his assessment of her—and of the advisability of letting his sister remain with her.

"Since you have never written your brother to ask whether you can live with me, how can you be certain he will refuse you? And why did you tell me you had written him of your complaints about Lady Neldane's school when you had not? It pains me deeply to discover you lied to me."

Clearly stricken by Georgina's reproach, Melanie reluctantly crossed the slate terrace toward him. She looked as though she were advancing to her execution.

She bore little resemblance to her pretty mother except for a pair of bright blue eyes and hair the shade of ripe wheat. A thin, gangly girl, her narrow face was marred by an ill-proportioned mouth.

Her upper lip was very thin, while her lower was excessively generous. This defect was made all the more prominent by her habit of pushing her lower lip out in a sullen pout.

Now was no exception. All the animation Justin had seen in her face when she'd greeted Georgina had vanished at the sight of him.

As his sister reached the French windows where he stood, her eyes widened and she blurted in surprise, "I have never seen you look so . . . so shabby."

"Thank you, my dear sister," he retorted dryly, "but I had far more important business than my appearance fully occupying both my mind and my time."

"What business was that?" she asked as, with dragging steps, she passed through the French windows into the dining parlor.

"Your disappearance." He stroked the rough stubble on his jaw thoughtfully. "What have you to say to me on that score?"

Melanie stared down at the floor, poking at some invisible spot on the carpet with her toe. "Nothing." Her voice was flat, robbed of the enthusiasm he had heard in it earlier.

"You owe me some explanation, Melanie, for the apprehension your disappearance caused me."

Her head snapped up, and her gaze finally met his. "Apprehension," she scoffed. "More likely you were delighted, thinking yourself rid of me."

Holding his temper in check, Justin told her quietly, "You could not be more wrong. You were entrusted to my guardianship, and I take your welfare very seriously. Why did you run away from Lady Neldane's?"

"I hate that boring school and everyone at it! I am miserable there." She glared at him defiantly. "And if you send me back, I shall run away again!"

He suspected that having succeeded once, she would do precisely as she threatened. He had not thought she had so much spirit. "Why did you not write me of your unhappiness, Melanie?"

Her pouting lower lip protruded even farther than usual. "Why waste my time writing fruitless letters? I knew you wouldn't care in the slightest about my feelings. All you want is not to be bothered with me!"

This accusation held enough truth that Justin was thrown on the defensive. He said sharply, "I might have cared very much if you had presented me with good reason for hating the school.''

But would he have? Justin's conscience prodded him. He'd been so certain he'd done what was best for her by sending her to Lady Neldane's, he might well have dismissed her complaints as those of a spoiled, slow-witted child who had not the least notion of what most benefited her. "So far you have explained nothing to me.''

Her face set in that sullen obstinacy he hated.

"Why waste my breath?'' she scoffed.

Justin prayed for patience. Before he could respond to her, the door to the dining parlor opened, and Penford strode in.

"Ah, Lord Ravenstone, I see . . .'' He broke off as he saw Melanie. "So you have turned up, have you, puss? Thought you would. What a fright you gave your poor brother.''

Penford turned to Justin. "Well, my lord, now that your sister is here, there's no need for you to rush away. You both must stay the night.''

The offer was highly tempting. Justin wanted nothing so much at the moment as to soak in a hot bath. *And have Georgina wash his back.*

Hiding his amusement at that outrageous, but intriguing, thought, he said, "You are very kind to offer, but I do not wish to impose upon you. I will lodge myself and my sister at the inn in Umberside.''

"No need of that,'' Penford assured him. "You will be far more comfortable here.''

Justin smiled. "I am certain we would.''

"Then, it's settled,'' Penford said. "You will stay here.''

Miss Penford started for the door. "I will see to rooms and order hot baths.''

Melanie, clearly anxious to escape her brother, followed Georgina from the room.

After they left, Penford said cheerfully, "I must warn you Georgie's feathers are still somewhat ruffled that you thought she would welcome your invitation to become your mistress."

Startled that he should know of this embarrassing *faux pas*, Justin said, "As her father, you seem remarkably unconcerned about my mortifying mistake. I had hoped she would not comprehend my meaning."

What must she think of him? But why should Justin care in the least? His vanity had never been flattered by whatever a lady of quality thought of him.

Yet he did care very much, and that baffled him.

His discomfort seemed to amuse Penford. "When Georgie came home that day and related your conversation, I had either to tell her the truth or let her believe you hopelessly mad."

Justin groaned. "I believe I would have preferred her to think the latter."

"Nonsense, 'twas a good lesson for her."

"How so?"

Before Penford could answer, his daughter appeared in the door. "Lord Ravenstone, your chamber is ready. I will take you up."

Her father said, "I will see you at dinner, my lord."

"I am afraid I left London in a great hurry," Justin said apologetically. "I ordered my valet to follow me with my clothes in my traveling coach, but I do not expect him to arrive before tomorrow afternoon. Although I carried a change of clothes with me, unfortunately they are for riding, not dinner."

"'Tis of no consequence," his host assured him. "We do not stand on ceremony here at Penfield. We eat informally in this room rather than in the state dining room, which we find too grand and intimidating. All I ask is that you not keep me waiting for my dinner."

"That I will not do," Justin promised with a slight bow.

As he accompanied Miss Penford across the inlaid marble floor of the entrance hall, he said, "I am surprised you came for me yourself, Miss Penford."

"I did so only because I wanted a moment to plead on your sister's behalf," she replied as they started up the stairs.

Justin should have known it was not for the pleasure of his company.

"Please allow Lanie to live here at Penfield, my lord. If you won't do that, pray at least hire a tutor for her rather than send her back to that dreadful school. She has a good mind, and she deserves better."

Justin swiveled his head so abruptly toward Georgina that he nearly tripped on the next step. "As nearly as I can tell, she is as much a ninnyhammer as her mother was."

Anger flashed in Georgina's eyes. "You are dead wrong, my lord! I grant you her mother was a foolish, spoiled, extravagant nitwit . . ."

That coincided perfectly with Justin's own estimation of his stepmother, and he suddenly found himself in surprising charity with Miss Penford. She was proving to be an astute woman.

". . . But Lanie has inherited your father's intelligence," she continued.

Well, perhaps she was not as astute as Justin had begun to think. He said acidly, "Not only would my father have disagreed with you as strongly as I do, but he would have been grievously insulted."

"Overestimated his intelligence, did he?" she queried archly as they reached the upper hall.

Justin might have reacted angrily had he not seen her eyes, shining with laughter. It was all he could do to stifle the most ridiculous impulse to bend his head and kiss the tip of her delightful, upturned nose.

"Why are you looking at me in such a peculiar way?"

"You have the most charming smile," he replied as she led him down the hall.

"Oh, no, my lord! Pray, do not try to distract me from my purpose with baseless flattery."

That affronted him. "I rarely flatter women and never with baseless inanities. Indeed, I am well known for my rude, uncivil tongue."

"You sound as though that were an achievement!" Her tone told him she did not admire such an attribute.

"But at least you know that if I compliment you at all, you are assured it is the truth."

"How comforting," she said wryly, "and an assurance that few of your gender can give. Most men will lie shamelessly to a woman if they think it will gain them an advantage."

He could not deny that. "But I am not most men."

"Are you not?"

Her incredulous tone wounded Justin. "No," he rumbled softly, "why would you think I am?"

"Your opinion of a woman's intelligence is as common among your peers as it is fallacious."

"I grant you it's common, but I dispute it's fallacious, although I will concede that every rule has its exceptions." Certainly Justin could not fault Miss Penford's intelligence.

"How generous of you!" She smiled sweetly.

"Then you will agree to a tutor for your ward?"

Feeling as though he had somehow stumbled into a concealed trap, Justin said sharply, "I agree to nothing."

"Yes, I have noticed you are a most disagreeable sort," she said mockingly.

Justin was not used to having his words turned against him like that, and he scowled at her. "You have the tongue of a hornet."

"How odd." She smiled impudently at him. "I did not know hornets had tongues."

Torn between exasperation and amusement, he shot back, "And I marvel that you have not been throttled by now."

"Fortunately for my longevity, not everyone agrees with your assessment of my tongue."

"And *I* do not agree with the odd notions about women you have instilled in my sister that have placed her in considerable danger."

"In danger? What on earth are you talking about?"

"About you leading her to think it is perfectly acceptable for a girl of her tender years to journey alone on a public stage. I shudder to think of what could have befallen her."

"So do I, and I assure you I never encouraged her to travel in such a manner. It is quite unfair of you to say I did. I also begged her *not* to run away from that dreadful school. I even went to the trouble of warning you she would likely do so if you did not remove her from it, but you would not listen to me. She needs a tutor."

"Miss Penford, I am a reasonable man, but—"

She interrupted, "If that is so, then why are you being so unreasonable about your sister's education?"

"Unreasonable! You are the one who is being unreasonable!" he sputtered.

"What is so unreasonable about wanting her to receive the same quality of education you were given?"

"A man is educated to make his way in the world, while a woman is educated to make a comfortable and loving home for her husband and children. Science and higher mathematics will not help her in that endeavor."

"In other words, a man is educated to serve himself, and a woman, to serve others!" she cried indignantly.

"You are trying to turn my sister into a damned bluestocking!" Good God, if that happened, no man would ever want her. Justin would be stuck with her forever. He pictured himself sinking into old age, chained to his sister's silent, sullen presence in his home.

This thought so appalled him that he snapped angrily, "You will make her as unmarriageable as you are."

He wanted to cut out his tongue even before he saw the stricken look in Georgina's expressive eyes. But the hurt was quickly gone, replaced by anger.

"I am unmarried by my own choice," she said frigidly. "As I have told you, I want nothing to do with marriage. I know you will find this impossible to believe, my lord, but I actually received several offers for my hand that I rejected."

Not impossible at all, Justin realized with an odd pang that felt rather like jealousy. "From whom?" he demanded before he could check himself.

"That, my lord, is none of your affair." She glared at him. "You clearly do not believe any man could have been so misguided as to offer for a *meddling ape leader* like me, but you shall have to accept my word that it is true."

She stopped beside the open door to a bedchamber. "Here is where you will be staying. I hope you find it comfortable." Both her tone and her expression told Justin she hoped nothing of the sort.

He bowed to her, saying mockingly, "Your kind concern overwhelms me. I will see you at dinner."

"Unfortunately," she retorted as she turned on her heel and walked away from him, her head high and her back rigid with anger.

Chapter 9

S till seething, Georgina sailed down the stairs.
Her emotions toward their maddening guest
bounced about like a ball in a lively tennis match—
up, down, then up, and now decidedly down
again—very far down.

So Ravenstone thought her unmarriageable, did
he? She could not believe how much that had hurt
her, though she did not fully understand why it
should have caused her such pain. Certainly the
Earl of Ingleham and Lord Plimpton had said much
worse to her after she had refused their hands, and
she had only laughed at their fulminations.

At the bottom of the stairs, she went directly to
the library, certain she would find her father there
at his writing table, and she was right.

The interior walls of the large, comfortable corner
room, Papa's favorite at Penfield, were lined with
built-in bookcases between Corinthian pilasters. On
the exterior walls, French windows alternated with
more bookcases set between the pilasters.

"Papa, why did you invite that dreadful man to
stay the night here?"

He looked up from the letter he was reading. One
of his bushy gray eyebrows rose questioningly.

"Ravenstone? Dreadful? I hardly think so, Georgie. Nor can you say he has no regard for his sister. He was clearly most anxious about her today and unwilling to rest until he had found her."

"That's only because he knew it was his duty to locate her."

"You do not find a man admirable who takes his duty as seriously as Ravenstone does?"

Her father sounded disappointed in her, and Georgina had to concede he had a point. She, too, had been impressed by the earl's concern for his missing sister. But after the last several minutes Georgina had spent verbally sparring with him, her improved estimation of him had vanished.

Now she was so out of charity with him that she said acidly, "Had he performed his duty before Lanie ran away, he would not have had to rush around the countryside trying to recover her. Please, Papa, promise you will try to talk him into letting her remain here?"

"I will try," her father replied, "if you will promise to be fairer to him."

She frowned. "What are you talking about?"

"You have disliked Ravenstone intensely for years, long before you met him, thanks to the tales Melanie's mother told you of him."

Georgina could not dispute her father's observation. Her dislike of Ravenstone had been based not merely on his neglect of Lanie, but on what the girl's mother had said about him, particularly about his cruel treatment of his late wife. "Lanie's mama was also Ravenstone's stepmother," Georgina reminded her father.

"And you quite rightly regarded her as a silly pea-brain. You would not have accepted her word on anyone else's character. Why do you think her description of her stepson was accurate?"

The question brought Georgina up short.

After she left her father for the kitchen to check on dinner, she was still puzzling over his query.

She remembered in particular calling on Melanie's mother in her bedroom at Dorton Hall a few months before she died. Her ladyship had suffered from a mysterious ailment that rarely permitted her to leave her bed.

"Justin would not allow his poor wife Clarissa to go anywhere." His stepmother shivered and pulled the bedcovers higher about her. "I should have gone quite mad if I'd been her. Ravencrest was so isolated, and Clarissa hated Cornwall as much as I did. But my horrid stepson kept her a virtual prisoner there."

"Why?" Georgina asked.

"I think he was insanely jealous of her. Clarissa was a very beautiful woman."

Lanie's mother leaned back against the thick wall of pillows that had been placed behind her back and closed her eyes as though calling up Clarissa's image in her mind. "Men instantly lost their hearts to her. But not Justin. He did not even attempt to disguise that he had not a shred of affection for her."

"Then why did he marry her?"

The invalid's eyes fluttered open again. "Oh, he was well paid to do so. It cost her father fifty thousand pounds to procure Ravenstone's agreement to marry his daughter. He would not settle for a shilling less."

Georgina wrinkled her nose in disgust at this revelation.

"Lord knows, Clarissa had suitors aplenty who would have happily wed her for nothing, but her father was determined that she would marry Ravenstone."

"Infamous!" Georgina cried.

"Yes, it was. Clarissa was barely seventeen when her father forced her to wed him. Once my stepson had her father's money, he cared naught for her. Indeed, he loved to be disobliging. If poor Clarissa particularly wanted something, he delighted in denying it to her. He took great pleasure in making her cry."

Georgina was shocked. "What a terrible man. I would have run away from him and returned to London."

"But poor Clarissa could not, for she had not a pence. He denied her access to so much as a shilling of *her* own considerable inheritance and forced her to dress in little better than rags. Why, he even took her beautiful jewels away from her."

Georgina was appalled.

"And he was such a critical man, always finding fault with the way Clarissa ran the household. He took an instant dislike to me because I defended her."

Hearing how husbands like Ravenstone, Ingleham, and her Aunt Margaret's spouse treated their wives had strengthened Georgina's determination never to marry.

"You see why I cannot bear the thought of my darling Melanie falling into his hands," her ladyship said. "If he would treat his wife that way, what would he do to a half sister he hates?"

"Surely, he does not hate Lanie!" Georgina cried.

"I am convinced he hates almost everyone, unnatural man! Unfortunately, my husband left my inheritance and my daughter's in his clutch-fisted heir's hands. We must rely upon his generosity, and he has none, except perhaps to his dreadful brother, Henry."

The dowager countess dabbed dramatically at her eyes with a lace-trimmed handkerchief. "Justin gives us nothing, and we must be a burden upon my poor parents. Oh, it breaks my heart."

To assure the critical Earl of Ravenstone would find not a single thing to disparage about tonight's dinner, Georgina spent more time than usual in the kitchen with the cook. Then she personally supervised the laying of the table. Finally she spent another half hour arranging the large bowl of freshly cut flowers she intended for the centerpiece.

She told herself she was going to such pains because she wanted to convince Ravenstone that he need have no concern about leaving his sister at a well-regulated house like Penfield.

But that wasn't entirely true. He might think Georgina unmarriageable, but she intended to show him that she ran a household that many a married man might envy.

Justin, heedful of his host's request that he not be kept waiting for his dinner, came down several minutes before the appointed hour.

Having bathed, shaved, and changed into his clean riding clothes, he felt considerably refreshed and in a more sanguine humor. He could not ask for a more comfortable and pleasant apartment than the one that Miss Penford had assigned to him.

Despite her justifiable anger at him, she had sent her father's valet to Justin with a well-sharpened razor and an offer to assist him in any way he could.

Hard on the valet's heels, servants had arrived with his bath and a copious supply of very hot wa-

ter. Justin was delighted, for it was the way he preferred his bath.

Still he could not help wondering wryly whether
Miss Penford might have hoped to scald him.

Or to have the valet unman him with the razor.

A footman showed him into a withdrawing room
adjacent to the dining parlor. Justin hoped Georgina
would be there alone so he might ask her pardon
for his rude remark about her being unmarriageable. It had been as cruel as it had been false.

To his dismay, however, the withdrawing room
was deserted, save for his sister in a sprigged muslin gown with gigot sleeves puffed to enormous
size. Her expression told him she was equally unhappy to see him.

"Good evening, Melanie," he said with a genial-
ity he did not feel. The cheerful, inviting room was
furnished with sofa and chairs covered in a pink,
green, and brown floral print. He seated himself in
a chair facing hers.

His sister stared down at the pale Aubusson carpet, mumbling something he could not understand.
As on every other occasion he'd tried to converse
with her, her face was settled in its customary sullen
lines, and she showed no inclination either to look
at him nor to talk to him.

Yet Justin had seen a very different girl that afternoon, and he wondered how to summon her
forth from the silent shell in which Melanie barri-
caded herself whenever she was with him.

But he had little talent for small talk and even
less idea of a subject that would be of mutual interest to both him and his young half sister, twenty-
one years his junior.

She continued to stare down at her feet as though
they were of the greatest interest to her. He contem-

plated the dinner ahead with trepidation. Surely she would attempt some conversation during dinner and not sit like a silent, stupid log, but his past experience with her did not permit him much optimism.

Anxious to break the strained silence between them, Justin said abruptly, "Would you be so kind as to enlighten me on why you were unhappy at Lady Neldane's?"

Melanie poked at the carpet with her toe and said nothing.

After a silent minute had passed, he said in exasperation, "Melanie, answer me."

"Why? You will only ridicule my reasons," she cried bitterly, her gaze remaining fixed on the abstract pattern she was drawing on the carpet with her toe.

"You cannot know that until you tell me." Justin struggled to hang on to his temper. "I might find your reasons quite persuasive."

"Not if they come from me."

Justin realized with a twinge of guilt that perhaps she had a valid point. "Try me. I may surprise you."

And himself, too.

But she did not accept his challenge.

When Georgina and her father entered the withdrawing room, a tense silence reigned there between Ravenstone and Lanie. When brother and sister saw Georgina and her father, the intense relief on both of their faces was so comical that she had to bite her lips to keep from smiling.

Justin rose to greet them. Now that he'd bathed, shaved, and changed his clothes, Georgina could not resist remarking with a smile, "How much you have improved since last I saw you, my lord."

He looked at her smiling mouth so oddly that, for a moment, she thought he must have taken umbrage at what she'd said.

Then he replied wryly, "I clean up well."

Too well, Georgina thought, admiring the breadth of his shoulders and the strong, muscular build revealed by his perfectly tailored riding clothes—and cursing herself for even noticing.

He stiffened under her scrutiny. "I must apologize again for failing to bring proper apparel with me."

"It does not signify," she assured him with another smile. "As my father told you, we do not stand on ceremony here."

Once again, he looked at her mouth in that odd way. She wondered uneasily whether she could have something stuck in her teeth.

Her father offered his arm to Melanie, and Justin did the same to Georgina. When she accepted it, however, he did not immediately follow her father and his sister into the dining parlor but held her back.

He said in a voice so low only she could hear it, "I want to apologize for my cruel, slanderous remark to you this afternoon, Miss Penford."

His surprisingly gentle, contrite tone sent a shiver of pleasure through her. Caught by surprise, she inquired tartly, "Of which particular remark are you speaking, my lord?"

"Perhaps I deserve that," he said ruefully. "I am talking about calling you unmarriageable. It was most insulting of me and patently untrue. Please, forgive me."

The grace and clear sincerity of his apology astonished her. The tennis ball that had been her bouncing emotions for hours now took a sudden high jump upward. She said lightly, "I merely thought it another example of the rude, uncivil tongue of which you boasted."

"I was not boasting," he retorted. "I was merely assuring you that I do not indulge in false flattery."

They belatedly followed her father and Lanie into the dining parlor. The round table, swathed in spotless white linen and set with covers for four, was bathed in soft candlelight.

She saw Ravenstone's attention immediately drawn to the center of the table, where she had placed the bowl of flowers upon which she had labored. He gave an unconscious nod of approval that made her feel rewarded for the time she had spent on them.

Lanie sat opposite Georgina and the men to the side of each of them. The diameter of the table was not large, facilitating conversation.

As the footmen served them lobster soup, Lanie said, "How unfortunate you were able to attend only one of Mr. Lyell's lectures in London, Georgina. I know how much you wanted to hear them."

"I own I was dreadfully disappointed to be barred from the remainder. However, I am happy to be back in Sussex."

"Do you not find the country dull?" Ravenstone inquired.

"Quite the contrary."

"I am convinced, Miss Penford, that if I have any opinion, you will take a contrary one."

His lips turned up in a smile that softened his face, and her heart skittered. How handsome he was when he smiled. "Or perhaps, my lord, the difference in our opinions merely mirrors the profound difference in our characters."

"Perhaps," he conceded. "Do you not find that

time hangs heavy on your hands in the country, Miss Penford? What do you do to occupy yourself?"

"So much that I frequently wish for twice the number of hours in a day so I might accomplish all that I want."

"She gives much attention to running the household and to assuring my comfort," her father interjected. "I am very lucky to have such a clever manager."

Ravenstone regarded Georgina mockingly. "I had not suspected you were so domesticated a creature. What will chiefly occupy you this summer? Creating a fine piece of needlework?"

Georgina bridled at what she fancied was a note of derision in his voice. "I have no talent for needlework, my lord, and even less interest in it. My principle occupation this summer will be to explore a most promising fossil site I came upon shortly before I left for London. I have not yet had much time to investigate it."

"Promising in what respect?" Ravenstone inquired.

"I have found some uncommon remains."

"After dinner, you must show them to me," Lanie cried.

Her brother looked at the girl incredulously. Ravenstone clearly thought Lanie had not the slightest interest in such things, and that angered Georgina.

The footmen served the first course that included removes of salmon with green butter, spit-roasted ham, and chicken with truffles.

Georgina's father, whom she knew did not share her enthusiasm for geology, turned the conversation to politics.

"I was most pleasantly surprised last year when

you supported extending the voting franchise," he told Ravenstone. "I had thought you would oppose it, my lord."

"Not at all. Indeed, I did not think it went far enough."

"You did not?" her father asked in surprise.

"No. It still clings to the belief that property, not people, is what Parliament represents. I believe the opposite. I should like the vote to be extended to all fit men."

"But not to women, fit or unfit?" Georgina challenged.

"Women by nature are unfit for that responsibility," Ravenstone said coolly.

Odious man!

But before Georgina could dispute him again, he said, "The truth is, I have very little interest in politics. I find the subject boring."

"I suspect you find almost everything boring, my lord," Georgina retorted.

Her observation clearly startled him, but he said nothing.

"I see you do not dispute it," she said with a smile.

Ravenstone looked at her mouth as though something was caught in her teeth. Georgina hastily closed her lips and ran her tongue over them, but she could feel nothing.

Her father interjected hastily, "Would you be willing, Lord Ravenstone, to support the factory bill to limit child labor in the textile mills?"

Knowing how ardently her father supported this bill, Georgina expected that he and Ravenstone, who no doubt opposed it, would argue.

Instead the earl replied, "I do support it most enthusiastically, but again I do not think it goes far enough. I would happily bar children from factories until they are sixteen years old, instead of only a mere nine.''

Georgina could not conceal her surprise at his answer.

Ravenstone looked at her with a gleam in his eyes. ''And the prohibition would extend to both boys *and* girls, Miss Penford.''

''How generous you are to my gender, my lord,'' she murmured with heavy irony.

Amusement glinted in his eyes. ''Yes, I am. More generous, I daresay, than it deserves.''

Arrogant, provoking man! Georgina regretted the dictates of etiquette that prohibited her from hurling every piece of china within her reach at her maddening guest.

Chapter 10

During dessert, Justin listened as Melanie eagerly plied Georgina with questions about people she knew in the neighborhood.

Since they were all strangers to him, he was excluded from the conversation. But Miss Penford's witty observations entertained him. He chuckled at such tart comments as "Mr. Tuttle spends so much time minding everyone else's business, he has no time to mind his own."

"And what of Mrs. Crockett?" Melanie asked. "Is she as disagreeable as ever?"

"Melanie, that is unkind of you," Justin said reprovingly.

Tense silence descended on the table as his sister pouted sullenly at him.

Miss Penford broke the quiet, saying with her brilliant smile, which instantly eased the strained atmosphere, "I sincerely doubt you would reprove Lanie if you knew Mrs. Crockett, my lord. She is the town shrew, who criticizes and abuses everyone. The only person who has ever met her exalted standards of conduct is herself."

Justin chuckled again. He enjoyed Miss Penford's tongue when it was not turned against him.

As Melanie and their hostess rose from the table at the conclusion of dinner, he wished he could accompany them into the drawing room and forego the male tradition of remaining in the dining parlor to drink port or brandy with his host.

Although he enjoyed the viscount's conversation, he enjoyed his daughter's more.

And she had the most beguiling smile he had ever seen. It lit up her face in a way that filled him with warmth—and a strong desire to kiss her charming mouth.

The dinner had been one of the best Justin had enjoyed in a country house, and he complimented Penford on it.

"Georgina sets a very fine table," the viscount answered. "When she and I dine informally, I prefer to adjourn with her to the library for my after-dinner port. Do you object?"

"Not at all." Justin wondered if Penford was a mind reader.

To his chagrin, however, both his hostess and his sister's faces fell at his response. Clearly the prospect of Justin's company did not please either of them.

Melanie said hastily, "Georgina, I cannot wait to see the fossils you found at your new site. I beg you to show them to me now while the men are enjoying their port."

"Yes, of course." Miss Penford turned to Justin. "Pray excuse us, my lord, while we go to my specimen room."

"Actually, I wish to see your fossils, too." Justin was curious to see what she had managed to collect, although he suspected they would be commonplace and uninteresting. "I will go with you. Will you accompany us, Lord Penford?"

"No, I do not share my daughter's enthusiasm for old bones. You can join me in the library when you are done."

Melanie followed Georgina out of the dining parlor and across the marble hall. Justin trailed behind them, admiring the sensual sway of Miss Penford's hips.

How pretty she looked in her gown of rich tangerine silk. Few women could wear that color successfully, but she was definitely one of them. It brought out the warm tones of her skin.

The gown's bodice was fitted at the natural waist except in the front where it dropped to a point. What a tiny waist she had. Justin was certain he could span it with his hands. And he itched to do just that—if only he could keep her piquant tongue silent long enough for him to enjoy the experience.

During dinner, the low-cut neckline of her gown had given him a tantalizing peek at her full breasts. He had found the view considerably more stimulating than a gentleman needed at the dinner table.

When they reached their destination, he stopped dead as he crossed the threshold and saw a huge skull and jawbone resting on a table in the center of the room. He was so astonished, he blurted, "Bloody hell, is that what I think it is?"

His sister exhibited no doubt whatsoever. "Georgina, I do believe you are right. You have found the skull of an iguanodon."

Justin's jaw dropped in surprise that his sister had instantly recognized what the skull must be. He would not have thought Melanie had the slightest notion of what an iguanodon was. Or a fossil either, for that matter.

Could it be that Miss Penford was right? He did not know his little sister at all.

"Yes," Georgina said proudly, "the teeth are exactly as Dr. Mantell described the ones his wife found, but only look how strange the jaw is." She picked up the object. "You see it has teeth only on the sides of its mouth and none at the front, which rather resembles a bird's beak."

Although Justin had read much speculation about these great beasts who had roamed the earth in prehistoric times, this was the first time he had actually seen any part of one's skeleton. He touched the strange jawbone wonderingly. "Where did you find this?"

"At an abandoned quarry on Penfield," Georgina replied, her eyes glowing with excitement and enthusiasm. "You can see why I am so eager to get back to work there. I hope to find more of the creature's skeleton."

Her luminous smile sent a wave of male desire through Justin that was at odds with his intellectual reaction to her discovery.

"Perhaps I will even find all of it," she said. "Would that not be wonderful!"

"Indeed it would," Justin agreed, excited at the prospect of new discoveries—and in more arenas than one.

With masterful self-control he tamped down his wayward thoughts about his hostess to concentrate on what she had found. "It is very possible you will, too, in light of how well-preserved the skull is."

He strode to the glass-topped specimen cases that lined the wall. Contrary to his expectations, Miss Penford's collection was far from commonplace. It contained a number of rare specimens, carefully labeled, that he had not seen before.

He regarded Miss Penford with new respect. She

knew as much about paleontology as she did about geological theories.

When Georgina pointed out a small fossil she had found near the iguanodon skull, Melanie confided, "I discovered one of these in a cave near Lady Neldane's, where several layers of strata were exposed."

"From what you have told me of her ladyship, I am surprised she would have permitted you to do any such investigating," Miss Penford said.

"She didn't. She was appalled that I would want to 'play in the mud and muck,' as she called it. I was forced to sneak out very early in the morning before anyone was awake."

"Were you never caught?" Miss Penford asked.

"Yes, I was, and it was dreadful." Melanie had clearly forgotten her brother's presence in her eagerness to unburden herself to her friend. "Do you know the stupid woman accused me of sneaking away to rendezvous with a lover?" Her voice rose in indignation. "Have you ever heard of anything so silly?"

Justin smothered a groan. So that had been the real nature of his sister's supposedly scandalous escapades.

"Even when I showed Lady Neldane the specimens I found, she refused to believe me."

Miss Penford pulled a face. "Stupid woman."

Justin was inclined to agree with her.

She gave him a speaking glance that unfortunately drew attention to him.

"Oh, I forgot *you* were here," Melanie squealed, clapping her hand over her mouth.

"How fortunate that was for both of us," he said dryly. He should have liked to hear more of his sister's candid confessions.

She stared at him blankly for a moment, then turned to ask their hostess about the strata in which she had found the skull.

Justin marveled at how different his sister was in Miss Penford's company. She seemed to bring out the best in Melanie.

Indeed, the little wasp appeared more skilled at dealing with his sister than anyone else was, including himself. Her offer to let Melanie live with her at Penfield might prove to be the best solution he could find for his sister—and for himself.

"We had better go to the library," Miss Penford said. "We have kept Papa waiting long enough."

The library, a large corner room, was brightly illuminated by many lamps. Informal groupings of sofas, chairs, and tables, scattered about with an eye to the occupants' comfort rather than to display, made the room, despite its considerable size, as pleasant as the dining parlor had been.

Several pairs of French windows were set in the two exterior walls, but darkness had fallen outside, concealing the view they afforded. The night had grown chilly, and an inviting fire burned in the fireplace grate. Above it on the marble mantel was an ornate clock of Sevres porcelain and ormolu.

Lord Penford sat in a large tapestry-covered chair, reading a thick leatherbound volume. Beside him on a round Chippendale table rested a silver-and-glass wine decanter and a half-full goblet.

Justin was surprised to see a harp in one corner. He started to ask Georgina whether she played but checked himself. He was fond of music, but only when it was well-played.

Experience had taught him over the years that making such an inquiry of a young lady of the house almost invariably led to painful performances that, at worst, were ear-jarringly bad and, at best, indifferent—and always went on far too long.

Georgina and his sister sat on a sofa covered in the same tapestry as Penford's chair. Justin quickly took the chair closest to his hostess. He accepted the viscount's offer of a glass of port and found its quality to be excellent.

He sank back into the comfortable cushions of his chair. He was beginning to appreciate his sister's desire to live at Penfield. "Your daughter showed us her latest fossil discovery. It is extraordinary."

"Do not tell me I am harboring another geological enthusiast."

Justin grinned. "I am afraid so."

"I am surrounded and outnumbered," Penford said with a mock groan. "Tell me why you are so impressed by my daughter's latest discovery."

"The skull and jawbone are so large I believe, as she does, that they must be from a prehistoric iguanodon."

"How did it get that name?" Penford asked.

"When Mary Anne Mantell discovered some large fossilized teeth, the first known remains of an iguanodon, her husband, Dr. Gideon Mantell, realized they were from an unknown extinct animal," Justin explained. "Someone pointed out the similarity between the teeth and those of a Central American lizard called an iguana, and Mantell named the animal iguanodon, which means iguana tooth."

"'Tis said iguanodons were gigantic lizards, Lord Penford, perhaps as much as ninety feet long!" Melanie cried eagerly, her eyes bright with excitement. She turned toward Justin, apparently forgetting in her enthusiasm whom she was addressing. "I can scarcely imagine such a thing, can you?"

" 'Tis difficult," he agreed. "I certainly would not care to meet a live one."

"I wonder if a musket would have been successful in stopping one?" Penford mused.

"After seeing the jawbone with all those teeth that your daughter found, I would have preferred to be armed with the world's largest cannon," Justin said wryly.

Melanie giggled, the first time she had ever shown amusement at anything he had said.

Determined not to lose the moment, Justin asked, "What other fossils did you discover, Melanie, in the cave you explored in Kent?"

She stared down at her hands, clasped nervously in her lap, and did not reply.

He tried to ease her anxiety by remarking, "I once participated in a fossil hunting expedition in Kent, not far from where you were. We found some rare things there."

Justin launched into a description of them, and his sister's interest in the subject quickly outweighed her unease with him. Soon they were discussing various fossils they had uncovered.

Impressed by his sister's knowledge, he asked, "Where did you learn so much about this subject, Melanie?"

"From Georgina. She is a wonderful teacher."

Recalling her response to his kiss in London, Justin suspected she would be wonderful at other things as well.

He turned to her. To his amusement, she had blushed prettily at his sister's praise. "And how did you learn so much, Miss Penford? From your father?"

"Not from me," Penford interjected. "My daughter despairs of me, but I much prefer politics to geology and paleontology."

"I fear then we have been boring you," Justin said politely.

"Yes, Papa, we have, and now it is your turn to hold forth on your favorite subject."

"As you well know, Georgie, I need no encouragement to do that." Penford turned to Justin. "I should like to start by asking you a question, my lord. In light of your liberal views on child labor and suffrage, can I hope for your support of a bill I want to introduce in Parliament that would protect married women's property from the follies of their husbands?"

Justin stiffened. "Better a law to protect husbands from the cruel and extravagant follies of their foolish wives."

Georgina whirled angrily on him. "Husbands need no such law. You men hold all the power, and you arrange privileges, including those of marriage, only to benefit yourselves."

"Then why are women so desperate to catch a man in the parson's mousetrap?" These scornful words popped out of Justin's mouth before he remembered she had already addressed this question during her visit to him in London.

"I told you before, a lady weds for security and because it is the only respectable avenue open to her."

"And, if she can manage it, also for a title and the prestige it confers," Justin countered cynically.

"She does so if she is vain and foolish. If she is, she deserves what she gets!"

Miss Penford suffered from neither failing. Justin could not help admiring her sparkling eyes and glowing countenance. She was exceedingly pretty when she defended her views. "And a gentleman is forced to wed for an heir. But he has no way of assuring that the heir for which he married is of his own making."

"Nor has a good and faithful wife any way of assuring that her husband will not snatch from her the children she adores and never allow her to see them again."

"A wife who is good and faithful should have no worry on that score," Justin retorted.

"No, she *should* not, but she *does*!" Georgina cried passionately. "Under the law, a mother has no right to the children she has borne. You men reserve the advantages of marriage for yourself and the burdens for your wives."

Justin's own anger kindled at that. He remembered too well Clarissa's wild tantrums. "Pray, what is the advantage to being tied for the rest of your unhappy life to an extravagant, spoiled child in an adult's body who can never be pleased?"

Miss Penford's lovely little chin tilted stubbornly. "If a man treats his wife as though she is a child, she will fulfill his expectations."

"If she behaves like a spoiled child, how else is he to treat her?"

"Perhaps if he treated her as an adult, she would act like one," Miss Penford shot back.

Justin noticed his sister gaping at them.

"Georgie, my dear," her father interjected dryly, "let us not refight the battle of the sexes tonight. Despite your views on women rights, my lord, may I still count upon your support for the factory bill?"

"Yes, although I wish it would give children more protection than it does."

"But in politics one must settle for the possible," Penford said with a sigh. "At least it will limit the hours children between nine and twelve can work to forty-eight a week, and they will be given two hours of schooling a day. Tell me, my lord, did you read Carlyle's 'Sartor Resartus' in *Fraser's* magazine?''

"Most interesting, was it not?" Justin replied.

A spirited discussion followed on the merits of recent articles and books. Not only did Justin discover that Miss Penford was remarkably well-read, but he was startled to find he held more opinions in common with her than he would ever have suspected.

Melanie contributed her own observations to the conversation, and they surprised him in their perception. He was more and more convinced Miss Penford was right in her contention his sister was far more intelligent than he thought.

When he saw his hostess hide a yawn behind her hand, he glanced at the ormolu-and-porcelain clock on the marble mantel and was shocked to see how late it was. He could not remember when a night had passed so quickly or the conversation been so lively.

"Melanie, you have had a long day," Miss Penford said. "You must be exhausted."

"Not at all." Melanie looked as unhappy as Justin felt that the evening was about to end.

"I fear I had not the stimulation of the common stage to keep me awake as you did today, Lanie. Pray, excuse me." As Miss Penford stood up, she asked Justin hopefully, "You will be leaving in the morning, my lord?"

He was startled at how little he wanted to do that. Generally he found country life exceedingly dull, but tonight had been a singular and most agreeable exception.

Justin wished Miss Penford would invite him to linger at Penfield, but she clearly had no intention of doing so. He could think of no plausible excuse that would permit him to remain.

Except his sister.

He said slyly, "Yes, my sister and I will leave in the morning. We do not want to impose upon your hospitality any longer than necessary."

"No!" Melanie wailed. "Please, please let me stay here with Georgina."

"You will leave when I leave," Justin said firmly.

"Why won't you let me stay here where I am happy?" Melanie dissolved into tears. Within a minute she was racked by sobs.

Justin, who regarded such a public performance as tantamount to blackmail, said sharply, "Have you not learned by now that I am immune to your tears? All you accomplish is to make me more determined to adhere to the course I have chosen."

Melanie jumped to her feet. "You are the cruelest man I have ever met!"

Normally Justin would have ignored such an accusation, but it angered him that his sister made it in front of the Penfords. He retorted sharply, "If you think that is so, Melanie, your acquaintance with men is very limited indeed."

She glared at him through her tears. "I hate you!" She turned and fled the room. Miss Penford followed her.

Penford, seemingly unperturbed by the contretemps, said calmly, "Melanie is at a difficult age. Another glass of port, my lord?"

Justin nodded.

Penford lifted the decanter from the table and refilled Justin's glass and his own.

"I must apologize for my sister's theatrics. She likes to use her tears as a weapon against me."

"Why not? They worked so well with her grandparents, I can understand why they became her weapon of choice." Penford sipped from his port. "Do you require anything more for your comfort while you are here?"

Justin smiled. "No, all my needs have been anticipated."

"My daughter does run an excellent house. I am most fortunate."

Justin recalled her claim about spurned suitors. "I am surprised a husband has not taken your daughter away from you by now."

"Several men have tried and failed."

"Who were the disappointed gentlemen?"

"Roger Chadwick, Sir Cecil Chadwick's sprig, came nearest to succeeding."

Justin's eyes narrowed. "I do not know him." So why should he feel such a dislike for this Roger?

"A fine young man," Penford assured him with a peculiar look that puzzled Justin. "Indeed, I have not entirely given up hope that Roger may yet prevail upon Georgie to accept him."

Justin's dislike of Roger escalated.

"Most likely the only two of Georgie's spurned suitors you would know, Ravenstone, are Lord Plimpton and the Earl of Ingleham."

Bloody hell. So that was why the poodle and the schnauzer had spoken so cruelly and untruthfully about her. She had rejected them. The pair sank even lower in Justin's estimation.

"Ingleham in particular could not believe Georgie would rebuff such a lofty marital prospect as himself and angrily demanded her reasons."

Justin could not help smiling. "No doubt, your daughter complied with her usual bluntness."

"Yes, she did. Ingleham was so enraged by her unflattering—but entirely true—reading of his character that I feared he would suffer an apoplectic seizure. Since then, he has defamed her to whomever he can."

As the scoundrel had done to Justin.

Penford paused as though considering how to proceed, then said, "As you know, my daughter would like to give your sister a home here."

Although Justin was becoming increasingly reconciled to this idea, he said politely, "I cannot allow Melanie to impose upon you like that."

"I have no objection."

Justin regarded him dubiously.

"Ah, I comprehend perfectly what troubles you. You are most concerned about your sister's welfare and properly so. You would not dream of leaving her here with us until you are convinced she is in good hands."

"I do not question *your* suitability," Justin said tactfully.

Penford cocked an amused eyebrow. "Only my daughter's?"

"I have some concern she might be an unfortunate influence on my sister."

"Georgie is an excellent influence on her," Penford assured him. "And it is not fatherly pride that leads me to say that. Had she not taken Melanie in hand, I fear your sister would have become quite impossible."

"Then I am most grateful to your daughter." Justin could not deny that Melanie had shown to greater advantage with Miss Penford today than she ever had before in his presence. His sister's lively demeanor and curiosity had astonished him.

"And without Georgie, your sister would not have developed that mind of hers."

That raised Justin's hackles, and he said coldly,

"The last thing I want is for my sister to become a bluestocking."

"Why?" Penford asked.

"They are so . . . so tedious." Justin managed to catch himself before he automatically said unmarriageable.

"Are they?" Penford cocked his brow quizzically. "You did not seemed bored by Georgie's conversation tonight."

Taken aback, Justin opened his mouth, then snapped it shut again. No, he had not been in the least bored tonight. How long had it been since he'd found an evening as interesting as he had this one. "I do not think of your daughter as a bluestocking."

"Clearly you mean that as a compliment to her, but Georgie would not take it as such."

"Most likely not," Justin agreed with a smile.

"If you have nothing urgent to take you back to London, Lord Ravenstone, I suggest you remain here at Penfield for a fortnight or two so you may observe your sister with Georgina. I am certain it will quiet your concerns."

The invitation had great appeal to Justin, although it sprang less from his concern for Melanie than from a reluctance to leave Penfield.

"Then, when you do leave, you will be able to rest easy that your sister will come to no harm here. Indeed, I think you will eventually agree that this is the best place for her."

"Perhaps I will stay."

"I shall be delighted to have your company," Penford assured Justin with an odd smile that puzzled him.

Although the invitation to stay longer was precisely what Justin wanted, he suddenly suspected the viscount of some ulterior motive of his own in extending his invitation. But Justin could not fathom what it could be.

Perhaps Penford hoped to sway him to support his radical legislation on married women's property rights.

But that would never happen.

Chapter 11

⟨ ∽◯◯∽ ⟩

Georgina lay awake far into the night, unable to banish Ravenstone from her thoughts. His apology for having called her unmarriageable had been so sincere that she could not help but be appeased by it. For the most part, he had been charming tonight, everything a hostess could wish for in a guest.

For her part, Georgina was embarrassed that she had not immediately appreciated his provocative teasing of her during dinner for what it was. But his stepmother had convinced her that he was devoid of humor.

His attentive conduct toward his sister had surprised her. He'd displayed considerable patience in coaxing Lanie to talk to him. Clearly, though, she did not understand his dry humor.

Having seen the way she acted toward him tonight, Georgina wondered whether his sister might be at least as much at fault as he in the estrangement between them.

Georgina had been pleased to see he had not been manipulated by Lanie's deplorable tactic, which she had learned from her mother, of bursting into tears when she was denied something she wanted and sobbing until she got it. This behavior exasperated Georgina as much as it did Justin. If a woman acted like a spoiled child, she deserved to be treated like one.

Although Georgina was a long time falling asleep, she rose early the next morning and dressed quickly.

Ravenstone and his sister's arrivals the previous day had left Georgina no time to visit the site where she had found the iguanodon skull.

Anxious to reassure herself that no one had discovered and tampered with the spot in her absence, she decided, despite the chilly morning, to visit it immediately after she had breakfast.

Lanie, who loved to stay abed until late into the morning, would not be awake for hours, and Ravenstone, like his sister, would undoubtedly be a late riser. Georgina would be back before they came down to breakfast.

She wondered whether her father had succeeded in persuading the earl to let Lanie remain at Penfield with them. Certain that Papa, who was always an early riser, would already be at breakfast, she hurried down to the dining parlor. She found him there, filling his plate from the dishes on the sideboard.

"Did you succeed in persuading Ravenstone to let Lanie stay with us?" she asked as she sat down at the table.

Her father turned away from the sideboard, his plate full, and took the chair beside hers. "Some success. Melanie will not be leaving us today."

"Oh, Papa, that's wonderful. Thank you."

"Nor will Lord Ravenstone."

Georgina, who was pouring herself a cup of coffee from an ornate silver pot, looked up. "What?" she asked blankly.

"He will remain here for a fortnight or two."

"A fortnight or two?" Contrary emotions buffeted Georgina. She told herself she was dismayed that he was not leaving, yet some subversive part of her was delighted at the news. "You cannot be serious, Papa."

"Watch what you are about, Georgie," he said in alarm.

She looked down to discover that she was pouring coffee into her saucer instead of the cup.

"I am very serious," her father assured her. "Ravenstone is staying, too."

Georgina reached for a clean cup and saucer. This time she succeeded in pouring the coffee into its proper receptacle, though her hand was strangely unsteady. "But Ravenstone despises the country."

"Does he?" Her father stirred cream into his own coffee. "He showed no such distaste when I invited him. He accepted immediately."

"What possessed you to invite him?"

"I believed it the only way we can persuade him to let Melanie live with us. In view of that, I did not think you would object."

"I cannot conceive why he would have agreed to stay."

For an instant, a sly, roguish gleam danced in her father's eye. It was the look he had when he was plotting some noble scheme, designed to benefit an unsuspecting recipient. What was he up to now?

"He accepted because he is quite rightly concerned about leaving his sister here until he has assured himself she is in good hands and will be happy here. Were you Ravenstone, you would feel the same way."

"Were I Ravenstone, I would not have ignored and neglected my sister as he has."

"Then, 'tis even more important that he should continue on here with her. They are little more than strangers to each other, and you must strive to help them become better acquainted. Ravenstone demonstrated yesterday he is concerned for her welfare. Perhaps when he gets to know her better, he will grow fonder of her and more attentive."

"I doubt it." But even as the words left Georgina's mouth, she recalled his efforts the previous night to converse with Lanie. She resolved to do her best to reconcile them.

As soon as she finished breakfast, she set off at once for the abandoned quarry where she had found the iguanodon skull and jawbone.

After several minutes of brisk walking, she skirted the base of a hill on a path that led into a narrow valley. Her destination, a shallow, horseshoe-shaped quarry gouged into the hillside, was directly in front of her. Loose dirt had accumulated at the bottom of the horseshoe, partially covering a knee-high wooden box.

An examination of the area convinced Georgina that the site had not been disturbed since her last visit. Not only was everything as she had left it, but hardy stalks of meadow oat-grass and sedge growing at the bottom of the quarry had not been trampled upon.

Although she had intended merely to check to make certain the site was in good order, she had donned beneath her skirt the pantaloons she wore when digging for fossils.

She'd put them on in case she encountered problems. But now that she was here, she could not resist spending a few minutes trying to locate additional bones from the iguanodon.

Georgina stripped off her skirt, revealing the black pantaloons beneath. Bending over, she opened the cover of the wooden box and pulled a pick from among the tools inside.

"Very sensible dress, Miss Penford."

Georgina, who thought herself entirely alone, jumped at Ravenstone's resonant voice behind her.

Conscious that in their relative positions, the part of her anatomy most visible to him had to be her bottom clad in tight-fitting pants, she straightened like a shot, dropping the pick. It tumbled to the ground with a thud.

Turning around, she saw Ravenstone still eyeing her hips. He grinned at her. "And very provocative."

She felt herself blushing beneath his warm perusal and her heartbeat accelerated. A stray lock of curly black hair dangled down on his right temple, and she had the oddest urge to push it back.

"How did you get here?" she demanded, surprised that he could have come upon her so quietly. She had not heard a sound until he spoke.

"The same way you did, on foot."

"I am amazed that you are even out of bed yet."

He chuckled. "I am not as dissolute as you think me. I always rise early in the country. I was coming down for breakfast when I saw you set out, and I decided to tag along."

"Had I wanted company, Lord Ravenstone, I would have invited you."

He laughed, a rich throaty sound that sent a shiver of pleasure through her.

"Which is why, little wasp, I did not make my presence known to you earlier." He studied the horseshoe-shaped walls of the quarry. "I wanted to see where you found the iguanodon remains."

"Now you have."

He raised his thick black brows at her tone and grinned. "And now I may leave? Oh, no, you will not rid yourself of me that easily."

Nor was Georgina at all certain she wanted to do so.

Still smiling at her, Ravenstone brushed a stray lock of hair from her cheek. Excitement spilled through her at his gentle touch.

"Tell me, do you wear trousers only when you are digging for fossils or do you shock your neighbors, as George Sand has shocked Paris, by going about in them publicly?"

"My neighbors' sensibilities are quite safe. Have you read her novel, *Indiana*?"

His grin faded. "Yes, the woman is as outrageous in her views as she is in her dress."

Georgina fired up at that. "Why? Because she champions the right of women to love and to be independent?"

"I am startled that your father would permit you to read such trash."

"Papa has never censored my reading."

"Perhaps he should think about doing so."

"He is not such an old fossil as you are."

The sudden glint in his eyes betrayed her shaft had struck home. But instead of retaliating, he said, "Speaking of fossils, I assume that is where you found the skull and jawbone."

Ravenstone pointed to an elongated indentation near the left edge of the horseshoe-shaped wall where she had chiseled the iguanodon skull free from its rock grave.

She nodded.

"This quarry is not very large," he observed. "Why was it abandoned?"

"My father ordered it closed for safety reasons when he inherited Penfield upon his brother's death. The quarry had been plagued by a series of accidents in which two workmen were killed and several others were injured."

The earl looked down at the pick Georgina had dropped. "I see you intend to resume your search this morning. Why did you not bring a servant or two to dig for you?"

"Because they tend to swing the pick too vigorously, and I fear they might destroy what I seek even as they uncover it."

"A valid concern." Ravenstone removed his coat and waistcoat and tossed them over the open lid of the wooden box.

Georgina's eyes widened and her stomach fluttered as next he unknotted his neckcloth, removed it, and threw it on top of his coat. He began undoing the top buttons of his shirt.

Dear God, was the man going to strip naked before her? She felt herself blushing. "What—what are you doing, my lord?"

He bent down and lifted the pick from the ground where she had dropped it. "I think you will find I wield this instrument with suitable care."

"I am astonished you wield one at all." She had never known an earl who would not have considered it far beneath his dignity to do so.

"I have been on a number of fossil searches," he explained. "Experience has taught me, as it has you, to use the tools myself rather than risk damage."

He began poking gently at the hillside above his head, to the right of where she had found the jawbone.

Georgina was relieved to see how carefully he worked. She pulled a chisel from the wooden tool-box.

"Why did you choose this site to dig, Miss Penford?"

"The strata here is very like that in which Mrs. Mantell's iguanodon teeth were found in Tilgate Forest."

He gave her a quick approving glance. His approbation generated a warm glow within Georgina, which surprised her. Why should she care?

Ravenstone returned to his efforts with the pick while Georgina probed with the chisel. "Papa says you are considering letting your sister live with us rather than sending her back to Lady Neldane's."

He paused in his explorations and turned to look at her. "Yes, I am."

She met his gaze. "I hope you will, my lord. It will be so much better for her than that dreadful school."

"Even if I reject your offer, I will not send Melanie back to Lady Neldane's." Ravenstone went back to chipping carefully away at the quarry wall with the point of the pick.

"You won't?" Georgina cried in surprise and joy. "What led you to that decision?"

"I concluded you were correct about it not being a fit school for her."

He was still working with the pick, so Georgina could not see his expression. She was astonished that a man of his arrogance and contempt for her gender would have conceded that she, a mere woman, could be right on any point.

"Then why would you not let Lanie live with us? Are you afraid of being criticized for not providing a home for her yourself?"

He stopped his work and again turned to look at her. "By now, I am quite used to being criticized for not keeping my ward with me. I was roundly censured after my father died for giving in to her mother's pleas that they be allowed to return to live with her parents here in Sussex. I was married at the time and so had far less excuse than I do now for not requiring Melanie to remain under my personal supervision. In retrospect, perhaps I should have."

"Why did you not do so?"

"Her mother refused to live in Cornwall, and I heartily disapprove of a mother being separated from her daughter or from any child when it is very small. Melanie, who was only a year old then, was both." He frowned. "Why the devil are you looking at me like that?"

Georgina was gaping at him, unable to believe what he had just professed. "I own I am stunned you think that way, Lord Ravenstone. Most men have not the slightest compunction about denying mothers their children, no matter how small they are."

"I told you before, I am not most men," he said with a wry smile that charmed her. "But clearly I have not yet convinced you."

"No, you have not." But he was making more progress than she would have thought possible twenty-four hours ago. "Why do you hesitate to leave Lanie here?"

His face was troubled. "Frankly, I am loathe to foist my sister, who is my responsibility, off on your father and you." He placed the head of the pick on the ground and leaned on the handle. "But what the devil am I to do with her?"

"Could she not reside with you at your country

seat in Cornwall?" Georgina suggested, knowing
Lanie dreamed of living in the home where she'd
been born.

"No, because I very rarely go to Ravencrest anymore." He ran his fingers distractedly through his
thick, unruly black hair. "I cannot in good conscience send her to live somewhere without my being there, too, to supervise her welfare.
Furthermore, the estate is quite isolated, and I fear
she would be very lonely."

Georgina could not fault him for this reasoning.
His blunt confession of his concerns pleased her,
and she decided to be equally frank. "I cannot argue
with you on either count, but perhaps you should
at least take Lanie to Ravencrest for a visit."

"Why?"

"Since her grandparents died, she has felt bereft
of a home and roots." Georgina glanced skyward,
her attention caught by a pair of kestrels wheeling
and hovering in search of prey. "Lanie is most anxious to see the house of her birth. She says she does
not remember it at all."

"I would be very surprised if she did, for she has
not seen it since she was a baby. My stepmother
hated Cornwall and, once she returned here, she refused to visit it again."

Her ladyship had also disliked her stepson and
repeatedly branded him as heartless and clutch-
fisted to Georgina.

"As for taking my sister to Ravencrest, I should
think the last thing she wants is to travel anywhere
in my company." Ravenstone's dark eyes were
troubled. "Have you not noticed how sullen and
silent she is with me? Last night was the first time
I ever succeeded in coaxing as much as a giggle out
of her."

Remembering her resolve to try to bring him and his sister to a better understanding of each other, Georgina said carefully. "Lanie does not understand your dry humor, and she is afraid of you."

"What the devil have I ever done to make her afraid of me?"

He was clearly so genuinely bewildered that Georgina felt an odd surge of compassion—and something else she could not define—for him. She had to squash a sudden desire to place her hands comfortingly over his much larger ones resting on the pick handle.

"For one thing, you have not given her sufficient opportunity to know you. Her mother died when Lanie was nine." Reproach crept into Georgina's voice. "Why did you not reclaim your ward then?"

"Two reasons. First, Melanie, her grandparents, their vicar, and their solicitor all wrote me such pleading, heartrending letters, begging me not to destroy entirely my poor, grieving sister's happiness by removing her from the only home she remembered."

Georgina had forgotten until this reminder how terrified Lanie had been after her mother's death that her stepbrother would take her to live with him.

"I listened to them against my better judgment." He sighed. "I had serious doubts about her grandparents keeping her."

"And well you should have." Georgina paused to watch as one of the kestrels swooped down to snatch up a mouse.

As the hawk soared off with his prey, she continued, "Did you not consider it your responsibility to visit your ward with some frequency to ascertain whether they were fit to have her and she was happy with them? I do not need the fingers of one hand to count the number of times you visited Lanie at Dorton Hall while her grandparents were alive."

His mouth tightened. "I know that was remiss of me, but I was bombarded with monthly letters from my sister telling me how happy she was living with her grandparents and begging me to let her stay. Even then, perhaps I would have come more frequently had it not been made so apparent to me when I did that I was not at all welcome. Melanie seemed to hold me in particular aversion."

Of course, she did. His stepmother had painted him as a miserly, heartless monster to Lanie. After her mother's death, her grandparents had harped to her that her half brother was cruel and uncaring and wanted nothing to do with her.

He hoisted the pick and turned back to study the quarry wall again. Apparently struck by some new idea, he nudged at its base with the toe of his boot.

Georgina was still thinking about Lanie. "You said, my lord, you had two reasons for not bringing your sister to live with you after her mother's death. What was the second?"

He turned his head toward her. "I was a widower by then and living a bachelor's life in London, hardly the proper atmosphere for a nine-year-old girl. She needed the freedom of country living and its fresh, clean air."

So, in making that decision, Ravenstone *had* thought of his sister's welfare. This realization mollified Georgina.

"I do not think any child should be required to breathe the soot of London," he continued. "Have you noticed when they are, how often they develop chest complaints?"

Georgina was astonished that *he* had noticed. "Since you dislike the London air so much, my lord, why do you stay in the city instead of going to your estate in Cornwall? Does the countryside there displease you?"

"Not at all." His face assumed a wistful, faraway look that inexplicably tugged at her heart. "The land is beautiful." He lapsed into a brooding silence.

Georgina was surprised to discover how much she ached to offer him comfort—and ached, too, to trace the sharp planes of his fascinating face. Finally she prompted, "If it is so beautiful, why . . ." She broke off, realizing the impropriety of asking such a personal question.

"Although the countryside is lovely, I cannot say the same about the house at Ravencrest. It is drafty, uncomfortable, and inconvenient. I hate it!"

Such intense pain shadowed his eyes that Georgina instinctively touched his arm in sympathy.

Both his outburst and her response clearly surprised him. And the latter, at least, seemed to please him.

She said gently, "I suspect your hatred of the house, Lord Ravenstone, springs from much deeper roots than mere discomfort and inconvenience."

He frowned. "Such as?"

From what I heard of his wife, she would have soured any man on marriage. Those words of Nancy Wilde's coupled with the abhorrence for wedlock that he had expressed in London prompted Georgina, always frank to a fault, to answer, "Unhappy memories, perhaps of your late wife."

Ravenstone's harsh face froze, and he snapped, "I discuss my wife with no one."

He grabbed the pick, turned back to the quarry

wall, and attacked it vigorously near its base, clearly taking out his anger and pain on it. His reaction assured Georgina she had correctly guessed the source of his unhappy memories.

The sun, surprisingly warm for this early in the day, shone down on them. Sweat from Ravenstone's exertion soon stained his white muslin shirt, turning it clinging and translucent.

Georgina stared in admiration at the ripple of powerful muscles in his shoulders, arms, and back as he worked. He was as well made a specimen of manhood as she had ever seen.

As she watched him, a puzzling heat twisted too deep within her to have been generated by the sun. Once again, she seemed to experience trouble catching her breath. And she shivered as she remembered how gentle and exciting those strong, capable hands of his had been as they had touched her in London. The heat within her intensified.

He continued his fierce assault with the pick, sending stones and dirt flying, until a concerned Georgina protested.

Justin paused and looked at her. "I will do no damage," he insisted.

A film of sweat from his labor covered his face. Her fingers itched to wipe it away with her handkerchief, itched for some excuse to touch his dark pirate face.

He leaned the handle of the pick against the wooden box where he had laid his clothes, grabbed his neckcloth, and ran it over his face.

He looked down at the dirty smudges on the formerly immaculate cloth and winced. "I hope my valet arrives today with my clothes, or I shall have to presume upon your father's wardrobe."

"Papa will not mind," Georgina assured him.

He lifted the pick again. "I am working below where I am certain the skeleton would lie in the hope the stone and dirt above will began to erode and break away when it rains, revealing more bones."

"But what if you are wrong about its position?" she demanded as he again attacked the hillside.

His rhythmic strokes did not slow. "I am rarely wrong, Miss Penford."

Her budding goodwill toward him wilted. *Insufferable, arrogant man!*

Chapter 12

Justin set out across Penfield in a westerly direction even though his destination, Umberside, lay to the northeast. His pace was leisurely, for he was in no hurry.

He still wore the clothes he'd had on at the quarry. Sweat had plastered his shirt, open at the neck, to his body. He knew that dirt streaked his face and his hair badly needed combing. He looked like a common laborer, which was what he wanted to appear to be during his visit to Umberside.

His efforts to unearth more bones at the quarry had produced no tangible results. Yet he had shown himself to be of value to Miss Penford, although, he thought ruefully, only as a manual laborer.

Unlike most of his fellow peers who thought physical exertion beneath them, Justin enjoyed excavating a geological site where he would be the first to uncover some fascinating bit of prehistoric evidence.

Even more had he enjoyed Georgina's company. At least he had until she guessed far too accurately what lay at the heart of his reluctance to return to Ravencrest, even for a visit. He and Clarissa had spent their marriage there, and he could not remember that miserable time without pain.

Yes, Miss Penford was entirely too intelligent and perceptive for his comfort.

Yet perversely, as Justin ambled toward the village, he could not seem to put her out of his mind. When she had touched his arm so comfortingly, it had been all he could do to keep from taking her in his arms.

He breathed deeply of the fresh country air and tried to fix his thoughts on his search for the reclusive Douglas. But the image of her bending over the wooden toolbox in those tight pantaloons popped into his mind. Desire had bolted through him, and he'd remembered all too well what it had been like to have that cute derriere squirming provocatively on his lap that day in London.

The bewitching baggage might have a wasp's tongue, but she had an angel's body. And damn, but he wanted to make love to her.

But an affair with an unmarried lady of quality was out of the question unless he intended to marry her. It would violate Justin's code of honor to do otherwise.

And he would never marry again.

Justin pursued his roundabout way to Umberside in order to observe Penfield. He could find no fault with what he saw. The estate bespoke an attentive and careful owner—the kind he used to be at Ravencrest.

Now, though, it was far too long between his brief visits to the estate he loved because he loathed the memories its house held.

Justin did not reach Umberside until midafternoon, thanks to the circuitous route he took through Penfield. He went into a tavern on the outskirts of town, finding it deserted except for the proprietor and two male patrons.

As Justin expected, the customers' appearance was as rough as his own. His dirty face and stained shirt, open at the neck, excited far less attention than if he had been better washed and attired.

The proprietor set the tankard of ale Justin ordered in front of him. "New hereaboot, ain't you?"

"Aye, I've come to visit a cousin," Justin replied. "Can you give me the direction to his home? His name's G. O. Douglas."

"Ne'er heard o' him," one of the customers, a middle-aged man with an ill-kempt red beard, volunteered.

This wasn't the answer Justin wanted to hear. He turned to the man. "Have you lived here long?"

"All me life. No one around here by that name."

"Nay, there ain't," the tavern keep seconded. "But you ain't the first man to come lookin' for this Douglas. Some fine gentlemen been in here inquirin' after him."

The critical way he eyed Justin announced as plainly as words that he did not think him in the same class with the other men who'd been looking for Douglas. "One o' them were an Oxford don, but e'en he, smart as he were, couldn't discover this Douglas."

Justin frowned. Why the hell did no one know the man? "But Douglas receives his mail here, and Umberside is the address he gives on his letters."

"If that be the case, best try Simon, the post rider what fetches the mail," the tavern keep advised. "Maybe he can tell you."

"An excellent idea." Justin took a swallow of ale from his tankard. "Your village is larger than I expected and looks to be most prosperous."

The bearded customer set his tankard down. "Aye, 'tis, thanks to Lord Penford."

His companion, a wiry man with a long, hooked nose, spoke for the first time. "Me came here from the north. People here don't 'preciate how lucky they are, having him for their landlord and master.

The bearded man said, "His lor'ship's daughter even set up a school for the children. Me grandson is learnin' to read, somethin' me ne'er had a chance to do."

"Weren't always like this," the tavern keep interjected. "Before his lor'ship's father and older brother died, 'twas hard times for the villagers and Penfield's tenants."

"Aye," the bearded man agreed. "Our lives would be awful different now, and not for the better, had the present lord's older brother not been carried off by the ague. He was very like his father."

"And different as night and day from his younger brother," the bearded man said. "Couldn't ask for better than our present lord and his daughter."

"That's high praise indeed," Justin remarked.

"And well-deserved," the tavern keep assured him.

After Justin left the tavern, he walked to the house of the post rider but found no one there. He then went to the inn where his inquiries about Douglas met with more assurances that the man could not possibly live in Umberside.

Obtaining paper and ink from the innkeeper, Justin hastily scrawled a note to the post rider and returned to his house, where he slipped the missive beneath the door.

As Justin walked back toward Penfield, he pondered the mystery of G. O. Douglas and what he should do next to find the man.

As he neared the house, however, his thoughts reverted to Miss Penford. It surprised him how much he looked forward to her company.

Georgina strolled along the path that led from the house through a grove of beech trees toward Umberside. As she emerged from the other side of the grove, she was surprised to see Lord Ravenstone striding toward her. He looked as dirty and unkempt as he had when they had returned from the iguanodon site.

No, he looked worse, for the black stubble on his unshaven face was more pronounced now. "My lord," she demanded in consternation, "have you been digging at the iguanodon site again without telling me?"

Her question seemed to surprise and irritate him. "Certainly not. I would not go there without you. It is your discovery. I only wish to help you uncover it." He frowned. "Why would you think I had gone there?"

"Because you look as though you have been digging again."

He glanced down at his clothes, and comprehension replaced perplexity in his gaze. "Such a fine day called for a ramble over the countryside. I was so scruffy, I decided it would be best to walk before I bathed and changed clothes, for I would only have to do it again when I returned."

She accepted his excuse without comment and would have continued on her way, but he caught her arm lightly with his hand. "Will you be so kind as to walk with me back to the house? I would be pleased to have your company."

Georgina was secretly flattered that he should want it, but she declined.

"Please," he coaxed with a teasing smile that turned her will to custard. "Only think, I may lose my way back to your house, and you will have to send out searchers for me. It will be so much easier for you to take me there now."

She could not resist his smile. Turning, she started back with him.

"You did not answer my question last night, so now I must ask it again. Where did you learn so much about geology?"

"Mostly from my tutor. He was a fine teacher. Mama and Papa knew how much I loved the subject, and they hired Gareth partly because he was so knowledgeable about it."

"You were on a first-name basis with your tutor?" Ravenstone inquired, his voice suddenly cold.

"Oh, yes, he was too young for me to call him Mr. Davis. And Gareth had nothing of the stiff, stern pedagogue about him. I could not have wished for a better, more agreeable, more charming tutor."

Georgina wondered why Ravenstone's eyes narrowed to slits. "And this is the man you propose to hire to tutor my sister?"

"Yes, it is. You will not find a better man."

"Would I not?" he snapped.

Georgina looked at him in surprise, baffled as to why he should sound so angry.

When Justin, freshly bathed and shaved, came down to dinner that evening, he was attired in proper dress. His coach, carrying his clothes and his valet, had arrived that afternoon, shortly before his return from Umberside.

The withdrawing room was empty, and a few minutes elapsed before his sister appeared in the doorway. When she saw him, she looked alarmed and started to back out.

Justin instantly stood up, saying genially, "Don't run away, Melanie. I want to talk to you."

She stopped, her expression reminding him of a trapped, frightened rabbit. Seeking to relieve her distress, he smiled at her. "I assure you I am quite harmless. Come and join me."

She looked at him dubiously, then moved reluctantly into the room and sat down as far away from where he stood as she could manage.

He promptly strode over and took a chair opposite hers. His proximity clearly unnerved her. Miss Penford had been right about Melanie's fear of him. But why should she be afraid of him? Surely he'd never done anything to her to inspire such a reaction. And financially, he'd been far more generous to her than most brothers would have been.

Justin reached out and took her small white hands in his larger ones. She started at his touch and would have jerked away from him, but he would not let her.

"I am not going to eat you, little sister. Can we not deal together better than this?"

Her eyes widened in surprise. For a moment, hope flickered there, dispelling their customary sullenness. "Will you let me live here with Georgina?"

"I have not yet decided."

Her face grew as dark as the sky during a torrential rain. "You mean to send me back to Lady Neldane's!"

"I mean to do no such thing. Even if I rule against your living at Penfield, I promise you I will not return you to her school."

Melanie's face brightened. To his relief, he saw he'd forestalled the storm of tears that had been about to burst over his head, but then her face darkened again.

"What is it now?" he inquired.

"You mean to send me to another dreadful school, as bad or worse."

"I may well allow you to remain here at Penfield."

He was taken aback by the joy that shone on her face, but it soon faded into suspicion. "You don't mean that. You are merely teasing me most cruelly."

"No," he said, startled she would think that. "I am not the ogre you clearly think me."

The undisguised skepticism in his sister's eyes wounded him. Before he could pursue the subject, however, Miss Penford and her father appeared, and they went into dinner.

Nevertheless, Justin determined to get to the bottom of his sister's animosity toward him.

Chapter 13

Georgina spent much of the next two days with Lanie and Ravenstone at the abandoned quarry, searching for more iguanodon bones.

Although they returned empty-handed to the house at the end of that time, Georgina felt she had achieved an important goal of hers, although one that had nothing to do with fossils. Justin was clearly impressed by his sister's enthusiasm and eagerness to search for more of the skeleton. He was discovering that Lanie was not the stupid girl he had thought her.

As they neared the house, Lanie said, "I want to see the new kittens that were born in the stable yesterday. Come with me, Georgina."

"Not now. I must get back to the house, but you go ahead."

Georgina waited until Lanie was out of earshot before asking Ravenstone, "Will you go riding with me this afternoon, my lord?" She had a reason for extending the invitation, and she feared Lanie's presence on the ride might hamper what she wished to accomplish.

He looked surprised and pleased by her request. "I would like that very much."

An hour later, as they rode across the downs, he asked, "Where are we going?"

"I thought I would show you some of Penfield that you have not yet seen." She had a very specific destination in mind, but she had no intention of disclosing that. Better to surprise him when they reached it.

Cantering past well-tended fields greening from the spring planting, woods thick with oak and beech, and a pasture of grazing cows, she watched Justin survey everything with assessing eyes.

"Your father's estate is very prosperous and well-managed," he remarked approvingly.

"It is now, but it was not always so. I fear my grandfather and Uncle Christopher, my father's elder brother, were not very attentive. They spent far more time running up gaming debts in London than in administering Penfield."

Ravenstone turned to look at her. "Ah, yes, gambling—the endemic disease of the English aristocracy."

His disgusted tone surprised Georgina. "I take it you do not suffer from that particular affliction, my lord."

"No, I rarely gamble and never for high stakes." His eyes narrowed, and his voice took on a bitter shading. "My father, however, suffered from the malady."

Justin said no more, but from his expression, Georgina suspected that he must have paid a dear price for his father's gaming.

"When Uncle Christopher died, he left behind nothing but debts. Mama and Papa had to work very hard to reclaim Penfield from the wretched condition into which he and grandfather had let it deteriorate. Fortunately Mama was the heiress to a great fortune. She and Papa applied some of it to improving the estate and to discharging my uncle's debts."

They slowed their mounts to a walk as they climbed toward the crest of a hill. When they started down the other side, Justin pointed toward the remains of a sprawling stone house in the hollow below. The roof over much of the structure had collapsed and so had portions of some of the walls. "What is that?"

The reason Georgina had asked him to go riding with her, but she said only, "It was the original manor house at Penfield."

"The one you live in now is a vast improvement. How long ago was the new one constructed?"

"My parents built it after my uncle died."

"'Tis that new, is it? I'd not guessed. Such fine workmanship is all too rare in these modern times."

"My parents employed only the best."

The road they were on led down to the ruins of the old house. When they reached the partially collapsed walls, Justin dismounted and helped Georgina down from the speckled mare she rode.

They wandered about, picking their way through debris that littered the ground from the crumbling roof and walls.

"As you can see," Georgina remarked, "this was one of those houses that was strung together over the decades by various owners with vastly different tastes and no overall plan. Papa said it was as difficult to find one's way through the maze of rooms here as through a London slum."

"That's much the way it is at Ravencrest."

She smiled. "So I gathered from your remark about its inconvenience."

"Did your parents build the new house because

they found this old one too awkward and anti-quated?"

"No, they did so because Papa hated this house. It was filled with so many unhappy memories for him that he could not bear to live in it."

Justin's head snapped toward her. He clearly suspected it was no coincidence she had brought him here.

And he was right. Listening to him when he had confessed his hatred for the house at Ravencrest, haunted by unhappy memories, Georgina had been struck by the similarity between his loathing for it and what her father had felt for the house in which he had been raised.

Papa, too, had not wanted to return to Penfield to live after his elder brother's death. But her mama had been wise enough to realize it was the house, in which he had endured such childhood misery, that he hated and not the entire estate.

Georgina suspected from the affection with which Ravenstone had spoken of Cornwall's beauty that he felt much the same as Papa had. If Justin built another house there, he might find the estate more agreeable, perhaps even make it a home for himself and for Lanie, who so desperately wanted one.

Georgina returned his questioning gaze squarely. "Mama suggested they build an entirely new house on a more propitious site, far removed from the old residence."

Ravenstone looked so severe that she wondered if he was angry at her. Then his harsh piratical face suddenly relaxed into a broad smile, and a strange, appreciative glow flared in his eyes. The change in him took her breath away.

Her gaze was fixed on his face instead of where she was walking, and her toe caught on a fallen brick in her path. She stumbled over it.

"Careful!" With lightning reflexes, Justin caught her before she could fall. His arms encircled her and lifted her against his hard body, steadying her. Heat sizzled through her at this contact, and she involuntarily quivered.

Hardly knowing what she was doing, Georgina turned in his arms and glanced up at him. Fearing her voice would betray the stunning effect he had upon her, she dared not speak her thanks for his quick action, and she smiled them instead.

He gazed hungrily at her mouth, and she felt an answering hunger within herself. Her heart accelerated.

Why, he wanted to kiss her.

And she wanted him to do so, wanted to feel his sensual mouth on hers so much she ached.

At last she admitted to herself what she had refused to acknowledge before. Ever since their first kiss that day in London, she had wanted Ravenstone to kiss her again, to make her feel once more the marvelous sensations she had then.

He raised his gaze to her eyes. They stared at each other for a long moment, tension crackling between them like summer lightning. His brown eyes turned warm and soft and luminous.

Slowly his lips lowered toward hers. Georgina raised her own to meet his.

His kiss was all she had wanted and more. Hot and plundering, it stoked in her a longing for something more, for something she instinctively knew would both feed and slake the fiery ache within her.

Some minutes later, the barking of dogs and the baaing of sheep penetrated Justin's ardor, and he forced himself to break off their wild kiss.

Looking toward the road that had brought them to the old manor house, he saw two dogs herding a small flock of sheep down the hill toward them. A shepherd with a staff brought up the rear.

Justin stepped away from Georgina, silently cursing the two- and four-legged intruders. She looked as dazed as he felt by the passion they had just shared.

What the hell was wrong with him? He was a sophisticated man who had enjoyed his choice of the most skilled courtesans in London. Yet none of those highly experienced women had made him feel the way this spirited innocent did. She embraced passion with the same enthusiasm she did everything else.

He looked down at her. Rebellious curls had escaped her hat and were tumbling about her pert, shining face. At that moment, he thought her the most beautiful woman he had ever seen.

Struggling to hide how much their kiss had affected him, Justin gestured toward the ruined structure. "Why did your father hate it so much?" He cursed the telltale huskiness of his voice.

Georgina could not seem to find hers at all. Indeed, he was not even certain she had heard his question. The dreamy, sensual glow in her eyes betrayed how deeply she, too, had been moved by their kiss. Enormously pleased, Justin waited a silent minute before he repeated his question.

This time she focused her eyes on him and answered. "He spent a most unhappy childhood there. He and his brother were very different. Not only was Christopher the heir and favorite on whom his father doted, but he was as big and strong and as frightfully proud and high in the instep as his sire." She paused and poked at a brick fragment with the toe of her boot.

The sheep were close to the old house now, and Justin saw the shepherd eye them curiously.

"Papa, on the other hand, was frail and sickly as a child, and that was anathema to Grandfather. He used to make fun of Papa, referring disparagingly to him as the runt of the litter and an embarrassment to the Penford name."

Justin winced at such cruelty. At least his own father had not been that, only indifferent.

Still baaing loudly, the flock of sheep passed the old house. Justin took Georgina's arm, and they resumed their stroll among the ruins.

This time, to Justin's disappointment, she kept a careful eye on the path ahead of her. He would have welcomed her stumbling a second time so he could take her in his arms again.

She said, "Mama told me both Grandfather and Uncle Christopher were stuffy dolts who never understood how brilliant Papa was. He prevailed upon his father to send him to the University of Edinburgh. Grandfather sneered at Papa's 'bookish' interests, but he was happy to be rid of him. And Papa was overjoyed to escape to a more congenial atmosphere. He loved the university."

"I wager it was there that he acquired his radical ideas."

Georgina nodded. "My grandfather was so incensed by them, he forbade Papa to return home until he recanted. He even rewrote his will to leave everything to Uncle Christopher with nary a shilling to Papa. But Papa did not care. He would not be coerced into abandoning his principles."

Justin suspected Georgina would be equally as strong and unyielding in the face of intimidation.

"And so your father held fast to them?"

"Yes, and then he met my mother."

"Who was she?"

"A Scottish heiress. Papa said she was the only woman he'd met whose intelligence matched his own. Her grandfather had made a huge fortune in shipping and trade that, in turn, was multiplied by her father's astute dealings. Papa became great friends with him. That's how he met my mother."

"Your paternal grandfather could not have been pleased by your papa's choice of wife, given her connections," Justin observed.

Georgina chuckled. "You're right. Although grandfather disliked the choice, Papa was not the heir. And after Papa's frail childhood, his father expected him to die long before his elder brother. So Grandfather did not care much whom Papa married as long as she was rich."

"Which your mother was."

"I think Grandfather hoped Mama's fortune would end up in his hands after Papa died. How welcome Grandfather would have been then at the London gaming tables."

To Justin's relief, the noisy flock of sheep vanished over the hill on the other side of the hollow. "But things did not work out quite as your grandfather expected."

"No, he died unexpectedly only a few weeks after my parents were married. My uncle, who was still a bachelor, followed him to the grave a year later, the victim of a putrid sore throat that worsened into a fatal inflammation of his lungs."

"And your father became the lord and master."

"Yes. Mama used to say Grandfather must be turning over in his grave, even though Papa is a far better custodian of the inheritance than either his brother or father ever were. The estate declined shockingly under their stewardship."

Justin knew from the men in the tavern that what she said was true, not merely daughterly pride speaking.

"My grandfather and uncle were too busy gambling in London to be bothered with Penfield."

"An all too familiar story." It had been the same with his own father. After his grandfather's death, Justin had been forced to assume responsibility for running Ravencrest while, in London, his father gambled away the estate's income, which should have gone for much needed improvements.

"This house was already in such wretched condition by the time Papa inherited it that it would have cost a fortune to restore it." Georgina picked up a piece of rubble and, with a twist of her wrist, sent it skimming over the ruins. "When Mama suggested building the new house, Papa was delighted to let this one, where he was so unhappy, fall apart."

"A vast amount of your mama's fortune must have gone to finance the new mansion, bring the estate up to snuff, and pay off your uncle's debts." Justin looked at her searchingly. "No wonder you are so concerned about surrendering control of your inheritance to a husband."

She whirled on him, anger radiating from her. Caught by surprise, he took an involuntary step backward.

"How dare you imply my father squandered my mother's inheritance! Nothing could be further from the truth. He spent none of her money without her approval and often he did so reluctantly and only at her insistence."

"So your mother had not your concern that a husband would squander her inheritance."

"Mama had *no* concern that *Papa* would squander it."

"But she would have been more careful with another husband?"

"She would not have married another man. She often said, had she not met Papa, she would have remained a spinster. They loved each other so much." Georgina's voice softened, and a wistful expression stole over her face. "Their love was beautiful to behold."

Justin was convinced that such a love, if it existed at all between a husband and wife, could only be of very short duration. Now, though, looking at Georgina's face, he wondered if he could be wrong.

"Papa worked hard to increase Mama's fortune and establish his own with wise investments. He succeeded in both these goals. He did not marry my mother for her money. Indeed, he pressed her to leave it directly to me when she died, and she did."

"So you possess a great fortune in your own right, even before your father dies, do you?"

Her chin tilted at a stubborn angle. "Yes, I do. Does that make me more marriageable after all in your eyes?"

Hell, she needed no money whatsoever, not a farthing, to seem highly marriageable to him, and he disliked being reminded of his earlier, stupid assertion. "Miss Penford, I have already apologized for my cruel and slanderous remark."

Her face softened and so did her voice. "Yes, you have, and I have forgiven you. But I am unwavering in my determination not to marry. I will not cede control of myself and my fortune to a husband. The only man I would consider marrying is one like

Papa, and I am convinced such a man does not exist."

Justin was sorely tempted to take her in his arms and convince her that he, too, had unique qualities—ones she would find most pleasurable.

He was about to reach for her when she looked toward the sinking sun and said, "It's late. We must go back. Papa does not like his dinner delayed."

As Justin reluctantly helped Georgina remount her speckled mare, he asked, "Why did you bring me here today?"

She answered with her typical blunt honesty. "I hoped it would give you an idea of how to make Ravencrest more enjoyable for you." Her eyes crinkled as one of her marvelous smiles brightened her face. "You clearly love the estate, but loathe the house."

That was true. Justin was surprised and touched by her startling perception and tact in bringing him here to subtly offer him a solution to his dilemma over Ravencrest, one that would allow him to walk in contentment along the Cornish cliffs again and listen to the ever-changing voice of the sea.

As a boy, that had been his greatest pleasure, and after his marriage, his only escape from the turmoil in his home.

As Justin mounted his chestnut gelding, he even knew the spot he would choose for a new house. It was on a rise above the granite cliffs that plunged into the sea.

He would situate his bedchamber and library, the two rooms where he would spend the most time, so that he could observe the shifting moods of the sea and hear its siren song.

Georgina smiled at him. "You see how much

Papa loves his home here now. He hates to leave it.''

But he has you to make it comfortable and companionable for him. Justin could not help envying Penford.

When they adjourned to the library after dinner that night, Justin's curiosity overcame his dread of the painful performance his query might inspire, and he asked Georgina if she played the harp.''

Melanie answered for her. ''She plays beautifully.''

In light of his sister's lack of musical ability, Justin suspected her assessment was based more on loyalty than on her friend's talent, but he gamely requested Miss Penford to play.

He even managed to sound enthusiastic.

''Oh yes, Georgina, do!'' Melanie seconded.

But it was not until her father added his plea that she walked with visible reluctance to the harp.

Her attitude made Justin fear the worst, and he settled on a sofa, resigned to a tedious, perhaps even painful, interlude.

But as he listened to the lovely music rippling from her fingers as they stroked the harp strings, he discovered that Georgina had once again confounded him. If anything, his sister had slighted rather than exaggerated her friend's talent.

Justin sank back in the comfortable cushions of the sofa and let the pleasure of the music seep through him. He could not remember when he had last felt so contented.

As he listened, he studied Georgina. She looked particularly pretty tonight. Her thick dark hair was piled high on her head, with charming little ringlets tumbling about her face.

She wore an emerald gown that accentuated the

green flecks in her eyes, making them look more green than hazel. The gown's low, square neckline afforded him a most pleasing and provocative view of her full bosom.

He no longer wondered that she had received several offers for her hand. Her father's words echoed in his mind: *I have not entirely given up hope that Roger may yet prevail upon Georgina to accept him.* Justin felt a piercing stab of jealousy for the unknown Roger.

Although Georgina played for a considerable time, he was disappointed when she stopped.

"That is enough for tonight," she said.

"Please don't stop now," Melanie begged. "I could listen to you play all night."

For once, Justin thought wryly, he and his sister agreed on something.

He turned his attention back to Georgina.

Since he had been at Penfield, he'd come to look forward to her company. He smiled to himself as he recalled their verbal dueling. Few men, and no woman until Georgina, had dared stand up to him. Yet he enjoyed crossing verbal swords with a worthy opponent.

And she was a worthy one. Indeed, she was.

Georgina was full of fire and passion. If her kisses were any indication, she would be equally passionate in bed.

Her glorious smile, which crinkled her face and made it glow like the brightest star in the heavens, bewitched him. So did her delicious body. He yearned to hold it against his own again and to explore its every secret.

Yet she was the last woman on earth in whom Justin should have any such interest. But he could not seem to squelch it. He was attracted to her despite himself.

And he was a damned fool!

Miss Georgina Penford was no member of the demimonde as he had first thought, but an unmarried woman of high birth.

Were he to embark on the dalliance with her for which his body ached, it could have only one conclusion, an untenable one for him.

Marriage.

The word was enough to send another shudder through him. He would never marry again.

Although Miss Penford professed an abhorrence as strong as his own for marriage, he would wager his entire fortune that, were they to have an affair, she would happily spring the parson's mousetrap shut on him.

Justin could not, would not let that happen.

Chapter 14

On the afternoon of Justin's eleventh day at Penfield, he stood at one of the French windows in the library, watching sheets of rain beating down. This was the fourth consecutive day of such heavy rain that all outdoor activities had been canceled.

Until now, Justin would have considered spending four dreary days indoors at a country house the worst kind of purgatory and one he would do anything to escape.

But not at Penfield.

Not in Georgina's company. The eleven days had flown by, even the rainy ones. They'd had many lively conversations and arguments about everything from competing geological theories to the relative merits of Jane Austen's and Sir Walter Scott's novels.

Not only was Georgina's conversation scintillating, but she ran a most comfortable home—one he'd become increasingly loathe to leave. Justin wished she was a fraction as eager to keep him here as she was to keep his sister.

He heard the swish of a skirt behind him and inhaled Georgina's distinctive gardenia scent as it enveloped him. He turned toward her, but she was looking out the window at the rain.

"Will it never stop?" she inquired impatiently.

Justin smothered a smile. Usually he was the impatient one, but not now. He knew she chafed at the rain because it kept her from searching for more iguanodon remains. In their last moments at the site, before the rain set in, she had uncovered part of a huge foot with three toes that they both felt certain was part of the prehistoric beast.

"Patience, little wasp," he counseled. "If we are lucky, the rain will do some of our work for us by washing away the dirt and rock from the hillside above where I excavated."

Before the deluge had started, he'd concentrated on hollowing out the base of the quarry wall until it resembled a cave, very shallow in depth and height, but running some thirty feet in width, in the hope that rain, erosion, and gravity would aid them in their search.

Skeptical of his plan, Georgina had continued to work with her chisel in her usual, careful fashion. That was how she had come upon the foot.

Georgina ended her contemplation of the downpour outside and turned to Justin. "It would be wonderful if your idea works." Though her words were positive, her tone indicated she was highly skeptical it would.

He was startled by how chagrined he felt at her lack of confidence in him. "You should have more faith in me," he complained.

"But I have a scientific mind. I require proof of everything."

"Perhaps you'll have it when the rain stops."

"Oh, I hope so!" Georgina turned and gave him

a smile that reminded Justin of the sun breaking through the clouds.

She radiated warmth, and he instantly forgot the rain and the dreariness of the day. Who cared about that when he could bask in her magnificent smile? He ached to kiss her, ached to unleash her sweet passion that he had sampled first in London, then again that day among the ruins of the old house. Most of all, he ached to make love to her, but he would not pay the certain price for that—marriage. He'd learned his lesson with Clarissa.

His mouth tightened as he remembered how he had gone to the altar thinking he was marrying a delightful, complaisant beauty, only to see her shed that disguise like a snake slithering from its skin. He still shuddered at what had emerged.

"What is wrong, my lord?"

Georgina's voice penetrated his ugly memories, drawing him back to the present. She watched him with a puzzled frown.

She was too perceptive for his comfort. "Nothing," he claimed, "except I wish you would call me Justin."

He was surprised at how much he wanted to hear her speak his given name in her pure voice, for he found it as lovely as the music that flowed from her harp.

But instead of granting his wish, she asked, "Where is Lanie?"

"You are much more likely to know than I am. She does not confide in me."

"But she is growing easier with you."

"True." Justin had worked hard since his arrival at Penfield to improve his relationship with his sister, and Georgina had helped him in every way she could. "Part of the credit for that goes to you."

His image of Melanie as a sullen, silent, seemingly stupid girl had eroded during his stay at Penfield. The Melanie he observed in the Penfords' company was bright and talkative, rather than silent and sullen as she'd always been with him. He'd been astonished at her enthusiasm for finding more iguanodon bones. Melanie had worked alongside Georgina and him without complaint.

Indeed, the only complaint had been his. His sister's presence had prevented him from taking advantage of several prime opportunities to kiss Georgina.

Justin had decided to let his sister stay at Penfield, but he had told no one yet. If he admitted his decision, he would no longer have any excuse to remain here himself.

Georgina flashed him another one of her glowing, face crinkling smiles. "Lanie is even coming to understand your humor."

"Yes." He smiled ruefully. "Now I do not have to tell her more than once or twice a day when I am teasing her."

"She is too serious, but how could she be otherwise when she was raised by two elderly, inflexible grandparents who lacked any sense of humor or fun.

A perfect description of the Dortons, Justin thought. "I wish I had not left her with them. You were quite right to take me to task for doing so. Why do you look so surprised?"

"I am always astonished when a man admits to a woman he is wrong and she is right."

"Little wasp," he retorted. "Can you never resist an opportunity to sting me?"

Her grin was so entrancing that he could no longer ignore the lure of her mouth. He had been yearning to taste it again since the day she'd taken him to the old house. Slowly he lowered his head to kiss her.

"Georgina, there you are."

Justin's head jerked up at Melanie's words. Georgina stepped away from him with equal haste.

"Your papa is in the withdrawing room, looking for you," Melanie told her.

"Thank you, Lanie. I'll go to him. Please keep your brother company while I am gone."

As Georgina departed, Melanie ambled toward her brother.

"Do sit down." Justin said. When she complied, he took a chair across from her. As he did so, he noticed how dull her eyes were. She appeared to be ill and feverish.

"Are you feeling unwell, Melanie?" he asked.

Her eyes widened in surprise. "Yes. How did you know?"

"You look ill. What's wrong?"

"I can't stop shaking, my throat hurts, and I ache all over."

Justin rose to lay his hand on her forehead. Her skin beneath his fingers felt as though it was burning. He observed with a worried frown, "You feel very feverish. You should be in bed. Shall I summon a doctor for you?"

"You sound as though you care about me," she said with such bitterness he winced.

"I do care about you, Melanie," he said gently. "You are my sister."

She jumped up, tears glistening in her eyes. "Just because I'm your sister, does not mean you care about me. Mama says the only person you ever cared about was your brother, Henry."

Melanie fled the library before he could rebut her.

Justin went back to the French windows. The rain had lightened, and he saw a patch of blue sky in the distance, indicating the weather was beginning to clear.

He hoped the same was true about his stormy relationship with his sister.

When Georgina told Ravenstone the following morning at breakfast that his sister was too ill to get out of bed, he asked anxiously, "Should I send for a doctor?"

Georgina was both moved and pleased by his regard for his sister.

"It isn't that serious," she reassured him. "I doubt that it is much more than a bad cold. I have given her an herbal remedy to lower her fever and ease her aches. I am certain she will feel better by tonight. If she does not, then you may summon a doctor."

Ravenstone's forehead was still creased with worry, telling Georgina that he was not nearly as convinced as she was that his sister would quickly recover.

Georgina glanced out the French windows at the bright blue sky decorated with a few puffy white clouds. The rain had finally stopped early this morning, and she could hardly wait to resume her efforts to uncover more iguanodon bones.

She asked Justin if he wished to accompany her.

He frowned. "Are you certain Melanie will be all right?"

"Physically, yes, although she will be miffed that we have continued our work without her." She smiled. "Are you ready to go to the site?"

Justin nodded, taking her wrist and lightly stroking its sensitive underside with his thumb. She shivered with pleasure at his touch.

"It will be a muddy swamp there," he warned as he released her wrist.

"I care naught for that," Georgina scoffed. "I am far too anxious to get back to work."

His dark eyes were teasing. "What, a lady not afraid of the mud and muck?"

"I assure you I am fearless in the face of nature."

As they set out, she was glad for Ravenstone's company. Strange how much more she enjoyed her search when he was with her. Not only was he as excited about what they might find as she was, but she could theorize with him what the great beast and the prehistoric world in which it lived must have been like.

To her surprise, Ravenstone did not dismiss her ideas and opinions with the usual patronizingly male superiority but discussed them with respectful seriousness. He treated her as his equal not his inferior.

Furthermore, the scope of his geologic knowledge and understanding astonished and impressed Georgina as much as hers did him. He could discuss the most arcane theories with authority, and a great many other subjects, too.

She wondered how much longer he would remain at Penfield. Her father had said a fortnight or so, and their guest had already been here nearly that long.

And the longer he stayed the less anxious Georgina was for him to leave.

Never had she savored a man's company the way she did Justin's. But this was not what confounded Georgina the most. It was the man himself. What was it about him that made her tingle as though she had received a shock whenever he pushed back a lock of hair from her face, made her ache when he took her arm, made her want him to kiss her again—and made her yearn for even more intimate contact?

She did not understand the strange, powerful attraction for him that she had never felt for another man. She had not been so aquiver around Roger Chadwick, the only man she had ever been in the least tempted to marry.

"You are very quiet this morning," Justin observed. "What has you so deep in thought?"

Her usual frankness failed her, and she said, "I . . . I am wondering whether your theory about excavating at the base of the wall worked."

They walked on in silence. As Georgina and Justin neared the quarry, she increased her pace in her eagerness to reach it.

Had she known, when she left the site after finding the foot, that rain would prevent her from returning for five days, nothing could have dragged her away.

The only thing that had made her rain-enforced hiatus bearable had been Justin's company. He was a delightful guest, quick-witted and provocative. Their lively conversations ranged widely, and she had come to realize their minds were in greater harmony than she would have suspected.

As they reached the turn in the path where the quarry would be revealed to them, Georgina was so anxious to see it that she stepped ahead of Justin. As she made the turn, she stopped so abruptly that he bumped into her.

"Oh," she cried in a voice of awed wonder, "I cannot believe it!"

Chapter 15

"**W**hat is it?" Justin stepped up to Georgina's side so he could see what had so astounded her.

"Your theory was right!" she exclaimed.

Where Justin had undermined the quarry wall, some of the dirt and stone above had been carried away by the storm to reveal the upper portion of massive ribs curving out from the eroded hillside like gigantic fangs.

They were attached at the top to a huge vertebrate spinal column. Both the front and back of the column was still hidden within the stone, but enough of it was visible, at least fifteen feet, to give an indication of the monstrous size the beast must have been. For a moment, Justin could only gape at the sight, scarcely able to believe his eyes.

Georgina recovered her voice first. "Look what we have found! An iguanodon skeleton! I am certain of it!"

Justin was every bit as euphoric over the discovery as she was. "It's truly awesome," he said in wonder.

She whirled around to face him. In her elation,

she threw her arms around him and hugged him fiercely. He hugged her back.

With her provocative angel's body pressed against his, a bolt of lust, as strong as he had ever felt, shot through him.

Her expression told Justin she was so overcome with happiness at finding the skeleton that she was oblivious both to the effect she was having on him and to the impropriety of her embrace.

She broke away from him and ran toward the skeleton. He could think of no other woman he knew who would have reacted with the exuberance that she did. He followed her more slowly, drinking in her contagious enthusiasm, delighting in her artless demonstration of joy and excitement, marveling at her vibrancy and passion.

But she did not get far at her initial pace. The rain had turned the dirt at the bottom of the wall into a slippery quagmire that proved slow going.

With each step, both she—and Justin behind her—sank above their ankles in the slime. The hem of Georgina's skirt was quickly weighted down with mud.

But she was clearly oblivious to her clothes, to the difficulties of forging ahead, and to everything else except getting closer to their amazing discovery.

Justin watched her in amusement and admiration. Although she had assured him earlier that she was impervious to muck, he had not truly believed her. He smiled to himself. He should have known better than to doubt her.

While they struggled through the mire, she slipped and pitched forward. Justin reached out to save her from falling, but as his arms closed around her waist, he too lost his footing.

As they both tumbled into the mud, he managed

at the last moment to twist so that they landed on their sides.

They fought to achieve a sitting position, not an easy thing to do in the muck.

When they succeeded, they burst out laughing at the sight of each other covered in mud. Georgina's cheek and chin were streaked with grime, and she was coated on the left side of her gown from shoulder to hem.

Justin looked down at himself. His clothes were as dirty as hers, and he knew his face must be filthy as well.

Georgina was still laughing so hard she clutched her abdomen.

Justin, in turn, was charmed by a lady so happy and ebullient that she could entirely forget her appearance. "It is hopeless to try to work in this muck. We will have to wait for the ground to dry a little."

"Yes," Georgina agreed, clearly much disappointed. "And find a way to remove the skeleton from the rock."

Justin stared at the wall thoughtfully. "I think first we should determine how far that backbone extends in each direction, and where the legs might be. Then we can draw a line around the skeleton, and hire quarrymen to cut the entire block out to minimize the damage. They may have to cut it into two or three blocks, but no more than that."

"What an excellent idea," Georgina said approvingly.

He smiled. "So you agree with me."

"Yes, of course."

He thought of how disappointed his sister would be when she heard about their discovery. "I do not think we should tell Melanie about this," he said slowly. "She will be disconsolate."

Georgina gave him a startled look, then inquired in an oddly neutral voice, "What are you suggesting?"

"As soon as she is well, we'll bring her here to see it for herself as we first saw it."

"Oh, yes," Georgina cried, clapping her muddy hands. "I can hardly wait to see her face when she beholds it."

Justin grinned at her. "Careful, little wasp, that is the third time in succession you have agreed with me. It could become a habit."

"Not likely," she retorted gaily as she attempted to extract herself from the mud.

Regaining their feet, however, proved difficult, for the mire offered them no support as they tried to scramble up.

Their hilarity increased as they floundered about, giggling and cavorting like two small children in the first snow of winter.

Justin looked at Georgina's laughing face, and a wave of affectionate warmth rolled through him. Dear, delightful Gina. He understood now why Nancy Wilde called her that. It fit her better than either Georgina or Georgie.

When at last she managed to gain her footing, mud clung to her gown, weighing it down so that it revealed her slender body far more intimately than she could have suspected. Justin gulped at the sight and fought against the desire that chewed at him.

"We look like a couple of beached whales," she said.

He quirked his eyebrow. "You do not in the least resemble such a mammal, and I am greatly insulted if you truly think I look like a mass of blubber."

Her cheeks pinkened beneath the smudges of mud. "No, I don't think that at all."

Her suddenly husky voice sent another rush of desire through Justin, and it was all he could do to keep from kissing her. Or more.

When they finally regained their feet, they pushed their way through the mud toward the path that led back to the house.

Before quitting the site, Georgina turned for one final look at the protruding ribs of the skeleton. "I can scarcely believe it."

Justin stared down at her face, smudged with dirt. He wiped his muddy hands against a clean spot on his shirt and pulled out his pocket handkerchief to wipe the streaks away, seizing this excuse to touch her soft cheek.

With her eyes shining, her smile at its most brilliant, she asked breathlessly, "Is it not the most magnificent thing you have ever seen?"

No, not nearly as magnificent as your smile!

Justin looked at her seductive mouth that he'd been aching to kiss again. He could no longer resist the temptation.

As he slowly lowered his head, their gazes met and locked.

Gina's eyes widened, first in surprise, then in anticipation.

Why, she wants me to kiss her! This realization intensified Justin's own desire. Her lack of coyness delighted him.

Their lips met, and he kissed her hungrily, unleashing a passion in them both that soon had them melding their mouths together in a wild mating that went on and on until they were both panting for breath.

As Justin's desire spiraled higher, he was thankful for how muddy the ground was. Otherwise he did not think he could have restrained himself from laying Gina down upon it and making love to her.

When their kiss ended, her expression defied analysis.

Justin looked at her warily. He did not think she was angry, but he decided he'd better apologize just in case. "I am sorry."

"You are?" She looked perplexed. "Why? I thought it was quite wonderful."

He laughed, charmed by her candor. He'd never known a woman so lacking in artifice and pretense. "Indeed, it was wonderful."

"Then why are you sorry?"

"Actually, I'm not," he admitted.

"Then why did you say you were?"

"When a gentleman gets . . . er, carried away with a lady, he is expected to offer his apologies to her."

Her face crinkled, her eyes shining with teasing laughter.

Justin adored that wonderful smile.

And her enticing lips.

"So occasionally, my lord, you remember you are supposed to be a gentleman?"

"Little wasp! How you delight in stinging me."

At that, she laughed again, a melodic sound that reminded him of chimes ringing out pure and clear on the fresh morning air.

He longed to kiss her once more, but she turned back to the path. Justin could not help himself. He put his arm around her and squeezed her affectionately.

As they headed down the path again, he could not remember when he'd felt so joyful and light-hearted and carefree. Probably not since he was about nine when his grandfather had begun training him in earnest for his future role as earl. Justin had loved the old man, but he'd been a hard taskmaster.

When they passed under a horse chestnut tree, a gust of wind shook the leaves, still wet from the rains, sprinkling them with water.

Gina raised her face to the drops, breathed deeply, and laughed with delight. "'Tis such a pleasure to be out after the rain has stopped." She glanced at him, her brilliant smile lighting her face. "Everything smells so fresh and clean."

Justin stared down at her in admiration. "What an unusual woman you are, Gina!"

She grinned at him mischievously, her eyes sparkling. "I do not know whether I should consider that a compliment or an insult."

"Very definitely a compliment, Gina."

"Why do you call me that? Nancy is the only person who has ever done so. She says it fits me better than Georgie or Georgina."

"And she is absolutely right," Justin said, desperate to kiss her lovely smiling mouth again. He thought of what it would be like to have her in his bed.

But it could not be. He was not such a fool that he would trade a few weeks or months of passion for a lifetime of marital boredom—or worse— which would follow. No woman could be as ideal as Gina seemed.

He recalled her avowed determination not to wed either. "What is behind your strong distaste for marriage?"

"The inequities it holds for a wife," she replied without a moment's hesitation.

"Inequities!" To Justin they were all on the husband's side. He must support his wife's extravagant habits, deal with her tantrums, and wonder whether the son she bore him was truly *his* heir.

Gina ignored his incredulous exclamation. "And what is behind yours, my lord?"

"Experience," he said brusquely. "You say women must marry for security, yet you have no intention of marrying. Have you no concern for your own security?"

"I told you women marry for security; I did not say marriage gave it to them. All too often, rather than gaining security, they lose what little they had. In my case, I would have a great deal to lose. Marriage would rob me of security, rather than provide it."

"How did you come to that *remarkable* conclusion?" he asked sardonically.

"You imply it is an erroneous conclusion, but it is not. I am an heiress to a great fortune. So long as I remain single, I control it." Her candid gaze met his. "But if I marry, control passes to my husband. I no longer would have any say in how my money was being managed—or mismanaged. If I married a man of Lord Ingleham's character, he would rapidly squander it, and I would be powerless to stop him."

Justin was chagrined that he could think of no good argument to rebut her. He contented himself with saying, "I am happy to hear that at least you do not believe, as so many silly females do, in that nonsense called romantic love."

She stopped dead on the path. He halted, too, and they faced each other. "To the contrary," she said, her eyes flashing angrily, "I believe very much in it."

That astonished him, for she was such an intelligent woman. "You would wager your happiness on such an ephemeral notion?"

"You confuse lust with love, my lord."

"They are one and the same!"

"Only for those who have not a generous heart. Indeed, love is the only reason I should ever consent to marrying, for I have seen the joy and pleasure it brings to both parties in a marriage."

"And I thought you a sensible woman." His scornful statement brought an angry flush to her face.

"More sensible than a jaded cynic like yourself, my lord, who thinks only of his pleasures."

"What a pretty notion you have of my character, ma'am!"

"What other notion am I to have, since by your own admission, you do not believe in love? That means you cannot have experienced it."

"You cannot experience what does not exist," he snapped.

"Love requires mutual respect and trust, and I think you, my lord, find it impossible to respect and trust any woman."

"Love such as you describe does not exist between a man and a woman. You seek a fantasy, a mirage."

"No, you are wrong!" she cried passionately.

He raised a skeptical eyebrow. "Am I?"

"Indeed, you are! I have witnessed such love firsthand in my own parents' marriage, and it was a joy to behold." Her expression turned pensive. "But I concede it is excessively rare. I know I shall never find a man like Papa."

Justin smarted at how clearly he failed in Gina's estimation to measure up to her father.

She started down the path again. They walked in tense silence the remainder of the way to the house.

Chapter 16

Georgina carefully probed the rubble at the base of the quarry wall, searching for any bones that might have washed down during the rains.

Three days had passed since she and Justin had made their momentous discovery, but this was the first day that the area had dried sufficiently after the heavy rains for them to work.

The tension that had arisen between them as they returned to the house after finding the skeleton had dissipated by that night, and now they worked companionably several feet apart at the bottom of the bluff.

They had ascertained the intact portion of the skeleton—the ribs still attached to the spinal column—would be too large to bring into Georgina's workroom or, for that matter, to fit through any of the entrances to the house.

The only building on the estate large enough to accommodate the huge skeleton was a big old barn adjacent to the newer, smaller stables that had supplanted it. The barn was used only for storage now, and Georgina had put men to work to clear room in it for her discovery.

Other men were building an ingenious dryland sled, long and low to the ground with runners rather than wheels, that Justin had designed to transport the blocks containing the skeleton to the barn.

She looked up at the partially exposed ribs and longed to set to work revealing more of them, but she and Justin had agreed that work would be better done in the barn.

Now they were concentrating on determining the creature's dimensions so they could paint a line that would tell the quarrymen where to cut.

Georgina glanced over at the enormous leg bone that Justin had unearthed a half hour earlier. He'd found it very close to where she had discovered the three-toed foot before the rains began.

She said, "By tomorrow, your sister should be well enough for us to bring her here." Although Lanie was still a bit weak and achy from her illness, she had been enough improved to come down to dinner the previous night.

"She's looking much better, but she's still a little pale, and she has lost weight," Justin observed. "I noticed at dinner last night how poorly her gown fit. She has outgrown her wardrobe, and she needs a new one."

"I am surprised that you noticed, my lord," Georgina murmured.

Justin flashed her a provocative smile. "I assure you I notice *everything* about a lady."

Georgina felt the heat rising in her cheeks at the appreciative perusal he gave her.

"Do you have a good dressmaker in this neighborhood whom I can employ to refurbish my sister's wardrobe?"

"Yes," she said hesitantly, "a very good one, but she is rather expensive."

He shrugged, clearly unperturbed. "I can afford it."

His response surprised Georgina in light of his stepmother's claim that a more clutch-fisted man never existed. "Lanie will be delighted."

Georgina felt something in the earth and worked eagerly to free it from the rubble. It proved to be another elongated bone, but not so large as the leg Justin had found. Then, following the direction in which the bone pointed, she unearthed what appeared at first glance to be the skeleton of a five-fingered hand, far too large to be human.

A closer look, however, revealed that what she had thought was a thumb was instead a strange, sharp-pointed horn. "Justin, come look at this!"

He hurried over and dropped to his knees beside her. "That's clearly the horn Gideon Mantell described protruding from the iguanodon's nose, rather like a hippopotamus's," Justin observed, pointing to the object.

"But I saw no place on the skull where it could have been attached," Georgina objected. "And if that's what it is, I should think it would be much larger. I believe Dr. Mantell was wrong. I think the horn must have been part of the iguanodon's hand."

She expected Justin to scoff at her, but instead he eyed her with obvious approval and respect. "I think you're right! But five fingers? And it is so different from the foot you found, which was larger, and had only three toes."

Delighted that he so readily accepted her theory, she pointed to the long bone above the hand. "And this must be the bone to which the hand was attached. It is smaller than the leg bone." She stared at him in wonder. "It must mean that the creature could walk on two legs, otherwise I would think the front and back extremities would be more alike."

"My God," Justin breathed, clearly awed. "Considering the size of the bones, the creature must have stood three times higher than even a tall man."

"I hope the sled and the barn will be ready when we need them."

"Oh, they'll be ready," Justin assured her. "It will take at least five or six days here to determine the skeleton's dimensions approximately enough and to set the quarrymen to their work."

"Surely not that long!" Georgina protested, anxious to begin sooner than that the delicate work of extracting all of the skeleton from its stone coffin.

But Justin's estimate proved to be optimistic. Eight more days elapsed before Georgina could finally gaze up at the blocks of stone in the barn. She turned to Justin. "Your idea of the sled was brilliant. We could not have gotten the stones here without it."

He winked at her. "You see I have my uses." He looked around. "Where did Melanie go?"

"The dressmaker was waiting to fit her with the first of the new gowns you ordered for her. She is incredulous and overjoyed at your generosity."

"Incredulous?" Justin sounded puzzled. "I don't understand why she should be."

"Only think, you totally ignored her all those years until her grandparents died. Poor thing was so unhappy living with them!"

Justin frowned. "But her letters assured me she

wanted to remain with them. Why did she not write me how she really felt?"

"Perhaps if you had bothered to answer her letters to you, she might have been more willing to confide the truth to you."

He looked bewildered. "But I wrote her four times a year when I sent her quarterly pin money."

It was the first Georgina had heard of his having sent letters or money to Lanie.

"I told her in my letters that if she was unhappy about anything that was within my power to make better, she should not hesitate to write me. But she did not even acknowledge my offer nor once thank me for the pin money."

Because, unless Lanie had deceived Georgina, she had not received a single one of his letters. Nor had his sister known of the money he had sent her.

But then Lanie had lied to Georgina about having written her brother that she was unhappy at Lady Neldane's. Georgina decided against saying anything to him until she could question Lanie and ascertain the truth about the letters and the money.

"Would you walk down to the pond at the bottom of the hill with me before dinner?" Georgina asked Justin when she ran into him in the upstairs hall late that afternoon.

"Of course," Justin agreed with a quick penetrating glance at her. "I can see the pond from the window of my bedchamber, but I have not been to it."

They strolled along a serpentine path that meandered through scattered oak, beech, and elm trees down to the lake. Roses of Sharon, their bright yellow flowers beginning to open, bordered both sides of the walk.

Justin waited until they were halfway down the

hill before he said quietly, "I assume you had a reason for suggesting this walk."

"Yes, I did." Georgina had spent the past half hour in a private conversation with Lanie. "I wish to discuss your sister with you, and I wanted to make certain I was not overheard."

One side of his mouth pulled up in a sardonic half-smile. "Are you about to resume your campaign to convince me Melanie should remain here?"

"No, something else entirely. I just had a long talk with her, and I want to discuss with you what she told me."

"Did she tell you why she regards me as such an ogre?" he asked teasingly.

"I did not need to ask her that," Georgina said bluntly. "I already knew. For years her mother and grandparents painted you as one to her."

Justin stopped and swiveled his head. "Bloody hell, why would they do that?"

Georgina halted, too. "Poor Lanie was not happy with them. Her mother was a weeping, whining, self-proclaimed invalid who paid no attention to anyone but herself."

Justin shot Georgina an appreciative look that told her he agreed with her assessment of his stepmother.

"Lanie's grandparents doted on her, but they were very rigid, very dull, and totally devoid of humor. My parents and I used to dread invitations to dinner with them."

"Believe me, I understand perfectly."

Georgina bit back a smile at Justin's fervent tone. Clearly he had suffered through one or two of those dinners, too. "From the time Lanie was quite small, she loved to come to Penfield to get away from the dreary, joyless atmosphere at Dorton Hall."

He looked bewildered. "If that was the case, why did she write me all those glowing letters about how happy she was there?"

"That is what I asked her today." Georgina resumed walking toward the pond. "Those letters were actually dictated to her by her grandmother. And as I suspected, Lanie never received a single one of your letters to her."

"What about the pin money I sent with the letters?" he asked, clearly shocked.

"She saw not a shilling of it."

A harsh expletive escaped him. Then, looking embarrassed, he apologized to Georgina for his language.

"Her grandparents' actions deserve such a response."

"Do you have any idea where the money went?"

They passed a mock orange tree, its fragrant flowers perfuming the air with the scent of orange blossoms. Georgina took a deep breath before plunging ahead. "I suspect her grandparents appropriated it to pay for your sister's expenses, since you would not."

"What do you mean I would not? In addition to sending Melanie pin money, I sent her grandparents a large sum each quarter for her expenses."

Georgina stopped again and looked at him in surprise. "You did?"

"I did. We are talking about a very large amount of money over the years."

So he had not been so clutch-fisted with Lanie's inheritance as had been alleged.

"What the hell did they do with it?" he demanded. "Have you any idea?"

As Georgina considered his question, she stared silently at the scene before her. The far side of the pond had been carefully landscaped to form a pleasing, colorful prospect from the house.

Rhododendron, now adorned with great clusters of purple flowers, were massed near the water's edge. Behind them rose two varieties of maples. Their leaves, green now, turned to a blaze of red and yellow in autumn. Behind the maples, horse chestnuts climbed still higher against the sky.

Georgina finally said hesitantly, "I dread to give voice to what I suspect, for I have no proof."

"Under the circumstances, I believe I have a right to know your suspicions."

"Perhaps you do," Georgina said thoughtfully. "Dorton was an incompetent manager, and he was deeply in debt. I recall that Dorton Hall was in sorry condition when Lanie and her mother returned to it. Not long after that, though, he began extensive repairs and refurbishing. Papa wondered at the time how Dorton could have come by the money to pay for such expensive improvements."

"So I most likely expended an enormous amount repairing Dorton Hall," Justin said so angrily that he startled a yellow-breasted blue tit into flight from a nearby tree.

"But it is not you who paid for it," Georgina reminded him. "Rather it was your sister's inheritance."

"My sister has no inheritance!"

Georgina stared at him incredulously. "Surely you are joking."

"No, I am not," he said as they reached the pond at the bottom of the hill. Several white swans glided gracefully over the water.

"You see why we call it Swan Lake," Georgina said, "although I admit 'tis stretching the definition of a lake."

"Yes, it is," Justin agreed.

"I cannot believe your father would have made no provision for Lanie," Georgina said, returning to that subject.

"It's true. The only provision my father made for her was to appoint me her guardian."

"So you claim the money you sent for Lanie's care and pin money came out of your own pocket?"

"It is not a claim, it is the truth," he said coldly.

"But we were told she received a large inheritance from your father for which you were trustee."

"By we, you mean you and your father were told that?"

"Yes, and Lanie, too. It is what her grandparents and her mother said."

Justin's face grew even grimmer. "So Melanie thinks that in addition to totally ignoring her all those years, I stole an inheritance she never had?"

"Worse than that. Her mother and grandparents drummed into her that you were a cruel, uncaring man who persuaded your father to make you her guardian in order to usurp her inheritance."

"Far from persuading him to make me her guardian, I was unaware he had done so until after his death. Had I known his intention, I would have done my best to decline a position for which, I am certain you will agree, I am highly ill-suited."

"Perhaps not as ill-suited as I first thought." Georgina's estimation of Ravenstone was improving in strides as large as an iguanodon's must have been.

She smiled at him, and his gaze fastened on her mouth the way it had before he'd kissed her. Warmth spiraled through her at the memory.

"He also named me guardian of my brother, but I had expected that, since I had been Henry's de facto guardian for years. You see my father had no time for his children."

"What about your brother? Did your father leave him anything?"

Justin looked at her, then away at the swans on the water, and finally back at her. "A modest bequest."

"Outrageous he would provide for a son, but not a daughter!"

"I agree," Justin said, surprising Georgina. "But he had two reasons for not doing so."

"What were they?"

"First, Dorton had extracted a most generous marriage settlement from my father, who felt it should provide more than enough to take care of both my stepmother and Melanie. Second, my father bitterly regretted marrying Dorton's daughter."

"Why?" Georgina asked.

"She looked so like my own mother, he was infatuated with her at first sight and impetuously offered for her hand three days later. After their marriage, he discovered that despite the physical resemblance, no two women could have been more different in temperament and understanding."

"So he left their daughter nothing."

"Actually it would have made no difference if Father had done so. He died in debt with no money to fund the bequest to Henry. If Ravencrest and the other estates had not been entailed, he no doubt would have lost those, too."

"So after your father's death, you supported both your wards?"

"Or thought I was," he said ruefully. "I did not mind, although it was difficult the first two years. It took me that long after Father died, and was no longer bleeding the entailed estates dry, to restore them to profitability."

Georgina regarded the complex man beside her with growing respect.

And, God help her, growing affection.

"Where is Henry now?" Georgina asked as they strolled along the pond.

"At my estate, Woodhaven, in Berkshire. I acquired it eighteen months ago after it had fallen into a sorry state. Henry has a passion for restoring such properties, and he has done a remarkable job there, although he's not finished yet."

"What will he do when he does?"

"He can either keep it for himself or sell it and use the profit to buy himself another distressed estate to return to good order. The choice is his."

They walked along the water's edge in silence for a few minutes before Georgina said thoughtfully, "I think Lanie's grandparents must have feared you would try to exert your guardianship rights, and Lanie would welcome the chance to escape Dorton Hall."

"Whereupon they would have lost their rich source of income," he said bitterly.

"Precisely. So they did their best to paint you in the worst possible light."

"And succeeded."

"Yes, and succeeded."

"What did Melanie say when you told her about my letters and the pin money?"

"I did not tell her. I merely questioned her as to whether she had ever received any letters or money from you. You are the one who should tell her the truth." She smiled at him. "Shall we return to the house?"

*　*　*

As he and Gina entered the house after their stroll to the lake, Justin cursed himself for not having spent more time over the years with his sister. Had he done so, he would have learned of her grand-parents' duplicity.

Gina said, "I forgot to tell you, Papa has invited a friend of ours to dinner tomorrow night. I am certain you will find him a welcome relief from the tedium of our company for so long."

"It has been anything but tedious," Justin said with absolute honesty. Indeed, he could not think of when he had ever been more entertained.

"You need not flatter me," she said. "After the company you enjoy in London, you must find us provincial."

"Not at all. I told you once that I never indulged in false flattery. *Never.*" He smiled at her. "Am I acquainted with your guest?"

"I think not, for he likes London as little as I do, and never goes there. His name is Roger Chad-wick."

I have not entirely given up hope that Roger may yet prevail upon Georgina to accept him. Justin glanced at her sharply, but her countenance was serene, be-traying no special emotion toward Roger.

"His father's estate is near here."

"How close by?" Justin asked, his jaw clenched.

"A few miles distant."

Not nearly far enough away.

"Roger is a charming man," Georgina continued. "I am certain you will like him."

Not bloody likely.

Chapter 17

~~~~~~~~~◦◦◦~~~~~~~~~

When Justin went down to dinner that night, his sister was alone in the withdrawing room, seated on one of the floral sofas.

As he crossed the room to her, Melanie started to rise, but he said, "No, please don't get up."

Choosing a chair near her, he pulled it closer to the sofa and took her delicate white hands in his own larger, darker ones. Her head snapped up in surprise.

"Melanie, Miss Penford told me you never received any of the letters I wrote you while you were living with your grandparents, nor the pin money I sent you. Is that true?"

Her incredulous expression gave him his answer. No words were necessary. Damn her grandparents for their avarice and mendacity.

When she finally recovered her voice, she asked in a choked voice, "W-what . . . what did you write me about?"

"Among other things, to inquire whether you were happy at Dorton Hall and to tell you that if you were not, I would make other arrangements for you."

Her face betrayed first astonishment, then doubt.

He said gently, "Since the only letters I received from you spoke of how happy you were at Dorton Hall and begged me not to remove you from there, I had no notion this was not true."

Tears welled up in her eyes. "Grandmama told me what to write, and I copied down her words."

"Why did you go along with her, rather than writing me the truth?"

"I was afraid of you."

"Why? What did I ever do to you that would make you fear me?"

"Grandmama—and Mama, too, before she died— described the ghastly way you treated your wife!" Melanie shuddered.

Justin fought to smother the anger that flamed within him at those lies. Knowing how much Clarissa had delighted in falsely abusing him to whomever would listen, Justin did not need to seek the details.

He'd forgotten how much under Clarissa's spell his witless stepmother had been. No one could have been more charming and convincing than Clarissa when it suited her purposes. He said sadly, "Generally every story has two sides, Lanie, and your mama heard only my wife's."

Her mama certainly had not heard his side, for he discussed Clarissa with no one. It went against his code of honor to broadcast his difficulties with his wife.

"They—they warned me you would be even crueler to me if you decided to take me from them."

"And you believed them?"

Something about his sorrowful tone must have touched her, for she looked at him with such hope in her eyes that he swallowed hard.

Then she shuddered and jerked her hands from

his. "Of course, I believed them!" Anger and defiance flashed in her eyes. "Why should I not? You had already stolen my inheritance from me."

He took her chin gently but firmly in his hand and held it so that he could gaze squarely into her eyes. "I swear to you, Melanie, as God is my witness, that I never robbed you of anything."

"But they said you'd stripped me of my inheritance, keeping it for yourself and your brother, and left me a penniless orphan."

"I did nothing of the sort."

"You mean I still have an inheritance from Papa?"

She looked at him with such happiness and relief in her eyes that he had not the heart to tell her the truth. Instead he released her chin and said quietly, "You are not penniless."

He would see that she was not, and she need never know the unhappy truth that her father had not provided for her.

Melanie jumped up and began to pace in front of him in agitation. "They said you hated me."

Justin stood up, too. "Why would I hate you?"

"Because Papa loved my mama and me better than you and your brother." Her expression turned wistful. "Mama said Papa adored her."

Her mama clearly had deluded Melanie about her father's sentiments and perhaps deluded herself as well, but Justin also kept that to himself. As for his father, he'd paid no attention to any of his children except when they could be of use to him.

"I never hated you, Lanie," Justin said gently, "but you acted as though you hated me."

"I was afraid of you! Can you blame me, what with the stories Mama told me about you. Then on the very few occasions you saw me, you were so stiff and silent!"

"So were you," he reminded her. "I do not converse easily with strangers. Frankly I had not the slightest notion of what to say to a schoolgirl."

Lanie looked at him as though she were seeing him for the first time. "Did you truly send me pin money?"

"Yes." He told her the generous amount he'd sent each quarter.

She gaped at him, clearly stunned.

"Oh, Lanie, if only you had written me of your unhappiness. I would never have left you at Dorton Hall."

At that, she burst into genuine tears and sobbed as though her heart would break.

Unable to stand her misery, Justin took her in his arms and hugged her to him, folding her head against his shoulder. He held her and comforted her as though she were his child. "I am sorry, Lanie, so terribly sorry," he murmured.

Georgina's own eyes misted with tears as she watched Justin soothing his sister. She had been in the dining room, making certain all was in order for dinner. When she opened the door to the withdrawing room, she overheard the final part of the conversation between Lanie and Justin.

Now she stood in the doorway between the two rooms, uncertain whether she should go forward or retreat. So engrossed were sister and brother with each other, neither of them noticed her there.

Justin continued to murmur tenderly to Lanie in a voice so low Georgina could not make out his words. Gradually Lanie's tears subsided. Justin pulled out a pocket handkerchief and gently wiped the tears from her face.

Her woebegone face broke into a smile, and she hugged him fiercely. He hugged her back.

Georgina stepped back into the dining room to give them privacy. But at that moment, Justin looked up and saw her. Before he could speak, the other door opened and her father bustled in.

At the sight of him, Lanie backed a little away from her brother. Georgina's father offered Lanie his arm and led her into the dining room.

As Justin took Georgina's arm to follow them, she whispered, "Why did you not tell Lanie the truth— that she has no inheritance."

"I did not want to hurt her."

That night, Georgina lay awake for hours, trying to make sense of her windmilling emotions toward Justin.

Thanks to Lanie's mother and grandparents, Georgina had hated him until she had met him. Then attraction had warred with dislike in her. But as she'd come to know him better since his arrival at Penfield, her animosity toward him had faded.

And the attraction had continued to strengthen.

A lump that seemed the size of an iguanodon's egg rose in her throat as she recalled the tender scene she had witnessed in the withdrawing room between Justin and Lanie.

Nor could Georgina push from her mind the marvelous, heated sensations that rocked her in Justin's arms. His kisses excited her, thrilled her, filled her with an aching yearning to experience more.

Justin is highly accomplished at giving a woman enormous pleasure. He was the best lover I ever had.

Initially Georgina had been skeptical of this claim

of Nancy Wilde's, knowing what tricks memory can play. But now she was far more inclined to believe it.

The right man could bring you enormous joy and pleasure and happiness.

Was that true, too? She wanted to learn the truth about Nancy's contention. Georgina told herself it was her scientific mind at work. She prided herself on being a rational, objective investigator of earthly phenomena. She determined to embark on an experiment to ascertain the dispassionate, scientific truth about what Nancy claimed.

Surely the strange ache within her when Justin held her in his arms and kissed her had nothing to do with her eagerness to undertake her scientific study.

Nothing at all.

Perhaps she would feel that same yearning in the arms of any man to whom she was attracted. The latter was rare enough. She'd found most of her suitors, like Plimpton and Ingleham, repulsive.

But the one other man besides Justin to whom she'd felt any attraction, Roger Chadwick, would be coming to dinner the next night.

In the interest of scientific investigation, she would determine whether his kisses would make her feel as Justin's did. Roger was such an obliging man, always eager to do whatever she asked of him. If she explained her scientific experiment to him, he would surely be happy to cooperate.

When Georgina finally drifted off to sleep, her dreams were haunted by dark eyes set in a harsh pirate face framed by black hair as unruly as it was curly.

*   *   *

Justin tried to persuade Gina to go riding with him the following afternoon, but she refused. "With a guest coming tonight, I have too much to do overseeing dinner. Besides, I want to be here when Roger arrives."

Jealousy shot through Justin. He was not used to having a lady refuse his invitations in favor of another man, and he did not like it.

If she would not accompany him, he thought irritably, he would ride alone, using the opportunity to query those he came across as to whether they knew G. O. Douglas or where he lived.

He would also try to run to ground Simon, the post rider, who had not responded to the note Justin had left him, inquiring where Douglas lived.

When Justin reached Simon's cottage, the post rider, a short thin man with bowed legs and small suspicious eyes, answered the door.

"I am Lord Ravenstone. Why have you not responded to my note about G. O. Douglas?"

"Weren't nothin' to say. Don't know who he is. Ne'er laid eyes on him." Simon turned to go back into his cottage.

"Just a moment," Justin ordered in a voice that stopped Simon in midstep. "At least tell me where his house is."

Simon turned back to face Justin. "Don't know that neither."

"You must. You deliver his mail to it."

"I don't," the taciturn Simon answered.

"Then what do you do with his mail?" Justin pressed.

"Give it to a friend o' his."

"What is his friend's name?"

"Ain't at liberty to say. Can't tell you no more."

He went back into the cottage and shut the door
behind him.

Justin muttered a string of sizzling expletives as
he walked away from Simon's cottage.

He had no more success with any of the other
people whom he asked about G. O. Douglas. Most
looked at him blankly. They all denied having ever
heard of the man.

Justin returned to Penfield just in time to witness
Roger Chadwick's arrival in a chaise and four. Why
the hell had Roger shown up so early? Dinner was
still two hours away.

Georgina looked particularly pretty in a gown of
jonquil yellow silk tied with a large orange bow that
displayed her lovely figure most enticingly. She
greeted Chadwick warmly.

Far too warmly!

To Justin's dismay, Chadwick had the face and
the physique of a man who cast ladies into swoons
of admiration. He reminded Justin of a statue of
Apollo, the mythological god of the sun, music, and
poetry, that he had once seen in a Greek temple.

Justin had not expected Chadwick to be so handsome. No, not handsome—*pretty*—with his slender,
perfectly sculpted face, Justin thought scornfully.

Roger clasped Gina's hands tightly. The look he
gave her left no doubt that his interest in her had
not cooled.

Seething silently, Justin watched them. Had
Roger come to renew his offer to marry her?

He continued to hold Gina's hands, staring at her
face shining with that luminous smile, which crinkled her face so beguilingly.

Jealousy gnawed at Justin that she looked at
Roger with such warmth. Determined to end their

damned hand-holding, he stepped forward with his own hand extended.

"I am Lord Ravenstone. I do not believe we have met."

A few seconds passed before Roger could manage to tear his gaze away from Georgina's face. With obvious reluctance, he relinquished her hands and shook Justin's.

She introduced the two men, then said, "Come, Roger, I will show you to your room."

"How kind of you," he said with a smile that made Justin grind his teeth. "I am anxious to make myself presentable to you."

With his bright blue eyes, golden hair, and perfect features, he was already too bloody presentable for Justin's peace of mind.

Roger took Gina's arm, and they started toward the marble staircase.

"I'll go up with you." Justin hastily moved to the other side of Georgina. "I have just returned from riding and must change, too."

As they climbed the steps, he expected Gina to at least ask him where he had ridden, but her attention was focused on Roger. She plied him with questions about himself and his journey to Penfield.

Justin felt as though he were invisible to his two companions.

And it infuriated him.

When they reached the door of Justin's room, Georgina said in a tone that clearly dismissed him, "We'll see you at dinner, my lord."

Justin watched from his doorway as she led Roger farther down the hall. As she turned to leave him, she murmured something. Justin could not hear what she said, but it brought a delighted smile to Roger's face.

Justin stalked into his bedchamber and ordered a bath in a tone that made his valet eye him with trepidation.

Georgina and Roger followed the path, bordered with Rose of Sharon, that wound between scattered trees down to Swan Lake.

She'd given much thought to when she would have the best opportunity to conduct her scientific experiment with Roger. After dinner would be difficult, for everyone would move into the library or the drawing room. What possible excuse could they give to go off alone?

No, she'd decided, better to do it before they gathered in the withdrawing room for dinner. Roger always came in midafternoon when he was invited to dinner, so they would have time. That was why she'd declined Justin's invitation to ride with him.

When she'd left Roger at the door to his room, she'd asked him to walk with her to Swan Lake as soon as he had made himself presentable.

The invitation had clearly delighted him, and he'd instantly accepted, telling her he'd join her in twenty minutes.

He'd been a man of his word.

As they strolled toward the water, Roger said, "I was surprised to receive an invitation to dinner from your father."

Georgina, too, had been surprised that Papa had extended one, for she suspected that he was not overly fond of Roger.

"I had thought you and your father planned to remain in London longer, but the city's loss is Sussex's gain," Roger said, smiling.

"I much prefer it here to London."

"I know you do, and so do I." He paused, then asked with surprising sharpness, "How long has Lord Ravenstone been here?"

"Since the day we returned from London."

"He accompanied you from the city?" Roger sounded alarmed.

"No." She explained how Justin had come to Penfield in search of his sister.

"But that was almost a month ago. Why is Ravenstone still here?"

"Papa and I are trying to persuade him to let Lanie live with us. He wants to assure himself she is in good hands and happy here before he agrees to leave her."

"From all I've heard of him, I would not think he would care in the least where he leaves her."

Roger had heard the Dortons' and Lady Ravenstone's complaints of Justin. Georgina felt compelled to defend him. "Oh, he is much more caring than Lanie's mama and grandparents made him out to be."

"I never thought to hear you speak so kindly of that man. I was certain you hated him."

"That was before I met him."

Roger gave her a perturbed, searching perusal. "How did he change your mind?"

"I discovered he's very different from what I thought," she replied absently, her mind focused on how she should broach the subject of her experiment. Usually never at a loss for words, she was having difficulty coming up with an explanation of it to Roger.

Yet she could not test what she felt for Justin on anyone else. Roger was the only other man to whom she'd felt even a mild attraction.

They reached the edge of the pond and stopped

to watch the swans gliding over the water.

"Why did you ask me to take this stroll with you?" Roger asked abruptly.

Never one to dissemble, Georgina answered frankly, "I hoped you would kiss me."

His stared at her with such astonishment that she felt the heat of a blush rise in her cheeks.

"Are you funning me again, Georgina?"

"No, I am very serious." She felt herself coloring even more hotly.

An odd triumphant gleam lighted his eyes. "Far be it from me to refuse you anything you want—especially that." He put his hands lightly on her shoulders, and lowered his mouth toward hers.

Georgina waited expectantly to feel the same rush of excitement and aching yearning that she had when Justin kissed her.

But when Roger's lips touched hers lightly, almost tentatively, and then withdrew instantly, she felt only disappointment.

His kiss must have been too brief. Looking up at him from beneath her lashes, she murmured, "Please kiss me again and, pray, this time do not make it so quick."

She wondered why he looked so pleased by her request.

"Your wish is my command," he murmured as he obediently settled his mouth on hers again.

This kiss, although longer, still lacked the hunger and passion and excitement of Justin's. Georgina wanted to groan in dismay.

If only Roger would open his mouth a little more. Perhaps if she kissed him in that fiery, demanding way Justin had kissed her, he would react as she had.

Georgina pulled Roger into her arms and applied

all the technique that she had learned from Justin.

It worked.

But not quite in the way Georgina had expected.

No yearning tied her in knots, no excitement twisted like lightning through her, no ache deep inside pained her.

But from the ardent way Roger returned her kiss, he felt far more than she did.

Justin stepped out of the bathtub in his dressing room and wrapped himself in the robe that his valet handed to him. He looked out the window over the grounds toward that pond ridiculously named Swan Lake. A bright splash of jonquil yellow along its shore caught his eye.

Gina—with that damned Apollo.

As he watched, Roger placed his hands on her arms and bent his head down to kiss her. Jealousy ripped through Justin, even though the kiss lasted only an instant and seemed more friendly than romantic.

Just as he began to breathe normally again, Georgina and Roger kissed a second time. No one would mistake this kiss for one between old friends.

Nor did it end quickly. Instead it went on and on.

In the grip of a strange fury, Justin cursed like a Jack-tar as he grabbed the pantaloons his valet had laid out for him and yanked them on. He ran into the hall, fastening them as he went.

"My lord, where are you going like that? You are not dressed!"

His valet's scandalized exclamation yanked Justin out of the red fog of his anger. He looked down at himself and retreated hastily into his bedchamber.

Earls of the realm did not run around the countryside half naked.

Justin went back to the window. Georgina and Roger were no longer kissing. They had started to walk slowly up the hill toward the house.

Justin told himself he wasn't jealous.

Hell, no, he wasn't.

Not at all.

He'd kill the bastard if he ever saw him kissing Gina again.

Chapter 18

J ustin went down early for dinner, intending to be the first person in the withdrawing room, but he discovered Roger Chadwick had beaten him there.

They silently eyed each other with mutual dislike.

Roger looked especially *pretty* tonight with his wavy blond hair brushed carefully forward over his forehead, Justin thought scornfully. His royal blue coat accentuated the blue of his eyes.

His clothes, elegantly tailored in the latest style, would have passed muster at a London assembly. The coat was long in back but cut away at the waist in front. Its collar and lapels were faced in a darker, contrasting shade of blue. The front of his white linen shirt was heavily frilled, and he wore his stock tied in a large neat bow at the front of the neck.

Justin itched to tie the bow considerably tighter.

Roger broke the silence. "Good evening, my lord. Miss Penford tells me that you have come to Penfield to determine whether to allow your sister to live with her."

Eager to hear what Roger would say about Gina, Justin remarked provocatively, "Yes, but I have my doubts about doing so. I find Miss Penford a most unusual young lady."

"I fear Georgina does have some eccentricities," Roger answered, apparently taking Justin's remark as criticism of her. His tone was that of an indulgent father speaking of a spoiled child he humored. "Lord Penford has been much too lax with her."

"Do you think so?" Justin asked.

"Oh, yes, but once we're married—"

Justin cut him off. "I was not aware that felicitations were in order. I understood Miss Penford had refused your offer of marriage."

Roger shot him a triumphant look that made Justin's hands double into fists that he was hard pressed not to use to rearrange Apollo's pretty face.

"Georgina had a change of heart this afternoon," Roger said smugly.

A fury, hotter and more intense than Justin could ever remember, engulfed him like a raging wild fire.

"As I was saying," Roger continued in a tone that set Justin's teeth on edge, "once we're married, I will take her firmly in hand and train her to be an excellent wife and mother."

Controlling his rage with iron determination, Justin said, "I sincerely doubt any man could train Miss Penford to be something she does not wish to be."

"You are much too pessimistic, my lord."

Justin raised an eyebrow. "Am I?"

"She wants only a firm and forceful husband, which I assure you I will be. You must bow to my superior understanding of Miss Penford. We have known each other for years."

Obviously Roger's understanding of Gina—regardless of the many years he'd known her—was inferior to Justin's. Why the hell would she have accepted an offer from this condescending prig?

Georgina approached the withdrawing room on leaden feet. Her scientific experiment with Roger had disappointed her enormously. His kisses provoked none of the shimmering, aching excitement that made her hunger for more as Justin's did.

Worse, Roger's triumphant expression as they'd walked back to the house afterward—rather like a wily cat who had trapped a mouse—disturbed her.

When she entered the withdrawing room, Justin was talking to her father. Lanie, a moonstruck expression on her face, was staring at Roger, who, in turn, had his eye on the door. As soon as he saw Georgina, he rushed to her side.

"How lovely you look tonight." Roger touched the ballooned sleeve of her gown, a cream silk figured with roses of various hues, which had been her father's birthday present to her.

At that moment, Justin turned toward them. His savage expression when he saw Roger's hand on her sleeve startled Georgina.

" 'Tis beautiful," Roger murmured.

Georgina was uncertain whether he was talking of her gown or only her sleeve.

"And my lady wearing it is even more beautiful," Roger added, a proprietary note in his voice.

But she hardly heard him. Her attention was focused on Justin who was crossing the room to them.

He was less colorfully dressed than Roger, in black trousers and coat over a plain white waistcoat and shirt. A scowl darkened Justin's face. Never had he looked more like a pirate to Georgina. He lacked only a black eye-patch.

As he reached her and Roger, dinner was announced. Justin immediately took her arm, and a familiar tremor of excitement raced through her at his touch.

Roger, who had not been so quick, protested, "I shall take her into dinner."

"Precedence dictates otherwise, *Mr.* Chadwick," Justin said coolly.

Roger flushed at this reminder of his lower status.

Georgina was about to say that precedence would not be observed tonight when she realized she much preferred Justin rather than Roger at her side during dinner. She held her tongue.

Her father had decreed that dinner would be served tonight in the state dining room. Since he disliked that room as much as she did, she'd instantly inquired his reason.

"The table in the dining parlor is too small to seat three guests comfortably."

She started to point out that they often had as many as four guests at it very comfortably, but he forestalled her, saying, "I want no argument."

Georgina stared at her father in surprise. He never acted in such a peremptory manner.

"I also wish you would wear the gown I gave you for your birthday. It is most attractive on you, and you never wear it."

She never wore it because its low-cut neckline and tight-fitting bodice forced her to wear stays, which she despised. But it was a lovely dress, and she put it on to please her father. It also required her to put on the matching shoes that pinched her feet.

As Justin escorted her into dinner, he whispered, "I thought you never wore stays."

Her startled gaze snapped to his.

His eyes glittered with mockery and anger. "A

day of more than one first for you, is it not, Miss Penford?''

His sarcastic comment baffled her, and they reached their places at the huge table in the state dining room.

Since fifty feet separated the table's head from its foot, Georgina had ordered the five covers placed together at one end. Her father sat at the head, Lanie and Roger on one side of the broad table, and she and Justin on the other.

As they ate, her gaze often lingered on Roger. Although shorter and more slightly built than Justin, he had a most pleasing countenance, and she could not understand why she felt nothing for him when he kissed her. Perhaps she should give Roger one more opportunity so she could verify her finding.

Hers were not the only eyes on Roger. Lanie, clearly smitten with him, could not seem to tear her gaze away from his handsome face.

Oddly, Justin's features pleased Georgina more. Roger's were too perfect, too bland. She found Justin's dark face with its harsh lines, chiseled planes, and sensuous mouth far more exciting.

Especially now when he seemed to be in an inexplicable, silent fury. He looked so threatening that he clearly unnerved the young liveried footman serving him. Each time the poor man was required to approach Justin, he looked as though he were being forced to walk the plank.

Georgina noticed that his hands trembled as he filled Justin's wineglass.

Dinner was a much more subdued affair than on any night since Georgina and her father had returned to Penfield from London. She blamed this partly on the cavernous size and ostentation of the dining room, which tended to make the diners speak in hushed tones as though they were in a cathedral.

But it was more than that. She herself was too busy trying to understand the effect Justin had on her, while Roger had none, to contribute much to the conversation. Justin glowered through the meal, while his sister stared at Roger in adoring, tongue-tied silence.

What conversation there was did not please Georgina. Her father asked Roger about agricultural concerns and encouraged him to discuss at length how to improve the quantity of a dairy herd's milk production, which she found excessively dull.

She would have thought her father felt the same way, but he encouraged Roger to discuss it at such tedious length she feared her eyes would glaze over. She had never realized before how boring Roger could be.

This was by far the least entertaining dinner since Justin and his sister's arrival at Penfield. So, as the footmen began to serve dessert, a trifle that had been built up to impressive height, Georgina was astonished to notice her father regarding his companions with a satisfied expression, as though the dinner were a grand success.

The nervous footman stepped between Georgina's and Justin's chairs to serve the dessert. Unfortunately he lowered a generous portion of trifle just as Justin reached out for his wine glass, and their hands collided. The footman started, the trifle tilted toward Justin, and the top layer of syllabub slipped off the confection and down into his lap.

The servant, clearly unnerved by the mishap, dropped the bowl, and it overturned, dumping the rest of the trifle into Justin's lap as well.

The culprit took one look at his lordship's face

and fled the room in terror. Seeing Justin's expression, Georgina was half tempted to do the same.

But she was made of sterner stuff. In her haste to forestall mayhem against the poor footman, she seized her napkin and tried to mop up the gooey mess of Naple biscuits soaked in sack, custard, and syllabub that oozed across Justin's lap. "I'm so sorry," she murmured.

Suddenly her wrists were caught in a grasp of iron that sent a little shiver through her.

"I think, Miss Penford, you had better let me deal with this." Justin's tone was dry, yet it had an odd husky quality to it that made her look up at his face in surprise.

His furious expression had vanished. Instead his dark eyes glowed with the heat she'd seen in them when he kissed her. She felt as though his gaze was melting her body into fluid.

She had such difficulty catching her breath that she hardly noticed as he firmly placed her hands in her own lap.

When he had managed to remove the worst of the mess, he stood up. Ugly splotches marred his waistcoat, coat, and trousers. "If you will pardon me, I must change."

He left the dining room and did not return by the time they finished dessert.

Georgina's father and Roger escorted her and Lanie into the library. She longed for some excuse to go upstairs so she could shed her torturous stays. Too bad the spilled trifle had not landed in her lap.

The night was unusually warm, and the French windows in the library had been opened to admit a slight breeze.

Before Georgina could seat herself, Roger said to

her, "It's such a nice night. Will you join me for a stroll in the garden?"

She opened her mouth to refuse before she remembered such a walk would give her another chance to test the effect—or lack thereof—of Roger's kisses upon her. A serious scientific investigator, she reminded herself, should always replicate her initial findings.

As they stepped through the French doors into the garden, Georgina looked up at the moon, only a sliver short of full, brightly illuminating the night. *Yes, it is a lovely night, and Roger is not the man I want beside me.* She was more than a little shocked by how much she did *not* want to repeat her experiment with Roger. Georgina feared this betrayed a dreadfully unscientific prejudice.

"I have never seen you so quiet as you are tonight," Roger observed.

She searched for something to say. Roger had always professed a great interest in her geological work, and she told him, "I have made the most exciting discovery."

He stopped and turned, smiling at her with smug triumph that puzzled her mightily. "Yes, I know you have."

"You know about the skeleton I found? Who told you?"

"Good God, you found a skeleton?" Roger looked shocked. "My poor darling, you must have been horrified."

Horrified! Darling! She gaped at him.

"Do you have any idea who the poor soul might have been? Has someone been missing in the neighborhood?"

"No, no, not a human skeleton," she said impatiently. "An iguanodon's."

Roger looked at her blankly.

Georgina remembered Justin's excitement, which had been every bit as intense as her own, over her discovery.

Roger asked politely, "What is an igua . . . how do you say it?"

"Iguanodon." Georgina tried to swallow her disappointment at his lack of genuine interest.

"What is it? I'm afraid I have no idea."

"It was a huge prehistoric animal." She distinctly remembered telling Roger about iguanodons several months ago, and he'd professed great fascination with them.

He gave her a patronizing smile. "Don't tell me you are still mucking about"—his tone told her how distasteful he found that—"searching for such things. I thought you would have surely tired of that by now."

His condescension shocked her. He had never acted this way to her before. "I will never tire of it!" she cried.

Roger gave her an indulgent look that said as plainly as words that he knew better.

Dismayed, she said, "You told me you were interested in fossils and geology."

"I was willing to humor that odd start of yours." He took her hands in his own and squeezed them. "My dearest Georgina, when we are married, you will be far too busy caring for your husband and our children to have time for such peculiar unladylike pursuits."

Disbelief and astonishment bubbled up in her like a hot mineral spring. She felt as though she was seeing Roger for the first time, the real Roger who had been hiding behind an obliging, genial facade. "Marry you?"

"Oh come, darling, you do not have to act coy. Your kiss this afternoon told me how passionately you feel about me and how much you regretted your earlier refusal of my offer."

Horrified that he could have so misconstrued her kiss, she said weakly, "Roger, I was only conducting a scientific experiment."

"You don't fool me for an instant."

Roger gave her a smile of such smug superiority, she longed to slap him. She was so angry that it did not register on her that he was lowering his head. Just before his mouth closed over hers, he said, "We will be married as soon as the bans can be published."

Justin bounded down the stairs, clad in fresh clothes. It'd been damned difficult for him to subdue the response of his body to Gina's unwittingly provocative ministrations as she tried to mop the trifle from his lap.

He went into the library, but Gina and Roger were not there. His anger flared anew when Lanie told him they were walking in the garden.

Gina had hardly said a word at dinner. She'd been too damned busy watching Roger across the table. And all through the meal, Roger looked at her like the cat who'd just lapped up his fill of the finest cream, while Justin seethed.

Lanie said dreamily, "Oh, Justin, isn't Roger the handsomest man you've ever met?"

Bloody hell, even his fifteen-year-old sister was under that damned Apollo's spell! He hung on to his temper by a frayed thread, determined not to harm the fragile rapprochement he and Lanie had attained. "Not quite that handsome," he told her dryly.

She looked so disappointed that he added hastily, "He has the kind of face that appeals more to a woman than a man." Especially, apparently, to Gina.

Justin noticed that Penford, occupying his favorite chair, had a triumphant gleam in his eye. *I have not entirely given up hope that Roger may yet prevail upon Georgie to accept him.* And now his hope had come true.

Justin said abruptly, "I could use a bit of fresh air, too."

He strode through the garden. Hearing the murmur of voices to his left, he moved toward the sound. He came upon Gina and her companion just as Roger said, "We will be married as soon as the bans can be published."

Fury as hot as molten lava poured through Justin's veins. So, despite Gina's protestation that she would never marry, she'd accepted Apollo's offer.

When Roger kissed her, she did not attempt to evade him.

Justin was damned if he'd watch another passionate kiss between the pair. "Lovely night, is it not?" he said in a booming voice.

Gina jumped away from Roger. "Yes, yes, it is," she said, glaring at Justin, clearly angry at him for intruding on her romantic interlude.

Both she and Roger obviously wanted Justin to disappear, but instead he said smoothly, "I know you won't mind my joining you."

Roger looked as though he wouldn't mind strangling Justin. And so did Gina.

Too bad, he thought angrily. He intended to get her alone and persuade her she was making a terrible mistake, accepting that smug bore. How could a woman as intelligent as Gina not see that Roger would be exactly the kind of husband she did not want?

The three of them, with Gina in the middle, walked in strained silence under the bright, nearly full moon.

Suddenly a squirrel darted across the path in front of them. Gina started and gave an alarmed little cry.

Longing to feel her soft curves against him, Justin seized this flimsy pretext to pull her protectively against him. His arm brushed the underside of her soft breasts.

Surprise apparently paralyzed her, for a minute went by without her trying to move away from him.

"Georgina," Roger said sharply, "this is most unseemly."

She hastily tried to step away from Justin, but he held her firmly to him for another few seconds like a male animal marking his territory.

When he released her, Gina shivered visibly. "It's chillier out tonight than I thought." She turned toward the house. "I am going back to the library. You gentlemen can continue your walk if you wish."

"Allow me to escort you back to the house."

She started to protest, but Justin said firmly, "I insist."

Once they were back inside, scarcely a word could be coaxed from Gina. Talk languished, and Justin belatedly comprehended how much the conversations he had enjoyed since his arrival at Penfield had depended upon her contributions.

When it came time to retire for the night, Justin left the library first. In his anger and haste, he went up the marble staircase two steps at a time. He did not stop at his own door, but continued on to Gina's.

Looking up and down the hall to make certain no one was around to notice him, he stepped into her room and quietly closed the door behind him.

A single lighted candle illuminated the area near the door, but its meager flame had not the strength to dispel the darkness that cloaked the farther reaches of the large room. He breathed deeply of Gina's gardenia scent that lingered in her chamber.

Justin was going to have a very private talk with her. By God, he was going to save her from making the terrible mistake of marrying that boring, patronizing prig Roger Chadwick.

He'd do whatever it took to convince her.

Georgina inhaled a deep breath of relief as Justin left the library. Now she had to get Roger alone before he went upstairs.

Why did Justin have to come into the garden at that most inopportune moment? Not that she hadn't been happy to have him interrupt Roger's kiss. It had quickly confirmed that he stirred none of the feelings in her that Justin did.

But Justin's ill-timed appearance had given her no opportunity to disabuse Roger of his ridiculous notion that she would marry him. She had intended to do so immediately. If she needed any additional proof she was making the right decision, it came a few minutes later, when the squirrel startled her.

The sensations that rushed through her as Justin held her against his hard body, his arms brushing the bottom of her breasts, so shocked her that she had been paralyzed.

Yet her attraction to Justin was far more than her

physical reaction to him. She'd thoroughly revised her earlier opinion of him. He was a good, generous, and honorable man. She would not have to worry about him feigning interest in a subject to indulge her as Roger had.

She loved her discussions and arguments with Justin. She loved the boyish enthusiasm and excitement he'd displayed when they'd seen the iguanodon skeleton. She loved the tender way he'd comforted his sister the previous night.

She loved Justin.

This realization dumbfounded her.

She had failed to heed Nancy Wilde's warning against falling in love with a man like him who did not believe romantic love existed. Georgina could never marry such a man. She wanted a husband who returned her love and would respect her as she respected him.

Not that Justin would ever ask her to wed him. He was adamant that he would never marry again. She told herself that given his contempt for love, his decision was for the best.

But perhaps he could be taught to love. Perhaps she could show him that romantic love truly existed. She had to try. Her own happiness demanded it.

But what if she failed? She swallowed hard and told herself that if she did, she would at least have had the opportunity to explore the turbulent currents the man she loved unleashed within her when he kissed—or even touched—her.

Justin is very accomplished at giving a woman enormous pleasure. Georgina wanted to sample that pleasure, to determine whether it could possibly be as wonderful as Nancy had claimed. Her scientific curiosity demanded she study this strange phenomenon firsthand and determine its validity.

And why should she not do so? She was an independent woman of considerable fortune, who made her own decisions.

Men could—indeed were *expected* to—have liaisons outside of marriage. Georgina chafed at the freedom men allowed themselves but denied women, whom they regarded as their property. It was so unfair! She would not abide by their self-serving strictures.

"Good night, Georgie. Shall I escort you up to your room?"

Her father's voice pulled her from her roiling thoughts. Looking up, she saw that Lanie had already left the drawing room, but Roger was still hovering near the door. She must talk to him before she went upstairs.

"No, Papa, don't wait for me. I want a few minutes alone with Roger."

Her father looked alarmed, and for a moment, she feared he would object, but then he left the room. As he did, she hurried to Roger.

"I am sorry, but you misconstrued my motive this afternoon in kissing you. I truly was conducting a scientific experiment and nothing more. I cannot accept your very flattering offer."

The initial disappointment in Roger's expression quickly gave way to anger. "Don't be a fool, Georgina! God created woman to be a man's wife, his helpmate, and a good mother to his children. It is both her duty and her whole purpose in life."

Roger could scarcely have said anything that would have been more detrimental to his cause. Through clenched teeth, Georgina said, "Just as man's whole purpose and duty in life is to be a woman's husband and a good father to *her* children."

He frowned at her. "Sometimes, Georgina, you have such eccentric notions, I wonder why I bother with you."

Anger flooded her, washing away the guilt she felt over rejecting him. "Pray, do not bother with me, Roger. By your standards, I am eccentric. You deserve a wife who believes as you do and who does not entertain views that embarrass you. Your happiness depends on a much more complaisant wife than ever I could be."

With that, she turned away. He caught her arm and forced her to face him. She glared at him. "Take your hands off me."

And he did.

She marched upstairs to her bedchamber. The night's emotional turmoil had taken its toll, and she wanted nothing so much as to push off the shoes that pinched her feet and shed her gown with its voluminous skirts that made her lower body feel as though it were shut up in an oven.

Most of all, she wanted to rid herself of the dreadful stays. By the time she reached her door, she was already unbuttoning the cuffs at her wrists.

As she stepped over the threshold of her bedchamber, she kicked off her painful shoes, vowing never to wear them again.

She shut the door of her room, which was so large the single candle by the door only illuminated part of it, and pulled up her skirts to unfasten her petticoats. Georgina gave a sigh of relief as they tumbled to the floor. She stepped over them, already undoing her bodice in her haste to shed her miserable stays.

She started violently when a husky, oddly choked male voice from somewhere in the blackness beyond the reach of the candlelight, said, "I think, Gina, you may wish to wait a few more minutes before you dispose of any more of your clothes."

Chapter 19

"Justin?" Gina squeaked in surprise, hastily clutching the bodice of her gown together with her hand. "What are you doing here?"

"We must talk privately," he said, thankful she was not the typical hysterical woman. If she were, she'd be screaming the house down now, and Justin would not have blamed her.

He had intended to make his presence known to her immediately. But, dammit, he hadn't expected her to begin stripping off her clothes the moment she crossed the threshold. He'd been so nonplussed that his voice had failed him.

Not that he hadn't enjoyed the show. He had.

Too damned much, he thought ruefully, trying to ignore the throbbing in his groin. He rose from the chair, hidden in the darkness beyond the reach of the candle's dim flame, where he'd sat waiting for her.

She snatched up the candlestick holding the lighted taper and headed toward him. "You could have talked to me downstairs. You should not be in—"

"I said privately," he interrupted, his own anger rising as he recalled the scene he'd witnessed in the garden. "I see once an eligible, handsome man made you an offer, you quickly forgot your determination not to marry."

In the halo of light cast by the candle she held, she looked stupefied by his scornful words. "What are you talking about?"

"I am talking about Chadwick." Justin made the mistake of dropping his gaze from her face. When she'd grabbed the candlestick, she'd clearly forgotten that her hand had been holding the low cut bodice of her gown together. Now it gaped opened, offering him a breathtaking—and arousing—view of her lovely breasts.

It occurred to him that he was treading in highly dangerous water. Were he to be discovered in her bedchamber now, given her present state of undress, everyone would be certain he'd been trifling with her. Justin would have no choice but to marry her.

Better me than Chadwick.

Bloody hell, had he lost his mind?

Justin hastily grabbed the two sides of her bodice to refasten it. As he did so, his hand inadvertently brushed the soft skin, sweet and smooth, of her breast, and he felt the tremor that shook her at his touch. He excited her as much as she did him.

His tongue seemed to cleave to the roof of his mouth and his manhood swelled. It took every bit of willpower that Justin possessed to force himself to close her bodice instead of removing it altogether.

He reluctantly dragged his gaze back to her face and tried to conceal his lust. "So you have accepted Chadwick's offer of marriage."

Gina frowned at him. "I am not going to marry Roger."

Justin was astounded at the surge of relief and

joy that swept over him at Gina's denial, but he was still wary. "Then perhaps you had better tell him so."

"I did before I came upstairs tonight." She looked puzzled. "Why would you think I was going to marry him?"

"He told me so. I saw no reason to doubt him considering that passionate kiss this afternoon by Swan Lake. What was that all about?"

Gina hiked her shoulders up in a dismissive shrug. "Merely a scientific experiment."

"If that was a scientific experiment, my name is Isaac Newton!" Justin retorted, outraged by such a ridiculous claim. What kind of a flat did she take him for? "Never have I seen two people derive so much pleasure from *science* before."

If only that were true, Georgina thought. Gazing at his face, Georgina thought it as stormy as the North Atlantic in winter.

"And because you and he shared a moment of passion together, did you believe yourself in love with him?"

"No, I did not! Unlike you, however, I *do* believe in love." Especially now when she realized how much she loved Justin. Georgina tried in vain to swallow the lump that had swelled in her throat. She had to make him believe in love, too!

Still scowling, Justin asked, "When Roger wanted you to participate in his *scientific experiment,* what did he tell you its purpose was?"

"Oh, he did not ask me to kiss him. I asked him. It was my experiment, not Roger's."

The violent look in Justin's dark eyes stunned Georgina. She felt as though she were being swept into a tumultuous and uncharted ocean.

"Whom else have you invited to take part in this

scientific experiment of yours?" Justin's voice was low and ominous.

"No one . . ." Her voice trailed off at the murderous look in his eye.

"Why did you not ask me to participate?" he growled.

She would not admit to him that he had inspired the experiment.

When she failed to answer, he said, "No matter, I volunteer." He took the candlestick from her and set it down on a chest of drawers. "I am always delighted to do whatever I can to advance *science.*"

His arms closed around her in a hard embrace, and his mouth settled on hers in a deep, punishing kiss that plundered her mouth and sent her senses reeling.

Her legs no longer seemed capable of supporting her, and she was suddenly thankful that Justin was holding her so tightly to him.

When he finally lifted his head, releasing her mouth, his eyes glittered with passion, and he looked as wild as she felt.

"How does that compare to Roger's kiss?" he growled fiercely.

Like a diamond to a cheap paste imitation.

When she did not reply, he released her from his embrace, his eyes glittering dangerously. "Perhaps this will help you decide."

Justin took her face in his hands, his thumbs lightly caressing her cheeks. He kissed her again, this time more gently, coaxing her mouth to respond to his. And it did.

Along with every other particle of her being.

She returned his kiss as passionately as he gave it. The ache in her body intensified.

He dropped his hands from her face to her bodice, but she was so lost in their kiss she scarcely noticed.

When he removed his lips from hers, she groaned in protest. Then she groaned again, this time in delight, as his mouth scorched an erotic trail down her neck toward the low-cut bodice of her gown.

But it did not stop there. As his warm hand moved beneath her breast and gently cupped it, his mouth closed over its rosy tip. She belatedly realized he'd unfastened her bodice again.

As he gently suckled her, a firestorm of desire roared through her body, and a cry of bliss escaped her lips.

He lifted his head.

"Don't stop," she begged. "You make me feel so . . . so . . ." She could not think of a word that would adequately describe the vortex of sensations that engulfed her.

His husky laugh sent a shiver of pleasure through her. He moved his mouth to the peak of her other breast while his hand continued to massage and tease the first.

Georgina moaned and twisted in delight, only to have her stays prod her painfully, reminding her that she still wore them. "Please," she murmured to Justin, "unlace my stays. They're hurting me."

He lifted his head, and she turned so that he could comply with her request. But instead of doing so, he turned her back to face him. His dark eyes were troubled.

"Gina, we must stop this madness now," Justin warned, at the knife edge of his control.

"Why?" she inquired breathlessly, looking up at him with such a luminous expression on her pixie face that he could not seem to catch his breath.

Scarcely conscious of what he was doing, he tore

his neckcloth away and opened the top buttons of his shirt, gulping in air and her sweet gardenia scent. "Because if we don't, little wasp, I very shortly will no longer be able to stop myself from making love to you."

Her eyes widened. "Really?"

"Really!"

Taking his face in her hands, she smiled at him, that magnificent smile that made him forget his own name—and all else, including every scruple he possessed.

Her sparkling eyes met his. "Make love to me, Justin. I want you to do that."

And he wanted to do so more than anything he could think of. After such an invitation, why should he not do as she asked? She wanted him, and he ached for her, ached to feel her soft, sweet body convulse around him.

Justin felt as though he were a randy seventeen-year-old again. It flashed through his mind that he was stark, raving mad to even consider doing what she asked. The price he would have to pay for this night would be so much higher than the brief pleasure he obtained.

But damn it, he wanted her, wanted her more than he could ever remember wanting any woman. In his frenzied hunger for her, nothing else mattered.

And if he refused her request, would she seek out that damned Roger Chadwick for further "scientific" experiments?

That enraging thought drove the last vestige of restraint and sanity from Justin's mind. He asked hoarsely, "Are you certain, Gina?"

Still smiling, she nodded. "Very certain."

Yes, she was. And certain, too, that she loved this

man as she would never love any other. Her heart and her body cried out for him. She wanted to experience that enormous joy and pleasure Nancy Wilde had described. She wanted to explore fully the tumultuous excitement and pleasure Justin aroused in her. But most of all, she wanted to prove to him that love was no mirage. She wanted to win his heart as he had won hers.

Georgina's breath caught as Justin's smoldering eyes suddenly blazed with decision and passion. He pressed her against his long, hard body. She felt the soft lawn of his shirt against her as his mouth closed on hers with such hunger and intensity that his fiery ardor sparked her own.

She returned his kiss as fervently as he bestowed it, scarcely heeding his hands at her back until he slipped off her stays and tossed them aside.

"Oh!" she gasped in surprise. "However did you manage that?"

He chuckled. "Don't ask."

He drew a step away, pushed back her bodice, and leisurely studied her breasts that he had bared. Georgina felt herself turning crimson at his perusal. No man had ever seen her like this before. Embarrassed, she raised her hands to try to shield her breasts, but he grabbed her wrists.

As he tugged her arms down to her sides, he murmured, "Don't try to hide such beauty from me, my sweet."

Startled, she looked up at him, silently challenging his observation. The heat and the appreciation in his dark eyes stunned her.

He smiled at her expression. "Yes, you are beautiful," he insisted, his voice strangely thick, as though his tongue had suddenly swelled.

His compliment melted her embarrassment and doubt like butter over a fire.

He bent his head and took her breast in his mouth again. Lightning flashes of pleasure bolted through her. The yearning deep within her grew painful in its intensity.

As his mouth and tongue toyed with her breast, his warm hands, so strong yet amazingly gentle, moved over her body, filling it with such quivering excitement, she moaned, then moaned again.

He lifted his head and looked down at her. His knowing smile made her blush again. Embarrassed, she ducked her head, and her gaze fell on the curly black hair that poked from the opening of his partially unbuttoned shirt.

Georgina longed to see him as he was seeing her. Her hands moved to his shirt front, unfastened the rest of its buttons, and pushed the material away.

She could not resist running her fingers lightly through the thick hair on his muscular chest. It was silkier than she had expected. She loved the contrast between the hard strength of his chest beneath her fingertips and the softness of his hair as it curled around them.

When she traced his dusky nipple with the tip of her index finger, he groaned as though she had hurt him. She looked up, surprised. Instead of pain, she saw a dreamy pleasure in his dark, half closed eyes.

Justin shrugged out of his shirt, letting it fall to the floor. She admired the ripple of powerful muscles in his shoulders and arms as he did so.

"Like what you see?" he asked lazily.

She nodded, too nervous to speak. Then her gaze fell on a vertical scar, puckered and faded, on his shoulder. She lightly ran her finger over it. "What caused this?"

"Don't ask," he said roughly and promptly kissed her with hard passion. He pushed her unfastened gown off her shoulders and it joined his shirt on the floor. Now she had only her stockings and shoes left.

Without warning, one of Justin's arms went round her shoulders and the other caught her behind her knees. He lifted her into his arms, carried her to the bed, pulled back the covers, and laid her on it. He removed her shoes and stockings and dropped them on the floor.

The gleam in his eyes as he gazed down at her intensified her nervousness, and she unconsciously reached for the sheet.

Justin demonstrated no such modesty. He sat on the edge of the bed, removing his own shoes and stockings. As he stood up, his back to her, his pants dropped to the ground, and he stepped out of them.

Georgina gulped as she caught sight of his muscled back, narrow hips and trim behind. He sat down on the bed again, lifted the sheet, and slid beneath it.

"You did not extinguish the candle," she reminded him.

Justin rolled over to face her and smiled. "I won't allow the darkness to hide you from me." He kissed her, a long, hot kiss and began to caress her tenderly.

His hands roamed slowly over her body, and his mouth followed suit. Her senses reeled at the exquisite pleasure his exploration gave her. Justin was revealing secrets to her of her own body, amazing secrets that she had never known before.

She gasped as his finger slipped inside her and probed her secret passage.

He frowned at her.

"What is it?" she asked in alarm.

"Has a man ever made love to you before?"

"Of course not!" she exclaimed, affronted that he should think it necessary to ask. "I never . . ." She managed to stop herself before she finished the sentence . . . *loved a man until you*. She could not bear to have him mock her love for him.

His finger continued to move inside her in a way that sent excitement spiraling through her.

"You never what?" Justin pressed.

She could think of no answer that would not reveal the truth, so she said evasively, " 'Tis not important."

"Perhaps it is to me," he said gently. "You never what?"

"Never wanted to do so before."

Her answer seemed to please and satisfy him. He kissed her and his tongue began to explore her mouth while his finger moved at the same seductive tempo.

Georgina closed her eyes. She would not have believed such exquisite torment could exist. What he was doing to her was immensely pleasurable, yet she felt as though something was missing, as though she were scaling enormous heights yet could not see the summit, hidden in an obscure mist.

Suddenly he withdrew his finger. She started to protest only to discover he was replacing it with another part of his anatomy, a much larger, harder part. Her eyes flew open in surprise and dismay.

Justin looked as though he were in pain, his face set, his breath coming in pants, his jaw clenched. Yet he was watching her intently.

"Relax, my sweet." His voice was hoarse and

strained, yet gentle. " 'Tis always uncomfortable for a woman the first time, but if you relax, it will go easier for you."

She tried to follow his instruction and succeeded initially. But as he slowly, carefully deepened his invasion, her discomfort increased, and she moaned in protest.

"Forgive me, I hate hurting you," he whispered as though he wished he could absorb her pain into himself. "Perhaps it will be better this way." He suddenly plunged deep inside her.

She cried out, but his mouth had closed over hers, sealing off the sound. He murmured soothingly to her and bathed her face with quick, tender kisses until she relaxed again.

He began to move within her slowly, carefully. After a few moments, she forgot her hurt and all else as tension and pleasure built apace within her.

His tempo gradually increased, grew frenzied, adding more fuel to the remarkable fire that was consuming her. She felt the sweat of his body mingle with her own.

Her body tightened and suddenly exploded in a crescendo of spasms so powerful she gasped, at a loss to understand the forces unleashed in her body. She felt like a blazing meteor arcing across the heavens. Opening her eyes, she saw Justin's startled expression a second before his body, too, convulsed.

When their tremors had stopped, he lifted himself away from her and settled beside her, studying her face. She looked at him in wonder. Nancy had not exaggerated. If anything, she had severely understated her claim. Enormous pleasure did not begin to describe what Georgina had just experienced.

Justin smiled as he pushed a damp curl gently back from her cheek. "I don't need to ask whether you enjoyed it." He sounded pleased and smug.

"It was . . ." She stopped, searching for a word that could possibly do justice to the bliss she had just enjoyed, but she could not find one.

He grinned at her, a mischievous, boyish grin that eased the harsh planes of his face and sent her heart galloping.

"Don't tell me that for once I've left you at a loss for words, little wasp?"

She nodded.

He chuckled. "What a delight you are."

Justin fitted his lips to hers in a kiss so tender her heart welled with love for him.

Then he pulled her tightly against him. They were both on their sides, their bodies touching from shoulder to foot. She loved the comforting texture of his skin against her own.

Justin awoke as the first hint of dawn penetrated the windows of Gina's bedchamber. She was cuddled against him, her warmth mingling with his.

What an incredible aphrodisiac she was for him. He had made love to her three times before they went to sleep, and now his body was already eager for yet another encore.

It had been a glorious night, a night of pure madness, of insane passion. A remarkable, unique, unforgettable night. He had never experienced another like it.

In the faint light, he studied Gina's sleeping face on the pillow beside him. Her ardor had matched his own.

Justin thought of the highly skilled and talented courtesans with whom he'd had liaisons over the years. Not a one of them had given him the extraordinary pleasure this passionate pixie had.

He smiled down at her. So sweet, so innocent.

Then his smile vanished as he thought of the consequences of this night he had spent in her bed.

Bloody hell, what had he done?

The madness that had consumed him last night, that had compelled him to violate his own code of honor as he had never done before, had burned itself out.

Now, he thought bitterly, he must pay the price for his reprehensible fall from grace.

And that price was marriage.

Justin had sworn he would never wed again. Now he must do so. It was the only honorable course open to him.

Yet as he looked at Gina and recalled their night together, matrimony did not seem so odious to him.

You were happy enough to marry Clarissa, too, a nagging voice reminded him. *You thought her charming, thought you loved her, thought she would make you a fine wife. And look at the agony you brought down on yourself.*

Chilled by his memories, he rolled away from Gina and left the bed. For the first time since Clarissa's death, he felt the terrible despair that had gripped him like an iron fist during their marriage.

How could he have been so damned stupid? He silently gathered up his scattered clothes from the floor, cursing himself for his idiocy.

Despite Gina's protestations that she would never marry, Justin knew full well she would be as eager to embrace matrimony this morning as she had been to embrace him last night.

She had trapped him, clever little wasp.

In that moment, he hated her.

Chapter 20

Half asleep, Georgina shifted on the bed, seeking the warmth of Justin's hard body. Unable to find it, she opened her eyes and discovered he had left her bed.

Blinking sleep from her eyes, she looked about the room, illuminated now by the dawning day. Justin had picked up his scattered clothes, laid them over the back of a chair, and was quietly dressing. He already had his pants on and was fastening them.

She stared in silent admiration at his long, lean body and wished it was still beside her in the bed. Her eyes focused on his chest with the thick dark hair curling over it.

He reached for his shirt. As he did so, the ripple of muscles in his shoulders and arms fascinated her. She longed to jump from the bed and run her hands over the bare skin of his torso, absorbing his warmth and his strength.

Her gaze rose to his harsh face. Dark stubble covered his jaw, and his black hair, thick and curly, was badly tousled. He reminded her so much of a pirate this morning that she shivered a little.

He pulled on his shirt, hiding his muscular torso

from her admiring eyes. It was all she could do to keep from protesting aloud.

Her heart beat erratically as she recalled the rapture she had experienced last night in his arms. Georgina's love for Justin overflowed.

But something he'd said just before he'd made love to her the final time nagged at her. "I cannot believe this." He'd sounded incredulous and disgusted with himself. "I would have thought it impossible, but I ache to make love to you one more time."

She swallowed hard. Clearly they'd had opposite reactions to the ecstasy they'd shared. While she burned for more, he was flummoxed that he should still want her at all.

As he buttoned his shirt, he glanced at her, and their gazes met. His expression was so bleak and icy that she felt as though an Alpine glacier was inching over her heart.

"Why are you dressing now?" she asked, pushing herself into a sitting position.

"Cover yourself!" Justin sounded angry and harassed.

Georgina had forgotten that she was naked. Stung by his tone, she hastily pulled the sheet above her breasts. Last night he had wanted to look at her. This morning she seemed to revolt him.

Struggling to keep her hurt from her voice, she asked again. "Why are you dressing? It's scarcely dawn yet."

"Servants rise early," he replied curtly.

"Ah yes, it is best that you not be caught in my room." Georgina tried to smile, but she could not manage it when this man, who had made such wonderful and tender love to her only hours ago, now looked and sounded so harsh and hateful. "Papa would not be happy."

She shuddered at the scowl Justin gave her. She felt as though the glacier had just swallowed her up.

"You need not worry," he told her sharply. "I will request your father's permission to marry you this morning."

She looked at him in astonishment. "What are you talking about? You don't want to marry me."

His sensual mouth that had given her so much pleasure during the night tightened. "No, I don't. There's nothing I want less."

Georgina felt as though he'd just split her heart with an ax.

"But you leave me no choice."

"*I* leave *you* no choice!" she cried, so indignant that she unconsciously let the sheet drop.

The sudden hot glitter in Justin's eyes alerted her to what she'd done, and she hastily pulled the sheet up again.

"It was not I who brought up the subject of marriage, my lord. If you are concerned about compromising my honor, you need not be."

" 'Tis my own that concerns me. Marriage is the price I must pay for last night."

"Why do you say that?"

"Surely the answer is obvious." His voice was limned with bitterness. "I cannot steal a lady's virtue without paying the piper. My conduct is even more reprehensible to me because you are my host's daughter. Never have I abused another man's hospitality so abominably as I have your father's."

Georgina felt such pain that she could not catch her breath for a moment. So much for thinking she could eventually teach this man she loved so much to love her in return! Justin did not care about her at all, only about making reparation for misusing her father's hospitality.

"You did not 'steal' my virtue." Her voice now was as cold as his. "It was *I* who asked *you* to make love to me."

Her response clearly surprised him. "True, but I should have resisted you."

"And why did you not?" Georgina held her breath, hoping, praying that he would admit affection for her had been responsible.

"My lust overrode all else, including my good sense."

He might as well have physically struck her, his reply hurt so much. Fighting to keep her voice from betraying her misery, she asked, "What about love?"

He snorted derisively. "What we had together last night was lust, pure and simple. Why must women—even one as intelligent as you—always try to wrap it in romantic gauze, rather than face up to what it really is?"

Georgina felt as though an iguanodon had just trampled her heart. Perhaps Justin had been in lust last night, but she'd been in love.

He might not know how to love, but she did!

She would not be such a fool, however, as to confess her love to him. She would not give him that trump card to use against her in his decision to wed her to assuage his conscience. Her love for him must remain her secret.

"You disappoint me, Gina. You are turning out to be like every other woman. Now, because I have bedded you, you fancy yourself in love with me."

"Believe me, I do not *fancy* myself in love with

you, not at all!" she sputtered, so angry at him she could scarcely get the words out.

The vehemence of her answer clearly startled him. "I am glad to hear that," he said with a stiffness that betrayed he was not nearly as pleased by her reply as he thought he should be. "Not that it matters much."

"Why, pray tell, does it not matter?"

"Thanks to my stupidity and lack of control last night, I must marry you." Justin turned away from her, tunneling his hand through his thick unruly hair. "We will be wed as soon as I can arrange a special license."

Georgina wanted no man who said he'd bedded her out of stupidity, then told her he must marry her only to satisfy his honor. She fought to hold back the hot tears of anger, disappointment, and hurt that threatened to well up in her eyes and complete her humiliation. "No, we won't be married by special license. Or any other way! I refuse to marry you."

His mouth opened, then closed again without emitting a sound, her response clearly shocking him into silence. Did the arrogant man think any woman would welcome his offer, no matter how grudgingly it was made?

With two quick strides, he reached the bed and sat down on its edge beside her. She held the sheet tightly about her chin.

"But you must marry me. Bloody hell, Gina, don't you understand? I've ruined you."

"I do not care in the least." Her head angled proudly, defiantly. "Pray, don't give it another thought."

He looked like a man goaded beyond endurance. "Gina, I am trying to do what's right by you. Don't make it more difficult for me than it already is."

"You are trying to do what will placate your own conscience," she cried furiously. "And I want no part of it! Furthermore, I am more to blame than you are in last night's fiasco, for I asked you to make love to me."

"*Fiasco!*" Justin sounded mortally offended.

Well, so was Georgina, and she lashed out at him. "Tell me, my lord, does your code of honor apply to your housemaids, too, or only to unmarried females of quality?"

The anger in his eyes told her that she had grievously insulted him. *Good!*

Tit for tat!

"I have never required a maid nor anyone else who is dependent on me to satisfy my needs," he said icily, jumping up from the bed. "Neither do I seduce another man's wife—any man's, regardless of his rank in life. And when I do make a mistake, as I did last night, I do not evade my obligation, even though it may be the last thing I want to do."

"My lord," Georgina said with asperity, "if you think branding me a mistake, an unwanted obligation, and the last thing you want will reconcile me to marrying you, you are dead wrong!"

He had the grace to flush. "It's you who's wrong. You will have no choice but to marry me once your father learns what happened last night."

"My father would never force me to marry anyone against my will. And the *only* thing I ask of you as a result of last night is that you not tell him about it. It will cause him great heartache. And I vow to you that if you do that, I will never, *never* marry you."

Justin again ran his hands distractedly through his unruly black hair. "Why are you so damned stubborn? You have the most to lose. I am trying to help you."

"Well, stop trying! I do not want your help!" *I want your love!* "And I will *not* marry you."

"Why the hell are you so opposed to marrying me?"

"I told you before that if I marry at all, it will be to a man I can love and trust and respect and a . . ." She broke off, stunned into silence by the fury that suddenly twisted his face. The remainder of her sentence, *a man who, in turn, loves, trusts, and respects me*, went unspoken.

Justin jumped up from the bed, snatched up his coat from the chair back, and stalked from the room without another word.

Justin avoided Gina until dinnertime, his wounded pride still bleeding from her rejection of his offer to marry her.

Her refusal did not negate the necessity of his wedding her, although it made doing so all the more bitter for him. It was the only honorable course open to him. And he was not a man to shun his duty simply because he disliked it.

He would, he decided grimly, simply have to persuade her.

And he might as well start now.

He recalled with burning chagrin her remark about last night's "fiasco," which had been another blow to his pride.

No woman had ever complained of his lovemaking before. He'd sworn he'd given Gina as much bliss as she had given him. How could she call it a fiasco?

Because she didn't know how good it was, but he did. And that made him all the angrier.

So he was a man she could neither love nor respect, was he? Damn it, she might at least have given him credit for trying to do what was right by her.

True, his offer to her had been clumsy and ill-worded. After having made love to her, he had thought she would be eager to marry him, if only to save her reputation. He had not dreamed she could have any objection.

Certainly no other woman would have balked. But then, he reminded himself, Gina was as different from other women he'd known as the sun was from the moon.

At least Justin did not have to worry that she was spending the day with Roger Chadwick. A silent, glowering Roger had left Penfield immediately after breakfast.

Justin did not tell her father what had occurred between them. He'd decided that Gina was right. Penford would not compel her to do anything.

And Justin was becoming well enough acquainted with his strong-willed little wasp that he did not doubt if he told her father, the maddening, intransigent female would keep her vow never to marry him.

He'd not seen her since he left her chamber that morning, and he felt some trepidation about how she would act toward him when he saw her in the withdrawing room before dinner.

She greeted him with a cool smile. During the meal that followed, she was her usual lively, witty self. If she was still angry at him, she hid it well. Perhaps by now, she had come to see the necessity of accepting his offer. Even if she had not, he might be better able to persuade her now that her anger had cooled. He'd have to try.

After dinner, she was prevailed upon to play the harp for their entertainment. A few minutes before they would retire for the night, Justin slipped from the room and again made his way to her chamber to wait there for her.

Stealing inside, he sat in the chair he had occupied the previous night.

He waited until Gina entered the room and closed the door behind her before he stood up. "What, no undressing tonight?" he teased. "How disappointing."

She started. "You frightened me, my lord!"

"Surely after last night, we are sufficiently well acquainted for you to call me Justin," he said dryly.

Her eyes widened, then narrowed. "You are not nearly so well acquainted with me as you seem to think."

Her cool answer frayed his temper. "What the hell is that supposed to mean? We know each other as intimately as a man and a woman can."

"Physically, yes, but true intimacy involves much more."

"Such as?"

"Sharing what's in our hearts and minds, sharing our hopes and fears, our triumphs and failings." She walked slowly, unsmilingly, to him. "Tell me, my lord, do you mean to sneak into my room every night now?"

Her tone made him want to grind his teeth. It also boded ill for his mission, but he forced himself to smile at her, hoping to coax one from her in return. "In spite of all good reason, the prospect has considerable appeal."

"Does it now?" Her voice turned sultry, and her lips widened in a mischievous smile.

He stared at her irresistible mouth, hungering for

the taste of it. Unable to stop himself, he bent his head and kissed her gently, tenderly. She kissed him back.

Memories of the previous night danced tantalizingly in his mind. Gentleness gave way to heat; tenderness, to hunger.

Justin wanted her. God, but he wanted her. And Gina showed no more inclination to stop him than he had to stop.

He had to have her. What did it matter if he slept with her again. The irreversible damage had been done the previous night.

Justin unfastened her bodice, and she attacked his neckcloth and the buttons of his shirt. They left a trail of clothes scattered as they made their way to the bed.

Aching with need, he began a frenzied foreplay. She astonished him with how quickly she was ready for him. Justin entered her, and once again they soared together.

Afterward Georgina lay in Justin's arms, spent with the pleasure he had just given her. He nuzzled her ear with his tongue. "Marry me," he whispered softly.

How much she wanted to accept after the ecstasy they had just shared, but she could not do so until he gave her his love as well as his passion. She forced herself to say firmly, "No."

"Damn it, Gina—"

She laid her fingers lightly over his mouth to silence him. "Listen to me, Justin, you asked me to marry you, and I refused you. You need feel no shame. You tried very hard to do the right thing, but I will not let you. You have satisfied your honor. Let us simply enjoy each other for now."

He looked at her as if he could not believe his ears.

She smiled at him. "Given your aversion to marriage, you should be delighted I have no interest in you as a husband, only as a lover." *Until you can return my love.*

The scowl on his face indicated he was far from pleased. He looked as though she utterly baffled him.

"Why?" His voice was no longer a gentle whisper, but a sharp demand. "Why do you refuse me?"

Were Georgina to tell Justin her most important reason—that he did not love her—he would merely insist again that she was a foolish female who mistook love for lust.

She could not bear that. Nor could she stand to have him ridicule her love for him as a foolish feminine illusion.

Instead she would outline her other doubts to him. "I do not believe we would suit."

"Why not?"

"You are a man used to having his own way, while I am too independent to play the submissive, simpering wife, obedient to your every wish. I refuse to sacrifice my freedom, to become your chattel at the mercy of your whims, with no right to my fortune or even my own children. If I am to marry at all, it will be to a man who respects me and my mind and encourages me to develop it instead of stifling me in a straitjacket of rigid propriety."

"Do you truly believe I would 'stifle' you and rob you of your fortune and your children?" he demanded hotly.

Georgina remembered his stepmother's accusations against Justin. Once she had believed them. Now she no longer did. But she wanted to know the truth, and she wanted to hear it from his own lips. "I was told you were very cruel to your late wife."

His eyes narrowed. "Cruel? How so?"

"Do you dispute that you denied her access to her own fortune?"

"No, I do not dispute that!"

His angry answer shocked Georgina. She had been so certain he would deny it. Much agitated, she wanted to get up and pace the floor, but she dared not, for she was naked beneath the sheet. "And did you keep her a virtual prisoner at Ravencrest?"

"No!" he snapped.

Georgina waited expectantly for him to explain what he had done, but he did not. "What is the truth in that regard?" she pressed.

He sighed wearily. "Gina, I told you before I do not discuss my wife or my marriage with anyone."

That ignited her own temper, and she lashed out at him. "And you are mad to think I would marry a man who keeps secrets from me. I insist upon a husband who regards me as his dearest friend, his partner, his equal, and who trusts me enough to confide everything to me."

"Gina—"

She cut him off angrily. "Nor would I ever marry a man who acted as you did toward your first wife. Is that why you wish to marry me, my lord? To appropriate my fortune as you did hers?"

Justin's jaw visibly clenched, and he flushed with anger. " 'Tis you who does not trust me enough! If you believe all that you've heard about me, why the hell did you decide to give your virtue to me?"

When she did not reply, his eyes narrowed to slits

and he grabbed her arm roughly. "Answer me, damn you!"

She retorted recklessly, "It was part of an experiment."

For an instant, he regarded her as though she were raving mad, then his hard eyes glittered in a way that, had she been more timid, she might have feared for her safety.

"And what was the nature of this experiment for which you used me as an unwitting guinea pig?" he growled.

She eyed him uneasily. He was in such an angry, unpredictable mood that she decided to evade answering. "I refuse to say until I have finished collecting and analyzing my data." She jerked back at the undiluted fury in his expression.

"And what other men do you intend to ask to participate in this particular aspect of your experiment?" His voice had gone from hard to deceptively soft—and very, very dangerous.

Determined not to let him intimidate her, Georgina said airily. "I have not yet decided."

The murderous look in his eyes prompted her to add hastily. "I may not need more data. You may have provided me with enough."

"Damned right, I have!" he growled. "And to make certain, I'll give you some more *data!*"

Justin yanked her against him and his mouth took hers in a furious, punishing kiss.

Passion blazed between them, his kiss gentled, and they began another kind of communication—long and slow and infinitely satisfying.

Later, as Gina lay sleeping, exhausted by their tumultuous lovemaking, Justin left her bed, dressed, and returned to his own chamber, where he stared moodily through the window at the night's dark silhouettes.

So Gina thought he had been cruel to Clarissa. What a joke that was!

He thought of what had transpired tonight with Gina. Once again, she had savaged his pride. So she'd made love with him merely as part of some idiotic experiment, had she?

Not only could she not love or respect him, but she regarded him as some damned *experiment*! He'd never been so mortified in his life.

Then he'd gone a little crazy at the possibility she might ask Roger Chadwick or some other man to participate in her experiment as Justin had.

You tried very hard to do the right thing, but I will not let you.

Yes, he had tried very hard, and now he felt not shame, but an enormous frustration. He would willingly marry her to protect her from censure and ruin, and she would have no part of it. How could such an intelligent woman act so stubbornly contrary to her own best interests?

You should be delighted I have no interest in you as a husband, only as a lover.

And he was delighted, he told himself furiously.

So damned delighted that he itched to throttle her.

Chapter 21

In the barn, Justin stopped chiseling at the stone encasing the long neck of the iguanodon skeleton to watch Gina, some twenty feet away from him at the hip section of the prehistoric beast.

It'd been three days since he'd learned she'd wanted him to make love to her merely as part of some fool experiment. He'd been so angry that night, he'd told himself he would not touch her again. And he had not. He'd tried to ignore her.

He could have more easily ignored the sun. Her marvelous smile and his hunger for her melted his resolve like snow beneath the sun's hot rays. Now he tried valiantly—and in vain—to ignore his aching desire for her.

He had thought it wiser to work at a considerable distance from Gina. Lanie had been working with them, but she'd left a quarter of an hour ago for another fitting of the clothes he'd ordered for her.

Gina was staring at the skeleton with such a puzzled expression that Justin asked, "What is it?"

"The iguanodon had hip bones like a bird's."

Forgetting his vow to keep his distance from her, he strode to her side. Her scent of gardenia wafted over him, intensifying his ache.

"See"—Gina ran her finger along a section of pubic bone that pointed backward as a bird's did—"and the front of the mouth was rather like a beak." She looked up at Justin with eyes full of wonder, her own luscious mouth slightly parted. "Is it not amazing?"

In that moment, he knew he could no longer resist her.

No longer wanted to try.

He kissed her, and she returned it, fanning the suppressed embers of his desire into a conflagration that consumed his resolve, his doubts, his hesitations, and every other obstacle in its path.

Her words echoed in his mind: *Let us simply enjoy each other for now.*

Why should he deny her that request—and himself as well?

After that incident in the barn, Justin could not stay away from Gina. His life at Penfield assumed a pattern in which by day he, Gina, and Lanie slowly reclaimed the iguanodon skeleton from the rock that had held it for eons. By night Gina and he made love. Marriage was not mentioned between them again.

As they left the barn one afternoon more than a fortnight later, Justin looked back at the massive skeleton. By now its giant curving ribs were fully exposed. "It reminds me of the bleached and rotting timbers of an old wooden ship turned upside down."

Gina's smile glowed. "What a perfect description, Justin."

As they entered the house by a side door, a woman, a stranger, came down the hall toward them. She walked with a weary gait, yet Justin judged her to be only a few years older than himself. Once she must have been quite pretty. Now, however, her thin face was haggard and such sadness haunted her eyes that his heart went out to her. Clearly she had endured some great tragedy.

She was simply dressed all in black from her unadorned bonnet to her shoes. Justin surmised she must lately have lost her husband or a child and was still in mourning.

Gina's face lighted with joy when she saw the woman. "Aunt Margaret! Oh, how happy I am you have come."

The two women embraced lovingly. Margaret's sweet smile in response to her niece's warm greeting could not vanquish the unhappiness from her eyes.

When Justin reached the women, Gina said, "Aunt Margaret, this is Lord Ravenstone. My aunt, Margaret Dodd. She is my father's youngest sister."

After Justin and Margaret acknowledged the introduction, Gina said, "Since you are here, Aunt Margaret, I assume your dreadful husband is away from home."

Justin had not heard such loathing before in Gina's voice for anyone. The pain in Margaret's eyes deepened at her niece's mention of her spouse. "Yes, he has gone to London for a fortnight. He will be back on the twenty-seventh."

"If you are lucky, he will meet with a fatal accident on the road," Gina said acidly.

"You must not say such a thing about anyone," her aunt scolded.

"You are far kinder than I am—indeed, far too kind. The world would be a better place for his elimination from it, and well you know it."

His little wasp never minced words. Justin wondered what her aunt's husband could have done to merit such condemnation from Gina.

"How did you get here, Aunt Margaret? Why did you not have Papa send a carriage?"

"I had not planned to come, but Mr. Moran, the rector at Cumberdale, insisted upon bringing me here. He refused to take no for an answer. He said I looked so poorly that he was convinced I needed to get away."

Justin silently agreed with the rector and blessed him for his perception and kindness to the poor woman.

Gina took her aunt's arm in her own. "I'm so happy you listened to him and came to us. You look exhausted, though, from your journey. You must have a nap before dinner. Do go up to your old bedroom while I ask cook to brew you a tisane. I will be up in a few minutes."

Margaret headed toward the staircase. Justin watched Mrs. Dodd climb the steps, her back hunched and her feet dragging as though she had scarcely the energy to navigate the steps.

The terrible grief he had seen in her eyes haunted him. She looked like a woman who had been through hell.

Nor had he seen Gina betray such hatred for anyone as she did for her aunt's husband. He turned to ask her why she felt as she did, but she was disappearing into the kitchen. He followed, stopping a few feet short of the door and waited. A delicious melange of food odors—roasting meat, potatoes, and a cherry pie—tantalized his nose and his stomach.

When Gina came out of the kitchen a few minutes later, she frowned when she saw him. "Why are you here?"

He fell into step beside her. "I'm curious why you despise your aunt's husband so."

"Words fail me when it comes to describing what a cruel man Sebastian Dodd is."

"Bloody hell, your aunt is married to *him*?" Justin stopped dead in his tracks he was so shocked. "No wonder she looks so unhappy."

Gina stopped, too, and shot him a surprised look. "So you are not an admirer of his."

"No, I always thought him eccentric. Now I am convinced he is mad."

She eyed him approvingly. "My own sentiments precisely. What brought you to this conclusion?"

"He has grown increasingly odder the past two or three years. The last conversation I had with him a month or two ago was highly disturbing. He was suspicious of everyone, certain they were plotting terrible deeds against him. And the wildness in his eyes was unnerving. The longer we talked, the more alarmed I became. Why did your father allow his sister to marry Dodd?"

"Papa had no say in the matter."

Gina looked up and down the hall as though to make certain no one else was in earshot. No one was, but still she lowered her voice so much Justin had to strain to hear her. "I told you, did I not, that my father was estranged from his parents?"

Justin nodded.

"My grandfather was a terrible judge of men. When he died, he named his good friend, Sir Thomas Kempton, and Papa's elder brother, Christopher, as her co-guardians and the trustees of her inheritance until she married with their approval."

Justin knew Kempton to be an addlepated old fool who mistook appearance for substance. "What about after Christopher died? Did your father still have no authority?"

"Grandfather stipulated that if one of the co-trustees died, all authority would be vested in the sole remaining one." Gina resumed walking, and Justin followed suit. "He expected Kempton, who was his own age, to die first, but instead Christopher followed grandfather to the grave within a half year."

"Leaving Margaret in Kempton's hands?" Justin asked.

Gina nodded. "She had several suitors, but none of them was rich enough to suit Kempton, and he turned them all away."

Justin and Gina reached the entrance hall with its great pillared arches and pastel frescos. Two maids were cleaning there, and Gina fell silent again.

She did not resume talking until she and Justin reached the first landing. "When my aunt was twenty-four, Kempton arranged a marriage for her with Dodd. My father strongly objected because he'd never liked Dodd and thought him strange."

"But Kempton would not listen to your father?"

"No, Dodd was rich as Midas and that was Kempton's only consideration. Papa had no legal power to thwart the marriage."

"What were Margaret's feelings?"

"That was ten years ago and—"

"Good God, she is younger than I am," Justin said in surprise, "and I thought her older."

"She has aged dreadfully the past two or three years. When she married Dodd, he was still sane and quite charming. Even if that had not been the case, however, my aunt is the sweetest natured of women and capable only of seeing the best in a person."

Justin could not resist interjecting with a grin, "Unlike her termagant of a niece."

Gina pulled a face at him but did not respond verbally to his provocation. "Aunt Margaret resolved to marry Dodd and devote herself to making it a happy union. But with a man like him, that was not possible even for a woman of Margaret's goodness."

"I recall they have children, do they not?"

"Yes, two girls, now seven and six, then a son born three years ago. They are the greatest worry to her. The boy was born after Sebastian had begun to sink into madness. A month or two after little Seth's first birthday, his father began to question the baby's paternity and falsely accused Margaret of adultery."

"Perhaps the charge was not false." The moment Justin said this, he regretted his hasty words. He was startled to realize he was so accustomed to finding fault with the wife in a marriage that it had become automatic with him.

Gina glared at him with such fire in her eyes that he wondered his eyebrows were not singed.

"If you knew my aunt at all, you would never utter such an ugly slander!"

Justin thought of the ineffable sadness that haunted the woman's expression. "I agree. I owe your aunt an apology."

They had reached the top of the staircase and the hall that led to the bedchambers. Gina stopped and faced him. "Indeed, you do! Dodd banished her from their home without a pence to her name. Papa has been supporting her since then."

"Why did your father not give her a home here at Penfield?"

"He offered, but she is so terrified for her children's physical safety at their father's hands that she refuses to leave the vicinity of his estate when he is in residence there."

"Surely Dodd would not hurt his own children," Justin protested.

"When he flies into one of his rages, he is capable of anything. I don't expect you to understand that. No one who has not seen him that way could."

"Oh, I understand all too well," he said so grimly that Gina gave him a questioning look. But he said nothing more, keeping his terrible memories to himself.

"Sebastian once beat my poor aunt so badly for *smiling* at one of their male dinner guests that he broke her nose and blackened her eyes. She could not open them for a week."

"Bloody hell!" Justin exclaimed, truly shocked. "Do the children tell her he abuses them?"

"Sebastian has not allowed my poor aunt to see them since the day he threw her out. But she cannot bear to leave the area when he is at home. She lives in constant terror that she will hear one of the children is at death's door from his cruelty."

"She has not been permitted to see her children for two years?"

Gina nodded. "Even when Sebastian is gone to London, as he is now, the servants dare not go against his orders that her children be kept from her. But at least when he is away, she does not have to live in dread for their lives."

Justin was appalled at the thought of three small, innocent children at the mercy of a madman. "No wonder your poor aunt is so unhappy. Can nothing be done?"

Gina turned left and started down the hall. "You know as well as I do, my lord, that a mother has no rights against her husband regarding her children, no matter how dreadful a man he is."

Justin had never questioned the justness of that until this moment. But then he had not known a father like Sebastian.

"And you say marriage is not a trap for a woman," Gina said bitterly.

For the first time, Justin could truly appreciate why Gina should fear the power marriage gave a husband over his wife and family. "I see why you distrust matrimony. With such a terrible example in your own family, I cannot blame you."

"Do you admit then that wives, who are utterly powerless against their husbands, suffer the worst in a marriage?"

"I am willing to admit that they *may* suffer the worst, but few husbands are as bad as your uncle."

"Perhaps few husbands are as insane, but they can be as cruel. You have only to look at poor Lady Ingleham to see that."

Remembering that Ingleham had been one of Gina's spurned suitors, Justin said, "I understand Ingleham was once so enamored of you that he sought your hand in marriage."

"You may be sure it was not me he was enamored of, but my inheritance. The arrogant scoundrel thought I would be overjoyed at an offer from him. Like you, he thought his title far outweighed in importance anything I would bring to the marriage."

"You slander me if you think me like Ingleham. Nor have I ever thought my title recommended me as a good husband, although a number of young ladies would disagree with that."

"Not all of my gender are wise," Gina retorted, "any more than all of yours make good husbands."

He smiled. "*Touché,* little wasp."

Gina disappeared into her aunt's room, and Justin went back downstairs, intending to pick up a book from his host's library.

He entered the room, thinking it unoccupied. When he was two or three steps inside, however, he heard a man's voice say urgently, "My lord, you must do something. I am convinced that Mr. Dodd in one of his rages will soon kill his poor, innocent son and perhaps his daughters as well. I do not . . ."

Justin spun around just as the speaker, a man with thinning sandy-colored hair and a cherubic face above a clerical collar, saw him and broke off in midsentence. Mr. Moran, Justin presumed.

Penford sat opposite the stranger, his chair pulled close. He, too, looked at Justin.

"My apologies for intruding," Justin said. "I was not aware anyone was here. I will leave you."

"No, stay, Lord Ravenstone," Penford said, his tone more an order than a request. "You are a clever man. Perhaps you can think of some way to solve this dilemma." He gestured for Justin to take a chair near his own. "This is Mr. Moran, the rector at Cumberdale, near the estate of my brother-in-law. He kindly brought my sister here today."

Justin sat down on the chair his host had indicated. "I met your sister a few minutes ago. I was shocked to learn to whom she is married. I won't mince words. I think Sebastian Dodd is a madman."

Penford gave him a grateful look. "I knew you were an astute man. All three of us agree that Dodd is insane. Mr. Moran came here today because he fears Sebastian will mortally harm one or more of his children. He wants me to do something to prevent that, but I know of nothing that I can legally do, given a father's rights over his children."

"Nor do I." Justin turned to Moran. "Why would

you think that Dodd would harm his own children?"

"He already has. I called at Dodd Park the night before he left for London." The cleric shuddered visibly. "I found him whipping his eldest child, Maggie, who is only seven."

"Good God, for what transgression?" Justin asked.

"For trying to protect her three-year-old brother. His father had already whipped him so viciously that I think he might well have killed the boy had Maggie not tried to stop him, and had I not come to call."

Justin felt sick to his stomach. The image arose in his mind of another cringing, terrified boy and an older sibling, this one a brother, who'd been determined to protect him.

"I am terrified that when Mr. Dodd returns from London, he will kill that poor little boy," the cleric warned. "Mr. Dodd is wrongly convinced the boy is not his son. Anyone who knows his kind, good mother will tell you that is ridiculous."

Justin frowned, "Whom does he think the father is?"

"The devil," the cleric said sadly. "In his twisted mind, he thinks the child is the product of his sweet, innocent wife's liaison with the devil."

"Bloody hell!" Justin exclaimed in shock. "Where did he get such a bizarre notion?"

"He says voices, which only he hears, told him so. He claims these voices have instructed him to exorcise the devil and his spawn from the Dodd home. I fear he will beat the poor child to death in his efforts to do so."

"Perhaps now you can understand why I cham-

pion rights for married women," Penford said to
Justin.

Yes, Justin could.

The cleric sighed. "I have not voiced my anxiety
for the boy's life to his mother. You must say nothing in front of her. She is distraught enough already."

"Have you any thought on how I can save my
poor nephew?" Penford asked Justin.

None that was legal. Justin's chair faced one of
the bookcases built into the walls between Corinthian pilasters, and he stared absently at the rows
of leatherbound books.

Finally he said, "I will have to give it more
thought. I am certain I will come up with something." Yes, he would. He could not allow a madman to torment and perhaps kill an innocent child
not long out of the cradle.

"I pray that you can," Mr. Moran said. "I beg you
to act quickly. A delay may well prove fatal. And
it breaks my heart to see those poor frightened children cowering in that gloomy, drafty house."

Penford snorted. "That wretched old house by itself would be enough to frighten a young child,
even without their insane father."

"When was the house built?" Justin asked.

"Back in Tudor times," Mr. Moran answered.
"One old man in Cumberdale claims the house has
one of those secret passages that Catholics back then
built in their homes should they need to escape."

"Do you believe him?" Justin used a skeptical
tone to disguise his interest in this revelation.

Moran shrugged. "Old Abe is in his nineties now,
and he is often confused about things."

Justin asked, "Who controls your living at Cumberdale, Mr. Moran?"

"Sebastian Dodd," he answered wearily.

"You have much to lose by helping his wife," Justin observed.

"Yes," the rector agreed, "but my conscience will not permit me to stand by and do nothing."

Justin nodded in approval. "You are a good man, sir." *And I will do everything I can to see that the risk you have taken is not in vain.*

Mr. Moran declined Georgina's invitation to dine at Penfield, insisting he must return to his parish immediately. As he took his leave, she thanked him again for bringing her aunt to them. Then she went upstairs to dress for dinner.

That meal was a quiet affair despite Georgina's efforts to keep a light, cheerful conversation going. Both her father and Justin were silent and preoccupied. Poor Aunt Margaret looked exhausted despite her nap and seemed lost in her private nightmare.

Only Lanie gamely helped Georgina try to keep the conversation going, but even their lively discussion of Lyell's theories could not draw Justin out of his silence.

After dinner, he surprised Georgina by excusing himself from the gathering in the library. "I must write my brother Henry on a matter of great urgency," he told her. "It cannot wait."

"The post will not be picked up before noon," she warned him.

"I cannot wait for that. I will dispatch my groom at first light tomorrow."

Conversation flourished no better in the library than it had at dinner. When her father asked Georgina to play her harp, she readily complied.

As she played, she kept glancing toward the door

in the hope Justin, having finished his letter, would appear, but he did not. The ornate hands of the bracket clock inched slowly around until it was nearly time to retire. She launched into her final piece.

Midway through it, Georgina glanced up and saw Justin standing in the doorway. In his hand, he held a thick letter. He must have had a great deal to say to his brother.

Justin abruptly turned away and disappeared from the doorway.

When Georgina finished the composition, she rose and accepted her listeners' compliments, then bid her father and Lanie good night. Taking her aunt's arm, she walked upstairs with her.

"My dear niece, your harp never fails to soothe me and make me feel better," Margaret said as they reached the door to her room. "Please, if you are not too tired, come in and sit with me for a few minutes."

Justin handed the long letter he'd written Henry to his groom. "Deliver this to my brother at Woodhaven. Leave at dawn and ride as hard as you can." He pulled a leather pouch of coin from his pocket. "Change horses as often as necessary." He had given Henry much to do, and he had little time in which to do it.

"Yes, my lord. Your brother will be readin' this afore another sun sets."

After Justin left the groom, he passed by the library again. To his disappointment, Gina was no longer playing her harp, and the room was deserted. He went on toward the staircase.

When he reached the top of the stairs, he saw

Gina accompany her aunt into Margaret's room. He continued past his room to Gina's.

Another twenty minutes or more passed before she opened the door and stepped inside. In the pale candlelight, her eyes brimmed with tears. Justin had never seen Gina cry. She was always so cheerful and so strong that he jumped up and hurried to her.

"What is it?" He grasped her upper arms gently with his hands. "Why you are crying?"

She shook her head negatively and began to cry harder.

Usually Justin detested a woman's tears, but Gina's moved him deeply. They were clearly genuine, not an act designed to manipulate him as Clarissa's had been.

He wrapped Gina in his arms, tucking her head against his face and shoulder, comforting and soothing her, much as he had his sister that night in the withdrawing room.

"I'm sorry," Gina sobbed, "but poor Aunt Margaret suffers so. She adores her children, and she is terrified that her husband, in his madness, will maim or kill them. It breaks my heart to see her go through this torture."

Mrs. Dodd's fear was well-founded, but Justin kept that to himself. Something had to be done about her crazy husband, and he intended to do it.

"I do not know how Aunt Margaret bears it. If they were my children, I could not! I know I could not!" Gina looked up at Justin, tears streaming down her cheeks. "You see now why I refuse to marry. Aunt Margaret's experience is a compelling, indeed overpowering, reason."

Keeping one arm around her, Justin lifted her chin with the other so that she had to meet his gaze. "Surely, little wasp, you cannot believe that I would behave in such a cruel manner toward my wife and children?"

The doubt and pain that dulled her eyes as she looked up at Justin stabbed at his heart as nothing had in a long time.

"I don't know what to make of you," she confessed, sounding more uncertain and woebegone than he had ever heard her. "At the moment, all I know is that I want you to keep holding me."

Well, at least that was something, Justin thought, as he folded her in his arms again.

She gave a choked little sigh of pleasure as he held her against him. He stroked her and whispered soothingly until her sobs subsided.

When they did, he gently wiped away her tears with his handkerchief. She did not attempt to escape the arm he still had around her. Instead she nestled closer to him.

Justin was buttoning his shirt when Gina awoke the next morning and smiled at him, her face crinkling and her eyes glowing in the way he loved. She looked so enticing that he could not resist going over to the bed and kissing her.

One kiss led to another. "I shouldn't be doing this," he said. "It's past time I was back in my own room."

As he straightened and moved away from the bed, he thought of how good they were together in bed, the passion they shared.

But that was not enough for her. His mouth tightened. She wanted something that did not exist— romantic love. He turned back to her. "Have you ever been in love, Gina?"

His question clearly startled her. "Why do you ask?"

"You say you would only marry a man you love. But such love is a mirage, and that is the reason you have not found it."

Outrage flared in her eyes, and her glorious smile vanished. "Love is no mirage! I have been in love, and I know it is not!"

The sudden excruciating pain in Justin's heart took him by surprise. "Who was he, this man you were in love with?" he growled.

Her face hardened into stubborn lines. "I refuse to discuss the man I loved, my lord, just as you refuse to discuss your wife and marriage."

Justin knew by the set of her face that it would be useless to press her. The contrary little wasp would never tell him the man's identity.

"But I can assure you, my lord, that love is about so much more than mere lust. It is about companionship—not just physical but also emotional and mental—and about sharing values and interests. It is about mutual compassion, caring, support, trust, and respect. It is about creating a family."

"Then why the hell did you not marry him?" Justin was shocked by the sadness his question brought to Gina's eyes.

"Circumstances made marriage impossible. But do not tell me love does not exist because I know it does!"

"Why did you love him?"

"That, my lord, is not something I can rationally answer." Her voice was so cold it was a wonder Justin did not suffer frostbite. "Did you not say it was past time for you to be back in your chamber?"

He took this pointed hint to leave. As he hurried back to his room, jealousy gnawed at him. Who the hell had Gina loved?

Chapter 22

As Justin finished changing into his riding clothes, he wondered when he would hear from his brother. It had been ten days since his groom had galloped to Berkshire with his urgent letter to Henry. Justin had not anticipated an immediate answer, for he had given his brother much to do, but he had hoped to hear from him by now.

Time was running out for Justin's secret scheme to rescue the Dodd children. It was already the twenty-third, and Sebastian would be returning home from London on the twenty-seventh.

Justin opened the door of his chamber and stepped into the hall, looking quickly in both directions in the vain hope of catching a glimpse of Gina.

She had still been asleep when he'd left her bed this morning. He'd expected to see her at breakfast, but she'd not been there.

When he inquired, he was told she was still abed.

Not wanting to work on the iguanodon without her, he'd decided to ride into Umberside instead and had ordered a horse saddled and brought around while he changed into riding clothes.

Now, properly attired for the saddle, Justin hurried down the marble staircase, his boots clicking against the steps.

As he crossed the entrance hall to the door, a footman hastened to open it for him.

"Is Miss Penford about?" Justin asked.

"I have not seen her yet today, my lord."

Gina was uncharacteristically lazy today, Justin thought as he crossed the portico toward the gray gelding awaiting him at the bottom of the stairs.

When he was mounted, the groom handed him the reins. "Will you be gone long, my lord?"

"Two or three hours, I should think," he answered as he urged his mount forward. He turned the gelding toward Umberside, where he planned to try once more to coax G. O. Douglas's whereabouts out of Simon, the taciturn post rider.

Justin had been at Penfield nearly two months and had not yet uncovered a single clue to Douglas or where he lived. Everyone Justin had questioned, except for Simon, had denied any knowledge of Douglas.

But Justin had been dilatory about pursuing Douglas. He hardly thought of anything these days except Gina.

And never had his thoughts been in such confusion.

He still wondered who the hell the man she'd loved had been and what circumstances had kept them from marrying.

Justin forced his wayward mind back to G. O. Douglas. The man's initials spelled GOD. Perhaps Douglas had a twisted sense of humor. Could the name be a pseudonym he'd chosen with that in mind?

After mulling over that possibility, Justin had asked Gina the previous day, "Do others in the neighborhood share your deep interest in geology?"

"Only Lanie and my former tutor, Gareth, and your knowledge of the subject far surpasses theirs. That's why it's been a pleasure to have you here."

He could not help remarking dryly, "I hope that's not the only reason."

He was rewarded with a pretty blush.

When Justin reached Simon's home in Umberside, the wiry post rider answered the door. The strong smell of cooking cabbage poured through the opening as Justin asked Simon again about Douglas.

Simon squinted at his visitor. "Told you afore, ne'er laid eyes on the man."

"But you cannot deny he receives his mail here at Umberside."

"Don't mean I know him."

Justin pulled two shiny gold guineas from his pocket. "But you could tell me where his mail is delivered."

Simon's eyes widened greedily at the sight of the coins.

"It would be well worth your while to tell me where Mr. Douglas's mail goes."

" 'Tis delivered to Lord Penford at Penfield."

Justin stared at Simon. Bloody hell, had he been that close to the reclusive geologist all the time he'd been in Sussex? "Surely Mr. Douglas does not live at Penfield?"

Simon shrugged. " 'Tis not for me to say, but his lordship sometimes includes with his own letters some from Douglas, too."

The implications of this shocked Justin. Gina had lied to him! Douglas could not live at Penfield without her knowing him. Anger and disillusionment tore through him. His fragile trust and his growing respect for her suffered a severe setback.

Since her father had no interest in geology, Justin had not bothered to ask him whether he might know Douglas, but clearly he did. Who the hell could the man be?

As Justin rode back toward Penfield, he remembered a conversation with Gina.

Where did you acquire your interest in geology? Clearly, not from your father.

No, from my tutor . . . Gareth still lives in the neighborhood.

Gareth! Justin recalled now she had said the man's surname was Davis. He wondered whether Davis's middle initial was *O*. If it was, his initials would match Douglas's.

Justin was considerably more eager to meet the tutor now, but even less disposed to like him. If the mysterious Douglas was her old tutor, he must have been the man that she had loved.

Circumstances made marriage impossible. Marriage between a tutor and his student would have been out of the question.

The clerk cleared his throat loudly, dragging Justin from his confounded thoughts.

" 'Tis all I can tell you about Douglas." Simon's squinty eyes were focused on the two gold coins in Justin's hand. He gave them to Simon.

The man clutched them as though they were part of the crown jewels. "You'll have to ask his lor'ship to whom he gives the man's mail."

"Yes, I intend to do that." *The very moment I reach Penfield.*

Justin rode back to Penfield at a gallop. When he reached the Georgian mansion, he turned his lathered horse over to the groom and ran up the steps of the portico into the house.

"Where will I find Lord Penford?" he demanded impatiently of a liveried footman."

"In the library, my lord."

Justin burst into that room without knocking. Penford sat at a writing table, composing a letter. When he saw Justin, he half rose. "What is it, my lord? You look most agitated."

Agitated didn't begin to describe Justin's seething emotions. "I have been told that you both receive and dispatch G. O. Douglas's mail from here."

Penford studied Justin in silence for a long moment, then said quietly, "Yes, I do."

"What do you do with his mail when you receive it."

"Pass it along to its recipient, of course."

"Who lives at Penfield?"

"Yes."

Justin had been so close to Douglas all this time. He could not stifle his anger, and it echoed in his voice. "I insist upon your introducing us."

"I am sorry but I am sworn to secrecy. Without Douglas's permission, I cannot introduce you. I will ask for it, to be sure, but I doubt very much that it will be granted to me."

"How is it that you know him, yet your daughter who is so deeply involved in this estate does not? Or was she lying to me?"

Penford's expression hardened. "I have never known my daughter to lie," he said coldly. "What did she tell you?"

"That she knew no man by the name of G. O. Douglas in Umberside nor anywhere else in Sussex."

"My daughter did not lie to you. She does not."

Relief flooded Justin that Gina had been honest with him. "Yet Douglas lives on your estate."

"Yes."

"I don't understand," Justin said.

"If you but thought about it, I think you would comprehend."

"Is he living on your estate under an assumed name?"

"No, he is not. You disappoint me, my lord. I thought a man of your acuity would understand immediately. Now, if you will excuse me, I must finish this letter."

Justin left the library and went in search of Gina. He'd not seen her since he'd left her sleeping that morning, and he missed her. Perhaps she could make sense of her father's cryptic remarks.

He checked the drawing room and the morning room, but she was in neither. He inquired of the butler and a maid, but they did not know where she was. Finally, another maid told him she was in the long gallery.

He hurried there. One of the gallery's long walls was lined with full-length family portraits in gilt frames. On the opposite wall, landscapes and other scenes alternated with long windows that looked out on Swan Lake. Gina stood two-thirds of the way down the gallery, staring up at one of the family portraits.

Justin's mood lightened instantly. He hurried toward her, his footsteps announcing him. Gina turned. He was dismayed to see she looked tired and a little haggard. "Are you well?"

She smiled. "I am, only a little tired."

"I missed you at breakfast this morning. I've never known you to sleep so late."

"Everyone is entitled to sleep in now and then," she replied lightly. "Where have you been riding?"

"I went into Umberside." He looked up at the

portrait that she stood before. It was of a thin, plain woman with nothing to recommend her except her smile, which reminded him of Gina's. "Who is she?"

"My mother." Love shone in Gina's eyes as she stared up at the image. "She died when I was sixteen. Both Papa and I were devastated."

"My mother died when I was thirteen."

"How you must have missed her."

"I did not know her well enough to miss her."

"What?" Gina cried, clearly shocked.

"My parents spent nearly all of their time in London. I was raised at Ravencrest by my grandfather. On the rare occasions my mother visited there, she was too busy with social calls and entertainments to spend any time with her sons." Justin could not keep the bitterness from his voice.

Gina's eyes clouded. "I do not understand how a mother could ignore her own children like that. What about your grandfather?"

"He also died when I was thirteen." Justin smiled wryly. "I did miss him."

A portrait of Gina hung to the left of her mother's, and he studied it critically. The artist had failed to capture Gina's vitality and spirit. "It doesn't do you justice."

"Why, thank you. Neither papa nor I care much for it. He hounds me to sit for another artist, but I find it so boring that I keep making excuses."

He looked back at her mother's portrait. "What was your mama's name?"

"Olivia. Mama hated it. My father wanted to name me after her, but she would not hear of it. They compromised by making Olivia my middle name."

Justin glanced at a portrait of a large, ruddy-faced

man to the right of the late Lady Penford's visage. "Who is he? He looks as though he must have been a giant."

"He was. That's my maternal grandfather. The Douglas men were all large, but the Douglas women tend to be rather delicate like my mother."

Justin stared at her. The *Douglas* men. Georgina Olivia.

*I know no **man** named G. O. Douglas.*

You disappoint me, my lord. I thought a man of your acuity would understand immediately.

Justin gaped at her. "Bloody hell, *you* are G. O. Douglas!"

Chapter 23

❧

A ll color bleached from Gina's already pale face, and she kept her gaze fastened on her mother's portrait. "Surely, my lord, you cannot believe a mere female could be a geological theorist?"

"When that mere female is you, I can believe damn near anything!" Justin grumbled. He felt like the world's greatest fool for not having tumbled until now upon the "recluse's" identity. "Why were you not honest with me?"

"But I was." She finally turned and looked at him. "I told you I knew no *man* named G. O. Douglas, and I do not."

"And I imagine you could argue that you know no woman either. Granted *G* and *O* are your initials, but you borrowed your mother's maiden name."

" 'Tis mine too: Georgina Olivia Douglas Penford. I merely dropped my last name."

"Why?"

Gina's eyes narrowed angrily. "Come now, the answer is obvious." Bitterness edged her voice. "Had the editors of the *Transactions* known a woman had written my articles, they would never have published them. And if it becomes known now that I am a woman, I will never be published again.

Worse, my theories will be attacked because of my sex, not because of their merits."

Justin wished he could deny this, but he knew she spoke the truth. And until these past weeks at Penfield, he might well have been one of her vocal critics had he known the truth.

Gina continued to stare up at her mother's portrait. "The theories of G. O. Douglas are much discussed and praised. But the very same theories, if put forward by Georgina Olivia Douglas Penford, would be ignored and ridiculed. I loathe having to hide behind a male-sounding pseudonym, but what choice do I have?"

Justin could not argue with her. "None, I'm afraid," he agreed. She had every right to be angry and bitter. His own ire flared on her behalf.

" 'Tis a man's world," she said.

Yes, he thought with a sigh, it was. For the first time, he grasped what it must be like to be a woman like her with a fine mind, facing all those closed doors to education and professional recognition, doors that would have been open to her had she been born a male, doors that were open to men far less intelligent than she.

"I appreciate your unhappiness and frustration, Gina. "But for God's sake, could you not have told *me* the truth."

"Would you have believed me if I had?"

Justin searched his own mind, determined to answer her as honestly as he could. She deserved the truth. "Perhaps not immediately," he conceded at last, "but certainly within a few days of my being here."

"Would you truly?" Her voice was skeptical and tinged with sadness and doubt.

"Yes, I recognized very quickly that you were

quite unlike any other woman I'd ever met."

"A freak?"

"No, damn it! I meant that as a compliment. I know no other woman with your lively mind and superior intelligence." *Or your magnificent smile, which warms me like the sun. Or your passion both in bed and out of it.*

"Nonsense, you merely know no other woman who is so determined to express herself candidly."

"That too!" he agreed with a smile.

"Justin, don't you see that when men believe women are naturally inferior, they evaluate them through the distorted prism of this baseless prejudice. If we women are inferior, it is only because men have denied us education, opportunity, and power, even over our own property."

"Most women lack your strength and superior understanding."

"When men treat women as weak, frail creatures, they often become what they are expected to be. Look at how different Lanie is with you now that you treat her with respect."

Struck by the truth of this argument, Justin could think of no rebuttal.

"Don't you see, Justin . . ."

She said his given name so beautifully that he loved hearing it on her lips. He wanted to hear it again and again—for the rest of his life.

"Men cannot blame women for faults caused by men's treatment of them."

He smiled at her. "I will concede that. Still, few women possess your intelligence."

Again his compliment seemed to anger rather than please her. "You're wrong, my lord. Few women were blessed with parents as wise as mine.

They insisted on giving me an education usually reserved for a son."

He started to argue, but her expression silenced him.

"Only remember, how you once thought Lanie was stupid."

Justin was ashamed to remember how true that was. Had it not been for Gina, he would still think that. But she had shown him how wrong he'd been—in so many ways.

When Justin went into the withdrawing room before dinner that night, he found his sister standing by the window, looking out. Hearing him come in, she turned away from the window and started toward him.

"How pretty you look, Lanie," Justin said.

Her face lit up at the compliment, and she smiled at him. "Do you really think so?" she asked shyly.

"Indeed, I do," Justin assured her with absolute sincerity. The bodice, big puffed sleeves, and full skirt of her white muslin gown was embroidered with garlands of delicate flowers. "You remind me of spring in full bloom."

She smiled, clearly pleased by his compliment. "It is one of the gowns you had made for me."

When Lanie smiled as she was now, her protruding lower lip was not nearly so noticeable. She was much prettier than Justin had suspected when she had presented only a sullen, pouting countenance to him.

"You were very generous to me, Justin. Thank you."

Her gratitude surprised him. He realized how rarely a woman had ever thanked him for what he did for her.

Both he and his sister had drastically revised their views of each other during the weeks they had been at Penfield. Now they were friends as well as relatives.

Justin had decided weeks ago to let Lanie live with Gina and to hire a tutor for her, but he'd told no one. If he did, he would lose his chief excuse for remaining at Penfield. But he would not keep her in suspense any longer.

He reached out and took her hands in his. "Lanie, I have decided to let you live with Gina and to hire a tutor for you."

To Justin's surprise, Lanie did not look as wildly pleased as he had thought she would. "What is it? I thought that was what you wanted."

"Oh, it is," she hastened to assure him, "but . . ." She did not finish her sentence.

"But what?"

"But will I ever see you again?" Her voice cracked.

A lump rose in his own throat. "Of course you will." Justin wrapped his arms around her and held her tightly to him.

As he released her, Lanie gave him a pleading look. "Would you take me to Ravencrest sometime for a visit. I want so much to see the home where I was born."

The wistfulness in her expression touched Justin. "Certainly. I will take you with me when next I go there."

"You promise?" she cried eagerly.

"I promise!"

Lanie looked as though he had just bequeathed the entire estate to her. "Oh, Justin, I cannot wait. You have made me so happy!"

"What has he done to make you so happy?" Margaret Dodd smiled at Lanie as she came into the withdrawing room.

Gina's aunt looked a little more rested than she had when she'd arrived at Penfield. However, she was still far too thin, and sadness haunted her eyes.

Justin understood the terror she felt for her children's safety. Both she and her children deserved so much better than that cruel, crazy Dodd, and Justin intended to see they got it.

When Penford came into the withdrawing room a minute after his sister, he went directly to Justin. "Georgie tells me you have solved the mystery of G. O. Douglas."

"I feel monumentally stupid not to have realized it sooner," Justin admitted. "It was just that . . ." he broke off with an embarrassed shrug.

"Just that you could not conceive Douglas is a woman."

"Yes, I'm ashamed to admit. One mystery solved, but I still seek the solution to a second. Will you enlighten me?"

"If I can."

"Who was the man your daughter loved?" Since Georgina had told Justin about him, he'd been obsessed with learning the man's identity.

The question clearly surprised Penford. "I was not aware that she'd been in love."

"Well, she was. She told me so herself."

Penford looked even more surprised. "She did?"

"Have you no idea who it could have been?" Justin pressed.

"I can think of only one possibility, but it would be wrong for me to hazard a guess aloud, since I obviously know less about it than you do."

Justin frowned, certain that her father thought her former tutor that possibility.

* * *

Gina looked so tired at dinner that Justin was concerned about her. When the meal ended, she did not accompany them into the library but went up to her bedroom, saying she was terribly tired and wanted to go to bed early.

When Justin retired for the night, he decided against going to her. She was most likely already asleep, and he did not want to disturb her. Gina clearly needed rest.

But in his own bed, he found himself unable to sleep without her beside him.

After tossing about for at least two hours, Justin decided to go down to the library to search for a book to read. As he went down the stairs, he was struck by a sudden impulse to detour to the long gallery to look at the portrait of Gina that hung there.

When he reached the gallery, he discovered he was not the only occupant of the house who apparently could not sleep.

Lord Penford stood near the picture of his daughter. He was not looking at it, however, but at the portrait of her mother. Justin strode toward his host, his footsteps echoing on the polished oak floor.

The lighted taper Penford held in his hand illuminated his face. He was staring up at the likeness of his dead wife with a look of such love and loneliness that Justin felt a lump in his own throat.

Without taking his eyes from the picture, Penford confided, "I loved her more than life itself, and I miss her desperately."

Although Justin did not believe in such love, Penford's voice was so desolate and choked with grief that his absolute sincerity could not be doubted.

"Olivia was my inseparable companion, my dearest friend, my most valued advisor, and my greatest passion."

Penford looked at Justin for the first time. A sheen of tears dulled the older man's eyes.

"Olivia and I shared everything, dreams, problems, interests, ambitions. Life can hold no greater pleasure than to share it with such a mate. Sometimes when I cannot sleep or am deeply troubled, I come down here and talk to her portrait. I think she hears me." Penford's voice broke, and he could not continue.

Justin was unused to seeing a man of Penford's intelligence in the grip of such strong emotion, and he did not know how to offer him comfort. Besides, Justin suspected memory, which tended to recall the good and jettison the bad, had undoubtedly made the union in retrospect seem better than it actually had been. Finally he said, "Lady Penford gave you a fine daughter."

The widower looked over at the portrait of his daughter beside the one of her mother. "Yes, she did. Georgie is so like her mother, not so much in appearance as in her character, intelligence, and compassion."

"Their smiles were much alike, though," Justin observed.

"Aye, Georgie has her mother's wonderful smile. How blessed I am to have had such a wife and now such a daughter."

"You are," Justin agreed with considerable envy.

"My wife made me happier than any man has a right to expect."

"Indeed, I know no other man who boasts of such conjugal bliss," Justin remarked with irony.

"That's because most of the men we know marry for the wrong reasons—connections, fortune, and an heir—and they get what they deserve."

Penford's eyes beneath bushy gray eyebrows seemed to pierce into Justin's soul. "Or they are forced by parents into an arranged marriage, like yours, with a spouse they cannot love or respect."

Justin stiffened at the mention of his own marriage. "Although it's true my father arranged my marriage to Clarissa, he did not have to force me into it. She was beautiful, and I was young and randy. I mistook lust for love."

Clarissa's beautiful facade had vanished immediately after Justin had put the wedding ring on her finger, and he discovered to his anguish the real woman behind the lovely face. His passion for her evaporated along with any illusions about love.

Penford nodded sympathetically. "A frequent occurrence among the very young. Experience is a great teacher, but unfortunately we must commit our follies before we can learn from them."

"True." Clarissa had wasted no time teaching Justin the miseries that marriage could hold for the unwary. He studied his companion curiously. "What do you consider the right reasons to marry?"

"Mutual love, companionship, trust, and respect. My Olivia had a fine mind and a caring heart. She helped me to see what could be done and encouraged me to do it. Sometimes I think she understood me better than I understood myself."

Penford stared up at his late wife's image in silence. A minute or two ticked by before he spoke again. "Ours was a rare and satisfying relationship, a deep and lasting love that nourished us both. She trusted and respected me, as I trusted and respected her."

Despite Justin's skepticism about such love, he was moved by Penford's avowal—and envious.

"Having enjoyed such an idyllic marriage, I am surprised you have not remarried."

"I am not such a fool as that."

"Nor am I," Justin said bitterly.

"But our sentiments spring from very different reasons. I know I could never find another woman like my Olivia, while you fear you might end up with another like Clarissa."

Justin stiffened. "I do not discuss my late wife with anyone."

"I applaud your restraint, but I do not need you to tell me. Her eldest brother was one of my closest friends, and I observed firsthand her . . ." He paused, as though searching for a more tactful word. "—er, tempestuous disposition."

An apt description, Justin thought.

Penford continued, "I, on the other hand, was a very lucky man to find the wife I did. I sincerely doubt I could be so fortunate a second time. No, I much prefer my daughter's company to any other woman's."

So, Justin realized, did he.

"I pray Georgie will find a man strong enough and sufficiently free of typical male prejudice toward women to appreciate what a gem she is."

"She is so opposed to marrying, it won't matter."

"You are wrong, my lord. My daughter's objection has been to the men who have offered for her. She is wise enough not to settle for less than a man with whom she can have a marriage as happy and loving as what her mama and I had. I am confident that when she discovers him, she will marry him."

Penford covered his mouth with his hand to hide a yawn. "I think I will sleep now, my lord. Good night."

For a long time after the viscount left him, Justin

stared up at the portraits of Gina and her mother, considering what Penford had said.

Then, his thoughts in a whirlwind, he abandoned his intention of going to the library and retreated to his bedchamber to sort them out.

Gina and her father had turned Justin's views on marriage upside down. Had he been more mature when he married the first time and been allowed to choose his own bride, might he, too, have found happiness?

As he lay in bed staring into the dark, he thought of how different Gina was from every other woman he'd ever known, especially Clarissa. Gina fascinated him. To his surprise, he'd come to admire her determination to live life on her own terms and not bow to society's strictures.

Yet she was kind and gentle, too. He recalled how acutely perceptive she was of him. When he'd arrived at Penfield, she'd understood immediately why he thought he'd find his sister there and his concern.

Sometimes I think Olivia understood me better than I understood myself.

Olivia's daughter had sensed at once the conflict within Justin between his love for Ravencrest and his hatred of the house there. Not only had she grasped his dichotomy, but she had subtly showed him how he could remedy the situation.

Justin hadn't felt so alive in years as he had since Gina came into his life. The ennui that had gripped him for so long vanished when he was with her.

He, like Penford, needed a wife of compassion, intelligence, and understanding who shared his interests and concerns, his joys and sorrows, not just his bed, to have a truly fulfilling marriage.

And Georgina Penford was that woman.

He realized how much he wanted to marry her.

When he'd come to Sussex, he'd hoped to convince G. O. Douglas to journey with him to the Alps to test his glacier theory. Now Justin would take *her* there for their honeymoon.

Although romantic love was a silly illusion, Gina most certainly had both his respect and his trust, which she believed a happy marriage required. He would have no qualms about placing his own life in her hands.

If I marry at all, it will be to a man I can love and respect. . . . Believe me, I do not fancy myself in love with you, not at all!

What if she would not have him?

The thought chilled Justin.

Chapter 24

Justin did not fall asleep until dawn and awoke well past the usual time he went down to breakfast. He entered the dining parlor, hoping to find Gina waiting there for him. But she was not.

Swallowing his disappointment, he asked the footman presiding over the sideboard, "Has Miss Penford already been down to breakfast this morning?"

"No, m'lord, she had a tray sent up to her room."

"Is she ill?" Justin asked, much alarmed.

"I do not know, m'lord. However, it is most unlike her to have a tray sent up."

Justin's concern for Gina dampened his own appetite. As he left the dining parlor, he met his sister.

"For once, I am up before you," she said. "I am on my way to work on the iguanodon. Will you come with me?"

"Certainly." Better to keep himself busy in the barn than sitting about the house fretting over Gina.

As Justin and Lanie walked to the barn, she said a little timidly, "Please tell me about our brother, Henry."

"What do you want to know?"

"What he is truly like. I always accepted Mama's

299

description of him, which made me quite happy that I did not know him."

Clarissa's handiwork again, Justin thought bitterly.

"But what Mama said about you was so untrue," Lanie continued, "that I wonder now if what she said about Henry was as wrong, too."

Justin smiled at her. "I assure you Henry is a shy, amiable young man. I know you will like him very much when you meet him."

"Will I meet him?" Lanie looked up at Justin with troubled eyes. "Why has he never made the smallest effort to see me?"

Justin picked his words carefully. "He remembers your mama. She made it very clear how much she disliked him. Did you know that she refused to let him live with her and our father. It was a very painful rejection for a child of twelve."

"Oh, I understand perfectly how he felt," Lanie cried in a voice that cracked with emotion. "How dreadful of Mama. Oh, I do want to meet Henry."

"And you will," Justin promised. "When I take you to Ravencrest, I will have him join us there."

They reached the barn and set to work freeing more of the iguanodon from its stone tomb. They worked for more than two hours before Justin suggested they return to the house. He was growing increasingly concerned about Gina. He had expected her to have joined them by now.

When they reached the house, he asked Curwood if she had been down yet and was told she had not.

He went upstairs to change, wondering when Gina would emerge from her room.

His question was answered when he opened the door of his chamber. Gina was waiting there for him.

"What a charming surprise," he said, grinning.

"Usually I am the one waiting for you." Then he sobered. "Are you well? I was very concerned when I heard you'd had a tray sent up to your room this morning."

"I was a little unwell, but it quickly passed. I am quite myself again."

"I'm relieved." She looked well, too. Justin drank in the sight of her mischievous face and slender, enticing figure in a red-and-white checked gown of Caledonian silk. "Had I known you were waiting here for me, I would have been up much sooner."

"I have only been here a minute. I saw you and Lanie returning from the barn."

"To what do I owe the pleasure of this visit?" Justin's gaze fastened on her lovely mouth, and he ached to taste its sweetness.

"Your decision to let Lanie remain here. We must discuss—"

"I know one or two other things I would prefer to do first."

Gina did not try to evade his embrace, and he kissed her hungrily. She returned his kiss with the passion that so delighted—and aroused—him.

It did not take him long to divest them of their clothes. Gina clearly wanted him as much as he wanted her.

But Justin was determined to be patient, to take his time. He wanted to pleasure her beyond anything she had yet experienced. He wanted to convince her to marry him with his body before he asked her in words.

And so he made love to her first with his mouth, kissing her everywhere, and with his hands, tenderly caressing every sensitive spot, and finally with his body, moving in the timeless rhythm of passion.

He loved her slowly and thoroughly, bringing her to climax after shuddering climax.

If her glowing smile was any barometer, he'd succeeded in his aim.

He gently smoothed her damp hair back and caressed her face with his fingertips. "Marry me, Gina."

The smile instantly vanished from her face, and the frown that replaced it broke his heart.

"Justin, stop worrying about your honor."

"Honor has nothing to do with my asking you now. I am doing so because I want to marry you."

She looked at him with the strangest expression he'd ever seen on her face. It was beyond his deciphering.

"Why do you *want* to marry me, Justin?"

"We would suit very well."

She frowned. "Why do you think that?"

"Is it not obvious? We are both fascinated with geology. When I came to Sussex looking for my sister, I hoped that I would also be able to persuade G. O. Douglas to accompany me to the Alps to accumulate evidence in support of his . . . er, her theory. Let me take you there for our honeymoon."

When this enticement did not erase her frown, Justin said, "And I will build a museum to house the fossils you have found. The reconstructed iguanodon skeleton will be its centerpiece."

"Marriage is a lifelong commitment to each other, not a geological expedition or museum, Justin." She sounded exasperated. "What of mutual love, respect, and trust?"

"You have both my trust and my respect. I cannot give you a mirage, romantic love, for which I know you yearn. I will not lie to you about that, for I want total honesty between us."

To his dismay, her frown deepened. He tried a different appeal. "And only think how happy Lanie would be to live with us at Ravencrest."

"Much as I love Lanie, I will not marry any man to make *another* woman happy! Furthermore, you hate the house there."

"But I intend to do as you suggested, build another one there. I have the perfect spot for it, atop a bluff that overlooks the ocean. You will love it. I want you to help me design the house."

"You should build the house *you* want, Justin. I am sorry, but I cannot marry you."

"Why not?" he demanded hotly. "I promise I will make you a good husband."

Gina looked at him sadly. "The way you made your first wife a good husband? You admit you took her inheritance from her. I was told she was forced to wear little better than rags."

"Rags!" Justin echoed bitterly. "I invite you to visit Ravencrest to see closet after closet stuffed with Clarissa's clothes. She often never looked at them again after she acquired them."

"Did you take her jewels away from her? Did you keep her a virtual prisoner at Ravencrest?"

"Damn it, Gina, no more questions! I have already said more than I have ever allowed myself to say before."

"But—"

"No more questions!"

She turned away from him. "How can I marry you when you do not trust me enough to answer my questions?"

"My trust in you has nothing to do with my reason for not answering you, Gina. I told you before *you* are the one who does not trust me enough to reject the lies you've been told about me."

"But you admitted at least one of the allegations against you was true."

His mouth twisted angrily. "So you fear I will rob you of your inheritance, is that it? Given the ugly notion you have of my character, why did you want me as your lover?"

She said airily, "I told you why. It was a scientific experiment."

"Did love have nothing to do with it?"

Her eyes narrowed. "Why would you think that it did, my lord?"

Her cool answer rasped his already raw emotions. "My name is Justin, damn it!"

"I have never told you that I loved you, have I?"

Justin felt as though she had just lashed his heart with a cat 'o nine. "No, but you're the one who believes in love."

"Yes, I do. To find happiness in marriage, a man and a woman must love each other. And that love involves so much more than mere desire. It means a husband and wife who are true partners in life, who mutually respect and trust each other. That's why I will not marry you."

Another lash across his heart. Why the hell should it pain him so that she did not love him when he did not believe it existed?

"But you will sleep with me as part of some damned *experiment*!" Justin glared at her, concealing how much her answer had hurt him behind a facade of anger. "Damn it, I insist you tell me to what purpose I am being used as a guinea pig."

She was clearly reluctant to do so.

"Come now, where's that wasp's tongue of yours?" he snapped.

Gina's eyes flashed dangerously. "I wanted to determine the validity of something that Nancy Wilde claimed. I could not believe it could be so, and I wanted to test it."

"Just what were you testing?" His voice was quiet, ominously so; the calm before the storm.

Gina eyed him hesitantly.

"Tell me, damn it!"

"Nancy told me you were most accomplished at giving a woman enormous pleasure. I wanted to see if that were true."

It was as though Gina had buried her fist in his gut. It took him a second to regain his breath. "Well, was it true?" he ground out.

She blushed. "Yes."

Justin felt used, betrayed. "At least you admit that much!" Anger permeated him the way water soaks through a cloth dropped in a stream. He wanted to throttle both Nancy and Gina. "How many bloody times did it take for me to convince you?"

Her color deepened. "N-Not many," she stammered.

He raised his eyebrows. "The truth, Gina."

She dropped her gaze to his chest. "Once," she admitted, her face scarlet.

His fury rose like steam from the boiling contents of a kettle. He swung himself out of bed, grabbed his pants, and pulled them on.

"Where are you going?"

"Back to my chamber."

"But *this* is your chamber," Gina reminded him.

He stopped dead, feeling like an utter fool. "Then you can leave! I'll be damned if I'll make love to a woman who is using me merely as an instrument to provide her pleasure."

"Is that not what you used Nancy Wilde and your other conveniences for? If it was good for the gander, why should it not be good for the goose?"

"That was different!" he snapped.

"Why? Because you are a man?"

"Damn it, those were business arrangements. Those women were well paid to—"

"Are you saying I should pay you for the pleasure you give me?"

He was so insulted that he sputtered, "Bloody hell, no, that's not—"

"How much do you want, Justin?"

Gina rose as gracefully as a nymph from the bed, and his mouth went dry at the sight of her naked. She had a beautiful body, full-breasted and tiny-waisted. Her skin was as creamy and delicate as fine porcelain. He thought of what it had been like to have her shapely legs wrapped around him while he made love to her. Despite his anger at her, his body instantly sprang to attention.

She snatched up her silk gown he'd removed from her earlier and pulled it on. "What do you estimate you're worth, Justin?" She picked up her petticoats and the rest of her clothes from the floor where they'd been dropped. "What should I pay you for your favors?"

"Nothing! Damn it, stop being ridiculous, Gina. I don't want—"

"Of course not," she interrupted. "You want nothing because you have the control of your money and property. Unlike a woman, you are not at the mercy of a man's whims."

She whirled angrily and, with head held high, disappeared into the hall.

Justin punched his fist into his pillow in disappointment and frustration. He was at his wits' end with Gina. The contrary female was so damned stubborn and strong-willed.

The irony of the situation did not escape him. He who had avoided marriage like the plague now could not coax the only woman he'd ever wanted to marry to the altar. What would it take to get her there?

Georgina could scarcely hold back her tears until she reached her own bedchamber. She shut the door behind her and threw herself on the bed in a paroxysm of weeping.

When she'd asked Justin why he would want to marry her, she'd held her breath. Had he answered that he loved her, she would have accepted him instantly. Instead he'd talked of geology and of a home for Lanie.

Georgina had sworn she would settle for nothing less than a marriage of equality like her parents had. But unless Justin loved her, such a marriage would be impossible.

Love was the powerful glue that held the partners together through the ups and downs that were everyone's lot in life. Love gave them patience and tolerance and understanding. Love was like an oil that kept two parts moving together without friction.

She did not need his title or his money. All she needed was his love. She had to have that.

And she had expected to have it by now. She had gambled in taking Justin as her lover that she could prove to him in time that he was wrong about love. She would prove to him that he, too, could love. But by now, her optimism that she could do so was fading like the light after sunset.

She had gambled, and she had lost.

Much as she loved Justin, Georgina would not jeopardize her dream of a marriage like her parents' by wedding a man who did not return her love and trust. She had seen too many unions in which the spouses grew indifferent to or even came to despise each other.

Several minutes passed before she could manage to stop crying. What was wrong with her? Georgina had only contempt for weepy females, yet for the past two or three days she'd been on the verge of tears half the time.

Chapter 25

⌒⦿⌒

S hortly before dinner that evening, an express arrived for Justin. The messenger insisted upon personally delivering the thick letter into its recipient's hands.

Justin, who was summoned to the entrance hall to receive the letter, sighed in relief when he saw his brother's handwriting on it. At last! Justin had only two days in which to act before Dodd would return from London.

The coins Justin handed to the messenger elicited a grin and repeated thanks from the man as he departed. Eager to read what his brother had to say, Justin stood right where he was, beside a fresco of frolicking maidens and cherubs, and broke the wax seal.

He read through three pages closely filled with his brother's neat handwriting and examined the maps and diagrams that Henry had enclosed.

As Justin refolded the sheets, he smiled in satisfaction and slid the letter into a pocket of his coat, glad that he had sent Henry to Cumberdale. He had discovered everything Justin needed to know in his daring plan to rescue Mrs. Dodd's children.

But he had very little time left to execute it before

Sebastian returned from London. Justin would leave for Cumberdale tomorrow.

At dinner, Justin was polite to Georgina but said little. Yet he seemed more preoccupied than angry, she decided.

As they finished their soup, her father said, "You are very quiet tonight, Ravenstone. I hope the express you received before dinner was not bad news."

Georgina looked up in surprise. She had not heard about the express.

"No, good news," Justin said, "but I will be required to leave here in the morning for a business engagement to which I am committed tomorrow night."

For some reason, it was all Georgina could do to keep from bursting into tears at that news. What was wrong with her?

"Do you return to London?" her father asked.

"No, actually my engagement is near Cumberdale." Justin looked at Aunt Margaret. "I was thinking if you would be willing to leave two days early, I could drop you off there. It would not be out of my way, and I would be delighted to have your company on the journey."

"How very kind of you," Aunt Margaret exclaimed. "I shall accept your offer if you are certain I am not imposing on you."

"Not at all," he assured her. "We will leave about eleven-thirty."

Georgina studied Justin suspiciously. He was plotting something. She was certain of it.

But what?

* * *

After dinner, Justin asked that he and Penford re-main in the dining room to drink their port so that they could talk. He must tell the viscount what he planned for Mrs. Dodd and her children. Perhaps he could also pick up some advice from his lordship on how to handle his daughter. *God knows, I can use it.*

Gina rose from the table, clearly miffed. "So, my lord, you want to exclude us females from your company."

Justin hated it when she called him my lord. "Only for a little while. We will join you shortly."

Gina looked recalcitrant, but her father said, "Go along now, Georgie."

She obeyed him, but she clearly was not happy about doing so. At the door, she turned and gave Justin a look simmering with suspicion.

When the door closed after the women, Penford looked at him expectantly, but Justin could not think how best to begin what he had to say. He absently ran his finger down the side of his glass of port.

His host studied him with shrewd, penetrating eyes. "Does this have to do with my sister or my daughter?"

"Both," Justin said, thankful for this help. "I'll start with your sister." He briefly outlined what he planned for the following day.

When he finished, Penford asked, "Why are you undertaking such a perilous mission on behalf of my sister?"

Justin had asked himself that same question, and he answered Penford as truthfully as he could. "I cannot sit back and do nothing when innocent chil-dren are in danger. My conscience will not permit it."

"If anything goes awry in your plan, it would have most disastrous consequences for you," Penford warned.

"I know that. It is a risk I am willing to take. The alternative is unthinkable to me."

"I admire your courage—and your conscience. I am also more grateful to you than words can possibly convey." He paused. "I do agree with your decision against telling my sister what you want her to do until the last possible moment. It will save you considerable argument."

"That was my thought."

"I shall happily pay for the upkeep of my sister and her children. I do not want to impose a burden on your brother."

"That is not necessary."

"I consider it very necessary." Penford took a swallow of port. "Now, what have you to say to me about my daughter?"

"I wish your permission to marry her."

Penford did not seem in the least surprised by Justin's request. "You'd be better employed trying to win *her* permission."

Justin smiled ruefully. "I have been trying. I have asked her a number of times, and she continues to refuse me. But I am determined to persuade her to marry me."

"How do you intend to persuade Georgie if she has already refused you a number of times?" Penford asked bluntly.

"A good question," Justin conceded. He'd tried seduction but he'd been the one seduced. She'd even offered him money, for God's sake. He felt his face growing hot at the recollection. Only one thing was certain. The little wasp would never bore him!

"What is my daughter's objection to marrying you?"

"We do not love each other."

"Then why would *you* want to marry her?"

"I think we could have the kind of happy and fulfilling marriage that you and her mother had."

"Without love?" Penford sounded incredulous.

Justin nodded. "You see, I do not believe in romantic love. My marriage to Clarissa cured me of any such foolish notions."

"Why do you say my daughter does not love you?"

"She told me so quite explicitly."

"Did she now? What exactly did she say?"

"That she did not fancy herself in love with me."

"I see." Penford looked amused.

His reaction affronted Justin, who did not find Gina's lack of love for him at all amusing. He picked up his glass from the table and took a gulp of port. "You do not seem surprised by my request for Georgina's hand."

"I have been expecting it for the past month— since you and my daughter became lovers."

Justin choked on the port. "She told you?"

"No."

"Then how?" he sputtered.

"I am far more observant than you think, my lord."

Justin took a larger gulp of port. "I am astonished you made no objection. Why not?"

"If you are lucky enough to have a daughter like Georgie, you will understand some day."

"Do I have your permission to marry her?"

"Of course, but only if she accepts you. I have thought for some time you would make her an excellent husband."

"I wish she agreed with you. Perhaps you can help me. You won her mother's hand, and you say Gina is much like your late wife. What advice can you give me?"

"Ask Georgie to help you."

"To help me what?" Justin asked in astonishment. Ask a *woman* for help? He'd never in his life even considered doing so.

"To help you with your scheme tomorrow."

Justin set his glass down hard on the table. "How can you suggest that when not three minutes ago you warned me of the disastrous consequences that could befall me? I would not think you would want her anywhere near Cumberdale."

"I don't, but you must show her that you value and trust her."

"I would not want to marry her if I did not value and trust her."

"Of course, you wouldn't. However, actions often speak louder than words. Now, here is what I suggest."

A footman appeared at the drawing-room door. Breaking off her conversation with her aunt and Lanie, Georgina looked inquiringly at him.

"Your father wishes to see you at once in the dining parlor."

Georgina jumped up in alarm. What had Justin told her father that caused him to send for her now?

As she entered the dining parlor, both men stood, their faces grave, adding to her unease. She steeled herself. "What do you want?"

But it was Justin, not her father, who answered her. "Your help," he said bluntly.

Georgina stared at him in surprise, her heart leaping with hope and excitement. Had she not just heard him, she would never have believed that he would ask for a woman's help—and in front of her father, too! If he was sincere, it would mean so much to her. She appreciated how hard it must have been for a man of Justin's strength and self-reliance to ask a woman for assistance.

"How can I help?" Even if Justin had not asked her, something shimmered in the air, a sense of conspiracy, of adventure, and Georgina responded eagerly, anxious to be part of it.

"I want you to go with your aunt and me when we leave tomorrow. I need your help in persuading her."

"Persuading her to do what?" Georgina asked.

"After we leave tomorrow, I will meet my brother, Henry, at the Five Points Inn. I want him to take your aunt to Woodhaven, my estate in Berkshire that he is currently renovating. The property has a dower house where she can live very comfortably. Her husband will never find her there."

"But Aunt Margaret will not go with your brother. She will refuse." Georgina looked at her father. "You know that, Papa."

"So do I," Justin said. "That's why I need your help. I am counting on you to convince your aunt to accompany you and my brother to his estate. I believe she will be more willing to go, if you are with her."

"Nothing will ever persuade Aunt Margaret to live in Berkshire, far from her children."

"They will be there with her."

Justin spoke so quietly that the implication of his answer did not instantly register on Georgina. When it belatedly did, she gasped and looked toward her father for confirmation.

He nodded, clearly understanding her unspoken question.

Justin explained, "While you and your aunt go with Henry, I will continue on to Dodd House to get the children."

Georgina gaped at him. "How on earth do you think you will get Sebastian to give them up?" *But how wonderful for Aunt Margaret if Justin can manage it.*

A sardonic half-smile twisted one corner of his mouth. "It's better you not know, Gina."

She gasped as she comprehended his intention. "You are planning to abduct them! That's why you're going two days before Sebastian returns from London."

Justin said nothing, neither confirming nor denying.

Georgina frowned. "But why would you undertake such a dangerous course for someone you scarcely know?"

"I feel I have come to know your aunt quite well since she has been here. Nor will my conscience permit me to leave three innocent, helpless children with that madman."

Georgina felt as though her heart were bursting with love for Justin. If only he could love her in return.

"Will you accompany us tomorrow and help me persuade her to go to Berkshire with Henry?" Justin asked.

"Certainly!" Georgina intended to give him a good deal more help than that. She would not be left out of such a grand adventure. From the sly smile on Papa's face, she suspected he'd guessed as much.

"Good. I am certain she will go more easily with

my brother if you go with her to Woodhaven."

"I will only go as far as the Five Points Inn with her." Georgina was determined to be honest with Justin. "Then I am going to Dodd Park with you."

His features hardened into what Georgina had come to think of as his pirate face. "No, you're not! It's too damned dangerous for you."

She smiled at him. "Listen to me, please, Justin. You need me with you. Do you think those poor abused children will go off with a strange man they've never seen before? They know me."

"My daughter is right," Penford interjected. "Not only do the children know her, they love her. They'll happily go with her."

"You both have a point, but I cannot involve Gina in such a risk. I don't know what will happen when I reach Dodd Park. I will not put her in danger. Sebastian is a madman, capable of anything."

"But he will not be there," Georgina noted.

"No, but there will be hell to pay when he learns his children are gone."

"I am not afraid."

"No, but you should be, little wasp." His voice was surprisingly gentle, and the look in his eyes embraced her heart.

Determined to go with him, she cried, "Only think, how will you manage on the long trip to your brother's with three small, terrified children on your hands?"

From his expression, he clearly had not thought of that, and the prospect appalled him.

Georgina rushed in to widen this breach in his defenses. "Believe me, you will be delighted to have me with you then."

He smiled at her in a way that made her heart somersault. "I am delighted to have you with me any time, but I do not want to place you in danger."

"You asked me for my help. Now, let me give it to you."

Justin looked questioningly at her father.

"I think my daughter is right. Let her go with you."

Justin looked uncharacteristically uncertain. "If I do, will you promise to do as I say, Gina? I want nothing to go awry nor any harm to befall you."

She nodded. "I promise."

He still looked worried, but he said, "Then I'll take you with me."

Chapter 26

Georgina expected Justin to come to her that
night, but he did not. She yearned to go to
him, but she would not chance having him ask her
to leave, as he had this afternoon.

She recalled with amusement how shocked and
repelled he'd looked when she'd offered him
money. Poor Justin, he wasn't used to a woman
who was as independent as she was.

But as she lay in her lonely bed, her amusement
soon faded. She missed Justin's hard warmth and
comfort beside her too much, and she could not
sleep.

She'd been tossing and turning for more than an
hour when the door opened and shut so quietly she
wondered if she were imagining it. She turned as a
large figure glided through the darkness toward her
bed.

"Justin?" she whispered.

"Yes." He shrugged out of his robe and climbed
into bed beside her.

"Why are you here?"

He sighed wearily as he pulled her against him.
"It's either sleep with you or not sleep at all."

Georgina feared the same held true for her. She

snuggled against him, his closeness comforting and relaxing her. Within minutes she was asleep.

When she awoke the next morning, Justin was standing by her bed, tying the sash on his robe. His unruly black hair was disheveled, and a thick stubble covered his jaw. Her own dear pirate, she thought with a smile.

"Good morning." She held out her arms to him.

His jaw tightened as though he were steeling himself to resist her. Instead of accepting her invitation, he remained standing. "Marry me, little wasp."

She dropped her arms. "Justin, we have been through this before."

"What if you are pregnant?"

"I can't be," she gasped.

"No?" He raised a mocking brow.

That gesture angered her into saying, "And if I am, even more reason not to marry you. I will not allow any man to do to me what Aunt Margaret's husband has done to her and her children."

Justin looked so enraged that she involuntarily pressed herself against the bed.

"I am not Sebastian Dodd, damn it!"

She stared silently, defiantly at him.

"How could you possibly think I might be?"

She turned away from him, unable to meet his furious gaze.

His hand grasped her chin in an iron grip, and he turned her face back toward him. "So, out of the groundless fear that I could be another Sebastian Dodd, *you* would do to *me* what he did to your aunt. Keep my child from me."

Georgina gasped in dismay. She had not thought of it in that light.

"Damn you, Gina, would it not be just as cruel

and wrong for you to deny me my rights to our child as it would be for me to take him or her from you? A child needs both parents!"

She could think of no argument to counter this, which made her defensive, and she cried, "Dodd's children don't need a father like him!"

Justin looked as though she had stabbed him. He whirled and stalked from the room without a backward glance, slamming the door hard behind him.

Georgina pushed herself into a sitting position. Such a strong wave of nausea swept over her that she clapped her hand over her mouth and lurched out of bed.

What if you are pregnant? Dear God, could that be what was the matter with her?

She ran to the basin on the washstand and bent over it, every bit as sick to her stomach as she had been the previous two mornings. That was why she had not come down to breakfast either day.

The first day, she'd thought she'd recovered when the nausea disappeared about noon and did not recur the rest of the day. But the next morning, the nausea was back, once more vanishing shortly before noon.

Now it had returned again.

Thinking back, she calculated that her monthly flow, usually as regular as the full moon, was at least two weeks overdue. Her hand touched her stomach in wonder, and a volatile mixture of emotions that contained both elation and fear flooded her.

If only Justin loved her, she would be the happiest woman in England to be carrying his child, but he could not give her what he was convinced did not exist.

And what of his treatment of his first wife?

*You are the one who does not trust me enough to reject
the lies you've been told about me.*

But why would he not confide the truth to her?

Georgina burst into tears. She hated herself for
crying, but she could not seem to help it. She had
turned into a damned watering pot.

As Justin's coach sped through rolling green
countryside, Georgina listened quietly to him question Aunt Margaret about her husband.

Georgina had feared Justin might be so angry at
her that he would refuse to take her with him, but
he did not protest when she appeared at the coach
in her sapphire blue traveling gown.

In fact, he said nothing at all to her, merely
handed her into the equipage. After that, she might
as well not have been in the coach for all the attention Justin paid her. At least, though, her nausea
had disappeared before they started out.

Aunt Margaret never talked about her husband,
but Justin drew her out with such skill and sympathy that Georgina soon learned much that she
had not known before.

"How long has your husband been hearing these
voices of his, Mrs. Dodd?" he asked.

"About three years."

"What do they say to him?"

"He says they warn him of his enemies who are
under the devil's control and are attempting to destroy him." Tears glistened in Aunt Margaret's eyes
and her voice cracked. "The list seems to include
almost everyone. There's hardly a soul he does not
suspect."

Georgina took her aunt's hand in her own and
clasped it comfortingly.

"The servants told me he's become very like his

grandfather, who heard voices, too. By all accounts, Sebastian's grandfather was a cruel and capricious man. He did not hesitate to take a horsewhip to his servants or anyone else in his power who dared to displease him, including his only grandson."

She could no longer hold back her tears, and she cried, "I am so frightened for my poor babies."

As Georgina tried to comfort Margaret, hugging her and murmuring soothingly, she glanced over at Justin. The deep compassion he clearly felt for the distraught woman touched her.

Several minutes passed before her aunt could control her weeping.

"How old are your children, Mrs. Dodd?" Justin asked gently.

"Maggie, the eldest, is seven; Beth is six; and little Seth is three." Her voice broke again. "I have not seen him other than at a great distance since he was one. Now I cannot see him or the girls at all."

"Why not?" Justin asked.

"A few months ago, Sebastian ordered the fence of iron palings that surrounded the house at Dodd Park removed and a brick wall eight feet high erected in its stead. He said it was to keep his enemies out. I think, however, it was also to prevent me from catching even the smallest glimpse of my babies as I was able to do on rare occasions through the old fence."

The coach slowed, and Georgina looked out the window to see the reason.

They were approaching the Five Points Inn, a two-story, half-timbered building with a thatched roof. It had gotten its name from its position at a junction where roads radiated out in five directions like spokes from a wheel hub.

As the coach turned into the inn's enclosed yard,

Margaret cried in alarm, "Where are we? This inn is not on the road to Cumberdale."

"No, Aunt Margaret, it's not." Georgina took both of her aunt's hands into her own. "Listen to me. Justin's brother is meeting us here with his coach, and he will take you to Woodhaven, Justin's estate in Berkshire, where you will be safe from Sebastian."

"I don't care about myself!" Margaret's voice rose to a hysterical pitch. "Don't you understand, it is my children I want safe from him!"

"And they soon will be safe with you at Woodhaven, Mrs. Dodd, if you will accompany my brother," Justin assured her.

She stared at him in confusion.

A youth of perhaps sixteen with sandy hair and a freckled face ran up to the coach. He would have opened its doors for them, but Justin gestured him away. "My brother has not arrived yet. We might as well wait for him in the coach."

Margaret recovered her voice. "What—what do you mean about my children?"

Georgina squeezed her aunt's hands harder. "He is saying you must go with his brother who will hide you and your children from Sebastian."

"But where are my babies now?"

"They are still at Dodd Park," Justin replied, "but I will soon bring them to you at my brother's."

"But—"

Georgina interrupted. "You must trust Justin, Aunt Margaret. He will do what he says. Please go with his brother as he asks."

From the corner of her eye, Georgina caught Justin watching her with the strangest expression.

The sound of another coach approaching distracted her, and she glanced through the window as an old, battered black coach, sadly inferior to Justin's in appearance and luxury, rolled into the inn yard and stopped near theirs.

"But, Georgina, I—" her aunt's voice faltered.

"Do it, Aunt Margaret," Georgina said firmly. "It is the only way to make your children safe." She prayed that she spoke the truth.

"I'll go," Margaret capitulated. "I will do anything that might help them."

The door of the newly arrived coach opened, and a young man jumped down. With a broad smile, he started toward Justin's considerably more elegant equipage.

As the man approached, Georgina looked toward Justin. The affection she saw in his face for the stranger startled her.

Justin flung open the coach door and stepped out to meet him. When Henry saw his brother, his expression left no doubt he returned Justin's affection. They embraced warmly.

Georgina studied the newcomer. Henry bore only a small resemblance to his older brother. His hair was not as black as Justin's, his eyes were a lighter brown, and his nose was smaller and straighter.

Although the shape of Henry's face was much like his brother's, it lacked the hard planes that made Justin's so memorable to her. Henry was also four inches shorter and more slightly built.

Justin looked over the coach in which his brother had arrived and grinned. "You have followed my instructions most admirably. Where on earth did you find that disgusting coach?"

Henry chuckled. "Hidden in the very back of a livery yard in Lower Frampton. It's ordinarily dragged out only for large funerals. When I saw it, I was certain it was what you wanted."

"It's perfect." Justin said something else to his brother that Georgina could not hear. Henry promptly headed toward the inn door while Justin exchanged warm greetings with the coachman and the groom riding on the box of the shabby coach. He called them Monson and Cray.

"How pleased I am that you both will be with me today," Justin said.

Monson's round face broke into a smile. "Looking forward to helping, we are, m'lord."

Returning to his own coach, Justin assisted Georgina and Margaret down from it.

"My brother has gone to hire a private parlor where you can rest and take some refreshment before we leave." He guided the women toward the inn door through which Henry had disappeared.

The freckled youth whom Justin had waved away from the coach rushed now to open the inn door for them.

When they stepped inside, the proprietress led them down a narrow, unadorned hall to a plainly furnished room, dominated by a round pine table with a badly scarred top and four chairs. A wine-colored sofa had been pushed under the window, and Justin led Margaret to it.

"I believe this will be more comfortable for you," he said.

As she sank down on the sofa, Henry said, "I have ordered food and drink. It will be here shortly."

"Come, Henry." Justin nodded toward the door. "If you will excuse us, ladies, my brother and I will be back shortly. If the food comes before we do, don't wait for us."

Fearing Justin might depart from the inn without her, Georgina jumped up and hurried after them.

In the hall, Justin turned and frowned at her. "I promised I would take you with me, and I will. I am only going to explain to Monson and Cray what I require of them. Is it not time for you to display some of the trust for me that you urged your aunt to have?"

She deserved that. "Yes, it is," she said with a smile. She lightly touched his sleeve before returning to her aunt.

Georgina glanced out of the window above the wine sofa where Margaret sat and saw Justin, his brother, Monson, and Cray deep in conversation. Then Justin pulled a paper from his pocket and moved his finger over the surface, clearly pointing out something. She wondered what it could be.

A few minutes later, the proprietress came into the room to spread a white linen cloth over the scarred deal table. She was followed by two servants carrying heavy trays of food and drink. As they set the dishes on the table, Georgina realized she was famished now that her nausea had disappeared.

After the servants left, Georgina filled a plate with foods she knew her aunt would like and brought it to her, then returned to the table to do the same for herself. She took one of the chairs by the table.

When Justin and Henry came in a few minutes later, they, too, filled their plates.

Georgina hoped that Justin would take the chair beside her own, but instead he crossed the room and joined Aunt Margaret on the wine sofa. Henry sat down in the chair next to Georgina's.

She smiled at him. "I hope my aunt and her children will not be an intrusion on your privacy at Woodhaven. You must be quite astonished that your brother has taken such an intense interest in their welfare.''

"Not at all.'' Henry glanced at his brother, his love for him apparent on his face. ''Justin would never turn his back on a helpless child in need of protection. He is the best of men.''

Georgina was moved by this clearly sincere tribute. "You obviously love your brother very much.''

Henry smiled. "Yes, I do. I dread to think what would have happened to me were it not for Justin. He was far more of a father to me than my own ever was.''

"What do you mean?''

"Our parents paid little attention to us. They left us at Ravencrest from our infancy while they spent their time in London.''

I did not know my mother well enough to miss her.

Georgina was appalled that parents could have ignored their children like that.

"Justin says he was the lucky one because he had our paternal grandfather to raise him. I was very happy that I missed that luck and had Justin instead.''

Henry's smile reminded Georgina of Justin's. "Why do you say that?''

"Grandfather was determined that his grandson not turn out as his lazy, irresponsible son had. The old man blamed our mother for leading our father astray. He did not like women very much.''

Like his eldest grandson, Georgina thought.

"Grandfather was a fanatic about honor and duty and very strict with my brother. But he trained him well. He was very proud of Justin. I think he loved him in his way.''

"You think?'' Georgina probed.

Henry nodded. "Grandfather was one of those

proud, gruff men who think it unmanly to display any sentiment. They must always conceal their feelings. He died when my brother was thirteen. I was only four then, but I still remember how badly Justin took his death. It was the only time I ever saw my brother cry."

Henry's own voice wavered, and he paused, staring through the window above the sofa where Justin and Margaret sat, talking quietly. Georgina said nothing. Henry had given her too much to consider.

After a minute, Henry resumed. "When Grandpapa died, my father grudgingly returned to Ravencrest. But after our mother died there four months later, Father, who adored her, went off permanently to drown his sorrows in London's pleasures, leaving my brother and me behind in the care of indifferent servants."

"How terrible!" Georgina cried, aghast that grieving children—the younger one only four years old—bereaved of two of the most important figures in their lives, had been left alone like that.

"Not for me," Henry said with a smile. "I had Justin. He became my comforter, my protector, my teacher, even my nurse. I was a weak, frail child, too small for my age, and he watched over me like a mother hen. I think I would have died without him and his love for me. In every way but one, he was my father, and I could not have asked for a better one. Is it any wonder I love him?"

"No." Georgina pushed the word past a lump in her throat that felt the size of a boulder. When she trusted her voice enough to speak again, she said, "I hope your father at least left Ravencrest in the hands of a good steward."

"No, my father was heedless to all responsibility," Henry said bitterly.

"You sound as though you hate him."

"I do."

Georgina, so close to her own loving parent, could not imagine anyone hating his father. "Why? Because he neglected you as a child?"

"No, I hate Father for what he did to Justin. He robbed my brother of his childhood and his happiness. Justin protected me, but he had no one to protect him."

Georgina put her plate of half-eaten food aside, no longer hungry after Henry's revelations.

"Ravencrest was sadly neglected until my brother shouldered the burden of saving it. He wanted to go to Eton and Oxford to study natural philosophy. Instead he stayed at Ravencrest, taking on a man's responsibilities while he was still a boy and doing what my father was too lazy and frivolous to do."

Henry drained the last of his ale.

"You and Miss Penford seem to have much to talk about, Henry."

Georgina started. She'd been so engrossed in what Henry said, she had not noticed that Justin and her aunt had left the sofa.

"If you have finished eating, we must be on our way," Justin said.

She rose hastily. "Yes, of course."

When they went outside, the sun had at last poked through the clouds. The inn yard was deserted except for their two coaches and a black saddle horse tied to a post. The animal had not been there when she'd gone into the inn.

She turned to her aunt. "Don't worry, Aunt Margaret, we will bring your children to you,"

The two women hugged in farewell.

"Be careful," Margaret whispered. "I am so torn. I wish you would come with me, yet I know it will be easier for my poor babies if you are there."

"The most important thing is to get them away before Sebastian returns from London," Georgina said.

"Time to go." Justin took Margaret's arm and guided her toward his own carriage. "Henry and I are trading coaches. I will reclaim mine when we reach Woodhaven with your children." Justin handed her into his coach.

As Margaret settled herself, she said to him, "God be with you and my niece. May He keep both of you safe."

Henry climbed in after her, and Justin motioned for the coachman to depart.

As his equipage rolled away, Justin turned, took Georgina's arm, and led her to the shabby coach his brother had hired. As he handed her into it, her nose wrinkled at the stale odors of old food and older tobacco that permeated it. The coach's interior, like its exterior, was all black. Even the heavy curtains at the windows were black.

She slid across the cracked leather seat to make room for Justin. Instead of climbing in after her, however, he shut the door.

"Are you not coming?" she asked.

He gestured toward the black horse tied to the railing. "I will ride ahead on horseback."

"Why?" she asked, astonished at how disappointed she was that he would not be accompanying her. "Are you still angry at me from this morning?"

One corner of his mouth lifted in a half-smile. "Only mildly irritated, little wasp. I am riding ahead because I want to study Dodd Park before you arrive. I have alternative plans in mind, and I must decide which gives us the best chance of rescuing the children."

She suspected that he might try to do more than that before she got there. "Oh, Justin, please be careful. I—" She broke off abruptly. She'd nearly forgotten herself and told him how much she loved him.

He looked at her curiously. "You what?"

"I—I do trust you."

"Well, that's a start," he said dryly. "I'll see you at Dodd Park. Monson knows where to meet me." He turned and strode briskly to the horse at the railing, mounted, and rode out of the inn yard.

Chapter 27

According to the map Henry had drawn, the road Justin was following out of Cumberdale bisected Dodd Park, cutting off much of the estate's land from its house, which was situated about a mile from the village.

Ahead of him, a baggage wagon piled high with trunks and boxes traveled at a sedate pace. Beyond the conveyance in the distance, Justin saw the high brick wall that Margaret Dodd mentioned Sebastian had built around the house.

As he pulled around the wagon, he noticed another wagon carrying more trunks and cases turning into Dodd Park. An unhappy suspicion seized him.

He slowed his mount and said casually to the wagon driver, "Fully loaded, I see."

"Aye," the man said sourly. "Madman Dodd ne'er travels light."

His suspicion confirmed, Justin hid his alarm behind an indifferent expression. "I thought he was not due back at Dodd Park for two more days."

"Already there, he is. Came back early, more's the pity."

"Aye 'tis, and a good day to you." Justin urged

his mount to a faster pace, cursing his rotten luck. He'd hoped to have the children far away from here before Dodd reached home.

His return made Justin's scheme infinitely more complicated, dangerous, and difficult. He berated himself for agreeing to let Gina come. He never should have let her prevail upon him.

He slowed his mount as he reached the brick wall. Had he not been on horseback, the wall would have hidden much of the house and the grounds around it.

Not that the house was much to look at. Built of rough gray stone, it sprawled haphazardly across a flat piece of ground. Its few windows were small and set with tiny diamond panes of leaded glass. The monstrosity looked even more uninviting, drafty, cold, and uncomfortable than the house at Ravenstone. His heart ached for the poor children trapped inside.

He passed the house and continued along the road until he reached the corner of the wall. A path ran along the side wall, and he guided his mount onto it.

The house and grounds within the walls were exactly as Henry had described them. While Henry had been in Cumberdale, he'd heard about numerous incidents of Dodd's bizarre behavior. Everyone there called him "Madman" Dodd and took care to stay out of his way.

Only the very dregs would work for him. Several people had expressed concern to Henry for Dodd's children, whom he'd left in the care of "a drunken slut."

While in Cumberdale, Henry'd also visited Abe Doherty, the old man Mr. Moran had mentioned. Abe had told Henry of a secret passage built long ago that led from Dodd's bedchamber to a trapdoor hidden in a children's playhouse located behind the house just inside this brick wall.

Justin had intended to use this passageway to gain access to the house, thinking Dodd would be in London and his chamber empty. He'd left only a skeleton staff of servants at Dodd House while he was gone.

So now Justin would have to contend with Dodd's possible presence in his bedchamber and more servants about the house to notice an intruder.

Justin was not worried about getting himself into the house. That should be easy enough. He would make certain Dodd's chamber was empty before he emerged from the secret passage.

The most harrowing danger would come when he gathered the children from the nursery and took them to their father's room one floor down. Not only did they risk being spotted as he led the children from the nursery to the chamber, but Dodd, his valet, or some other servant might go into it while Justin was collecting the children, cutting off their access to the secret passage.

He reached the corner where the side and back walls came together, about forty yards behind the rambling old house. A road, so narrow it was scarcely wide enough for a wagon, ran between the high brick wall and a copse of goat willow and alder.

He turned down this road and soon reached a tall gate of heavy wood planks set in the back wall exactly where Henry's drawing showed it to be.

Several feet from the gate along the wall, Justin saw the crumbling children's playhouse that hid the trapdoor to the secret passage.

Henry had warned him it was not in good repair,

but he was shocked to see the small structure's old thatched roof had partially collapsed. Hunks of plaster had fallen away from the walls, exposing the wood lath beneath.

He hoped the hidden passage was in better shape than the structure that concealed it. If not, he was in for an even more difficult time than he'd yet anticipated.

Justin rode close to the gate. Leaning over it, he saw it was securely fastened by a heavy bolt, as Henry had warned it would be. The bolt was set only a foot or so below the top of the gate, where it would be difficult for anyone but a very tall man to reach it.

Justin dropped his hand down on the interior side of the gate and slid the bolt back. Then he rode into the copse on the other side of the road and dismounted. He led his horse deeper into the thick shrubbery, detouring around a small spring that bubbled up, creating a marshy puddle.

When he reached a spot where he was certain his horse could not be seen from either the road or the house, he stopped and tied the animal to an alder sapling.

Returning to the road, he crossed it and stopped abruptly at the smothered sound of a child crying in pain and fear.

The pitiful noise seemed to be coming from the playhouse, and he hurried silently along the brick wall to the sorry structure where he listened intently.

"Hush, don't cry, Seth," a little girl's voice pleaded. "We are safe here."

"I'm . . . so . . . afraid," Seth managed to get out between sobs. "What . . . if . . . someone . . . finds us . . . Maggie?"

"No one will if only you will stop crying."

"I's tryin'," Seth said. "But my legs hurt so I can't stan' it!"

"I know they do," Maggie said. "But if we keep quiet, no one will think to look for us here because we are forbidden to go inside."

"What if it falls down on us," another little girl's voice said. "I'm afraid."

"Not so loud, Beth," Maggie whispered. "I'm more afraid of what Papa will do to Seth. I've never seen Papa as bad as he was this afternoon." The child's voice quavered. "I was so thankful when Mr. Thomas came to talk to Papa, and he had to let Seth go."

"But we can't stay here," Beth complained. "What will we do?"

"After its dark tonight, I'll find a ladder so I can open the gate, and we'll run away."

Justin's cup of gratitude overflowed. His task would be infinitely easier now with the children already out of the house. Dodd's early return had turned out to be a blessing in disguise.

"Where'll we go?" Beth whined.

"To Mr. Moran. Maybe he'll help us."

"He won't dare," Beth said in a bitter tone. "No one dares. They're too afraid of Papa."

Justin's heart went out to the children hiding in the playhouse. Especially to Maggie. He knew the fear and desperation she felt. He had once been in her position, trying to protect a younger brother from harm.

"We have to try, Beth," Maggie retorted stubbornly.

"I don't want to. I'm afraid."

"We must for Seth's sake." Maggie's voice was

firm. "Papa doesn't whip you the way he does him."

Maggie had clearly inherited her cousin Gina's courage and determination, Justin thought.

"What if Nurse tells Papa she can't find us?" Beth asked.

"She won't notice we're gone," Maggie said scornfully. "She was starting on a full bottle of what cook calls blue ruin. You know when Nurse drinks that, she never pays any attention to us."

Justin hoped the wretched nurse drank the whole damned bottle of gin, passed out, and didn't wake up until morning.

He moved silently to the gate. As he pushed it, he cringed at the creaking of its seldom-used hinges.

"What was that?" Beth's frightened voice carried to Justin's ears.

"Sh-h-h," Maggie cautioned. "Someone is opening the gate. I hope whoever it is forgets to lock it."

Justin pushed the gate only wide enough for him to slip through sideways. Thank God for the elm trees behind the house that screened its windows from the back wall.

He hurried to the playhouse. Its door was only four feet high, and he dropped to his knees to look inside. He could see nothing but fallen thatch from the section of the roof that had collapsed. The resourceful Maggie must have arranged the reeds to conceal her and her charges behind them. Not the smallest sound disturbed the stillness.

Justin wondered what to do now. He did not want to frighten the children, and the entry of a stranger into their hiding place would surely do that. But he could not remain kneeling in front of the playhouse without risking detection. Gina would have been of help now, but mindful of the danger, especially with Sebastian Dodd back, Justin was still thankful he'd ridden ahead.

He whispered, "Maggie, I am a friend of your mother's, and I have come to take you to her."

"Is she here?" The girl's voice was suspicious.

"No, but she is waiting for you at my brother's house."

Silence.

"Do you remember your cousin Georgie who lives in Sussex, Maggie?" Justin asked.

"Oh, yes!" Maggie responded. "Where is she?"

"She will be here shortly with a carriage to take you to your mother," Justin said soothingly. "I have opened the gate, and I want to get you outside the wall before she comes. We will wait for her in the copse across the road."

He heard a shuffling sound inside the playhouse. A pair of eyes, bleak and blue, in a thin little face far too old for its years, peered out at him with fear and uncertainty. "Why isn't Georgie with you now?"

"I rode ahead on horseback to see if I could find a way to smuggle the three of you out of your house." Justin gave Maggie his friendliest, most encouraging smile. "I did not expect to find you had already smuggled yourselves out. Now let me get you the rest of the way to safety."

He held out his hand to the little girl.

"Don't go with him, Maggie," Beth hissed. "I'm afraid."

"Please, don't be afraid," Justin tried to reassure them. "I only want to take you to a place where you will be safe and happy with your mother."

Maggie hesitated, studying him with distrusting eyes.

"Can't we go, Maggie?" Seth begged. "I don't want Papa to whip me anymore."

She clearly could not resist her little brother's pathetic plea. Her chin fixed in a determined way that reminded Justin very much of Gina.

"You must take my brother first," she said.

"Certainly. I will carry him out. Then Beth and you follow me."

"I won't go," Beth said stubbornly.

"Then you will stay here by yourself," Maggie said. "Seth and I are going."

Her face vanished from the doorway for a few moments. Then she reappeared carrying her brother, who was so small and thin he looked considerably younger than three.

As Justin reached for him, she warned, "Be careful, he's all bloody."

Justin looked down and saw that Seth's legs were covered with lash wounds, some raw and bleeding, others rising in painful welts.

If Justin could have gotten his hands on Sebastian Dodd at that moment, he would have killed the bastard for whipping an innocent child like that. Mr. Moran had been right to fear what would happen to the poor boy when his father returned from London.

Justin took the quaking child in his arms and held him tightly. "Don't worry, Seth. I promise you that you are safe with me. And, I promise you, too, I won't hurt you."

"Don't leave me alone, Maggie," Beth pleaded from behind the fallen thatch.

Maggie turned back to the playhouse. "I must unless you come with us. I must get Seth away from Papa."

A minute later, a little girl, a smaller version of

Maggie, appeared in the doorway, her big eyes frightened.

Justin shifted Seth to one arm and held out his other hand to her. "I promise I won't hurt you, Beth. Come now, hurry through the gate."

She stood motionless for a moment, staring up at Justin. Then Maggie grabbed her arm and pulled her toward the gate. "Hurry up."

Beth reluctantly went along with Maggie. Justin, carrying Seth, followed them out and pulled the gate closed. He did not try to slide the bolt back into place, knowing he could not reach it from the outside.

He led the two girls across the narrow road and into the copse. After cautioning the children to make no sound, he carefully picked a spot where they could not be seen from outside the copse. He sat down on the ground with Seth on his lap and leaned his back against an alder tree. He gestured for the girls to do the same, and they did.

He held the boy tightly against him and stroked his blond hair comfortingly.

Justin wished he had something soothing to apply to the boy's legs. At the very least, though, they needed to be washed. He pulled a clean handkerchief from the pocket of his coat, decided it was too small, and tore off his neckcloth instead. He handed it to Maggie. "You'll find a small spring over there." He pointed toward it. "Wet this in it."

She did as he asked. When she returned, the cloth was soaking.

Taking it from her, Justin wrung it out. He tilted the boy's face up to his. "I hate to do this to you, Seth, but I must clean your legs. I am afraid it will hurt dreadfully, but I know you will be a brave little man about it and try not to cry."

After giving Seth a reassuring hug, he gently began sponging away the blood and rinsing the wounds.

"It burns so," the little boy whimpered, but he bit his lip and struggled to hold back his tears. His valiant efforts brought a lump to Justin's throat.

"I know it does, and I am very sorry to have to do this to you." Justin worked as quickly as he could.

When he finished, he said, "I am very proud of you, Seth, for being so brave." He hugged the child and could not resist dropping a kiss on the top of his blond head.

The child stared up at the man holding him with puzzled, questioning eyes, as though Justin were of some alien species that Seth had never seen before. Justin smiled reassuringly at the child and gently stroked his hair.

A minute later the boy threw his arms around Justin's neck, gave him a smacking kiss, and pressed his cheek against his benefactor's.

An astonished Justin felt his heart melting and tears burning at the back of his eyes. Good God, he hadn't cried since his grandfather had died. He clasped the thin child to him and made a silent vow he would ensure that Seth was never abused again.

After a while the boy, his voice so choked Justin could scarcely understand him, confided, "Papa says I's spawn o' the devil."

Pure fury coursed through Justin's veins. He sat the child on his lap again, and cupped the thin little face in his hands.

As Justin looked at the woebegone child, it was all he could do to keep his rage from his voice. "Your Papa is dead wrong, Seth. Something is twisted in his mind, and that makes him see things the opposite of what they truly are. You are not what your father says."

These words brought such hope to Seth's tearful eyes that it broke Justin's heart.

"W-what's I then?"

Justin, still cupping the boy's face, used his thumbs to brush away the tears that dripped down his pale cheeks. "You are a very special, a very precious treasure, a rare human diamond that brightens the earth. I have come to take you away from your papa because he does not appreciate the treasure he was given, and so he cannot keep it—you."

"Truly? I's a trea'ure?" the boy asked, clearly not quite daring to believe what he'd just been told.

Justin hugged the child to him. "Truly, Seth. Truly you are."

The child looked up at him, his face glowing as brightly as the diamond Justin had called him.

Holding Seth tightly, Justin prayed that Gina and the coach would come before the children were discovered missing and a search was launched for them.

One thing was certain. Sebastian Dodd would take Seth away only over Justin's dead body.

Chapter 28

The badly sprung coach, traveling at high speed on the road from Cumberdale, suddenly slowed and turned off on a country lane. Georgina frowned. Why had the coachman left the main road, which ran past the entrance to Dodd Park?

And why did he continue to move at such a snail's pace? When she called to Monson with this question, he answered, "His lordship ordered me to take it slow from here on so as not to attract undue attention."

She sank back against the seat and impatiently drummed her fingers against the worn leather seat, certain she could make it on foot faster. As she watched through the window on her right, she saw in the distance a steeple that looked like the one she had seen from her window when she had stayed at Dodd Park three years ago.

Georgina looked to the left, expecting to see the house through the window. Instead she saw nothing but a very high brick wall. It must be the one that Sebastian had built to keep his wife from seeing her children.

Her heart sank. The place was a fortress. How could Justin hope to get the children out of there?

Knowing him, though, he would somehow. But at what danger to himself? The sight of the prison-like wall had vividly brought home to her the risk he was taking and cast a frightened pall over her spirits. Where was he now? Had he already found some way in? Could this man she loved so be trapped inside even now?

She should never have let him ride ahead by himself. She should have insisted he take her with him. She was not used to bowing to a man's wishes. She had this time and ended up stuck in this coach moving slower than a lazy turtle.

The equipage came to a full stop beside the only break she saw in the brick wall, a closed gate of heavy wooden planks.

Georgina heard Cray, the groom, scrambling down from the coach box, but she paid him no heed. Her attention was focused on the gate to the left. She started as the door on the right side of the coach was flung open.

Justin's terse voice ordered, "Come girls, quickly!"

Georgina whirled around, weak with relief at the sight of him. "Justin, thank God, you're safe," she cried, her voice breaking with emotion.

He gave her a startled look as he thrust Seth at her.

Seeing the boy, her heart leaped with joy. How had Justin managed to rescue the children so quickly?

"Take Seth for me while I help the girls into the coach." Urgency permeated Justin's voice. "I want to get away from here before someone sees us."

She automatically reached out for the child and took him, but his face puckered.

"I want Jus'n," he wailed, reaching back toward the man.

"It's all right, Seth," Justin said soothingly. "Gina won't hurt you, I promise."

Two thin, bedraggled young girls, who were so altered Georgina barely recognized them as Beth and Maggie, ran up beside Justin. He lifted first Beth, then Maggie into the coach.

Georgina looked at Justin with profound gratitude that he had managed to rescue the children.

"Georgie," Maggie cried as she recognized her cousin. "Justin said you were coming for us!"

"Are you going to take us to our mother like he said you would?" Beth asked, doubt and fear in her voice.

"Yes, I am." Georgina prayed that they would be successful in spiriting the children away and that she would not be made a liar.

Justin walked to the front of the coach and talked in a low voice to the groom standing beside the horses. After a minute, the man disappeared into the copse, and Justin gave instructions to Monson on the box.

Seth began to cry. "I want Jus'n."

"And here I am." Justin climbed into the coach and took the seat opposite Georgina and Maggie. The instant the door closed behind him, the coach rolled forward.

Justin's cheek had a smudge on it, locks of his unruly black hair curled about his face, and his neckcloth was missing. He'd unfastened the top buttons of his shirt, and whorls of raven hair peeked from the opening. Georgina was seized by an utterly inappropriate desire to slip her fingers beneath his shirt.

Seth reached out to him. "I wan' Jus'n."

He took the child from Georgina and settled him carefully on his lap. Seth smiled shyly up at him, then nestled against his chest and sucked his thumb.

She'd been wrong, Georgina realized. The children clearly would have gone with Justin, even if she had not come. He had a way with small children that she had never suspected.

A horse galloped past them. Georgina recognized the groom, Cray, astride the black that Justin had hired at the Five Points Inn. "Where is he going?"

"To do some errands for me," Justin said. "He will catch up with us later."

Georgina dropped her gaze to Seth and, for the first time, noticed the ugly red gashes and welts on his legs.

"Dear God, what happened to him?" she cried, horrified.

"His legs don't look nearly so bad as they did before Justin washed them," Maggie confided.

Georgina's gaze rose to Justin's grim face.

"Sebastian returned two days early from London," he said.

Georgina felt nauseated. "He did that to Seth?"

Maggie answered her. "Papa whipped him. He only stopped 'cause his steward had to see him."

"Is that when you ran away?" Justin asked as he gently smoothed Seth's tousled blond hair.

Maggie nodded. "Papa kept screaming at Seth that he was gonna whip the devil out of him." The little girl began to shake and her teeth chattered as though she had caught a severe chill.

Georgina put her arms around the child and held her close, murmuring softly, "You're safe now."

Tears rolled down Maggie's cheeks. "I was so afraid of what Papa would do to Seth."

"You were very brave." Justin smiled at Maggie.

"You made it many times easier for me to spirit you away."

She smiled wanly at this praise. "I didn't feel brave. I was so afraid Papa would discover us."

"Where did you find them?" Georgina asked Justin.

"Hiding in what's left of that playhouse against the back wall. It was a magnificent piece of luck. I heard them talking as I went to the gate."

"I wish this coach could go faster," Beth said fretfully.

So, most fervently, did Georgina, but she knew why the coachman was going slowly.

"It will soon," Justin promised.

"What happened to your neckcloth?" Georgina asked him.

Maggie answered for him. "He used it to wash the blood from Seth's legs."

Several minutes later, they heard a speeding coach thundering up behind them. The children froze, and Seth started to wail.

Justin hugged the boy to him. "Don't be afraid, Seth. I promised you I wouldn't let anyone hurt you, and I won't."

Seth stopped wailing and tried to smile, but he could not quite manage that. He reached out and grabbed one of Justin's thumbs tightly in his fist.

The coach rushed past them. As its clatter faded in the distance, the children visibly relaxed, but Seth did not let go of Justin's thumb. Georgina watched the man and boy on the crackled leather seat opposite her in bemusement.

A little later, a horseman rode up beside their equipage and shouted at Monson, who slowed the vehicle to a stop.

Seth buried his face in Justin's waistcoat and began to whimper. "Don't worry, little fellow," he reassured the boy, "it's a friend."

The door opened, and Cray, the groom, handed two bags, one large and the other small, to Justin, then closed the coach door. The equipage immediately started up again.

Justin looked inside the large bag and handed it to Georgina. "Bread and cheese. Not much, but it will tide us over for the time being."

"I'm so-o-o hungry," Beth cried. "I want some."

Georgina broke off pieces of the food for the two little girls.

Justin pulled a small jar and two pieces of white cloth from the other bag. He showed the jar to Seth. "This is something to make your legs feel better. Will you let me apply it to them?"

Seth looked at him dubiously for a moment, then nodded.

"Good." Justin opened the jar and applied the salve it contained to the cuts and welts on Seth's legs with such care and gentleness that Georgina had to fight back tears.

If she had not already been convinced that his stepmother's tales about Justin had been lies, she would have been now. This man on the seat opposite her was no selfish, miserly tyrant who took pleasure in making others unhappy. He was generous and caring, a man capable of deep feelings.

Georgina felt ashamed that she could ever have believed his stepmother. Yet he himself had admitted he'd denied his wife her fortune.

She frowned, trying to reconcile a man who would do that with the one opposite her, treating a child, hurt in both body and spirit, with such tenderness. She concluded that Justin must have had excellent reason for acting as he had with Clarissa.

But why would he not defend himself against the false accusations?

When he finished applying the salve, he covered Seth's legs with the cloth.

"You didn't hurt me at all," the boy said, sounding as though he could not believe this himself.

"I'm glad," Justin said. "Would you like bread and cheese now?"

Seth nodded, and Georgina gave him some.

After the children had eaten their fill, Georgina entertained them with fairy tales and other stories of her own creation.

The food had made the children sleepy, and their yawns came with increasing frequency. Beth, sitting beside Justin, nodded off, her head falling to the side and bumping his shoulder, rousing her.

"We don't have much room, Beth," Justin said, "but perhaps if you lie down on the seat beside me and curl up, you will fit."

As the little girl complied, just managing to squeeze into the small space, he shrugged out of his coat. He smiled at Georgina and Maggie. "I don't know what to suggest for you."

Georgina did. "Maggie, if you use my lap as a pillow, you can lie down on this seat."

"And what will you do?" Justin asked Georgina when the two girls were settled.

"I sleep quite well sitting up."

He looked dubious but said nothing. He covered Seth with his own coat.

"Would you like me to take Seth for a while?" Georgina asked.

"No," the boy wailed, grabbing the front of Justin's shirt with his fists. "I wants Jus'n."

"I'll keep him." Justin smiled at Georgina in a

way that made her pulse race. "Try to get some sleep."

The words were hardly out of his mouth before she drifted off, exhausted from the day's excitement and traveling.

Seth's crying awakened Georgina. She opened her eyes. Justin's dark head was very near to Seth's blond one, and he was softly singing a lullaby to soothe the child as he rocked him in his arms. She had never heard Justin sing before. He had a rich baritone that filled her with pleasure and soon lulled both Seth and her back to sleep.

Georgina awoke with a start as the coach jerked to a stop. She saw Justin on the seat across from her, watching Seth who was still sleeping in his arms.

Her heart turned over at Justin's tender expression. This man might scoff at *romantic* love, but he knew how to love.

She whispered, "What if Dodd discovers where Margaret and the children are hiding? He will take them away from her again."

Justin's face hardened into steel determination. "No, he won't. He may be very rich, but I have the power to destroy him. If he dares come near these children again, I will see him in Bedlam where he belongs."

Maggie, her head in Georgina's lap, stirred and opened her eyes. "What is it?"

"We have reached Woodhaven, where your mama is," Justin said. He nudged Beth to awaken her.

Georgina heard footsteps running to the coach and the door flew open. The dim light of the carriage lamp illuminated Aunt Margaret's frantic face.

"Mama!" Maggie cried, throwing herself at her mother who, with tears streaming down her cheeks, hugged her tightly. Beth, who by now was awake, reached for her mama, too.

Little Seth's eyes fluttered open. He glanced with sleepy disinterest at the trio hugging and crying, turned his face into Justin's chest, and went back to sleep.

Behind her aunt, Henry's worried eyes peered into the coach. When he saw his brother, relief lit his face. "Thank God you succeeded, Justin. We have been so worried about you."

Justin smiled wearily. "It went far easier than I thought. My luck was in tonight."

Margaret helped her two daughters down from the equipage, then held out her arms to Seth. "And my baby." The love and longing on Margaret's face as she looked at her son nearly reduced Georgina to tears.

Justin slid across the cracked leather seat and handed the sleeping boy to his mother, then stepped down from the coach and turned to help Georgina.

"You look exhausted," she told him as she alighted. "You did not sleep at all, did you?"

"No," he admitted.

Aunt Margaret hugged Seth to her as though she could not quite believe he was real. "So long, so long," she murmured brokenly. "How I have prayed for . . ."

The rest of her sentence was lost in Seth's wild wail. The little boy had awakened, and he looked at his mother with terror on his face. "Where's Jus'n?" he screamed. "I wants Jus'n."

"I'm here, Seth," Justin said, going to him.

The child twisted in Margaret's arms and reached out for the man.

As she handed her son to Justin, the pain on Aunt Margaret's face tore at Georgina's heart. The little boy wrapped his arms around Justin's neck and clung to him.

"He doesn't remember you yet," Justin told Margaret gently. "And it has been a very difficult and unsettling day for him. Let me carry him into the house for you."

Henry led his guests inside the big brick house. Margaret followed with her daughters still hanging on her skirts. Georgina stepped inside next. Carrying Seth in his arms, Justin brought up the rear.

"What time is it?" Georgina asked.

"A little past two A.M.," Henry answered. "I know you are exhausted. Beds and hot water have been prepared. I will take you up."

As they followed him, Aunt Margaret said, "The children will stay in my room with me."

In the upper hall, Henry stopped and opened a door.

"This is our room," Aunt Margaret told her daughters. The three of them stepped inside, and Justin followed with Seth. The child had fallen asleep again, and his head lay on Justin's shoulder, his little face pressed against his neck.

"Justin, I've given you your usual room in the corner," Henry called after his brother. "I'll wait for you there after I show Miss Penford her room."

Henry crossed the hall and opened the door opposite her aunt's. "This is your room, Miss Penford. I trust you will sleep well."

"Thank you," Georgina said, looking longingly at the tester bed with its carved walnut canopy.

As she was undressing, she heard muffled male

voices in the room next to hers and surmised that must be Justin's chamber. Exhausted, she fell into bed and went promptly to sleep.

Sometime later, she awoke to the sound of Seth screaming. She fumbled groggily for her wrapper so she could go to him. By the time she found it, however, Seth was quiet again, and she sank back into sleep.

The next thing she knew, daylight streamed through her windows and the clock on the mantel told her it was two hours past her normal time for rising.

As she got up, the now familiar nausea swept over her. She rushed to the basin stand in the corner, barely raising its folding top that served as a splashboard in time.

Georgina could deny the truth to herself no longer. She was pregnant.

She wanted the baby so much. It was, after all, the result of her love for Justin.

But what was she to do about its father? He wanted to marry her, and she would happily do so if only he could love her.

All her life, she had dreamed of a marriage like her parents'. Now she must choose between that dream and a man she loved so much, but who mocked the idea that true love could exist between a man and a woman.

Yet he was a man capable of great love and compassion. He'd shown her that with his brother and sister, and with Aunt Margaret's children. But he could not extend his love to a woman and wife.

Could Georgina someday succeed in teaching him to do so? Did she dare take that chance? If she failed, she would be living a nightmare instead of her dream.

Yet as Justin had pointed out to her yesterday, she had no right to deny him his child. It was just as wrong for her to withhold her baby from its father as it had been for Dodd to keep his children from their mother. What was she to do?

Chapter 29

When her nausea began to subside, Georgina dressed. Color always raised her spirits, and she was thankful she had brought a gown of vivid scarlet silk with her.

She tried the connecting door to Justin's chamber. It opened, and she peeked into the darkened room. Not wanting to wake him if he were still sleeping, she quietly slipped inside and moved toward the bed. Justin lay on his side, his arm protectively over a small bundle next to him.

Moving silently to the bed, Georgina discovered the bundle was Seth, his blond hair, fair complexion, and thin little body a touching contrast to the big, black-haired, muscled man beside him. The child had pressed himself tightly against Justin, his little fists clutching the curling black hair on the man's chest.

Georgina, moved to the depth of her soul by this tableau, gulped and fought back the tears that threatened. Her heart overflowed with love for Justin. He would make a wonderful father.

Her hands settled protectively over her stomach. She pictured Justin lying with their baby—a chubby little boy with his father's dark eyes, raven hair, and wonderful grin—as he lay now with Seth.

In that moment, she knew that no matter what the price to herself, she could not deny their baby its father. She loved Justin far too much to withhold his child from him.

He might not love her, but he would love their child and be a good father to it. Justin was right. Their baby needed the love and care of both parents.

Furthermore, she would never love another man as she loved this one. That love gave her the courage to gamble.

Yes, she would marry Justin.

Although doing so might cost her her dream of a union like her parents had, she might, just might, attain it with him.

Surely a man capable of such love and caring for children could learn to extend that love to a woman. She was determined that in time she would win his love.

Until she did, her love for him would have to be enough to forge a marriage that would bring them both happiness and fulfillment.

She watched the sleeping man and child for several minutes before she went back into her own room.

Still a little nauseated, she decided to steal out of the house for a walk, in the hope the fresh air would make her feel better.

At the bottom of the staircase, she ran into Henry. He greeted her with such cool reserve that she inquired in surprise, "Have I done something to offend you?"

He studied her for so long Georgina wondered if he would answer.

Finally he asked, "Why do you refuse to marry my brother?"

Caught by surprise, she almost let slip that she now intended to do just that. She could not tell Henry of this decision before she told Justin. "I—I feared he would not make a good husband," she stammered.

Henry frowned, clearly affronted on behalf of his brother. "I assure you he would make a wonderful husband."

"Would he?" Hoping to learn more, Georgina made herself sound skeptical. "I heard differently about his first marriage." She hated to probe like this, but Justin would not tell her. What else could she do?

"You heard wrong. Believe me, I was there, and Justin had the patience of a saint with that terrible woman. You must have heard Clarissa's false version of their marriage."

"Certainly I have not heard Justin's. He refuses to talk about her or their marriage."

"Of course he does. Honor and integrity are very important to him. In his view, for a man to discuss his wife or his marriage with anyone else is dishonorable. That's why my brother never defended himself against Clarissa's outrageous lies."

So that was the reason for Justin's silence—a highly laudatory reason.

My trust in you has nothing to do with my reason for not telling you, Gina. You are the one who does not trust me enough to reject the lies you've been told about me.

Guilt poked at Georgina. Justin was right. She who had demanded trust from him had not fully given him her trust in return.

"Who told you that my brother was cruel to Clarissa?" Henry demanded.

"Your stepmother."

"That ninny! I don't think I ever met a more stupid woman. She spent no more than three or four days total in Clarissa's company, and she believed every lie that witch told her. But enough. Justin would not appreciate my talking of it to you. Let me show you into the breakfast room. You will not leave it hungry."

Her stomach revolted at the thought of food, and she said hastily, "Pray forgive me, but I have forgotten something in my room, and I must go back to get it." She turned and fled up the stairs to her chamber, barely making it to the basin in time.

Later, as Georgina lay on her bed, she heard her aunt and Maggie talking in the hall outside her room. By now Georgina was feeling better again. She rose and went into the hall.

As she bid them a good morning, the door to Justin's room opened quietly, and Seth slipped outside. He was clad in a makeshift night garment that she suspected from its size must be one of Henry's shirts. The boy's bare toes peeked out from beneath the white linen.

He rubbed his eyes sleepily, then reached out for his sister's hand. "Maggie, I's hun'ry."

She took his hand. "As soon as I've dressed you, we'll go down to breakfast."

As the two children disappeared into the room assigned to them, Margaret said sadly, "Seth prefers Maggie to me."

"That's because she's been caring for and protecting him the past two years," Georgina said. "Why was Seth not sleeping in your room?"

"I hope your asking means that he did not awaken you with his screams," her aunt replied. "The poor baby had such nightmares after we put him to bed. About five A.M., he woke from another one, and I could not quiet him. He doesn't remember me, and he's afraid of me. It breaks my heart."

Georgina hugged her aunt comfortingly. "He will soon know and love you again."

"I hope so. He screamed for Lord Ravenstone, who fortunately heard him and came running before Seth woke up the whole house. The moment his lordship picked him up, Seth quieted, but then he clung to the poor man and would not let him go. Not even Maggie could coax Seth into going to her."

"He seems to have become very attached to Justin."

Aunt Margaret nodded in agreement. "Finally, Lord Ravenstone said that if we were to get any more sleep, he had better take Seth to his chamber with him. I didn't hear another sound from my poor baby after that."

Maggie and Seth, who was now dressed in the rumpled clothes he had been wearing the previous day, appeared in the doorway.

"Have you had breakfast yet, Georgie?" her aunt asked.

"No, but I'm not hungry," she replied, retreating toward her room. "I fear all the traveling yesterday left me feeling not quite the thing."

Georgina shut herself in her room again, thinking of Justin and all that Henry had told her of him both today and at the Five Points Inn.

Tears burned her eyes as she pictured the lonely boy who had been forced to be a man and shoulder a man's burdens before his time.

Chapter 30

More asleep than awake, Justin groggily reached for Seth and discovered the child was gone.

He detected a faint scent of gardenia and forced open one eye. Gina was sitting in a chair near the windows. Her gown, the same bright shade of scarlet she had been wearing the night he had first seen her, offered a bright splash of color in the darkened room. His heart turned over at the serene, dreamy expression on her pixie face.

He propped himself up on one elbow. "I hope you intend to continue this practice of stealing into my room, but I wish you would come farther than that chair." His voice was still hoarse and rough from sleep.

She stood up. As she approached the bed, Justin pushed himself into a sitting position. "Where did Seth go?"

"To breakfast. He has become extremely attached to you."

"Especially to my chest hair," Justin said wryly. "What were you thinking about just now?"

She settled on the bed beside him, her eyes

gravely studying his face. "I was contemplating what name we should give our child."

An entire pot of strong coffee could not have banished his sleepiness more thoroughly. "You *do* know how to wake a man up! Are you telling me we've made a baby?"

She nodded, her face anxious.

He was so filled with wonder and elation that he could not find his voice. He placed his hand gently, reverently on her stomach, still so flat that he could scarcely believe his child was growing there.

After a moment, she asked, "What name would you like to give him if he's a boy—"

"You can choose whatever given name you want, but his surname is damned well going to be Alexander."

"If that's what you want," she said placidly.

"Of course that's what I want!" Her serene mood baffled Justin. He studied her suspiciously. "You know that can only happen if you are my wife?"

"I know."

His heart did a wild dance of relief and elation. "So you've decided to marry me after all?"

"Yes." Her voice was choked, and tears glistened in her eyes.

His joy instantly evaporated. He jerked his hand away from her stomach. "Don't look so damned happy about it!" His voice was raw with the bitter hurt he felt. "Still afraid I'll steal your inheritance?"

"No," she said quietly, her gaze meeting his. "I do not believe your stepmother's allegations against you. I asked you about them because I wanted to learn the truth from you. Instead you admitted denying your wife access to her fortune. I was shocked and dismayed, especially when you refused to explain further."

He went very still. "And now?"

"Now I know you had to have had an excellent reason for doing what you did. You are too good and honorable a man to have done so otherwise."

Hope sprang up in the barren garden of his heart, but he ruthlessly weeded it out. He had been disillusioned too often. "Why have you changed your mind and agreed to marry me?"

"Because you were right, Justin. It would be very wrong of me to deny our child his father." Her voice wobbled. "Our child needs both his parents."

Crushing disappointment gripped him at the realization he faced another marriage in which his bride wed him for reasons that had nothing to do with her feelings for him. At least Gina did not lie to him, as Clarissa had done, by professing to love him.

A strained silence descended like a wall between them. Finally Gina said, "I think you will make a wonderful father."

"But not a wonderful husband?"

Justin watched her swallow convulsively. A single tear escaped the corner of her eye and trickled down her cheek. He felt as though it was a sword slicing through his heart.

In his pain, he lashed out. "And what of your vow not to marry unless you found a man with whom you shared mutual love, respect, and trust?"

Her only answer was more tears trickling down her cheeks.

He hid his own misery behind contempt. "But you will break your vow, abandon your dream, in order to give your child a father, one who also conveniently possesses a title and a fortune. You disappoint me! You are like every other damned woman!"

Fury blazed in Gina's eyes. She swiped angrily at her tears. "You are dead wrong, my lord! I am breaking my vow and marrying you, even though you don't love me, because *I* love *you*. I love you far too much to deny you our child!"

Justin gaped at her, so stunned that he could not immediately comprehend the full import of her words.

Gina jumped up from the bed. "All I want is your love, damn it, nothing else! I don't need your wretched money. I already have a fortune of my own that will keep me and our child in great luxury the rest of our lives. Nor do I give a fig about your title. Society bores me to tears."

She glared down at him. "As for giving up my dream, Justin, I warn you I am not! No matter how long it may take me, I am determined to win your love as you have won mine."

He was too dazed to speak. *She loves me!* He felt as though a chorus of nightingales was singing those words over and over in his heart. That such a fascinating, vital woman loved him so intensely that she would compromise her dream humbled him, thrilled him, awed him.

And made him happier than he'd ever been in his life.

"I warn you, Justin, I am going to lay siege to that fortress you have erected around your heart to keep love out." She tossed her head defiantly. "And I *will* breach it. I *will* prove to you not only that true love exists but that marriage to a woman who loves you as I do can be both happy and fulfilling."

She whirled angrily away from the bed, her full skirts billowing, and started for the door, galvanizing Justin into action. He grabbed for her and managed to catch a piece of scarlet material, jerking her to a stop like a filly that had reached the end of her tether. He hauled her back to the bed by her skirt.

"Let go of me," she snapped.

Instead he pulled her down on the bed and wrapped her in his arms so tightly that her struggle against him was futile. He tried to kiss her, but she turned her face away. He settled for nuzzling her ear, then whispering into it, "You are magnificent, little wasp, when you are in a temper."

Justin nipped at her earlobe. "Now, instead of telling me, why don't you show me how much you love me?"

She turned her face back to him, and he promptly captured her lips, kissing her with all the hunger that was in his heart. His passionate little wasp responded as she always did—with fiery ardor.

He unfastened her gown and quickly divested her of her other clothes. Justin had nothing to shed for he was naked beneath the sheet. Gina joined him there, and he started to pull her down beside him, but she would not let him.

"No, Justin, it's my turn. You asked me to show you how much I love you. Now let me do so."

And she did, using her lips, her tongue, and her hands with such thoroughness that he did not think she missed a single inch of him. He'd never had a woman make love to him with such intensity and sheer delight, with such determination to give him pleasure.

And she succeeded beyond *his* wildest expectations. His whole body quivered with sensation.

He was in heaven.

He was in hell.

He would die if she did not take him soon. His manhood throbbed urgently.

Justin looked up at her as she straddled him, her

brown hair tumbling about her bare shoulders and breasts in wild waves. She reminded him of a pagan love goddess unleashing her magic on him.

He reached up and filled his hands with her breasts, kneading them gently as he teased the pink crests with his thumbs. "You're sublime," he breathed with absolute sincerity.

Her moist lips parted in amusement. "From the man who never indulges in flattery."

"It's the truth! Oh-h-h," he groaned and his body went rigid as she started to take him inside her with torturous slowness.

She began to move over him in a steady rhythm while he gritted his teeth, trying to stave off his release.

When her pace quickened with increasing rapidity, he could last no longer. He shuddered over and over, helpless in the grip of a shattering climax. She convulsed around him, prolonging and intensifying his own response until he thought he might die from sheer pleasure.

Afterward as she lay in his arms, she breathed, "Oh, Justin, I love you so much."

He held her close to him, smoothing back her hair, damp from the heat of their passion. "When did you finally decide you loved me?"

"Not finally," she contradicted. "I knew weeks ago." She turned on her side and snuggled against him, her breasts pressing to his chest. "I would never have asked you to make love to me if I did not love you beyond measure."

He frowned. "Then why did you tell me you didn't?"

She stroked his cheek tenderly with her hand. "I told you nothing of the sort. I said I did not *fancy* I loved you, Justin. I *knew* without a doubt that I loved you."

"And who was the other man you once loved?" He hated himself for asking, but he had to know. He did not want to wonder every time she smiled at another man whether he was the one.

"What other man?" Gina's face crinkled into that marvelous smile of hers. "The only man I have ever loved, Justin, is you." Her smile faded. "But I could not tell you and have you mock my love. Oh, Justin, I could not have borne that!"

He understood how she had felt, how well he understood. Now he owed her the truth, owed her the same candor that she had given him. "I have never discussed Clarissa or our marriage with another soul before, but as my future wife, you do have a right to know what really happened."

She put her index finger to his lips to silence him. "You do not have to tell me, Justin. I trust you."

He kissed her finger. "I want no secrets between us, but I ask you not to tell anyone else."

"You have my word," she promised.

He let go of her and pushed himself into a sitting position on the bed. She followed his example except, to his disappointment, she held the sheet up around her. He would have much preferred the view had she let it drop down to her lap as he had.

He put his arm around her and held her against him. "Our fathers arranged Clarissa's and my marriage. I learned later that mine was well-paid for doing so. I was twenty, and she was barely seventeen but already a beauty in addition to being an heiress."

"You did not want to wed her?"

Justin's somber gaze met Gina's. "But I did. I won't deny it. I welcomed our marriage. No one could be more charming than Clarissa when she wanted to be. She seemed to be a complaisant, well-behaved young lady, eager to please her prospective husband. She talked very little, but I attributed this to shyness."

He reached out and took Gina's hand in his own. She continued to hold the sheet up with her other one.

"Clarissa seemed to be everything I thought I *should* want in a wife. Naive young fool that I was, I believed myself in love with her, and I believed her when she told me she loved me. Then we were married."

Gina's expression was troubled. "But Clarissa did not love you?"

"No, she lied to me at her father's instruction. I was not allowed much time with her until we were married. Her father took no chance that I might discover her true nature before we went to the altar. Had I known it, nothing could have compelled me to marry her. My father knew what she was, but in his greed to collect the money hers had offered him, he said nothing."

In his agitation, Justin tunneled his free hand roughly through his hair. "Clarissa always had to be the center of attention and have her own way in everything. She flew into irrational, uncontrollable rages at the smallest provocation. One never knew what would set her off."

He felt Gina tighten the pressure of her hand on his, offering him silent comfort. "Perhaps if I'd been older, I might have known better how to deal with her, but I had never seen anyone behave like that, and I was stunned. In her tantrums, she was a danger to others, especially those whom she thought had no recourse against her, such as the servants.

Or an eleven-year-old boy who was too small for his age.''

Gina gasped. ''Your brother?''

''Yes, she hated poor Henry. A few months after we were married, she tried in one of her rages to stab him with a dagger.''

''Good God!'' Gina exclaimed, her eyes round with horror.

''She would have succeeded had I not heard her screaming at him. I managed to wrestle her away, and she stabbed me instead.''

Gina pulled her hand from his and lightly touched the puckered scar on his shoulder. ''So that is how you got this.''

Justin nodded.

Gina twisted and lowered her head to kiss the scar tenderly.

It was such a sweet and loving gesture that it was all he could do to keep from abandoning his story and making love to her again, but he forced himself to continue. ''To ensure Henry's safety, I tried to send him to live with my father and his new wife in London, but Lanie's mother refused to let him live with them.''

''How terrible of her,'' Gina cried. ''No wonder you disliked her.''

''In retrospect, I think Clarissa was jealous of Henry because I loved him. Her behavior killed my affection for her within a few weeks of our marriage, and I was not good at hiding my feelings.''

Justin's gaze met Gina's squarely. ''I did not refuse Clarissa access to her inheritance so that I could spend it myself. I did so to preserve it.''

''You need not explain, Justin. I know you did what you thought best.''

Deeply touched by Gina's faith in him, he ran his

fingers lovingly over her cheek. "Thank you, but as I said, I want no secrets between us. Clarissa was the most extravagant creature I've ever known. She squandered such an enormous sum on herself and her clothes in the first three months of our marriage that I had to step in and put a stop to it. Had I not done so, she would have thrown it all away within another three."

His hand dropped away from Gina's cheek, and he paused. Only the song of an unseen bird from beyond the windows broke the silence.

"I did not take *her* jewels from her. They were the Ravenstone family jewels, which were handed down to me and must pass down to my successor upon my death. I took them from her after she attempted to pawn them in retaliation for my putting her on a strict allowance."

Gina took his hand and squeezed it again.

"She wanted me to take her to London, but I could not leave Ravencrest. I was desperately trying to keep the estate going while my father bled it dry, squandering everything he could get his hands on at the gaming tables and on his expensive new bride. That's why Clarissa accused me of keeping her a prisoner at Ravencrest."

Gina was clearly perplexed. "Why would a woman act as she did?"

"For years I asked myself the same question. I have you to thank for helping me find a possible answer."

"Me?" Gina echoed in surprise.

Justin nodded. "Yes, you made me understand a woman's helplessness and frustration at having no power or control over her life. I began to see that that could have been Clarissa's problem. Since she was a child, her tears and her tantrums never failed

to win her everyone's attention and her own way—
until she met me."

"But by then, her dreadful behavior had become
habitual," Gina said.

Justin nodded. "Clarissa's understanding was
limited, and she never comprehended that such behavior with me cost her more than it gained."

"Oh, Justin, what a terrible time you had." Forgetting the sheet, Gina let it drop and turned to hug
him so hard that he wondered wryly whether she
was trying to squeeze from him every last drop of
pain Clarissa had caused him.

Then Gina began to kiss him. He quickly forgot
everything but the titillating way that her breasts
pressed against him; her mouth devoured his, and
her gardenia scent teased his nose.

Almost immediately, he was as hungry for her as
if it had been years since they'd made love, instead
of only minutes. And from the gleam in her eyes,
she felt the same way.

This time they made love to each other, wild, ex-
uberant, tender love that propelled them into a
shuddering, rapturous climax that went on and on
like an earthquake that would not stop.

Afterward Justin lay joined with her, cuddling
her to him, unwilling to break the connection between them.

"I love you so much," she whispered.

Again he felt humbled and honored and infinitely
blessed that this remarkable woman, so vital, so
strong, so passionate, so determined, loved him.

He would do everything in his power to make
her happy. Never had he felt such a powerful desire
to protect and cherish a woman—or anyone else,
for that matter, since his brother Henry had been a
child.

But what Justin felt for Gina transcended anything he had ever felt for another person, even Henry.

He *loved* her with every fiber of his being.

This realization hit Justin with the force of an Alpine avalanche. He who had mocked love's existence was wildly in love with Gina. What a fool he had been not to have recognized the true nature of his feelings for her earlier.

He had once accused her of mistaking lust for love, but he grasped now that the mistake had been his. As his wise Gina had known all along, love was so much more.

Her love for him healed the terrible wounds that first his mother, then his wife had inflicted on his heart. Before he had even come of age, these two key women in his life had fueled his disillusionment with love, and he'd chosen to mock it as a mirage.

But now, the wonder of Gina's love for him opened his eyes to a searing insight about himself. Between them, his mother and his wife had left him unconsciously harboring deep in his soul the fear, never before admitted even to himself, that he was unlovable.

Gina's love for him removed the blinders from Justin's eyes even as it dissolved this previously unacknowledged fear.

He saw now that his selfish mother had not wanted to be bothered with her children. Clarissa had been incapable of loving anyone but herself. The fault had been theirs, not his.

Justin smiled as he recalled Gina's defiant promise that she would break down the walls around his heart. His determined little wasp had already done so.

Eager to tell her, he opened his mouth but closed

it again when he saw that she had fallen asleep. He lay watching her face, which in repose looked as young as a schoolgirl's, his heart bursting with love for her.

A lifetime would not be long enough for him to spend in her company. He could think of no better way to wake up every morning than to her glorious smile.

How ironic: he had spent so many years denying love's existence that he had not recognized it when it sailed into his life, clad in a scarlet gown and pelisse.

Georgina awoke with a start. Justin was lying on his side next to her, watching her with a smile of such tenderness that her heart leaped.

"So we're awake, are we?" His voice was husky with emotion. "It occurs to me that I have not made you a proper offer of marriage this morning, and I must remedy that, but first . . ."

He gathered her in his arms and kissed her gently, yet thoroughly. Then he said with a grin, "I know I should get down on bended knee to make my offer."

Her eyes sparkled with amusement. "Especially dressed for the occasion as you are. I confess I've never seen a naked man on bended knee."

"Nor will you now. I prefer to hold you in my arms like this."

"And I prefer you to do so," she assured him. "I love the warmth of your skin against mine—as well as everything else about you."

He smiled. "Just as I love everything about you."

A shadow of sadness fell over her heart. "You love all the parts of me, but not the whole."

"My dearest, dearest Gina, I love the *whole* of you,

too, with all my heart and my soul, with all my being.''

For a moment, she wondered if she had misheard him. His declaration was so unexpected—and so stunning—that it robbed her of speech even as it flooded her with happiness.

"I want you to be my wife, Georgina Penford, and so much more. I want you to be my lover, best friend, confidante, companion, and trusted advisor, as your mother was your father's. Will you be all those things to me as I will strive to be to you? Will you marry me, my one and only love?''

She had not misheard! Justin was offering her his love *and* the marriage she'd dreamed of having.

At last, she recovered her voice. "Oh yes, Justin, I will marry you. I love you so much, and I do want to be all those things to you.''

They hugged as exuberantly as they had done that day they'd first seen the iguanodon skeleton.

Justin nipped her earlobe lightly, then whispered, "But no more damned 'scientific experiments' with other men. I wanted to kill Roger Chadwick that night. I was half out of my mind with jealousy.''

"So that's why you let me seduce you," she teased.

"I was determined to have you any way I could get you, my love.''

My love. How those words thrilled her. "I assure you I have absolutely no interest in such experiments with anyone but you." She caressed his cheek lovingly. "You had no reason to be jealous of Chadwick kissing me, for it conclusively proved to me that I could not feel for him what I felt for you.''

Justin groaned. "I wish I'd known that then.''

Her eyes sparkled. "I'm glad you did not. You might not have made love to me if you had.''

"What a blind fool I have been, Gina. Convinced as I was that romantic love did not exist, it took me far too long to recognize the real reason why I felt so strongly about you, my dearest love."

She tenderly traced the arc of his black eyebrows with her finger. "Oh, Justin, I want so much to make you the happiest man on earth."

He grinned, his eyes adoring her. "But you already did, my Scarlet Lady, when you agreed to marry me."

Author's Note

For readers who wonder why I referred to the
giant skeleton as that of an iguanodon rather
than a dinosaur, this novel is set nine years before
Sir Robert Owen created the word dinosaurus (from
the Greek for terrible lizard) in 1842.

Sir Charles Lyell, Dr. Gideon Algernon Mantell,
and his wife Mary Anne, were well-known figures
in nineteenth-century British geology.

Lyell, the author of the three-volume *Principles of
Geology*, did deliver a series of lectures in London
in 1833. The first was open to both men and women,
but the subsequent lectures were closed to women.

In 1822, Mary Anne Mantell discovered fossilized
teeth of an iguanodon, a plant-eating, ornithischian
(bird-hipped) dinosaur that lived in the Cretaceous
Period of the Mesozoic Era. These first recognized
remains of a dinosaur came from a quarry in the
Tilgate Forest near Cuckfield in Sussex.

This was not, however, the first discovery of dinosaur remains in England. In 1677, the Reverend
Robert Plot of Oxford described a gigantic leg bone
that was probably from a dinosaur. In the early
nineteenth century, a large fossil jaw and other

bones of a meat-eating dinosaur, later named mega-losaurus by Dr. James Parkinson (who identified Parkinson's disease), were found in Jurassic sediments at Stonesfield in Oxfordshire.

Avon Romances—
the best in exceptional authors and unforgettable novels!